I0731089

STORY

Pretentiously Titled Series Book 1

GUS GWYNNE

WORKBOOK PRESS LLC
187 E Warm Springs Rd,
Suite B285, Las Vegas, NV 89119, USA

Website: https://workbookpress.com/
Hotline: 1-888-818-4856
Email: admin@workbookpress.com

Ordering Information:
Quantity sales. Special discounts are available on quantity purchases by corporations, associations, and others. For details, contact the publisher at the address above.

ISBN-13:   978-1-957618-73-9 (Paperback Version)
                978-1-957618-74-6 (Digital Version)

REV. DATE: 02/22/2022

Story

By Gus Gwynne

Dedicated to all the D&Ders – The ones I've known, the ones I've never met – Players, DMs, Game Designers, Module Writers, and All The Rest – This book is for all of you!

Table of Contents

Chapter 0: *Before*

Crown Sorcerer Emstone was a pale, bookish sort of man, slightly below average in height, and slightly above average in weight. His thinning hair was originally dirty-blonde, but age and stress had turned what was left of it a sort of dignified gray. He wasn't aged enough to look wrinkled, but he still gave an impression of age, and perhaps even of wisdom.

But it wasn't wisdom that had brought him his position as the leading sorcerer in King Yonind's court. It was sheer, raw mental force of will. His few admirers and his many detractors all said that he could bend a man's mind three times in a single afternoon, and all without saying a single word. No sorcerer in the kingdom was anywhere near so strong as he, and many a secretly rebellious noble lived in fear of the day Emstone might appear on their doorstep and twist their loyalties to suit his king's needs.

Socially, his most unusual trait was that he had only ever had a single wife. In a culture where men of power and wealth kept multiple wives and numerous concubines as the norm, he had only ever married one woman and never taken a single concubine. It was peculiar, but most people were too afraid of him to ever ask him why.

The result of that one marriage was what was on his mind right then. His wife had died in childbirth, but their daughter, Shina, had survived. Survived and grown into a magnificent specimen of womanhood.

A magnificent specimen of *unmarried* womanhood. One who somehow managed to chase away every suitor her father ever convinced to even try to woo her. Most noblewomen were married by the time they were fifteen summers of age, but Shina was in her eighteenth year and still living with her father.

It was his right as her father to make her marry anyone he wanted, but the most adept manipulator in the kingdom just couldn't seem to force his daughter to do anything against her own capacious and capricious will.

He was bound and determined that, this time, it would work. The Earl of Chara was coming for dinner, and Emstone was positive this would finally be the man he could marry his only daughter to. Besides having the noblest rank and title of any suitor yet, he was also fabulously wealthy from his tolls on the main north-south trade route of the eastern part of the kingdom.

Surely no young woman, not even his willful daughter, could just say no to someone like that! And, darn it, even if she did say no, he was her father, one of the most powerful men in the kingdom, and, for once, she would do as he said!

Thus braced for battle, he strode past the guards placed on Shina's quarters and gestured peremptorily for one of the door-slaves to open the curtained doorway for him. With firm steps, he barged into her rooms, determined to finally have his way and get her decently married off!

Since he hadn't told her they were having guests, he was surprised when he found her in her dressing room, surrounded by body-slaves who were busily getting her into an expensive gown and some costly jewelry he couldn't quite remember buying for her.

She was stunning! Her fox-red hair, her smooth, tan skin, her dark blue eyes, all framed by black and white silk and a prince's ransom in platinum and pearls.

Shina was busy berating one of the slaves for misplacing a hair pin, and a dark red palm-print on the slave's face vividly showed his mistress' displeasure. Everyone was in such a bustle and rush that nobody paid any attention at all to her father's entrance into the room.

Emstone was immediately immensely pleased.

"Shina, my darling girl! I'm so happy to see you dressing up for our guest!"

Shina glared at him briefly, a glance of scorn and contempt he had become accustomed to over the years. "What are you blathering about now, Daddy? What guest?"

Before he could get a word in edgewise, she gave an exasperated sigh and continued. "Not another one of your boring old men that you want to push me into bed with, I hope!"

He was stunned, and the look on his face was all the answer she needed.

"Daddy! You're horrible! They're all nasty, boring old men! I swear, I halfway expect you to hold my legs open and push them into me, you're so desperate to marry me off!"

She paused dramatically for a moment as Emstone's will melted in the storm.

"Well, Daddy, you'll just have to marry your guest yourself! I'm off to the ball at the Gaurdon house, and I won't be back till late."

She turned away from him and yelled at one of the slaves to hurry up with her shoes. When she turned back and realized Emstone was still standing there, she rolled her eyes and said in an exasperated voice, "Daddy, you can go now," pointing emphatically at the doorway.

His shoulders slumped in despair, the most powerful sorcerer in the kingdom retreated from his daughter's battlefield in total defeat.

The last thing he heard as he left that wing of the house was the slap of something hard hitting flesh and his daughter yelling, "No, you fool! The other diamond earrings!"

Back in his part of the house, a slave, eyes downcast to the floor, made the gesture that meant it wanted his permission to speak about a matter of the master's request. For a moment, Emstone wondered if maybe he should use slave-gestures to Shina, but then he remembered the slaps and bruises and knew it wouldn't help him enough.

"Yes?" he asked the slave.

"Earl Kunis of Chara is here, master. He has been seated in the north conversation room per your request, master."

Emstone took a deep breath to get his courage back, stood up straight, and determined that the evening would not be a total waste. Perhaps the Earl would have some stratagem to help them win his daughter – the man did have twenty-three wives already, and must know *something* of how to deal with women after all.

He walked his way through marbled halls and gilded foyers, past a dozen house-slaves caring for a horde of treasures and artworks. The Crown Sorcerer was a wealthy man, favored by the king, and it showed in how he lived.

The north conversation room was where he normally met with the wealthy and powerful who sought out his favor in reaching the king's ear. It was the richest room in the house, and would suit the earl well, he knew.

When he got there, the earl was looking out the window at the house gardens. They were pretty at that time of year, but not at their best. That was in the spring, when they'd be full of flowers and the sights and smells of ripe fruit. Still, it showed he was a man who appreciated the finer things of life.

Earl Kunis was a tall, thin man of about thirty years. As always, he was dressed in a slightly feminine fashion, with pale blue makeup around his eyes and lips and clothing dripping in silk and lace. As a noble of the kingdom, he was armed with a longsword, but his clothing and manner almost made it seem like he should have a woman's daggers on his belt instead.

Yes, Emstone thought to himself, *this is a man who must be able to understand women. He must be able to think like they do. Perhaps he can still help after all.*

***

Passet, second son of the Viscount of Mila, was smitten. The young woman he had just danced with was gorgeous, beautiful, witty, a skilled dancer, and, most importantly of all, the first woman who had ever paid any attention to him at all since puberty. She had even ignored the times his voice cracked! It was love and nothing would dissuade him from it!

He left the dance floor reluctantly, but he was too afraid of Duke Antain to deny him the floor with Shina, even if she was the love of his life.

No matter! She might be dancing with the duke, but he knew deep in his heart that she was his and would be no other man's ever! The smile she had given him at the end of their dance would be his treasure till he could win her for himself!

"Passet, you okay?" asked his friend, Hund, third son of the Count of Thurman.

Still floating on pure love, Passet greeted his best friend. "More than okay, my friend. I'm in love!"

Hund looked confused. "With who?" he asked skeptically.

"The red-haired goddess of my every dream, who blinds my eyes so they see only her grace and beauty on the whole dance floor," he said, pointing towards Shina, where she was dancing with the duke.

Hund looked where his friend was pointing, trying to ignore the awful poetry he'd just been subjected to, and then his eyes goggled when he realized who Passet was pointing at. "You have to be kidding, buddy! Please tell me you're making a joke!"

Passet looked seriously at his friend for a moment. "A joke? Why a joke? She's gorgeous, she's wonderful. Why shouldn't I fall in love with her?"

"Because she's such a world-class bitch that she's scared off every

4

single man her father has ever ensorcelled into spending time with her. Her dad can mind-bend people so they'll betray their best friends or die saving their worst enemy's life, but he can't keep anyone interested in her!"

"What?!?" Passet was shocked that his friend would use such language about his goddess.

"Her dad is the Crown Sorcerer. Lord Emstone himself! And even he can't stand her."

Passet paused. "Emstone! The Lord of Traitors? He forced one of my father's vassals to betray our family! That's *his* daughter?"

"Yeah. The very one."

Passet looked daggers at Shina. That serpent could never love. It was right that she should be dancing with the most vicious man in the kingdom, Duke Antain. They suited each other!

Chapter 1: *To Rescue a Fair Maiden*

Like all the best stories, this one starts with a damsel in distress, a dragon, and a mighty warrior.

The damsel, Shina of Berdonia, was being held captive in a castle hidden deep in the Silver Crown Mountains. Her kidnapper, Lord Antain, the Duke of Klosia, was using her to force her father, Crown Sorcerer Emstone, to betray King Yonind.

Shina was imprisoned in the highest room of the tallest tower of the castle, of course. The room was pleasant enough, with tall windows that let in plenty of sunlight during the day, and a nice view of the starry sky at night. It had comfortable furniture, and even a few nice decorations.

But it also had a steel-clad door, locked from the outside by a strong bar and guarded by the duke's men day and night. It had iron bars over the windows, and a sixty-foot drop for anyone trying to escape through them. The castle itself had high walls and strong gates and a multitude of armed men to keep rescuers out and damsels in.

From the windows, Shina could see the vast wilderness surrounding the castle. Even if she had, by some miracle, managed to escape the tower (impossible) and the castle (inconceivable), she would have been trapped in the mountains. They towered all around, covered in beautiful but deadly glaciers and deep woods hunted by dangerous beasts.

If she had, by some agency far beyond her own means, gotten through the woods and over the passes of the mountains, and was still alive, she would still have to cross the Icefloe Sea to get back to the kingdom. That sea was as infamous for its freezing cold waters as for its giant monsters. And the only ships crossing it would belong to the duke, or perhaps a few desperate pirates who would be more likely to rape and kill her than to help her get home.

The only way to avoid sailing the sea would be to travel hundreds of miles through deadly, untracked wilderness into the frozen north, to go around the east end of the sea. The whole area was notorious for the harshness of the land and the fierceness of the griffons and other monsters who preyed upon it.

Escape was thus impossible, and her father hadn't the courage to force the duke to release her. While her father loved her, his honor was too strict to betray his king, so it seemed inevitable that Shina was to die in this unassailable fortress.

Shina herself was a gloriously beautiful young maiden, with hair the color of a red fox, smooth, tan skin, shapely breasts, and nicely rounded hips. Men found her very attractive indeed. She had been well trained in the traditional womanly arts of dancing, singing, cooking, medicine, and knife-fighting.

She was used to being spoiled by her father, and was accustomed to a most pleasant life. Till her kidnapping, she had never faced hardship more harsh than a stern word on the most strict of disciplinary measures.

So, while her gilded cage would have seemed luxurious to many, to her it seemed barren and hard. At home, she was used to being surrounded by slaves who lived for nothing but her slightest whims. She had a wing of her father's house all of her own, a dozen rooms filled with luxury and rare artworks. She had a team of chefs who made sure all of her meals were delicious. She had been surrounded by loyal guards who had given their lives in a vain attempt to keep her out of the duke's vile grip.

In her prison, she ate no worse than the military officers in charge of the castle, but also no better. She had also discovered such rough living as having to attend to her own bath – they gave her hot water and soap and rough towels, but she had to scrub her own skin and there were no soothing scented oils to finish with.

She was used to being surrounded by slaves and thus having no real privacy, but the soldiers were not hers to command and she was scared of the lustful stares they gave her when she bathed or dressed. The duke had repeatedly promised that, so long as she behaved, the soldiers would not harm her, but her young mind had filled in the opposite: That he would let them have their way with her if she was anything but compliant with her captivity. The duke had never made any threats that they would rape her to death if she tried to escape, but she was convinced the threat was implied. The duke's ruthless reputation made that crystal clear and, she was sure, beyond doubt.

In the month since she had been kidnapped, she had learned to live with constant fear, but had not yet discovered the courage within to stand up to it. She had simply gone numb to it, and had lost that youthful spark of defiance, though she had not yet succumbed completely and begun to propitiate her captors.

Her kidnapping had been a simple matter. She had been asleep in her luxurious bed when suddenly armed men had torn down the curtains to her room, their swords running red with the blood of her guards and slaves, and had hit her over the head, tied her up and carried her off. From the roof of her father's house, a wyvern from the duke's coterie had carried her off to the docks, where she'd been loaded aboard ship, and then brought here.

She'd had a concussion for a while, and much of the trip was a blur of dizziness and darkness. She was sure she'd been kept below decks for most of the crossing of the sea, and she didn't remember much but seasickness from that.

By the time they came ashore in the north, she'd recovered from the blow to the head, and she vividly remembered the way she'd been manhandled into a cart and bundled off to the castle where she was being held.

She had only been in the tower for a few days. The guards didn't speak to her much, but they had informed her that the duke was on his way, and would be there in a couple of days. She didn't know what he intended for her, and she was terrified at being helpless in the power of a man reputed to be the most ruthless lord in a kingdom that had been forged in fire and blood.

Late on her fourth night in the tower, a sudden loud noise interrupted Shina's sleep. Light from the full moon was streaming in through the windows, and she looked around the room, but nothing seemed amiss.

She was almost convinced she'd dreamed the noise, and was about to go back to sleep, when suddenly the door to her room was smashed open.

A monster stood in the doorway! It was a huge beast! The moonlight glowed green in inhuman eyes and glinted from horns, scales and tusks on its almost reptilian face! Its giant bulk filled the whole doorway. Where a tall man could stand easily with room to spare, the monster crouched. Where a warrior could walk with easy clearance, it turned sideways to fit its gargantuan shoulders through. An ominous cloak billowed out behind it, almost enough to be a curtain for the doorway.

Shina screamed! She knew with horrible dread that the duke had sent this thing to brutally murder her!

"My father will pay for my return!" she cried. "Please! Please! I'll do anything! Please don't feed me to this thing!" She cowered beneath the covers, fear covering her body in sweat and setting her limbs to trembling! She knew that only the hateful duke's guards could hear her, but desperation drove her cries for mercy anyway.

The monster paused just inside the room. "Feed you to me? What's wrong with you? I'm here to rescue you!"

Shina was nonplussed. She hadn't expected it to speak. And then her stunned mind parsed out what it had said.

"W…what?" she tremulously whispered.

"I'm here to rescue you. So get out of that bed and let's get a move on! We don't have all night!" The creature's voice was a deep rumble, like a subterranean waterfall or a bass drum, but its speech was unexpectedly clear and well-articulated.

Shina was still in a state of shock, and the monster was in a hurry. So it quickly stepped over to the side of the bed, took a hold of her, and pulled her out from under the covers.

Shina tried desperately to cover her naked body with her hands as she turned bright red and shrieked in embarrassment. Her hands desperately fluttered around, trying to hide first this part and then that from the monster's gaze.

"Oh dear gods," muttered the monster. "Must I do everything myself?" Then it grabbed a blanket off the bed, wrapped her in it, and threw her over its shoulder as if the bedding were a sack. She was shocked by its strength as the monster handled her as easily and casually as a grown man would pick up a small puppy.

The next few minutes were a nightmare for Shina.

The monster ran down the tower stairs, and with each step she bounced against his back brutally. She curled into a small ball and wrapped her arms around her head to keep it from being knocked to pieces against his shoulder. She felt dizzy and trapped, but there was nothing she could hold on to and nothing she could brace against. Just a whirlwind of bashing over and over, with only the slightest gap to peer through.

The monster hit the door at the bottom of the steps and didn't even slow down. The door was built to withstand a battering ram, and was firmly locked with an inch-thick steel bar! With a titanic crash and a shriek of tearing metal, the steel hinges were ripped from their stone mounting and he smashed through the door without the slightest pause.

In a bound, he dashed across the courtyard towards the walls. Through a gap in the "bag", she briefly glimpsed a group of armsmen charging towards them, but the monster was moving far too fast for them to catch!

The monster reached the wall and leaped up the stairs, four or five at a time. Shina barely had time to scream as an archer on top of the wall fired his crossbow at them. Shina stared at sure death for the briefest moment, and heard the arrow hit flesh, but the monster just kept running up the stairs.

Shina could see the crossbow arrow sticking out of the monster's neck. Dark blood, black looking in the moonlight, began to drip from the wound, and she was sure it would die any moment now.

The monster reached the top of the wall, still running flat out. She thought it would attack the archer, who was hurriedly reloading his crossbow. But it didn't! Instead it took two long steps to the edge of the parapet and leapt off the wall!

They fell straight for the ice-cold moat and spikes at the bottom of the wall, fifty or more feet below them, and Shina's mind dropped from panic to shock as rapidly as her body, still on the back of the monster, plummeted towards certain death!

But they had only fallen a few feet when suddenly gigantic wings spread from under the monster's cape and their fall became a swift glide towards the edge of the forest!

Shina's heart felt like it was climbing up her throat to block her breath!

She looked around wildly as they sped through the air towards the trees. A brief look back showed her four or five men staring in wonder at the escaping duo.

She saw one raise his crossbow and take aim straight at her. Her battered body braced for the pain she knew the arrow would hit with, and then they were amidst the dense fir and pine trees and she couldn't see the castle any more as it disappeared behind the branches flashing past them.

She was too exhausted by the stress and adrenaline to realize that she was bracing for a crash, when they landed quite gently next to a huge fir tree.

The monster reached up with its free hand and took ahold of the arrow sticking out of its neck. Shina, who knew the healing arts, knew that the arrow itself was the only thing keeping the monster alive! If it hadn't killed already, then it was itself blocking the flow of blood, and would have to be removed carefully or it would kill even more quickly than leaving it in would.

"No!" she started to shout a warning.

Before she could say even one more syllable, the arrow had been ripped out and a terrible gush of blood sprayed out with it.

Shina stared as the blood flow stopped almost immediately. Even by the spotty moonlight in the trees, she could see the wound sealing itself before her eyes! In moments, it was gone, not even a scar left visible!

What sort of demon was this? And what horrible fate awaited her? Was she being kidnapped for some horrific ritual? It said it was "rescuing her", but demons were born to lie.

The monster shifted Shina's weight on its back and began to run into the woods. She had no idea where it was taking her, and she was in such despair and pain she could hardly care anymore. She just knew she needed to stop being bounced around, it hurt far too much.

"Please," she whimpered. "Please stop hurting me."

The monster stopped running and unslung the blanket-bag from its shoulders, then picked her up and set her on her feet. It looked her over and seemed to realize how badly it was hurting her.

It thought for a moment. "Can you run?" it asked.

Even as it asked, her legs collapsed under her and she sat abruptly on the hard, snowy ground. Through tears in her eyes and her voice too choked up to speak, she merely shook her head in a weary "no".

"Then I'll have to carry you. Sorry." He seemed genuinely contrite, and she realized he was right. The castle would have pursuit after them in a minute, and she knew that would only end in torture and death. She vividly imagined the duke's unspoken promise that, if she ever tried to escape, he'd let his men rape her to death. He'd never had to say it because she knew it was implied by the very fact of her captivity.

But Shina had a strength of mind that was finally beginning to rally to her need.

She looked up at the monster and saw, strange as it looked on such an alien countenance, actual concern there.

"Then carry me in front," she said wearily. Her mind raced. "If you tie the blanket around your neck and make a hammock of it across your chest, I can hold your arm or your neck to steady myself. Will that work? Can you do that?"

The monster didn't hesitate. It took the large blanket and tied it behind its massive neck. Shina felt she would freeze, sitting in the woods naked, while it worked on turning the blanket into a harness. After all the strange turns and violence of the last few minutes, her nudity in front of this thing no longer bothered her. There were bigger issues on her mind than modesty.

More rapidly than she expected, the monster had the blanket ready for her. She was surprised by how dexterous and artful its hands were, to accomplish such a task so rapidly and easily. From its size and ugliness, she had presumed it would be both clumsy and stupid. She realized now that it was far from either.

It picked her up and they worked her into the improvised papoose. She found she could kneel in it, suspended across his chest, and keep her head and arm free to grip him. But, as the monster began to jog into the woods, her arm grew bitingly cold in mere moments.

"You'll have to hold me," she said. And he did. His massive right arm took her weight effortlessly, and she curled her arm into the blanket, out of the icy night breeze. As he jogged along, his body heat seeped through the blanket and into her, and she began to warm.

She wasn't comfortable, but after a few minutes, her adrenaline settled down and she began to feel less panicked and shocked. Curiosity about her strange rescuer began to form in the recesses of her recovering mind.

"Where are we going?" she finally asked, after they'd been travelling for a few minutes. The monster seemed to have a definite destination, and seemed to know precisely how to get there.

"Into the mountains," he answered. "There'll be a blizzard up there tonight. That'll cover our tracks, and keep the duke's war griffons from hunting us."

"A blizzard?! But we'll freeze to death! These mountains are impassable during a blizzard!"

"Don't worry," he replied. "We'll work it out."

He ran along in silence for a while.

Shina couldn't relax or sleep, not being carried like this, not with the excitement and stress of the night thus far. She was in pain, bruised and strained by her earlier treatment, and she needed a distraction.

"Do you have a name?" she finally asked. She couldn't think of a better question, but it would have to do for starting some sort of conversation. The monster didn't seem short of breath, though he'd been running rapidly for almost an hour by that time.

"Ulak. Thag Ulak."

The name sounded crude and primitive to her, but she supposed it would be better than trying to address him as "monster" or some such. More polite anyway.

"Thag Ulak…. Does it mean anything?"

"'Thag' is just a name. It doesn't mean anything. 'Ulak' means 'monster' or 'terrible'. My stepfather gave me the name, since my mother was dead by the time I hatched."

Thag seemed unusually articulate for a monster.

"How did your mother die?" Shina realized it was an insensitive question even as she asked it. "Oh! I'm sorry! I didn't mean …"

"No, no, it's all right," he assured her. "My mother was a troll. She killed a couple of villages and ate them before my stepfather finally hunted her down and killed her."

"A … troll! Like, the kind that's ten feet tall and eats everything and can't be killed by mortal weapons? That kind of troll?" Shina's eyes were wide with surprise and her voice rose in a shrill squeak of shock.

Thag nodded and glanced down at her. "Yes. That kind of troll. Dumber than a box of rocks and deadlier than plague. That kind of troll." His voice was steady and calm, as if he'd had this conversation a million times before.

"But …," she paused. "You don't seem like a troll. You're big enough for one, but you seem…" she suddenly realized her comment was about to be incredibly offensive to a creature that had total power over her and just might think of her as a midnight snack.

"I don't seem stupid enough? Right?" Shina winced as he hit the mark dead on.

"Well, that's from my father. He was a dragon. A dark, evil dragon that ruled over a corrupted swamp. Smart, wicked, ages old, greedy, cunning, and extremely dangerous. I got my intelligence from that side of my family."

She might be mistaken, but she got a brief glimpse of his face, and he seemed to be grinning. Like he was playing a joke or something!

"You're kidding, right?"

"Nope," he answered.

She sputtered a moment, delicacy and manners warring with morbid curiosity, and then curiosity won. "But a dragon and a troll? How? I mean…" she realized she was actually blushing! How could she be asking Thag about how his parents conceived him?

"They were possessed by a demon when it happened," he said calmly, as if that explanation somehow made it all right.

Shocked silence was her only reply.

As they climbed further into the mountains, the night got colder and colder. Then, just as Thag had predicted, it began to snow. Lightly at first, but it built rapidly into a steady fall, and Shina could hear the wind begin to blow.

She had pulled a hood of blanket over her head, and was shivering horribly despite the blanket and Thag's considerable body heat. Every breath of the night air was an icy knife cutting her lungs, and every hint of wind seemed to slice through the blanket and cut directly to her frigid bones.

"H…h…how l…long," she stammered out through chattering teeth. She wasn't sure herself what she meant by it. How long would they survive? How long was he going to keep going before he froze to death and she died beside him? How long till … her numb mind didn't know and didn't care.

"Hush. We're almost there. You'll be okay in a minute. Cover your face with the blanket. Leave your eyes free if you can't take the claustrophobia."

She heard, but she didn't care and couldn't answer.

She fell asleep in his arms, carried like a tiny child, numbness and cold finally winning out over her hurts and bruises. She never expected to wake again. *"This is how you die of cold,"* she thought. *"You fall asleep, and then you feel warm, and then you just never wake up. I'll never wake up…."*

"Wake up," she heard a huge, rumbling voice say softly from a great distance. A hand the size of a dinner plate was gently shaking her shoulder. "Time to wake up."

It seemed to take forever to pull her mind out of the darkness. Waking up was the longest trip she'd ever been on. But finally, she opened her eyes and tried to look around.

Panic grabbed her! She was blind! She couldn't see anything but blackness!

She could feel the blanket against her skin. She could feel that she was lying down on some hard, bitterly cold surface. She could hear the wind moaning, but it seemed to be at a distance and she couldn't feel it.

But she couldn't see *anything!*

She began to thrash around, and Thag grabbed her arms to keep her from hurting herself. Drowning in the darkness, she grabbed his arm and gripped it as if it could somehow keep her afloat!

There was worry in his voice as he asked, "What's wrong?"

"I'm blind. I can't see! It's all black!" The pitch of her voice rose with each horrified statement. She was nearly screaming when she repeated, "I can't see!"

Thag took a firmer hold of her. "Nonsense. It's just really, really dark in here. You humans can't see in a dark cave, at night, with a blizzard going on outside. That's normal."

She calmed a bit. "A cave?" she asked, her voice plaintive. "Just a cave? I'm not blind?"

"You're not blind. It's a cave. I woke you up because you need to eat or you'll freeze to death."

"A cave..." she repeated quietly. "Just a cave."

She pulled the blanket tighter around herself. "It's cold in here, Thag. I don't know if you feel it the way I do, but it's far, far too cold in here for me."

"Cold doesn't much bother me . Trolls and dragons both like icy mountaintops just as well as they like tropical swamps. I don't pay much mind to either one.

"But I hadn't realized you'd be affected by it this much. That's bad.

"I thought getting you out of the wind and weather and getting you something warm to eat would be enough, but I'm beginning to doubt that."

Her teeth weren't quite chattering any more, but she was still bitterly cold, and knew she wouldn't survive the storm without some source of heat.

"Can you build a fire?"

"No wood in here. Even if I go get some, nothing to light it with anyway."

"Your father was a dragon. Can you ... you know ... light it that way?"

Thag was puzzled for a moment. Then he realized what she meant. "Ah. No. He wasn't that kind of dragon. I can spray acid around from glands in my throat, but he wasn't the fire-breathing kind."

Shina thought a moment. She reached out to where she thought Thag's voice was coming from in the dark. Her hand found him easily enough, and he was warm to her touch.

"You're warm enough," she said. "You'll just have to be my campfire for me, I guess.

"May I sit in your lap, Thag? If you can keep me up off of the floor, and we share some heat, I think I'll be warm enough to last the night."

Thag picked her up and then sat down, his back against the wall of the cave. They carefully wrapped the blanket around her, so only a small part of her face was showing through a gap for her to breathe through.

Then he handed her a warm bowl of hot soup. She took it, and it warmed her hands even though they were exposed to the chilly air. "How is this still hot?" she asked.

"My stepfather gave me a few gifts when I grew up and was ready to move out. One of them is that bowl. It produces hot soup or cold wine, either one. Whichever I want. Cleans itself out, too."

Ah. She understood that. Her father was a sorcerer, and magical implements were a common enough thing around their house. Most weren't anywhere near so practical, but it was a familiar thing in a night of confusion and terror, and comforted her just by that.

The hot soup felt good going down her throat and into her stomach. The heat spread quietly and pleasantly through her whole body and she began to relax and almost feel comfortable.

A gust of wind fluttered the edges of the blanket, and Shina shivered briefly. Thag took off his cloak and spread it over both of them. He truly seemed not to care about the bitter cold.

Shina shifted around a bit, trying to get comfortable. She'd never slept in a monster's lap before and it wasn't easy to settle down. Thag let her settle in, and was about to ask if she was all right, when he realized she had started lightly snoring. She'd fallen asleep without him even realizing it.

Chapter 2: *Getting Away with It*

When Shina awoke, there was faint daylight reflecting into the cave from the snow outside.

She yawned and stretched, then winced. Her muscles were sore and she was sporting dozens of bruises all over her body.

And she was free of the duke's gilded cage!

She was on the run, hiding in a cave in the mountains with a monster bred by a demon from two horrors, surrounded by hostile terrain, naked in snow-covered mountains, lost, bruised and battered, tired, hungry, and certainly being hunted by the duke's dedicated, well-trained, well-equipped, extremely hostile army. If she got caught, she was sure that torture and death would be the least of her worries.

But she had escaped!

And she wasn't alone. Her rescuer/captor/guard/companion was a monster, true, but he seemed to be at least a well-spoken monster. And unquestionably more competent at escaping through the frozen mountains than she would be on her own.

She wasn't sure how he'd measure up against a squad of the duke's soldiers, but she'd seen him smash his way through half a dozen of them with great ease.

And she was free!

If she died in the mountains, at least it would be while attempting escape, and not while rotting in that damned tower!

Having gathered her wits a bit and assessed her situation at least briefly, Shina looked around at the cave.

It wasn't bright in there. Enough sunlight was reflecting in off the surrounding snow that she could see, but it was still a cave cut deep into solid rock.

It was maybe the size of a medium house. The ceiling was fairly high, but Thag probably wouldn't have picked it if it weren't big enough for his extreme height. The floor seemed to be compacted dirt and was basically level and flat, and the walls were some dark stone. No way to tell what in this light. It was dry, and there were no columns or stalagmites or stalactites to indicate it had ever been significantly wet.

Other than Thag's presence, it was a perfectly boring cave.

In the quiet and half-light, she also got a better look at Thag than she'd had in the dark and excitement of the night before.

She was still sitting curled up in his lap, where she'd slept the night. His arms were wrapped around her and his huge torso loomed over her where she was leaning against.

His skin looked black or maybe dark gray, but that may have just been the light. His shoulders, above her, were covered in hard, heavy scales, almost like armored pauldrons. The scales came about a third of the way down his chest, but left a gap over his sternum below his neck. She saw that the backs of his hands and wrists were also covered in scales, with pointy little bumps in them over the back of the hands and onto the first knuckles.

He was wearing only a wide belt that went halfway up his stomach and a pair of leather, knee-length pants. The belt had numerous loops and small hooks on it for carrying things, and the pants were covered in a variety of pockets.

Below the pants, his shins and feet were also scaled, with gaps around the ankles themselves. His large toes were tipped by heavy, use-worn claws instead of toenails. The feet were more or less human-like in shape, just huge and scaled and clawed. She couldn't tell from where she was sitting in his lap, but she guessed he probably had thick calluses on the soles of his feet, and didn't need shoes or boots thereby.

Above his immensely wide shoulders and bull-like neck, Thag's head was truly monstrous. His massive jaw protruded forward several inches, giving him a predatory look. His nose was almost flat on top of that, and was covered by even heavier scales than his shoulders and chest. The wide nostrils puffed slightly with each breath, and the whole thing was more animal than human.

She realized he was looking down at her and she suddenly wondered if he'd slept at all. His eyes were in deep sockets and widely set, almost on the sides of his face. In the dim light of the cave, she couldn't tell for sure, but it appeared that his eyes were plain black orbs, with no iris, no white, just some dark color. Above them were heavy brows, bone-like and solid looking. From there, his forehead sloped back much more steeply than a human's would. She knew from brief glimpses the night before that the top and front of his head were covered with rough, bumpy scales, heavy and thick.

From the back of each side of his head, horns swept out and forward. They were thick at the base and tapered down to slightly rounded points after curving down and forward to slightly below his jaw-line. The horns didn't come forward of his face, and she thus assumed they wouldn't be useful for goring anything or in other offensive capacities. On the other hand, she could see scoring and scratches on them that looked like they might have been used to deflect blades that otherwise would have hit his face and jaw.

His arms, on either side of her, were thicker than her waist and roped with gigantic muscles. His legs, underneath her, were titanic and the muscle under her hips felt nearly as solid as the rock of the cave they were in. His chest, behind her back, rising and falling slowly as he breathed, was a gargantuan wall of muscle. Through her back, she could faintly feel his heart beating slowly deep inside him.

Shina wasn't warm, but between her blanket and Thag's cloak, and the steady warmth of his body against hers, she wasn't cold either. On the other hand, the tower had been very warm and comfortable, with a soft bed and down pillows and silk sheets. She'd had warm but plain meals as often as she asked for them, and nice wine or clean water to drink whenever she felt thirsty. It had expensive oak furniture and a good view of the sunset and the beautiful and majestic mountain. She'd had tailored silk clothing to wear. And guards outside with orders to kill her if she tried to escape, and bars over the windows, and a locked steel door between her and any freedom at all.

She preferred the cave and her one blanket, and the pangs of having missed breakfast, so long as it came with a chance, however faint, at freedom.

She reached a hand out from the blanket to feel the skin of Thag's arm. The light scales just above his elbow were rock-hard and slightly rough to the touch, but the exposed skin closer to the joint felt smooth and warm, with a pleasant, satiny texture almost like expensive leather. Despite the cold air in the cave and despite leaning against ice-cold rock all night, his skin was warm to the touch.

"We should breakfast," Thag suddenly rumbled. "And let me check if it's safe to go outside so you can relieve yourself out there. Otherwise, it's the back of the cave for that, and we'll just have to live with the odor."

With a jerk, she pulled her hand away from his arm, as if burned by the sudden realization that touching him that way was far too forward!

Shina quickly tried to recover her composure. "Yes, yes, definitely," she agreed.

Thag effortlessly picked her up out of his lap and set her standing beside him. She kept the blanket wrapped around herself, but her feet almost immediately began to feel uncomfortably cold.

When Thag stood up, she caught a glimpse of his back. Something seemed … not right. His shoulder-scales extended down across his back, covering the whole spread of his upper back and narrowing in a curve till, just above where his belt cut off her view of them, they were barely wider than his spine. It looked like she would expect … but, still, something wasn't quite right.

Thag stood up and stretched hugely. Muscles writhed under his thick skin, stretching till his joints popped. He bent backwards and then twisted forwards to each side, getting circulation going and stretching the cold and damp out from a night of leaning against bare rock.

Thag looked back at her sort of oddly, and she realized she was staring at him.

His face came into a patch of clear light from the rising sun, and she saw his eyes for the first time. They were deepest black, without whites or irises, and had a strange swirling look to them, as if some shiny black metal had taken liquid form and been stirred into motion, like oil on water. It was unnerving and brought home to her exactly how exotic her rescuer was!

Thag cautiously looked outside without leaving the cave entrance. After a minute of looking carefully, patiently, in all directions, he stepped out and looked up and around.

"I think we're safe. The duke's war-griffons will be out soon, but even they will take a little while to get this far into the mountains." He turned to her and gestured for her to join him.

Some snow had been blown into the cave by the storm, and she had to walk through it to get to the entrance. It felt like razors of cold were slicing into her delicate skin, but she inured herself to it and stepped up next to Thag, staying just inside.

In the better light, she could see that his skin was the dull gray of dyed leather, while the scales across his head, shoulders, hands and feet were the color of charcoal, and looked worn and rough.

But his eyes stayed that strange metallic black, liquid and alien.

He pointed at a nearby fir tree. "Leave the blanket here and run over to that tree as fast as you can. I'll keep the blanket dry so you can warm up quickly when you get back.

"Bathing will help your bruises heal, so grab a handful of snow and rub it over yourself. It'll be bitter cold, but you'll dry off fast enough in this air, and it will help your muscles feel better."

Shina was shocked. She blinked a few times and her mind ran over what Thag had just said, refusing to accept it. After a moment, she managed to blurt, "You want me to run around *naked* in the snow, rub snow all over myself, and then run back up here? Are you crazy?"

"Are you saying you would rather do your business in the cave we need to spend the day in? You can do that, but I would not recommend it. Even in this weather, it will reek, to say the very least." Somehow, his inhuman face managed to convey a look of puzzlement, an are-you-sure-you-know-what-you-just-asked kind of look.

"But … but … but …" she stammered, still trying to disbelieve what he'd said. "But I'll be *naked!*"

Thag, still puzzled, took a moment to answer. His deep voice was filled with hesitation as he explained, "If you run as fast as you can, get under that fir where there's no wind, and get back as fast as you can, you'll be fine. People do that kind of thing all the time in colder weather than this. For that matter, some of them go swimming in ice-water, and they're fine afterwards. They say it refreshes them."

He still obviously didn't *get it*. "But I'll be *naked*," she emphasized again.

And then she blushed when Thag suddenly laughed. "Naked? Yes, you'll be naked. In front of me," and he emphasized that last word by pointing at his inhuman face. "Lady, I'm not some farm-boy or courtier peeking into your dressing room through the curtains. I'm … this," and his hand motioned towards himself, emphasizing exactly how not-human he really was.

He chuckled and muttered under his breath, "naked", as if it were some great joke.

Shina was mortified that he'd figured out what she meant, and horrified that she'd begun to think of him as a man, instead of a monster. She realized that a small part of her had actually thought he wanted her naked so he could lust after her, and was disappointed that he didn't!

Oh gods! What am I thinking! She thought.

With a quick breath, she gathered her resolve, stepped out of the blanket into the frigid air, half-handed-half-tossed the blanket to Thag, and sprinted for the tree.

A million and one thoughts tore through her mind. *What was I thinking? Oh my gods I'm so embarrassed! I can't believe I'm doing this!* And, still in the deepest part of her mind, *I hope he is/isn't watching!*

When she got there, she crawled under the fir, and found that he was right. It was less cold under there, and she had all the privacy she could want. She shivered her way through, and did run a handful of snow over her skin, then crawled back out and sprinted back to the cave.

It was an uphill run, but a short one, and she got back only slightly winded. Her skin felt both cold and hot at the same time, and her pulse, pounding through her from the exertion, warmed her whole body.

Her breath was steam in the cold air, and on the run back, her mind had calmed down enough that she laughed to herself. As she got to him, she indicated her steaming breath and laughingly told him, "Look. I'm a dragon now too!"

Thag met her with the blanket held open, and quickly wrapped her up in it, then picked her up off the ground so her feet were no longer in the snow. He smiled back at her.

"Feeling a bit better?" he asked.

She smiled and realized she was. "Yes. Much. Thank you." It was just the polite thing to say, but she realized she really meant it. "Thank you, Thag. For rescuing me. For taking care of me."

Thag nodded his acceptance.

The day in the cave went quickly. After breakfast, more of Thag's magic soup bowl, they talked about Thag's plans for getting out of the mountains. They would travel by night, to evade the griffons. Thag said there would be snowstorms every night, and it would be rough on her, but it would keep their tracks from lasting in the snow.

He told her about the caves he had found, and how they'd stay in one each day for the next three days. Then there'd be a village, and a road. They could move faster there. He planned to go east and travel around the inland sea rather than take a boat over it.

He'd come over on a pirate ship, after intimidating them into taking him as a paying passenger, but he didn't think that would work for getting her back to the kingdom. They might try it if the duke's pursuit was too dangerous for the road, but it would be a last resort if they did.

They'd have to make plans after the village. Till then, it was just a straight path over the pass, but after that they would need to work out what to do. Shina was too tired to make the effort for plotting.

It wouldn't be safe. None of it would be safe. Shina realized, sadly, that she would never be safe again, not while the duke and the king were at each other's throats, but at least she would have options better than dying in a tower in the far north of the world.

Thag cut crude shoes, more booties or slippers than anything else, out of an edge of the blanket, and sewed them up so they would stay on her feet, using a large needle and some leather straps that he carried in one of his many pockets. He didn't have enough thread to make more clothes from the blanket, but it was better than being barefoot in the snow when she did need to walk.

She was slightly surprised that he had skill in such a thing, since she thought of sewing as a womanly craft. It wasn't till later that she realized she no longer doubted his hands, however huge and ugly they might be, would have the dexterity for detailed work like stitching. She was, after less than a day, beginning to take his competence in disparate things for granted.

They spent the afternoon talking of her life in a royal sorcerer's house, as a member of the minor nobility, and of his life as a vagabond and mercenary, living by his wits and strength on the roads of a thousand different lands. From some of the stories, she gathered he had spent time in the noble courts of some strange lands.

She learned that he'd been raised in the wild by an elvish druid, the same one who'd killed his troll mother and stolen his egg from her. He knew the ways of a thousand animals, and could mimic their calls and list off their habits, diets, and the details of how they lived their lives. He knew the properties of another thousand plants.

Indeed, he was the best-educated person she'd ever met, and she soon found herself sharing things even her closest friends didn't know. How she'd despaired of ever finding a suitor who didn't just want her to use her attractive young body and then discard her, or who were just looking for the wealth and political connections her father had. How so many of the men her father had chosen for her were ignorant and boorish, or, worse, boring.

Thag sympathized with her, though, as he pointed out with a laugh, he'd never had any suitors himself so couldn't really say he knew what it actually felt like. She giggled and pointed out that, as a man, Thag would actually *be* a suitor, he wouldn't *have* one. Thag wryly pointed out he'd be more likely to be the horrible monster some suitor had to rescue a fair maiden from and they both laughed at the image of that.

"Hard to court someone when I'd never get past 'hello' without the young lady in question screaming in terror and running for the nearest knight-in-shining-armor type," as Thag put it. Though he added, "Might actually be a good way to earn a bit of extra money. Offer my 'terrorize the girl into your arms' services to gallant young knights…."

Whenever Shina got cold, Thag had her get up and walk around the cave vigorously. Between that and periodic sprints to the tree, she kept warm enough. He had her sleep the evening, so she could travel all night. Halfway through, she got too cold from sleeping on the floor, and she crawled back into Thag's lap, just like the prior night.

As the sun went down, the wind began to pick up, and Thag said it was time to go.

Long before they reached the second cave, Shina was exhausted and frozen through.

Thag carried her as gently as he could, but the jostling shocked her bruises, the cold cut through the blanket like a knife, and the darkness and howling winds caused a sense of pervasive fear so instinctive she couldn't rationalize it away.

Soon, she was too worn out and frigid to care. The bouncing and the cold were just the way it was. Her exhausted mind couldn't conceive that it had ever been any other way or that it would ever end. The idea that she had ever been warm seemed like a vague dream.

When they finally reached their shelter for the day, Thag had to feed hot soup to her. She was too tired and her hands were too numb to hold the bowl.

Shina was wracked by dreams of being trapped in a small, dark place that was freezing cold. She tossed and turned constantly in her sleep, muttering little sounds that reminded Thag more of a small animal in pain than of human speech.

It was late afternoon when she finally woke up. Thag was holding her in his lap again, and she felt small and frail against that backdrop. She barely got up long enough to go eat and attend to necessities, and then she fell into another exhausted sleep.

Her youth and strong constitution were taxed to the limits over the next three days and nights. She spent her days shivering in frigid caves and her nights being carried through the terror of storm after storm.

Thag's alien eyes, which could see in the dark of a midnight blizzard, began to haunt her dreams. Even during her brief periods of wakefulness, she could see them burning behind her eyelids whenever she blinked.

What was he that he could do the things he was doing? A dragon? But why would a dragon rescue her? Why would a dragon care for her and help her eat, and catch her every time her shaking, numb legs gave out on her?

Why would a dragon hold her gently in his giant lap and carefully and conscientiously do everything possible to keep her warm through the bitter days in the caves?

And why would she feel safer in his lap than she ever had in her own home, even through the pain of unhealed bruises, bone-deep exhaustion, and frozen numbness?

She couldn't think, and consciousness seemed like too hard a struggle to be worth the fight.

And Thag kept on going. Night after night. Day after day. Cave after cave. Storm after storm.

Chapter 3: *Duking it Out*

Every soldier of the castle was in the courtyard standing at strictest attention. Every uniform was perfect. Every foot, arm, weapon, hand, was perfectly placed.

A cry from the southern lookout tower, "They come!" was accompanied by a quick semaphore of flags to let everyone in the surrounding land know the duke was on his way in. He and a few key officers and bodyguards were riding in on trained wyverns, accompanied by an escort of dozens of war griffons.

The officers of the castle knew what he was there for, and were prepared and braced for the worst. They had failed, and they expected to pay severely for it.

The duke landed first, jumping gracefully to the landing platform in the courtyard while his wyvern barely touched down and immediately sprang back into the air to let the next alight.

Duke Antain was a tall, muscular man with short, black hair and pale blue eyes. He kept a mustache, pencil-point thin with every hair meticulously in place. Some women found his dark, arrogant look and harsh face attractive. He always had perfect posture and a pantherish grace to his every move.

He was, first, foremost, and always, a fighting man who held his power through his own prowess on the battlefield, his cunning as a tactician and strategist, and the loyalty he commanded in the brutally competent ranks of his army.

Before any of the people with him had even disembarked, the duke was speaking urgently to the castle's top officers.

"I heard about her escape, and I want to know how it happened," he snapped.

"Sire, she had outside help. Something inhuman, we're not sure what, came in the night, killed thirty men, and escaped with her over the wall."

The duke thought for a moment. "You're not sure 'what'? Not 'who?', but 'what?'"

"Yes, sire. We have reliable reports from multiple men that her rescuer was much too large to be a man. One guard swears he shot it in the neck, at nearly point-blank range, with his crossbow, and that it didn't even slow the thing down.

"He got the best look at it, and swears it was some sort of demon."

The duke looked surprised. "He shot it from close range, and got a good look at it, and he lived? How did he survive?"

"It ignored him, sire. With his arrow sticking out of its neck, it ignored him and leapt off the wall. He and a few others saw it spread large wings and fly into the woods. Over that wall, sire," the man pointed to where Thag had jumped from the wall only three nights ago.

"Bring me that man. I want his report in person…"

***

The duke had heard all the reports. Some men he had questioned twice. Now he stood at the top of the wall, where Thag had jumped, and looked pensively out over the woods, towards the mountains.

"Captain," he said, beckoning.

The castle's captain knew his fate was about to be sealed, but he stepped forward immediately and bravely. The duke looked him over. *A good man. One of my best. And this thing made a complete fool of him. Best not to underestimate it!*

"Captain, I want you to know this isn't your fault. When I gave you this charge, I didn't think that her sorcerer father would send a demon to steal her from us. He normally refuses the dark arts, but I should have anticipated that the threat to his daughter would drive him to measures he would normally avoid.

"You've been using trackers and war-griffons to try to find them. It's a good start. We'll continue that, but I also have some … specialists … here. Some resources you don't have. Let's give them a try."

The duke had long since memorized the maps of the surrounding lands. "Add my griffons to yours. Send some in relay up and down the coast. They won't find her, but we have to look just in case.

"Your maps indicate four settlements within a week's travel from here. Have you checked those?"

The captain felt almost weak with relief. He was being forgiven! "Yes, sire. We checked with three already. They're pirates and smugglers, and they'd give her to us if they had her. They know we could crush them if we were forced to."

"And the fourth?"

"We can't really check with them, sire, but we don't really have to. You see, sire, it's a whole village of werewolves…"

Chapter 4: *Were Are We Going With This?*

Shina was not only awake, but was both terrified and furious! "We're going *WHERE?*" she demanded, staring furiously into Thag's eyes. She stood up to her full four-foot-eleven height and stamped her foot in anger.

Thag rumbled calmly. "A village full of werewolves. You need clothing, which they have, and we need some supplies, which they also have. And they'll have medicine for your bruises and fever, if I'm not mistaken."

Shina was reduced to sputtering since her mind refused to come up with any sort of answer to a statement so patently absurd!

"I'll go back to Duke Antain and his men! They'll torture and rape and kill me, but it'll still be better than being eaten alive by werewolves!"

Thag gave a long-suffering sigh. "They won't eat you. You thought I was going to eat you when you first saw me, and I haven't done it yet. Or do you think I'm taking you there so I can share you? Amount of weight you've lost over the last few days, you'd hardly be a meal for a whole village, much less me."

Shina pouted. She argued. She threw a temper tantrum until Thag just picked her up, stuffed her in the blanket-bag and started walking.

"You let me out of here!" she screamed, and punched him through the bag. "Ow! My hand!"

Thag had said there would be no storm that night, and he was, as always, right. The cool night air, without the usual freezing winds, was merely completely unbearable through the blanket, instead of the usual state of beyond-all-endurance.

After pouting and shivering for a few minutes, she finally asked, almost politely, "May I look out, please?"

Without stopping, Thag released enough of the top of the "bag" that she was able to stick her head out and look around.

It was dark, of course, since they were still traveling by night to avoid the duke's air patrols. Thag said they'd soon be outside the flying range of the griffons, and could start to travel by day at that point.

Her eyes adjusted quickly enough. They were getting used to slight

light in stone caves, and a starlit night wasn't too hard on them. Soon, she could see they were coming down from the mountains, following a stream bed, towards a lower valley.

As they got closer, she could see lights, as from windows, in the near part of the valley, and she surmised correctly that this was their destination.

"So why do werewolves have a village out here? Don't they normally roam around the woods in packs?"

Thag didn't reply right away. She knew by now that this meant he was considering her question seriously. Finally, after a minute or so of silence, he said, "Some do. This pack lives mostly as men and women. They have a village. They raise some animals – those that don't panic themselves to death surrounded by werewolves. Some of them hunt.

"Mainly, though, they're out here to stay away from mankind. They like it out here. They feel safer this way."

Shina was running a slight fever, and was exhausted by the rough treatment life had given her over the last few days. Though Thag had carried her almost the whole way, she felt like she'd run a marathon and was too worn out to argue more over their destination.

She was resigned to either living or dying by Thag's craft and strength, and she decided to just trust him and hope it wasn't misplaced.

They were still a mile away from the lights of the nighttime village when Thag stopped. He unhooked the blanket from his neck and set her down.

Thag stood straight up to his full height and threw his shoulders back. He stood with his feet apart and his elbows out to his sides. It made him look even bigger and more intimidating than usual, and she instinctively knew that was on purpose.

Thag sniffed a few times at the air, his head tilted slightly up.

Faster than Shina's eyes could follow, Thag spun around and lashed his left hand at a blur of darkness that was leaping through the air at his back!

His massive arm held the creature by the neck, effortlessly holding the snarling, struggling thing several feet off the ground.

Thag whirled again, and snarled at something in the darkness past her. A rumbling growl rose from his titanic chest and he loomed like some wild beast!

The thing in his hand yelped in fear as he hurled it into the dark, and she heard more yelps of surprise where it crashed, hard, into something out there that she couldn't see in the dark.

Thag spread his arms wide, the claws on his fingers fully extended. He shifted so he was standing over her where she crouched on the ground, his tree-trunk legs straddling her helpless body.

"I see you, were! Change now, or I kill every one of you, pup to dam! Smell me and know I can do it!" Thag challenged in a roar.

A pair of glowing, green eyes approached from the dark and Shina clung to one of Thag's legs in instinctive terror.

As they approached, the eyes rose up from the ground, and Shina saw the transformation twist its flesh. It started as a giant wolf, easily four feet at the shoulder, and smoothly shifted to a strong, rugged looked woman.

The woman was as naked as Shina was, but something about her said the cold was beneath her notice. Her whole body spoke of a noble disdain for mere cold, based on sheer, raw durability.

Six others, three men and three more women, stepped into the moonlight. All were naked, and none seemed to care. The six took places behind the first woman, granting her precedence. All looked ready to fight if she demanded it.

Thag looked to the right, straight into the dark woods. Shina couldn't see a thing there, but Thag snarled, in his rumbling, threatening, powerful voice, "You too, little bitch. Don't think I can't see you well enough to count every hair on your mangy pelt!"

In moments, an attractive young woman walked out of the darkness over there and stood, hands on hips, glowering at the giant in their midst. The other seven looked like full adults, but this one looked about Shina's age, perhaps even younger.

The first woman glanced at the younger woman, and then looked Thag full in the eyes. "We smell you, dragon-thing. What do you want with us? The way around our village is to the south. You can go that way without interference."

Shina had heard such arrogance in the voice of Duke Antain and a few of the king's courtiers. The threat in these people's stances made her wish Thag would just take their offer and head south.

Thag pointed down at Shina, where she crouched beneath him. "She needs clothing and medicine. You will provide that. She needs to rest for a few days, and needs to be safe from the duke across the mountains. You will provide that too. Then we will move on. Your territory is yours."

Shina thought for sure these proud people would be mortally insulted by Thag's demands and his threatening tone, so she was caught completely by surprise when the leader suddenly sighed in obvious relief and relaxed into a more comfortable stance.

The woman looked at Shina with intent concern in her eyes. "You poor thing! You look half-frozen! And you're hurt!" The were looked up at Thag indignantly. "What have you done to this poor woman? Why have you hurt her like this?"

Shina recovered just enough to protest, "It wasn't his fault! He saved me!"

The woman gave Thag one last accusing glance, as if she didn't quite believe Shina, and then, all-business, stepped over and helped Shina to her feet. Her companions, suddenly friendly and relaxed, started chattering amongst themselves and with her. Questions about how cold she must be and would she like something warm to eat, comments about "so-and-so has a daughter about her size," and a dozen opinions about whose house she should stay at.

The young woman who'd appeared last finally stepped in and took control. "You lot leave her to me! I'll get her indoors and warm, and then you can all bother her once she's slept! Can't you see she's about to pass out in front of us!"

The bustling crowd herded Shina with them, pausing only enough to wrap her back up in her blanket. When it was clear that she could barely walk, the young woman spoke up again. "Jack, you carry her. And be gentle about it!" The man she'd addressed swept Shina up into his arms and began to carry her.

Shina was too tired to protest that Thag should be the one carrying her.

Somewhere along the way, she fell asleep, or passed out. To her battered body, it was much the same.

When she woke up, the first thing she noticed was that she was pleasantly warm. She was wrapped in blankets made of bearskins, with heavy fur and a pleasant, leathery smell, lying in a soft bed in a wooden room instead of a cave.

There was light streaming in through a curtained window and the room felt safe and comfortable.

She stretched and her muscles felt relaxed. They tensed and relaxed comfortably under skin that felt clean and unhurt.

She felt good! It was the best feeling in the world to not hurt at all! To feel rested and warm and not the slightest twinge of pain was more luxury than the best room in her father's fabulous house!

The young woman from the night before (or was it longer ago than that?) stepped through the deer-hide curtain in the rough-timbered doorway to the room. She was smiling and looked genuinely happy. "Good morning," she said cheerfully. "How do you feel?"

Shina gave a contented sigh. "Well. I feel well. Thank you."

Seeing her in full light, instead of the moonlight-in-the-woods of their first meeting, Shina could see that the young woman was, indeed, about her own age. Maybe a year or two younger. She had short black hair, a pretty face, pale skin, and bright, cheerful brown eyes with a glint in them. Her body was slender and looked quite athletic. She didn't have Shina's heavy bust or wide hips, but she was still definitely feminine and quite attractive. She was taller than Shina, probably close to average height or a little more.

Her stance, her face, every move of her body, spoke of a sense of self-confidence and well-earned pride. And she almost glowed with an inner health that Shina could only admire.

Unlike the prior night, the young woman was wearing clothing. It seemed to be lightly-furred leather. Perhaps from a doe or some similar animal. It was dyed in bright patterns, and looked well-cut and masterfully crafted.

"Are you ready to get up and get some breakfast, or do you still need rest?" the young woman asked.

Shina decided she was ready to get up and said so. She pushed off the blankets and sat up. She felt marvelous, and wondered at how she could possibly feel this well after the last few days.

"I'm Shina, by the way. I don't know if Thag introduced us last night."

The young woman giggled for a moment. "Last night? Try three nights ago. You've been sleeping most of the last three days. I'm Lisa. Thag is out hunting with some of the pack, so we've got time to get you some food and fit you for some clothing."

All through waking up and getting breakfast, Lisa chattered like the teenage girl she was. Shina took a few minutes to get comfortable with the fact that she was having bacon and eggs cooked by a young werewolf in a log cabin in a village of weres, and then she settled in to the constant chatter herself.

Other young women started to show up a few minutes after breakfast, some with bits of clothing they hoped would suit her, others with this or that travel supply, all with cheerful banter and bright smiles.

Shina was trying on a pair of doeskin boots that seemed to fit reasonably well, when Lisa said something that stopped her dead in her tracks in the morning. "It must be nice having a mate like Thag. He's <u>such</u> a great hunter! He's been out with …" she stopped suddenly when she saw the shocked look on Shina's face. "What's wrong?"

"Mate?" Shina sort of squeaked, blushing furiously from the top of her head to the soles of her feet.

"What?" Lisa was genuinely confused.

"Mate?" Shina asked again. Her mind desperately tried to make sense of what Lisa was saying, but it just wouldn't connect. She wanted to say a million things, most of them excuses or lies, but she couldn't seem to get anything more to come out of her mouth than just the one word.

"Well, you certainly smell like it. When you were with him the other night, you smelled and acted like human girls do when they're around their mates. And he certainly protected you like an alpha does when her mate is threatened.

"I mean, it seems kind of strange for a male to be the alpha, but Thag definitely is, and you humans are kind of weird about the whole thing, with males leading most of your packs, so everyone just assumed…"

"Mate?" Shina repeated again.

"Yeah. He's great. What's wrong?"

Shina felt like she was about to die of embarrassment, but she finally got her thoughts together enough to speak. "But he's a … monster."

Lisa seemed to be waiting for Shina to say something that made sense.

"He's huge. And he has horns and fangs and he's not even human and …." She belatedly realized she was saying 'not even human' as if it were a negative thing, to a pretty young … wolf-monster.

She desperately gathered her bearings and her rapidly crumbling sense of self-reserve, and said, "He's not my mate, that's all."

Lisa looked dubious. "Ooookay, whatever you say," and dropped the subject.

Conversation the rest of the day was slightly more restrained, and Shina noticed that most of the young werewolf women were looking at her in a puzzled way, but she refused to bring it up.

Thag and the hunting party returned a little before sunset. They had spent the day with the weres driving large prey to Thag, who could bring down a moose or even a bear in a few seconds with his bare hands. It had been a very productive day, and they were dragging nearly a ton of fresh meat, bones, and hides on a sled pulled mostly by Thag.

The village rarely went hungry, even in the dead of winter, but with Thag's help, they'd brought in a month's worth of successful hunting in only three days.

The whole village met them as they came in, and everyone was very excited and happy with the results of the hunt. Male and female alike, everyone settled down to skinning, butchering, and all the other chores needed to turn this bounty into winter supplies.

They were gathered in the village center around a large bonfire. The sun had set early over the mountains, and it was a cold winter evening, but everyone was dressed comfortably and the fire and hot food and company made it a pleasant party. Shina was sitting on a bench near Lisa, while Thag sat on the cold, hard ground a few yards away. Torches and lanterns on poles provided extra light and warmth around the whole space.

The whole evening, Shina realized that the young women of the village were all interested in Thag. Most would start to flirt, then would notice her, and they'd bow their heads submissively and stop, instinctively avoiding challenging her.

Two of the young women, both closer to her age and older than the rest, were more brazen. They looked Shina in the eyes and gave a sort of silent challenge, then openly flirted with Thag. They were as frank about what they wanted as city prostitutes! It was shocking!

And nobody took them to task for it! No adult stepped in to make them stop being such sluts. No one even discouraged them.

One of the girls had her shirt open nearly to the waist, showing a shameless amount of cleavage. This wasn't like the natural nudity of the first night she'd been here, when the weres had shifted to their human shape from animal form. This was sexual in a way that Shina was both unfamiliar with and shocked by.

Thag bantered with and teased a few of the young women, and Shina found that she was actually getting jealous! This was just wrong!

"What is wrong with me? I'm getting jealous of were-bitches throwing themselves at Thag shamelessly! These hussies! How dare they! And why does it matter to me? I should just..."

Before she knew what she was doing, before she could lie to herself and make herself stop with some jury-rigged excuse, Shina stood up from the bench, walked over, and sat down in Thag's lap, perching herself on one of his immense thighs. In the caves, she'd slept there every night for warmth and safety, but this was something else, and she wasn't sure what.

Thag adjusted how he was sitting to let her get comfortable, and didn't even pause his conversation with some of the other hunters. He smiled at her for a moment, in a comfortable, familiar way, silently saying "hello", and put his arm around her body just like he always did.

She immediately felt warm and safe and strangely comfortable.

In a moment, Lisa was tapping Thag on the other arm and indicating he needed to make room for her to sit on his other thigh. Thag, surprised, looked at Shina as if for her permission. She smiled. Now that she'd claimed her territory, it seemed okay to share it with her new friend.

Shina and Lisa chatted for a while, while Thag discussed hunts and animals and scents and good fights with the village hunters, and the rest of the village wrapped up the chores on their prey.

It was the most simple, relaxed, friendly evening that Shina had ever spent.

Hours later, in moonlight, with the fire finally dying down, Thag picked up the two sleeping women from his lap, and carried them to Lisa's family's house. He couldn't fit through the front door, but Lisa's mother and father took the two young women from him and bundled them off to bed in Lisa's room. Shina protested sleepily as Lisa's mother led her into the house, but didn't resist.

Thag, wrapped in his heavy leather cape, settled down on the front porch. He chuckled to himself at the image of him being a watchdog in this village of werewolves, as he rested. Thag was dragon enough that he didn't sleep the way mortals do, but peaceful rest was something he cherished the rare times he could get it. He shut his eyes and listened and smelled.

His keen ears could easily pick out every set of lungs in the village. It was effortless for him to tell the one set of human lungs from the surrounding were ones. To any human observer, Lisa and Shina would seem to be a pair of young women tucked into a bed together, sleeping comfortably. In the dark of the night, once the torches had burned down, most humans would have had trouble telling the two apart. As close as they were to him, Thag could easily differentiate their breathing, and even the sounds of the two hearts.

The scents that filled his nostrils were ones of a sleeping village of weres, with that lingering scent of the young human woman. He was fond of her, which wouldn't have surprised her and would have pleased her. But he also thought of her as a child who needed protection, which would have bothered her had she known it, though she couldn't yet admit that to herself.

Of course, it was natural for him to feel that way about her, since he was nearly five centuries older than she was.

***

"Lisa! Shina! Wake up!" Lisa's father, Marty, was shaking both of them by the shoulders. He sounded urgent, but excited, not afraid.

"Wake up! Thag says there's someone coming, and you need to get up now!"

The sun wasn't up yet, and the only light in the room came from a small candle Marty had lit and put on a spike near the doorway. The candle was for Shina's benefit, since Lisa didn't need light any more than any wolf did to find its way around in a moonlit room.

As the two young women climbed out of bed, Marty continued, still excited. "Shina, you need to get dressed. It's cold out there and we don't have a fire going yet."

Lisa could tell her father was a little worried, his scent tinged with the slightest bit of apprehension, but not true-fear. "Daddy, should I dress, or just go out, or should I shift? What should I do?" she asked. Lisa was still young enough to ask for decisions to be made for her. She was calm and brave, but still a little unsure of herself.

He paused and thought for a moment. Finally he decided, "Dress. You can always shift later if Thag says to." It was natural for him to think Thag should make all the decisions – Marty was a beta and would do whatever the strongest alpha wanted. His own daughter, who was growing up to be a hunter, would one day soon be an alpha, and he would defer to her when she was, despite being her father and life-mate of her mother.

The two girls quickly cleaned and dressed and joined Thag and most of the weres at the edge of the village. All of the weres picked up the scent on the wind, just as Thag had. There was an edge of nervous anticipation to their waiting – enough that Shina picked up on the emotion even though she couldn't smell what they could.

Just as the sun rose over the mountains, Shina saw a person approaching the village through the woods, on foot.

She was upwind of the village, and all the weres were sniffing in anticipation. Some were in the shape of normal wolves – the size of large dogs but with yellow eyes and the look of dangerous predators. A few were in their war-form, like huge wolves from some ancient time, the size of ponies and with fangs inches long and razor sharp. About half were in human form, and about half of those were dressed in their finest leathers.

It occurred to Shina that she'd only been awake amongst these people for a single day, but she already accepted their casual nudity, out in the wind and snow on a bitter day. She would have been mortally embarrassed by them a week ago, but her experiences since her rescue had inured her to the prudish modesty she'd grown up with. For the weres, nudity in the snow was just the way they were, and their pride and the naturalness of it clothed them as much as was needed.

It was yet another bitingly cold day, and she welcomed the furs that they had given her. She was comfortable, and the clothing was amazingly supple and pleasant to wear. The bright sun, low in the pale blue sky, would do little to warm the mountain village on this winter day, and there was a slight but bitter breeze off the mountains. A few pale, fleecy clouds raced across the sky.

Thag, of course, stood at the head of the crowd of villagers. Their pack alpha, the first woman Shina and Thag had met in the woods, stood at his shoulder, mere inches back from his position. From stories yesterday, Shina knew this woman didn't have a human-name, and was the best hunter of the whole village. She had killed a mountain lion all by herself, an impossible feat, when she was younger than Shina was now, and had led the village bravely and skillfully for over a decade.

Finally, Shina could clearly see who was coming, and she was shocked!

It was a woman approaching them through the snowy woods. But what an amazing woman! She had pale, reddish-gold hair down to her waist, with the sides of her head shaved bald above her ears and up to her temples. She was tall and athletic looking, with long, perfect legs and graceful arms. Her face was beautiful in every feature. She was wearing a see-through green dress from her shoulders to her ankles, that covered a body that could only be called perfect. Covered it while still revealing every bit of it.

The woman had large round breasts that somehow didn't need the kind of support that they should have, and had ample well-rounded hips. Breasts and hips swayed with every graceful, sexy stride as she walked towards the village.

Around her waist, she had a simple golden belt made of flat plates linked together, and she wore a silver, or maybe platinum collar around her neck, almost like an armored gorget but decorative rather than functional. She wasn't wearing anything else, but her upper body was covered in brilliant tattoos, covering her upper chest and her arms down to her wrists. These also were on her outer thighs, from waist to knees.

As she came closer, Shina could see that the woman had bright blue eyes, beautifully shaped and made up with colored eyelids and long, dark lashes.

She was barefoot, and the dress made it plain that she wasn't wearing anything underneath the sheer silk. The whole outfit drew the eyes to the triangular patch of curly hair between her legs, and to her large pink nipples.

Shina had never seen anyone like this, nor any outfit like this. She was shocked. This went far beyond the nudity of the weres. The sexuality of it hit her like a slap across her face, and she felt plain and boring for the first time in her young life!

Shina was standing next to Thag, and the woman approached

the two of them. As she arrived, she gave Shina a look, peering deep into her eyes, that somehow made Shina catch her breath as a warmth spread through her body that she'd never felt before.

The woman's voice was a sultry caress. "Hello Thag. How are you these days?"

Shina was instantly burning with jealousy! Thag knew this creature? This gorgeous, sensual goddess? This embodiment of feminine sex! Oh gods, she suddenly felt crushed.

"Hello Koserana. What are you doing here?" Thag replied. He did know her! It wasn't fair!

"Saving your ass, big guy. Duke Antain is on his way with an army on wyvernback. They'll be here by tonight."

The weres were shocked and confused. "Here? He's coming here? What will we do?"

Koserana calmly looked around at them. "It's too many to fight, and they'll have silver and fight from the air, so you'll have to give them what they want." She pointed at Shina, "Which is her."

Thag's eyes narrowed and he reflexively took a slightly more aggressive stance. He paused for a moment. "Can we run, or is it too late for that? Or could you get her out of here while I distract them?"

Koserana didn't hesitate. "Not what I'm here for, big guy. I've got other work to do. I'm just here because I owe the wolves a favor from a while back.

"As for running, you could, but I doubt she'd be able to keep up. Her blood's not strong enough to fly, you know."

Shina was getting more and more confused with every statement. "What do you mean about my blood and flying? What work are you talking about? Are you saying I just have to give myself up and let the duke kill me?"

Thag put a hand gently on her shoulder. "We'll run," he rumbled. "If we fight, this whole village will be destroyed. And I can't protect you against a whole army. If we fight, they'll get you before I kill them all."

Koserana considered for a moment. She gave Shina another one of the glances that made her feel that strange warmth. Then she appeared to make up her mind.

She nodded and spoke, "Okay. You'll run. I'll keep the village as safe as I can. You'll need a storm to cover your tracks. Can she run in that?"

Thag replied, "I'll handle the storm. We're okay for that. We've done it before."

Thag spoke to the village leader. "I won't tell you which way we're going, so the duke's men can't force you to tell. He'll know that, so that should keep your people a bit safer. Send your young into the woods to hide. He won't be able to find them there unless he gives up on chasing us in order to hunt your people."

Weres sprang into action, some running to gather the pack's cubs and youth, others running to grab travel supplies for Thag and Shina. A few started a quick conversation with Koserana and Thag as Shina headed back to Lisa's house to get her things.

Lisa led Shina back to the house and they went in to get her stuff.

"I've got a few extra things for you, Shina," said Lisa. "Some more clothing, and a bag to carry it in. And a few things I'd like you to have." Lisa held out a leather strap with a large fang on it as a pendant. She looked embarrassed for a moment, then screwed up her courage. "This is one of mine. I'll grow it back, but you can have it to remember me by. I've never had a human friend before, and I want you to remember me."

Shina thought for a moment, then took the odd necklace and put it on. She leaned forward and kissed her friend. "I don't have anything I can gift back to you, but I promise I'll wear it and remember you."

The two young women hugged, and tried to keep from crying. They'd only known each other for a couple of days, but each had never had a friend like the other.

Finally, Thag finished his conversation with Koserana and the village elders. He came back to Lisa's house and pointed out that he and Shina needed to get going.

"Lisa, you'll need to clean our scent off of everything in the village. The duke will have animals with him that can track by scent."

Thag and Shina set off into the woods, walking together. It felt good to be on her own feet, but Shina knew that, when they needed speed and endurance, Thag would carry her again.

They hadn't gotten far when Koserana called to them to wait up.

Shina was expecting some sort of goodbye to Thag, but instead Koserana came straight to her.

She smiled and met Shina's eyes with her own. "I know we just barely met, but Thag told me a bit about you, and I feel like I kind of know you." Koserana leaned in and kissed Shina gently on the lips. The feeling had an electricity in it that Shina was not prepared for and which startled her. "If you ever get tired of the big guy, look me up. Okay?" She held Shina at arms' length, her hands on the younger woman's shoulders, and looked deep into her eyes.

Shina was flustered and a bit confused. "Um… sure. Yeah," she finally managed.

Koserana turned back to the village with barely a hint of a wave for Thag, and ran away gracefully and fleetly.

As soon as she was out of earshot, Shina turned to Thag and asked, "What was that about? What did she mean?"

Thag shushed her and gestured that they should get moving.

It wasn't until several minutes later that he broke his silence. "She could hear you, back there. She's got dragon ears, so it's polite not to talk about her anywhere close by."

He looked down at Shina, walking next to him at an easy pace for her. After a few seconds, he asked, "Do you really not understand what she meant?"

Shina could have sworn that there was a hint of embarrassment in Thag's voice and manner. The slightest hesitation, the tiniest tension in his face. She couldn't imagine why, but she knew him well enough to notice even that tiny hint. She'd never seen him anything but totally frank before, so it bothered her.

She stopped, turned to face him, and thought for a second. Was she missing something obvious? If so, it wasn't obvious to her. With a puzzled look on her face, she asked again, "I don't get it. What did she mean?"

Thag looked at her for a little bit and seemed unsure where to start. Finally, he shrugged his giant shoulders in a "no way around it" kind of gesture. "She's attracted to you. That's what she means."

Shina was still looking blank, so he decided to be more blunt, "She wants to seduce you and have sex with you." Shina blushed a deep shade of red and had a shocked look on her face. Thag continued, unperturbed, "She does that with lots of attractive women. She's usually more aggressive about it, but she apparently thinks you're mine right now, and she doesn't want to fight me for you."

Shina was stunned, and Thag had to gently direct her with his hands to get her walking again.

Over the next few minutes, she tried, several times, to ask more questions. Each time, she would get her mouth open, as if to start speaking, and then would stop and just keep walking. Once or twice, she got as far as "But…" or "What…" but no further than that.

Thag knew it would take some getting used to. Shina had led a very sheltered life and it was obvious she knew little or nothing about actual sexuality. Her shocked embarrassment when he first dragged her out of her bed back in the tower had told him the whole story on that part of her life.

He also knew, from her first question about his own parentage and other conversations, that she had a bit of a morbid curiosity about the subject. So it would be best to just frankly answer any questions she had and get her over being shocked by the whole thing. Sort of a "sink or swim" style.

Shina, meanwhile, was battling in her own mind in a million directions at once. Her first prudish thought was that a woman being sexual with another woman was perverse and even horrible. But the rush she'd felt when beautiful, sexy, gorgeous Koserana kissed her! But it was wrong! But it had felt good when Koserana admired her so warmly when they first met.

She was confused and unsure of herself, and Thag kindly let her sort it out for herself, willing to lend a hand if she asked.

They walked several miles before the end of the day, taking several rests for Shina. Thag seemed to be in no hurry, and merely walked silently alongside her.

Finally, slightly before it actually got dark, Thag stopped and said they needed to set up camp for the next few hours.

They picked a large fir tree and crawled into the hollow under its lower branches. It was a crowded space, but it would shelter them adequately for a while. As before, they shared Thag's soup bowl for supper, and then settled down with Shina in Thag's lap for warmth and comfort.

"Thag?"

"Yes?"

"How do you know her?"

"Koserana? We've crossed paths a few times. She's a mercenary. Usually works as a bounty hunter. But her jobs sometimes cross with what

I'm doing, so we've worked together a couple of times."

Shina seemed to be gathering up her courage. Her voice was tiny when she finally asked, "Have you made love to her?"

"No. I already told you, she does that with other women. You may not have noticed, but I am male," he said with a chuckle.

Shina stopped to think. It was something Thag was teaching her to do, and she was beginning to realize why he thought it was important.

"Thag?" she said again after a while, her voice sleepy.

"Yes?"

"If I ever do make love with anyone, I think I'd like it to be with a man, like you. But ..." she paused again. "But Koserana is so beautiful I think ... maybe ..." She didn't seem able to go on.

"I know," he replied softly. "I know."

Shina snuggled into Thag's lap, warm and safe. Tired from a day of walking, she was soon asleep.

Thag rested as the wind outside the tree began to howl and the snow began to fall, exactly as he had said it would. He knew the young girl had the beginnings of a solid crush on him. He just wasn't sure what to do about it.

Fear, even terror, or hatred, were the emotions he was used to from humans – he'd expected to spend the whole rescue dealing with her fear.

He wasn't prepared for affection.

He was accustomed to distant respect from other dangerous people, like the dragon Koserana. They weren't afraid, for a variety of reasons, these ones. They knew he was dangerous, but they accepted it.

The only person he'd ever had love from was his stepfather. Though centuries had passed since Llwddan died, Thag still missed him, but paternal love and loss hadn't taught Thag how to deal with a young girl being attracted to him.

Through the evening and into the night, as she slept peacefully in his lap, Thag wondered what he should do. As the night wore on, he found no answers, only deeper and deeper puzzlement.

Chapter 5: *Storms*

The duke, wearing silver-plated armor, arrived at the werewolf village early in the long winter evening. His riding wyvern set down in the middle of the village, along with five others, and he and his captains disembarked while the animals rapidly climbed back into the sky and took up a soaring pattern with the others of his flying command.

He had fifty men in the sky and another hundred in the tiny village and the woods around it. All were armed with silver-plated arrows and swords, and armored in silvered mail. Two of the men with him were also accomplished sorcerers.

Arrayed against a village of a few score hunters and peasants, even if they were werewolves, it was an overwhelming force. That was how the duke did all of his business – never by margins that left any hope to any potential rival or foe. If he couldn't overwhelm, he bided his time till he could, or pursued covert plans of treachery like the kidnapping of the royal sorcerer's daughter.

Some of his senior men, companions of years and a hundred battles, thought it odd that he was personally pursuing the young woman. Why not leave it to them? There wasn't anything he could do out here in the mountains and woods that they couldn't do just as well, and he had important matters back at home. But none of them were brave enough to risk his wrath by questioning him.

The duke was mortally concerned about Shina, for many reasons. Not the least of which was the manner of her rescue. How had they known where she was? How had one of his strongest castles been penetrated as easily as an army camp whore? The reports from the men of the castle, of a giant monstrosity that shrugged off crossbow bolts like mosquito bites – this scared the duke. Who of his rivals could buy such help? What would it do next? Why hadn't his – special ally – warned him of this?

While he was out here pursuing the escapee and her rescuer, was some well-informed, well-financed enemy of his moving forward on plans he knew nothing about? Was the whole rescue simply a ruse to get him away from the kingdom for a while?

Thoughts like this chased each other's tails through his mind, leading to a nervous anger that left a burning pit in his stomach and kept him awake at nights.

His thin excuse for kidnapping the girl, the one he'd told his men and had them tell her, that she was a coin to be used to buy the royal sorcerer's treachery against his king, was a bold lie. He knew that plan would never work, but it made for a good excuse with his allies – the ones he trusted enough to tell of this endeavor.

Damn his allies as cowards anyway! If they would openly proclaim for him, they'd have enough strength to fend off the royal armies and break away into a kingdom of their own. United under his command, they would be strong enough to break from the tyrant's reign, but separately they were held to the royal yoke as thoroughly and absolutely as slaves.

Thoughts like this had the duke in a rage. His men assumed he was angry about being forced to pursue her himself – even if they couldn't imagine why he would do so.

The man who had led the duke's forces into the village strode up to his duke and then dropped to one knee and bowed his head with a firm, "My lord".

"What have we got, lieutenant?"

"My lord, we've captured all who were here when we arrived. But they must have had word of our approach, since all that's here are a score of old men and women. There are tracks leading out of the village in all directions, mostly adults, a few wolves, several children."

"Any sign of our prisoner or the beast?"

"No, my lord. But one of the houses and a few areas of the village have been scrubbed clean of all scents. I'm sure my lord can see the implication."

The duke nodded, a satisfied look on his face. This was a clever man, no wonder his captain had recommended he lead the search. *Yes. The implication. Someone was here who the village wish to hide from me. Obvious, of course.*

"Have a flying patrol scout the area. They won't find anything, of course, but we should look anyway. Put the villagers we captured in silver chains and ship them off to the slave markets. They deserve worse for trying to thwart me, but it's all we have time for right now.

"If patrols find any of the wolves, kill them on sight.

"It's too late to fly the wyverns tonight, so make a camp here. Tell the men to loot anything they want. We'll burn the rest in the morning."

As the duke gave his orders, men sprang into action, barking directions at their own subordinates. In moments, the whole platoon was busy turning the small village into a proper military camp.

The duke took over one of the bigger houses – the whole house smaller than his usual bedroom at home, but better than the tents he usually had to live in when on campaign.

Late into the night, he and his best officers pored over the few scant maps they had of this area, and reports from the scouts who had overflown the whole valley as best they could. It wasn't much, but they were pretty sure which directions Shina and her rescuer had to be going.

The duke knew, now they were on the right track, that his flying squadrons would overtake the refugees by midday tomorrow. He just wondered what the beast had in mind for that. He was sure it would anticipate being intercepted. No matter how fast it was on foot, it was still forced to follow overland terrain, and must know it would be overtaken by aerial pursuers.

Thus far, it had shown itself to be dangerous, cunning, and faster than a good horse. It was rapidly crossing terrain that normally required flying mounts for any speed at all. Its assault on his castle had been fast, deadly, and effective. At first, the duke had wondered why it left living witnesses, but by now he understood that rumors spread by them to the other men had them all afraid – veteran soldiers who had iron nerves in even the most brutal battles were afraid to face the beast.

The duke knew he'd lose men in any attempt to recapture the girl, and every man lost getting his kingdom would be one less to help him hold onto it once it was his. That math was always on his mind.

It would, of course, be much easier and safer to simply kill both of them from the air. But he knew the horrible consequences that faced him if he did that. He fell asleep still working through his options, and dreamed of green eyes and a young woman.

***

Thag woke Shina when he felt it was time to get moving again. While she got ready for the night's hike, he crawled out from under the tree and took a look around.

He was looking at a bright flame, far back in the valley below them, when Shina came out and joined him.

She was quiet for a moment, till she realized what they were looking at.

"Oh gods, Thag!" she suddenly screamed. "Oh no! Oh no! That's the village isn't it! They're burning the whole thing!"

She looked up at him, imploring him to contradict her, begging with her eyes to be wrong. But they both knew she was right. It was the village that was burning, with everything and everyone in it. The distant fire was reflected clearly in the black mirrors of Thag's eyes, along with a profound sadness that crushed any hope of doubt she might have had.

Shina looked back at the distant flames.

"Come, little one," rumbled Thag. "We must be going.

"Most of the wolves will have fled into the woods. Koserana and the village alphas will have seen to that. They knew the risks they took in standing up to Duke Antain, and they took them bravely. We do them no service if we get caught after the sacrifices they've made."

Her plaintive voice was barely a whisper, "You could kill the men who did that." When he didn't respond, she went on, barely louder. "Why are you standing there looking at me when you should be killing those men?"

Thag merely looked at her. She stared back at him, grief and accusation marring her youthful beauty. He sighed, and then spoke. "Yes. I undoubtedly could. Some would get away, maybe to hunt you, maybe to flee to their homes across the sea. But I could kill many, maybe even most.

"And I might even kill the duke, though he'd probably just fly out of my reach on a wyvern. If I did kill him, he would deserve it for what he's done, and not just to you or those wolves.

"But, child, evil can't cure evil. Killing for food or necessity or defense of self and family, that's one thing. Killing for vengeance just begets more killing.

"If I kill the duke, the whole kingdom will fall into war. The nobles all hate each other, and the king is a dark-hearted man who would gleefully take one side or another in all their fights, so that he could clean up the pieces and loot the battlefields.

"Yes, I could kill them. And then I'd have to kill more. And then more. And more yet. It would never end. That was the path the battle-mages took, and it has spawned ruin for our world."

He looked dejected, his shoulders slumped, his head bowed, crouched down so his face was level with hers, his voice fading to a quiet whisper of distant thunder. From below his lowered brows, his eyes sought hers, and she had to strain to hear, "Is that truly what you wish, little one? War with the kingdom?"

Her first instinct was to tell him "yes" with all her heart, the temper of the spoiled, vitriolic girl she had been raised to be. But Thag had begun to teach her to think. She paused, and saw the pain in him. She knew, then, that Thag would do it if she asked. He would hate it, but for her he would drown the kingdom in blood and pain. Realizing that, Shina took her first step towards being a better woman than her father would ever have been able to raise.

Gently, she reached out and touched Thag's face, a light caress on his hideous cheek, where scales and lumpy flesh hid the wise soul she now knew lurked within. "No," she said simply but firmly.

Silently, the two looked once more at the flames back in the valley. Then they turned in silent and perfect accord, and walked noiselessly into the woods.

***

It felt like he had just barely gone to sleep when Duke Antain woke suddenly to the sound of screams – both human and that horrifying shriek that wyverns make when terrified and in agony. He was abed in his armor, with sword in hand, in case the weres attacked in the night, and he came awake instantly ready for battle!

The tiny bed in the closet-sized "master bedroom" of the werewolf headwoman's primitive hut was unfamiliar, and the room was totally dark, without the windows or night-lights most humans preferred, so it took him a moment to find the door, but then he was out and springing for the main entrance to the house!

Two of his bodyguards tore the door open from the outside just as he reached for it himself, but he brushed them aside and stepped out into the dirt path that passed for a main street through the middle of the village.

The whole village was in flames!

The very roof he'd just been under was beginning to burst with golden fire!

His men were running everywhere in a mad panic, some of them engulfed in searing flames, others simply terrified by whatever was going on!

And then, up in the air, outlined by its own fire against the night sky, he saw it! The beast had come to attack them!

Shocked, he stood and just stared for a moment! He could hear his men around him, babbling at him with noises that refused to settle into coherent words, but he ignored them completely as he watched the horrible beast soar through the heavens and come around for another attack.

It turned straight at him and spread its wings in awesome and terrifying grace. His mind saw that his men had been wrong about it – it wasn't some dark thing of the deepest night, it was gleaming and metallic and shaped like some winged serpent-thing out of a nightmare!

His men scattered, dropping their weapons and shields and running as the horrible monstrosity sped towards him!

But the instincts that had left him alive on a hundred battlefields didn't abandon him completely. He hurled himself to one of the mighty arbalests lying on the ground where a panicked soldier had dropped it, and, in a single swift move, he had it aimed at the creature.

The arrow he fired seemed to move in slow motion as it speared through the air straight into the beast's chest!

And then all his senses returned to normal speed as the beast screamed in agony and winged past him at a mad velocity! A diving hawk might move so swiftly!

The duke realized that his men had also been wrong about its size – this beast was no ten-foot-tall giant of twisted humanoid shape! Its body was no larger than a small pony, maybe a very large dog, and only its wide wings, long neck and serpentine tail made it look larger than it was.

He had hurt it! Maybe even killed it. His brief glimpse had seemed an eternity while it was happening, but even brief as it had really been, he knew that the arrow had pierced its scaly, coppery armor deep into the flesh of its chest, puncturing it downward from the shoulder into the chest itself.

He knew from his many battles that such a wound was often fatal, and he held the hope that it was this time too.

Then the moment was past, and the beast had flown off into the night, wounded and bleeding and hopefully dying.

The duke and his bravest men brought order to the survivors as quickly as they could. A swift check revealed that every wyvern he had was either already dead, dying, or so badly injured the only thing to do was the final mercy. Almost half of his men were dead with them, and a few more wouldn't see the sun rise again.

"The prisoners?" he snarled at one of his captains.

"Gone, my lord. They escaped during the attack."

"If any of their guards still live, I want those men nailed alive to the trees! Leave them for the wolves that they let escape!" he raged.

The captain blanched, but raced to obey, dismayed that the night had started so well and ended so terribly.

***

Thag and Shina had barely been walking for an hour, Shina walking next to him and setting the pace as briskly as she could, when suddenly Thag silently stopped her with a hand on her shoulder. She looked around apprehensively at the Stygian darkness of the woods, but she could neither see nor hear anything out of the ordinary.

Still, she knew her senses were far less keen than her companion's, so she waited while he appeared to be listening.

Suddenly he took her by her shoulders and leaned down to put his face level with hers. "Shina, listen to me carefully! Don't be afraid of what you are about to see! Don't be afraid!" His intent look and serious voice were more than enough to call up a deep dread inside her, but she swallowed and firmed her voice and told him she wouldn't.

What could possibly… and her mind filled with images of intangible dread and terror as she fought for courage. Anything that Thag thought might be frightening was surely too much for her!

And then she caught a brief glimpse of something like a titanic bat crossing the stars over their heads, and circling around where they stood. The sight itself was horrible enough, though it was but a shadow against the faint light of the night sky, but fear seemed to pour into her as if she were a vessel and it was coming in from outside!

Her father had taught her, when she was very young, to recognize the power of a sorcerous mind assaulting her senses, her reason, even her deepest emotions. She knew exactly what this was, and the disciplines he had trained her in from her earliest years (to his own dismay as she grew older) were automatic. Walls of intellectual force, purest will, and iron-hard emotional control snapped into place as she slipped into her defenses.

The relief of being freed from that external terror was enough to let her get a grip on even her own fear. Her defenses would not stop her own emotions, only those being forced into her by sorcerous means, but the sudden cut-off of the outside fear was enough relief to allow her to take control of her own emotions.

Thag would protect her, she knew, and that was enough.

The flying thing folded its wings and stooped to the ground, landing roughly. It lay there, in a heap, radiating pain and fear in equal measures.

Gods, it's strong! My father hasn't half its strength on his best days! she thought to herself.

Thag didn't even pause, but stepped right over to the thing, and put his hand on its serpentine head, as if to reassure and calm it.

In the dim light, Shina could only see that it was a medium-size animal – smaller than a horse, but bigger than most dogs. It was scaly, and the scales seemed to glint in the starlight. Its head, roughly serpentine, was at the end of a long, thin neck that connected back to a somewhat thicker body, which looked like it probably had the usual four legs, perhaps in a somewhat feline shape. She could tell it had a long tail behind it, like a lizard. And it had large, bat-like wings that also seemed to gleam like metal, as did most of its body.

Then, without warning, her vision seemed to blur where the creature was. Not quite like it had been immersed in mist, but not too unlike that either. The sensation made her eyes hurt for a moment, but it faded so fast she almost thought she'd imagined the whole thing.

And as suddenly as the mist had taken her sight, it was gone, and Koserana appeared in its place! She was kneeling on the ground, Thag's huge hand resting lightly on her head, just where the beast had been.

If Shina hadn't seen it herself, she would never have believed it!

Two nights before, she had stayed in a cabin owned by werewolves, but somehow her mind refused to accept *this*.

Her disbelief lasted only a moment, and then Koserana shattered the night with a scream of such agony as Shina had never heard in her life!

"*You fool!*" shouted Thag. "Shifting with that thing still in you! What were you thinking!"

He caught Koserana's head as she collapsed to the ground, her scream cut off as suddenly as it had started, cushioning her fall and keeping her from hurting herself further. He gently stopped her from moving her arm, where it would have made the wound worse, and cradled her head with his other hand.

Koserana's voice was feeble. "I got them, Thag. I burned them for what they did to my wolves. I got them!"

Shina was stunned! The burning village wasn't the duke, it was this … this thing!

Thag looked up at Shina, "Shina, noblewomen in your land learn healing. Can you help her?"

Shina's anger faded like a snuffed candle-flame as she realized she was needed. "Let me look," she said as she stepped up and tried to see what was wrong.

"It's too dark for me, Thag. I need light. Do I have time to build a small fire?"

"Do it."

The wolves had given her a fire-kit – simple dry tinder and flint that she could strike on a knife they'd also given her. It was simple to gather some dead branches from the ground around them, and it took only minutes to get a small campfire going.

Shina realized it felt really good to be doing something useful. Something she wasn't dependent on Thag or her father or anyone else for.

Thag gently carried Koserana over the small fire and lined up her head and shoulder near it so they were well lit for Shina's human eyes.

"Don't put her too close," Shina directed. " I don't want to burn her."

Thag smiled. "Gentle one, you can't burn her. You could drop her naked into a volcano, and she would swim through the lava like you would through water."

Shina looked at him, puzzled, but decided to pass up his riddle in favor of examining the horrible wound in Koserana's shoulder.

The shaft and feathers of a long arrow stuck up from the shoulder. Obviously the rest of the shaft and whatever head it had on it were deep inside the wounded woman's chest. Blood was seeping from the wound, not pouring, so she knew the arrow-shaft itself was blocking the wound closed. *It'll need to be removed carefully, or she'll bleed out.*

She remembered to check her patient's mouth for blood, to see if the lung was punctured, and was glad to not see any. It was a hopeful sign, anyway.

"Thag, is this the kind of arrow that you can't pull out? Can you tell?"

Thag knew what she meant, but he couldn't tell what kind of head it had on it, so he said as much.

A memory flashed through Shina's mind. She paused from inspecting Koserana's wound and looked up at Thag leaning over the two of them.

She squinted a bit at the side of his neck, then reached up to touch it where she'd seen him rip a crossbow arrow just like this one out of his own flesh. There was no scar, no sign there had ever been any wound.

And that reminded her incongruously of something else. "Wings!" she suddenly exclaimed. "You had wings!"

Thag was definitely nonplussed by this sudden announcement, seemingly coming from nowhere. After a moment, he recovered and gently asked, "What?" The look on his face was the first time Shina had truly seen him totally unsure what was going on.

"When we escaped from that castle," she pointed in a vague direction that may or may not have been towards the actual castle. "You had wings when we escaped. ..." she saw he was still confused and continued, "When we jumped off the wall, you had wings!"

Thag thought for a moment and then realized when she meant. "Ah. Yes. I'm part-dragon. I can't shift as completely as Chalkos can, but I can take a form that sort of has wings. Can't fly with them, but they are good for gliding off of walls." When he said "Chalkos" his head gestured towards Koserana, and Shina took the alias in stride.

A puzzle that had been bothering the back of Shina's mind ever since that night was finally settled, and Shina turned back to Koserana/Chalkos.

"I'm assuming she can't heal like you can, so I can't just tear the arrow out. The shock might kill her if it rips anything." She shook her head. "Thag, there's just not much I can do without a healer's kit."

"Would one of those help?" Thag asked.

She nodded emphatically. "There are magical tools in those. With one, I could cut into the side of her chest and see the arrow-head. Maybe even remove it if I have to. Then we could treat the rest of this.

"I've never done anything like that before, Thag. Maybe we should get her to a real healer?"

"Soldiers have those kits, right?"

"Yes. My father's guards always had one or two around."

Thag nodded. "Then I'll go get one." He took Shina by her shoulders. "Little one, you must guard her. She's as important as you are. We need you both alive. Can you guard her for a day or two?"

A heavy rock settled into Shina's stomach and her knees felt weak, but she managed to get a quiet "yes" out. Thag looked at her intently, as if he needed to assure himself that she really meant it. Then, to her pleased surprise, he put his gigantic arms around her and gave her a brief hug.

His eyes looking directly into hers from mere inches away, he smiled and nodded. "Yes, indeed you can." She realized he was proud of her and her spirits rose instantly!

He rumbled, "I'll be back in two days at most. Move her under a good tree. There'll be a storm tonight and you need shelter even if she doesn't." He took off his cloak and handed it to her. "Use this as a sleeping bag if you need to. She'll be a good source of heat if you need it.

"If I'm not back in two days, head east. Don't go back to the kingdom, they'll just hunt you down and kill you before you can get to your father. East. You understand? Look for Brad in Anytown. Brad in Anytown, if we get separated."

She nodded. East, not the kingdom, which was south and west. It made sense. Without Thag, the duke's men would certainly capture her if she went into the kingdom at all. There were independent city-states to the east, and maybe she could make a life in one of them if she had to.

Thag didn't have to tell her what his plan was. He was going to attack the duke's small army and steal a healer's kit from them. Despite what she'd felt only a few hours before, and despite what he'd said about fighting a war for her, she was sure the plan was risky.

"Will she get infected? Or is it true that only humans and natural animals get infected wounds? Will she get a fever?"

"No infection or fever. It's not just humans and animals, but she can't get an infection any more than I can. Dragons don't get infections."

Shina looked at the unconscious woman lying on the ground next to her. "*Dragons?*" she asked. "Dragons are real?"

"Ask her when she wakes up. Oh, and make sure she doesn't try to shift. That wound will only get worse if she does."

Thag looked at her one last time, smiled, and then turned and ran off into the woods, back the way they had come. In a second, he had flashed out of sight into the dark of the night.

Shina was again surprised at how *fast* he was! He was so big, towering over everyone and just massively solid, that even though she knew he could walk faster than her, it was easy to forget that he could run much faster yet.

He planned to retrace a full day's travel, fight a small army, and return, in "a day or at most two". She had only known him for less than two weeks, but she knew him well enough to know that he really did expect to do exactly that.

After a final glance in the direction her hero had disappeared into the night, Shina settled down to the chore of getting Koserana under a good tree, as Thag had directed. The woman was heavier than her, and she also had to avoid jarring or otherwise aggravating the wound. It wasn't going to be easy, but it had to be done.

Her father's daughter would have balked at the physical demands, and would have tried to browbeat Thag into doing the heavy lifting for her, or at best would have just given up on it altogether after a single half-hearted attempt.

The young woman Thag had hugged and been proud of, took a

deep breath to gather herself, and set to the task at hand with the conviction that it had to be done, and thus it would be done.

***

The distance Shina's best hiking pace had covered in most of a day, Thag retraced in a couple of hours. It was barely past sunrise when he arrived at the smoking remains of the village and found it completely deserted.

"The wolves probably won't come back here. They'll find another valley, even further from the 'civilization' they despise, and settle there," he thought.

It was just as obvious that the duke and his small army were retreating, heading back towards their own lands, largely along the path that Thag had taken.

He'd done it in a week, carrying Shina most of the way, and all of it through blizzard conditions. The weather would stay clear for the fleeing men, Thag knew, but it would take them at least a month to clear the mountains. Doubtless they didn't have the supplies for that. Though if not all of the duke's wyverns had been killed, some might come looking for him and bring some supplies. If they were very, very lucky.

The tracks were muddled enough that Thag could only tell it was a lot of men. Maybe eighty or a hundred, possibly slightly more or less. But no mounts, no beasts of burden at all.

He hadn't seen anything flying leave the ruins as daylight arrived, so he knew Chalkos must have gotten every one of the wyverns and griffons.

This was going to get very, very ugly for the duke and his men, and probably sooner rather than later.

***

Jenlaw took his night guard duty seriously. He was far enough into the woods that the other men's campfires wouldn't ruin his night vision, but close enough that a yell would easily carry to them.

The frigid cold of the air nipped at him through his heavy cloak and thick boots. His leather armor, though studded with silver spikes, wasn't so cold as heavier chainmail would have been, but he was still shivering, and had to stay moving to keep the cold at bay.

Like all the men, he knew they'd been soundly defeated at the werewolf village. Some of the men claimed the duke, Lord Antain himself, had killed the beast, but Jenlaw was quietly unconvinced. He'd never say anything, not where the duke or any officer might overhear him anyway, but there was a general grumbling that the thing had attacked them twice, once at the castle, once at the village, and both times it had killed men and then gotten away clean. Both times with a crossbow arrow in it – but if the first one didn't kill it, why expect the second one to?

Plus, just to make this more horrible than it already was, they were trapped on the ground, without support, and there were werewolves in the woods around them. Angry werewolves. Maybe silver studs in his armor and silver plating on his sword would help, but couldn't werewolves use crossbows just as well as men could, and would a few silver studs help against that?

He hadn't yet reckoned with their dismal state of food supplies. "Tomorrow" and "tomorrow night" were what officers worried about. Jenlaw was worried about *this* night and the werewolves that were undoubtedly in it.

Starlight, amplified by the crystal clear air and the snow cover on the ground, and his careful attention to preserving his night vision, were enough to give him a brief glimpse of something huge and dark racing out of the woods towards him, in near total silence and tremendous speed. The briefest image.

Soldier Jenlaw of Duke Antain's personal guard would never worry about werewolves again.

***

"My lord … um …," was enough to wake Duke Antain from his miserable sleep. He rolled over and looked up at the soldier who had addressed him. It was barely light out, the sun still rising over the high mountains to the southeast.

"Yes, Kierly? What is it?"

"Um … I'm … not really sure, sire."

The duke blinked the sleep out of his eyes and then stood up, stretching muscles and joints that were protesting the short sleep on the cold ground. The duke's cloak was enchanted to keep him warm and dry, so he wasn't as miserable as most of his men, but sleeping in chain-and-plate on rock-hard ground wasn't comfortable even after all the years he'd spent in the field on campaigns and battlegrounds.

He looked around, and saw that all eighty of his men were staring at something. They looked more confused than angry or afraid, so he trudged over, still yawning, to see what was up.

Men stepped aside as he arrived, and the duke took on the same puzzled look and stance they all had. What was going on?

At the edge of their camp, right between two small fir trees, there was a pile of dead animals. From what the duke could see, it looked like a moose and maybe two goats. They were obviously dead, recently so since they were fresh and still had all the skin and flesh on them, but what were they doing there and how had they gotten there during the night?

He looked around at all of the men, but they were all just as puzzled as he was.

This nicely solved their immediate food problem. There was enough meat there for all the men for several days, at least if it was rationed reasonably. *But how did it get there?*

"Did anyone see how this got here?" he asked, more puzzled than upset.

A chorus of "No, sire", "No, my lord", "Not me, sire", came from all around.

It was about then that someone noticed that Jenlaw and Kalco were missing. A quick search of the perimeter of the camp found Jenlaw tied to a tree, babbling about monsters.

Nobody could find Kalco at all. Though he had been huddled together with a few other soldiers for warmth during the night, they had all been asleep and nobody had noticed him leaving.

None of the other guards had seen a thing, and Jenlaw was incoherent.

This expedition, to capture a stupid escaped girl, had turned into one of the biggest disasters in Duke Antain's life, and he still couldn't figure out why.

And where the hell had Kalco gone, and where had this damn meat come from?

***

It was a couple of hours past dawn on the second day that Thag had been away. If he didn't return by the next sunrise, Shina would have to consider that he had failed and that she needed to finish her escape on her own. She wasn't worried about it yet, but she was worried about Koserana.

The wounded woman was slowly bleeding out. She was in such terrible pain that she stayed unconscious most of the time, and Shina had to struggle to keep her from moving around and making herself worse. She would wake up enough to drink a little hot broth every now and again, but Shina knew Koserana was dying, despite what little she'd been able to do to slow the bleeding and keep the wound from getting worse.

She was thinking about that when Thag appeared from between the trees. He was carrying someone over his shoulder, holding him by the legs with his upper body hanging behind Thag's back!

"What? Who?" she asked, delighted to see Thag but confused by his … cargo? prisoner? something else?

Thag sauntered up easily, breathing deeply but not winded by his long run through the night. He smiled and winked. "You wanted a healer's kit, so I brought one. This is the healer, and his kit is in this bag," and he handed her a small leather sack.

Shina, somehow, just couldn't think of a good response to that.

Chapter 6: *Go East Young Woman*

Thag gently woke Koserana up.

Shina was holding Kalco, the duke's best field medic, at knife-point. The poor man, confused by his kidnapping, and terrified of the giant monster that had done it, wasn't sure what was about to happen. He knew he was a dead man – he'd never betray his duke or cooperate with these enemies of his, and they would surely kill him when he refused.

Koserana slowly opened her eyes. They were bloodshot with pain and stress, and deep black rings around them stood out horribly from her pale, bloodless skin. For a moment, there was no recognition in the blank look she gave the giant half-troll.

"Thag?" she finally forced a hoarse whisper past cracked lips.

"Hey," he said gently, with care and affection in his deep voice. "This man here can help you heal, but you need to convince him," he pointed at the shaking soldier. He whispered, full of doubt, "Can you do that?"

Koserana blinked a few times, focusing her eyes on Kalco.

Shina was scared. She already thought of Koserana as a friend, and she was convinced she was dying right in front of her. She glanced away from her charge, Kalco, at Koserana's still-beautiful face, and was amazed to see the irises of Koserana's eyes change from bright blue to metallic copper! The eerie metamorphosis spread rapidly over the bloodshot whites of the eyes, and inward across the pupil, till all that was left were spheres that looked like they were made of bright metal!

Kalco suddenly stiffened where he stood, and Shina thought for a moment he was going to struggle. She braced herself to use her knife, held at his neck, if she had to. But he merely stood, ramrod straight and straining with every muscle.

A glance at his face showed his eyes locked on Koserana's, his pupils so dilated that there was only the faintest hint of a ring of color around them.

The metal of Koserana's eyes began to swirl, as if the copper spheres were somehow fluid despite still looking like solid metal. Solid metal that was in strange motion.

Shina knew where she had seen that before, and looked at Thag's gem-black eyes, looking like black crystal but always swirling and flowing. But where his flowed slowly and without direction, Koserana's were like two whirlpools, spinning faster and faster every second.

Suddenly Kalco spoke. "Oh! Mistress! How did you get so hurt?" He looked at Shina, his eyes still dilated unnaturally wide, and told her, with total conviction in his voice, "Let me go! I must care for the mistress!" He abruptly reached up to push the knife away from his neck.

Shina glanced at Thag, who quickly nodded his assent, so she let the man go.

Kalco grabbed his healing kit from Thag with a brief, "I need this for her!" and then knelt beside the wounded woman and began quickly and professionally to examine the arrow and the wound.

Thag whispered to Shina, "We should let him work," and gestured to indicate they should retreat behind one of the trees.

Thag paused to tell Kalco, "Call if you need help with her. We are dedicated to her service, as you are," then joined Shina on the other side of a large fir. They couldn't see Kalco or Koserana from there, the branches were too thick, but could easily hear Kalco muttering to himself.

Shina spoke quietly, "Thag, what did she do to him?"

"She made him fall in love with her. Not like romantic love, more like the love priests have for their gods."

"She can do that?"

Thag hesitated. "Of course she can. You've spent your whole life around a sorcerer. Aren't you familiar with that kind of thing?"

"Are you saying she's a sorcerer as well as a dragon and a shapeshifter, and whatever else she might be?"

Thag smiled. "Little one, all dragons are sorcerers and shapeshifters. Don't you know the history of magic?"

Shina shook her head. "My father said magic is from sorcerers, or from the old battle-mages. But all the battle-mages are dead, so it's just sorcerers now. And their magic is a gift from the gods to their favorite people. That's what he always told me."

Thag muttered something that sounded like, "Pompous buffoon," and shook his head in negation.

"Are healing kits fast?" he asked her as he sat down next to her.

She wasn't sure why he was asking, but answered as best she could. "It will probably take him at least a few minutes, maybe an hour or more. If he can even heal her. Thag, I think she's dying." Her voice caught on the last words and a tear came into her eyes.

"Ah. So we have a few minutes," Thag acknowledged. He continued, "Let me tell of how magic came to be and how people use it. He'll either save her or not. We've done what we can to save her, and standing here brooding about it won't help her.

"When the world was first being shaped by the gods, they made innumerable models, each a world, but only a piece of one. Some had seasons, some didn't. Some had day and night, some were either perpetually light or eternally dark. Some were large, with continents and oceans, some were very small, only a few hundred yards across. Some were made of fire, some of stone, some of water, some were just vortexes of air, and some mixed these together in various ways.

"This world," he pointed at the ground under them and then all around at the sky and the mountains and trees, "is made mostly of stone and earth, with seas resting on stone foundations. It has air above the seas and land, and enough fire below the land that we have some volcanoes and such around. Others are different.

"But the gods couldn't decide what the final world should be like, so they ended up with shards of worlds, but without a full world.

"Thousands of years ago, humanity was made in the worlds. Humans are made to act as little gods – able to create and to think and to rule over worlds, but not makers of worlds.

"Most humans are limited to their own shard. They can't even see the other shards except as stars in the night sky." Shina's face reacted to that, but Thag stopped her before she could interrupt him. "Most people think they live on spheres, for the shard-edges fold space and join themselves. They see the void as empty, instead of being full of other shards and power.

"But a few humans could see other shards. Those ones could also channel and direct, to one extent or another, the massive creative power of the void around the shards, that the shards themselves were made with.

This is where 'magic' comes from – it's the power used to create the shards themselves, and it can still shape them, and the things in them.

"The first people to use magic were the elves. They had a small mastery of it, and they used it to make their bodies beautiful and eternal. They don't really die unless they are almost completely destroyed. They don't get sick or old. The magic left in them, they use to master their arts and music and food. Some, like my stepfather, use it to commune with the spirits that are the craftsmen of the shards – the titans and elementals that build mountains and storms and seas and everything else that isn't itself alive.

"Next came the dragons and the wizards. The wizards use magic outside of themselves, far more powerful than the elves. There never were very many wizards, compared to the numbers of humans in all the shards, or even compared to the tiny portion of humanity that became the elves.

"Dragons are among the most powerful of magic users. They transformed themselves into far more alien beings than the mere cosmetic changes of the elves – powerful, graceful, deadly bodies that can blast toxic flames from their breath, can soar through the skies and even through the void to other shards, and minds that can bend the will of anyone weak enough and foolish enough to look into their eyes.

"Chalkos is one of those. She's a full dragon, the last one in our world – maybe the last in all the shards since Ariel left the shards with the demigod Gem. She can take on the human form that would have been hers if she hadn't been born a dragon, but her natural form, the form she was born to, is a beautiful creature with copper scales and wings and talons. 'Chalkos' means 'copper' in a language from another shard. 'Koserana' is the name she uses when the disguises herself as human – it means 'servant of my master' in yet another shard-language. She pretends to most humans that 'Koserana' is the servant of 'Chalkos', and very few people know they are really the same being.

"Sorcerers are the human descendants of dragons like her, with a touch of their power, but only a touch. That's what your father is."

Shina thought about what Thag had said, and then asked the question uppermost in her mind ever since he'd mentioned it, "What do you mean 'see shards as stars in the night sky?'"

***

"That's not what stars look like, Daddy," said the six-year-old girl.

She and her father were looking at a painting her father had commissioned for the house's front hallway. It was a night-scene of the city, with the front of the house in the foreground, a backdrop of the city skyline, and the top third of the wide painting was the night sky done in black velvet and tiny gemstones in the outlines of the more famous constellations.

Emstone, the girl's father, corrected her. "Well, of course they don't look '*real*'. Real stars twinkle and all that. But it's beautiful anyway, and that's what matters. Don't you like it, darling?"

Young Shina looked at it petulantly, and muttered under her breath, "It's still not what stars look like."

Her father gave a long-suffering sigh and went back to admiring the superb painting. His daughter, he knew, would grow up one day and would stop being so very difficult when she was more mature. Yes, he was certain of it. And the painting really was beautiful, especially the tiny shards of gemstone used for the stars. Very beautiful indeed, and quite satisfactory.

***

"What do you mean about stars?" Shina asked again.

"Stars. They're just stars, right? Everyone says they're little points of light in the sky that you can only see at night. Right?" Thag replied, his voice just dripping with innocence and absolutely no expression on his face at all.

He pointed up into the sky. "Like those up there, that make the Big Shark constellation. Everyone knows what stars are."

Shina play-punched him. "Damn it Thag! I'm serious!" her voice brooked no further teasing.

"What do you see up there, Little One? Where everyone else sees points of light in fanciful shapes and sweeps of hazy light, what do you see?"

Shina looked where he had pointed. "I see what I've always seen. And what I've always been told was just imagination. I see an island in the sky. I don't know how else to describe it. And island in the sky…" her voice trailed off.

Thag nodded and looked up at the sky.

Shina was quiet for a minute. Then, "Thag, what do you see?"

"I have dragon-eyes. I see a sky full of worlds. Islands in the sky, as you poetically stated. I see the currents and storms in the void between them. I see lands I can't go to because I'm only half a dragon, and even that half is tainted."

Shina heard the longing in his voice and looked at him, almost alarmed. "What do you mean, tainted?"

Still looking at the sky, not returning her look at all, Thag rumbled, "My father was a lesser dragon. His blood tainted by whatever his ancestry was. Nobody knows. My stepfather didn't. The lesser dragons can't do the full transformation. We can't fly…" he stopped for a minute or two. Shina waited. She wanted to comfort him, for she heard the sadness and longing in his voice, but she didn't know how.

Finally, he continued, "We're meant to fly. Dragons are, I mean. Fly between worlds. It's why the first dragons *became* dragons in the first place – to fly to the worlds they could see and nobody else could."

Shina had thought Thag a monster when she first saw him. Then she had thought him a hero when she understood he had rescued her. Now she realized he was a person. She had clung to him for safety many times, and taken shelter in his arms from storms and werewolves and the bitter cold of the northern nights, but this time she put her arms around his thick neck and *she* gave *him* a hug.

Neither spoke for a while. They didn't need to.

After a time, Shina spoke. "Thag, I don't care that my father paid you to rescue me. If you want to go, to find someone who can help you get to the stars, you don't have to stay with me. I don't know how, but I'll find my own way home."

Thag looked at her in complete surprise and shock. "Paid me? Your father? Where did you get that idea?"

"I thought he must have. You said you live as a mercenary and all that. I thought that's what you meant."

"Your father didn't pay anyone to rescue you. He sold two of your bodyguards into slavery in the mines, for the crime of being off-shift and asleep in the barracks when you were kidnapped, and let it go at that. He never even asked the king to help find you, much less hire anyone."

He saw the crushed look on her face and stopped. "I'm so sorry, Little One. You caught me off guard. I shouldn't have said those things. I'm sure your father loves you very much and wants you back...."

Shina stopped him with a finger on his lips. She swallowed, then wiped a brief, bitter tear out of her eyes. "No. No, I believe you were right the first time. My father and I never got along. I was pretty mean to him, and he was too busy being the Royal Sorcerer to be much of a father."

She raised her face and looked into Thag's eyes. She was touched by the concern on his face and the hurt in his eyes. He regretted hurting her. No one had ever cared for her that way before. "Thag, I was a pretty horrible person before. I don't think anyone would hire you to rescue me. And I don't think you're just 'muscle for hire', despite what you said before. You're too kind and generous and wise for that." Thag tried to interrupt, but she again put a finger against his lips to shut him up.

"I know, you want to deny what I'm saying about myself, but it's all true. And you want to protest about yourself, but that's all true too.

"I guess what I'm trying to ask is, why did you rescue me? Nobody hired you for it, right?"

Thag pointed at her finger, where it still rested on his lips, a question on his face. She giggled a moment and removed it. "You may speak now." They both smiled at the humor, weak as it may have been.

"Nobody hired me. I do sometimes work as a mercenary, but only when Sam tells me to. Before you ask, Sam is the first druid. She was a friend of my stepfather's, and she's the one with the plans. I can't tell you more than that, but I can take you to her if you ask me to."

"She would know why I can see 'shards' instead of 'stars', and she can say why I'm 'important', like you said a few days ago, and all that, right?"

"She can say."

Shina thought for a moment, but only a moment. "Is she another one of these fantastically beautiful women you're going to have to swear to me you haven't slept with after I meet her and get jealous?"

Thag chuckled and nodded, pleased to see her joking. "Yeah. She's ... something ... yeah."

Shina looked at him through narrowed eyes, sure he was having some sort of laugh at her expense, but that she'd have to wait to find out what.

"Okay," Shina said, when she realized no more was going to be forthcoming. "Thag, what do you really think about Koserana?"

"I think she'll live. According to the soldier I asked, the guy I brought is one of the duke's best battlefield healers. So she should be fine."

Shina looked suspicious. "That's not what I mean, and you know it."

If Thag could have rolled his eyes, he would have. "Shina, Little One, I already told you. It's not like that. Even if I wanted to, I'm not her type. Anyway, she's a bit immature and way too emotionally impulsive.

"Not that I can blame her for that. It's normal at her age.

"She's only about 130 years old, you know."

Shina gasped. "She's what?"

"Immature. Impulsive. Hasn't really grown up yet," he shrugged.

"No, I mean the part where she's one hundred …" she couldn't even finish saying it.

"… and thirty," Thag finished for her. "….about. The bandits that raised her didn't really keep a calendar, so nobody really knows exactly how old she is."

Shina just stared at him.

"What?" he asked.

"One hundred and thirty?"

"Yeah, that's very young for a dragon. If she had living parents, they'd consider her about … maybe a 'pre-teen', to use a human term."

"At one hundred and thirty?"

Thag saw that it wasn't getting through. "Shina, she's a dragon. You have to accept that. If she doesn't get herself killed through recklessness like the other night, she'll live practically forever. Dragons don't really finish growing up till they're at least a thousand years old. Don't let her human disguise fool you – that's a very little girl over there. By dragon standards."

"Wait a minute! When you say, 'she's only 130 years old', do you mean 'only' as in 'a dragon would say only', or do you mean 'only' like you think 130 is 'only'?"

"What?" Her question had lost him.

"Thag, how old are you?"

"What year is it? How long has Yonind been on the throne?"

"Yonind's been king for twenty-three years."

Thag quickly added it up. "Then I'm … let's see … five hundred and … seventeen years old." He nodded to himself as he mentally checked his numbers.

"You're five hundred years old?" she squeaked.

"And seventeen. Yes." He nodded again.

Shina just stared.

Then she started laughing hysterically, so hard that she started hiccupping.

Thag shook his head. *Women are strange*, he thought for neither the first nor last time.

***

A few minutes later, Kalco called Thag to come to him.

The man was near tears. "I can't save her," he told Thag, with a sob in his voice. "I can't get the arrow out, and if I don't it'll kill her. She'll bleed to death by tomorrow at latest."

Thag spoke gently. "Why can't you get it out?"

"I know the type of arrow. It's got a barbed head. If we pull it out, it'll tear her so badly she'll bleed to death in a few seconds. But we can't push it out because we'd have to push it to below her ribs, and that means pushing it through her lung and kidney. It'd kill her."

Thag thought for a moment. "Shina mentioned cutting into her side and removing the head that way."

"She's lost too much blood to survive while we tried to cut through her ribs. She'd be dead before we got to the head."

Shina was scared. She didn't want Koserana to die. But Thag just squatted down next to her and looked at her thoughtfully.

After a minute, he asked, "What if we got the arrow out without pushing or pulling? Could you save her if the wound were open for a few minutes, but with no arrow in it?"

Kalco looked up at Thag, a ray of hope in his gaze. "Can it be done? If you can use some sort of magic to destroy the arrow where it is, then yes, she can live."

Thag picked up Koserana's limp body effortlessly and stood up. He carried her a little ways and set her down on a rock outcropping, where she just lay, pale but with huge bruises around her eyes and the horrible arrow sticking out of her shoulder. No blood was coming out of the wound any more, but Shina knew the woman's chest was slowly filling, probably already impairing her lung's ability to inhale.

"Stand well away, both of you. This is going to be very dangerous," said Thag.

He carefully positioned Koserana so she was sitting up, her back resting against bare rock. Then he muttered something, and began to undress her. He handed her belt and dress to Shina, and then carefully removed the metal collar from her neck. Shina was surprised to see horrible scars that had been covered by it. But Thag's odd behavior was more of a mystery than the neck scars on her beautiful friend. What was he up to?

Again he muttered to himself. It sounded like "fumes" to Shina, but she couldn't be sure. He looked around as if searching for something, and then pointed in a circle around where Koserana was seated.

Shina saw the air ripple, and then a breeze came up and began to swirl where Thag had just pointed! In moments, a steady and gentle wind was making a tiny vortex around Thag and Koserana. What was he up to?

Thag positioned his head near Koserana's shoulder, just above it, and then blew firmly on the arrow. Yellowish-green mist came from his mouth, and the feathers and shaft of the arrow began to boil!

Shina had never seen anything even vaguely like it! In seconds, the exposed shaft was just gone, burned away by the fumes from Thag's mouth. Then he put his mouth to the wound and ... something ... she couldn't tell what.

"What is he doing," Kalco demanded of Shina. "Is he hurting her?"

"I don't know what he's doing. Trust him and wait." She looked at the kidnapped soldier and saw terrible concern on his face. He was perfectly willing to attack Thag to rescue his "mistress". *That's what my father does to nobles who dislike the king*, Shina realized. While it might save her friend's life, she was sickened by what it had done to this man. He was about to attack Thag, certain suicide, to protect someone he should actually hate. As Chalkos, Koserana had killed friends and companions of this man – she was his enemy. But magic had bent him, twisted his emotions and mind to Koserana's wishes. It was terrible in a way she had never thought of before.

As she assured the distraught man that Thag was trying to save his mistress, she promised herself that if she ever had any magic of her own, she'd never use it the way her father did. Koserana had twisted this man to save her own life – self-defense made it at least acceptable, though still ugly. Her father did this to keep a violent warlord rich and powerful and to make his own life more convenient, with no regard for the cost to others. *Never!* she vowed to herself. *Never for that.*

After only a few minutes, Thag took his mouth off of Koserana's shoulder, and, with a brief gesture banished the breeze he had called up. "Come here carefully," he told Kalco. "If you smell anything, step back away."

Shina sniffed at the air where she stood, maybe ten feet away, and smelled nothing but the usual forest smells. Idly, she wondered what it smelled like to Thag or what Lisa, her werewolf friend, would smell if she were with them. They could smell things no human could.

The soldier ignored Thag's warning and nearly leapt to Koserana's side, futilely trying to shoulder Thag out of his way till Thag stood and moved aside on his own. He saw that, where the arrow had been was now an open wound, bleeding lightly but freely. Swiftly, his expert hands used the enchanted implements from his kit, and he began repairing the damaged tissues.

"She'll need water. Lots of clean water, to replace the lost blood. And red meat. Fresh liver is best," he brusquely told Thag without even looking up from his patient. "Get those."

"Can she drink while you work?" Thag asked.

"Yes. It's okay for her to be awake now that the arrow is gone."

Thag got out his soup bowl and gently woke Koserana. "You need to drink now, Chalkos. Drink this." He placed the bowl at Koserana's lips.

The medic asked what was in the bowl, and seemed mollified when Thag told him it was soup broth, thick with nutrition and plenty of blood-iron. He nodded his head in brief approval, never having even looked up from where his hands were busy with the wound.

Koserana slowly sipped the rich broth. Shina knew how filling and satisfying that soup was, and how elusive its taste – she never could decide what meat it tasted of, sometimes like chicken, other times like beef, other times flavors she had never encountered outside of the soup itself. Always good though, and always strangely filling for just liquid.

Koserana drank and drank and drank. Far more than it should take to fill a human stomach, and then even more. For minutes that stretched on and on, she drank bowl after bowl of that potent broth. Finally, she stopped, took a deep breath, and opened her eyes to look up at Thag.

She blinked a few times, and then looked down at the ground and began to sob.

Kalco turned from the wound and looked angrily at Thag. "What are you doing to her?" he demanded!

"Is she healed? Will she recover the rest of the way on her own? Are you done?"

The man, a tight-lipped look of building rage on his face, nodded. "Yes! She'll heal the rest of the way on her own. But you're upsetting her! Leave her alone or I'll…" Thag hushed him by the simple expedient of covering the man's mouth with one huge hand.

Thag looked into the man's eyes and demanded again, "She'll heal the rest of the way without you?" The man, still silenced, nodded, though his eyes raged anger at Thag.

"Shina, if she needs more help, can you do it?"

With the arrow apparently gone, though she didn't understand how Thag had done that, Shina felt confident that she could and said so.

"Good," said Thag, then looked down at Koserana. "Let him go. All the way."

Koserana nodded, and her eyes flashed momentarily into liquid copper spheres.

The soldier's transformation was immediate and complete. One moment, he was angry at Thag for upsetting his "mistress", the next, he was confused and scared. A monster was holding him by the face, and a strange young woman sat on the ground in front of him, naked and pale and weak looking. He had never seen either of them before in his life, and the monster's giant, terrible face, with a mouth full of fangs and with terrible horns on the side, was only inches from him.

He was a brave man, this soldier of the Duchy of Klosia, medic of Duke Antain's own bodyguards, but this was too much, too strange, too horrifying, too sudden. He fainted.

Thag stood up to his full height and looked down at the unconscious man at his feet, then shook his head in exasperation. He put his hand out for Koserana. She still looked weak and pale and like she would start crying again, but she took his hand and stood up.

"Shina, keep an eye on him. Koserana and I need to talk privately."

Koserana looked dejected as Thag half-led, half-carried her away, her eyes downcast and her shoulders curled. But at least she was walking! Shina decided that was good enough for now.

Thag took Koserana far enough away that Shina wouldn't hear them. If anything went wrong, he knew he would still hear either her or the soldier. But he didn't expect to need to intervene. Shina was learning to stand on her own and soon wouldn't need him as a crutch.

Chalkos, on the other hand…

She started talking first. "Thag, I'm so sorry. I didn't mean to … whatever." She was genuinely contrite, but he needed more than that.

He started out gentle. She needed that. "Koserana, what were you hoping to do?"

"I don't know. I just got angry and they were hurting my wolves, so I wanted to hurt them. And I knew they were hunting you and Shina and I wanted to protect you too, so I …" she trailed off.

His voice was soft. "Beautiful One, you could have been killed."

She nodded, but couldn't speak.

"What would have happened if you had killed the duke, or left him stranded in the woods to die with his men? Humans can't live in these mountains like we can. He would have died, you know."

She nodded again, then gathered herself enough to think it through. He gave her time. "With the duke dead, his alliance would fall apart. King Yonind would crush them without the duke's leadership. It'd be another civil war, wouldn't it?"

Despite her youth, she had a dragon's wits behind those eyes.

"Yes. Another war in the kingdoms," he agreed with her.

She sighed and stood up straighter, accepting what he was saying. "And that would set everything back, make it all worse again."

Thag didn't need to say anything. She knew.

"Oh Thag! I'm so sorry. But they were going to hurt my wolves!"

He just looked at her.

After a moment, she looked down again. "They're not really 'my wolves', are they Thag? They belong to themselves, don't they."

She was learning. Slowly, but it would be enough, he hoped. She was so very young! A child's impetuous and tempestuous desires and emotions, ruling a mind and body that could smash small armies. The dragons had been crazy to take such power on themselves and their children, but it was thousands of years too late to worry about that. The shards needed her – not now, but in centuries when she was old enough to fly the void. It was possible that, one distant day, they could repair their damaged worlds. She would be key to that.

Thag changed the subject. They had covered what he needed. "You'll need to travel with us for a while, Koserana. Till you've healed inside, you can't shift. It'll be easier if you're with us."

She nodded, still thinking about what she'd done and how close she'd come to setting back plans that were centuries in the making. He let her, leading her silently back to where Shina waited.

As soon as they came out from behind the trees, Shina could see that Koserana was doing better. They'd only been gone a few minutes, but whatever Thag had done or said had put some spirit back in the young wom… dragon. She might as well get used to thinking of Koserana that way, and better to start right away.

Something was off, though, as she looked at her. Something… she thought about it, and then had it. "Koserana, what are your tattoos?"

The first time Shina had met her, back at the were village, the tattoos had been pictures of mountains and woods and streams, maybe a few wild animals. Then, when she'd been dying, the pictures had all been battle scenes – flames and men in armor and weapons. Now, they were pictures of the stars – and pictures of the way stars really looked, like islands in the sky.

Koserana smiled warmly and her eyes twinkled. "You like? They change when I think about things."

Shina turned Kalco over to Thag. Their prisoner had recovered while Thag and Koserana were gone, so she'd tied his hands behind his back. Shina walked over to Koserana and took a close look at the pictures on her friend's skin.

The pictures were amazingly well done. Beautifully colored inks, and with a sense of life to the pictures. She's seen paintings by master artists in both her father's house and the king's palace, and these were at least as good.

"They're amazing! How do you do that?"

Koserana smiled even wider. "You really think they're amazing? You like them?" Shina realized she really was like a young child emotionally. She'd seen that kind of wide-eyed pleasure on the faces of children many times, but adults don't really react that way.

"They're fantastic," she agreed.

"I can show you how. We'll just need some ink and some time alone and I can give you one if you want it." Her face was lit up by excitement and her eyes, bright blue and clear again, with the bruises around them already fading, were alight.

Shina wasn't sure what she was getting herself into, but she shrugged. "Sure, that sounds great."

Koserana laughed and hugged Shina tightly to her, then released her and yelled to Thag, "Shina's going to let me give her a living tattoo! Isn't that great?"

Thag looked at them and then shrugged and nodded. "If you both like. Why not?"

"Too bad I can't give you one too, Thag. Then we could all three have them. That would be nice."

Shina and Thag quickly discussed their plans and routes. With the duke off their trail, they could travel more easily now, and take a less dangerous path. They wouldn't need Thag's storms to cover their trail and discourage pursuit, and they could travel by day. Those two things alone would make it much easier.

Koserana would be with them, of course, at least for a while. They decided they would also need to take Kalco along with them, though they could dump him at the next village they came to. Letting him go while they were still in the mountains would be a death sentence – it would be kinder to just slit his throat, and neither of them wanted to do that.

Their first day of travel together, Koserana's shoulder and arm were still painful and she was still recovering from blood-loss, so they had to rest frequently and stop early. Shina did what she could with the healer's kit. They didn't trust Kalco with it, since it could harm as well as heal, and they didn't want Koserana to enchant him again – it wasn't needed – though she offered to do so. Offered loudly and in Kalco's hearing. It was childish, and Thag told her to knock it off, but she kept finding ways to tease their captive.

Shina was embarrassed by her friend's behavior, but then had to concede to herself that she hadn't been any better, much worse really, when she was growing up.

When they had a quiet moment alone, Shina asked Thag if Koserana was always like this. He admitted he didn't know her well enough to be sure, but pointed out that Koserana might just be showing off for her, Shina. Young women with crushes often act silly about the people they are attracted to, after all. Shina blushed, and Thag pretended to ignore it.

For a while, she argued with herself. *I wasn't that bad. Really.* Then she remembered how jealous she'd been, and how silly, back in the werewolf village.

Thag assiduously avoided noticing how frequently Shina blushed and glanced furtively at him for a few hours after they had that conversation about girls with crushes.

After the first day, they took to following a wide river. It was much easier going than tramping through the mountains directly. The river was bitter cold, but unfrozen, and rushed past them through many shallow rapids and small waterfalls. Though the water was fresh snowmelt, Thag still insisted that Shina boil it for herself and Kalco before either drank, pronouncing that it was healthier that way for humans.

Every few days, Thag would go out hunting for a few hours and bring back fresh meat for all of them. He himself ate almost exclusively from his soup bowl, but that couldn't provide four people with adequate food, especially since one was a troll and one a young, growing dragon.

Shina started out being shocked by how much Koserana could eat at every meal – her normal diet was more than enough food for four or five grown men. But on that prodigious diet, Koserana was rapidly growing healthier and stronger every day.

After a week or so, Koserana was strong enough to walk through the day. Like Thag, she didn't sleep nights, so the two of them kept watch all night. Shina often tried to stay up and be part of their late-night conversations, but after long days of walking she was so tired she would regularly fall asleep while the two dragons spoke about lands and people she had never heard of.

When Koserana was strong enough to guard Kalco – though he seemed to understand that "escape" meant merely either dying of exposure and starvation in the mountains or simply being chased down by Thag before he could hope to get far enough away to matter – Thag began to take Shina hunting with him when he went. He had captured one of the military arbalests the duke's men liked to carry, and he taught her to use it. She liked the time alone with him, and liked it when he stood behind her and guided her arms and hands to teach her aim.

The days were short and the nights were long, and the terrain along the river was still both rough and dangerous, so progress was slow, but Thag assured them that they were going the right way and would get where he wanted soon enough.

Shina realized, after a time, that one of the reasons Thag was so unflappably patient was that he had seen centuries of life and was used to just keeping going. She knew from their wild escape from the tower and over the castle wall that he was capable of rushing decisiveness when he needed it, but she recognized his willingness to take the time he needed as a strength, and tried to emulate it.

Koserana continued to flirt with her, but now it seemed it was more for something to do, to pass the time, than the infatuation she had seen at their first meeting. Shina found that the young dragon did have some of the emotional tempestuousness that all children have, but that she was also highly intelligent, amazingly knowledgeable of the world, and had a wicked but fun sense of humor.

Thag put up with a lot of little practical jokes from the young dragon – at first Shina thought it was just his usual patience, but then she realized he actually enjoyed being twitted. He'd never had many friends, and enjoyed the banter and the fun. She tried teasing him a few times herself, and found that she liked it.

Of her two companions, she found it odd but true that Thag, a half-troll who looked like he should be just some titanic thug, was the more scholarly. Koserana had a lot of "street smarts", but Thag had more book-learning as well as his vast supply of experience in the real world.

It took over a month for them to traverse the length of the northern peninsula and reach the river's outlet into the far northern seas. From there, they turned south and east, and Shina knew they would soon enter orcish lands.

Before they got very far on that leg of their journey, they found an isolated fishing village on the eastern edge of the Iceflow Sea, and let Kalco go on his way. Thag assumed he'd try to find some way back to his duke, but they'd be far away and completely out of the duke's reach long before the soldier could tell his tale to his lord.

***

Shina knew about orcs, of course. Everyone knew about orcs. Savage brutes, bound by a code of extreme battle-honor, they were the ultimate mercenaries. King Yonind employed a platoon of them, and used them in his most dangerous battles. Bigger and stronger than human men, their warriors were trained to fight as soon as they could walk. They never betrayed or abandoned their contracts, fighting to the death rather than breaking their sworn oaths. They neither offered nor accepted mercy.

She knew that orcs lived in a vast land in the east, past the Argent Crown mountains, where countless hordes of them lived and fought in great tundras and forests and mountains. The exact lands Thag had told her they had to cross.

She had learned enough to not ask him if they were going to kill and eat her, but she was still mortally afraid.

What she didn't know was that there were several cities on the borders between the orcish lands and the lands of men, where the two races mixed their lives and business. Not peaceful cities, no dwelling with orcs under its roof could be called peaceful, but civilized cities nonetheless.

It was to the greatest of these that Thag was leading them. The unofficial capital of the borderlands, the mighty fortress city of Anytown, with its teaming thousands. City of a thousand languages, where the unsavory of a hundred kingdoms and barbarian villages rubbed shoulder to shoulder on crowded walkways and in dark dens of every vice known to men, and a few more besides.

Getting to Anytown took weeks of hard travel through the northern hills. By the time they reached the outskirts, the soft girl that Shina had been raised to be was irretrievably gone, replaced by a strong woman, sure of herself and her friends, with hard muscles and the keen vision and dexterity of a predator. She'd lost the last of her baby fat long since and replaced it with a lean strength that could cover miles of the harshest terrain at an easy stride, and could sleep on the hard ground easily and comfortably.

Shina had been raised in one of the greatest cities the western kingdoms had ever seen, but her long months of near solitude had unprepared her for the city they finally arrived to.

And what a city it was!

The smell was the first shock. Shina had become accustomed to the fresh air of the northern woods and hills, and Anytown was filled with a reek of smoke, sewage, and the vast multitudes of sweating, breathing, belching, farting, pissing, shitting, just plain *stinking* people who swarmed her streets.

Countless fireplaces, smithies, and foundries filled the air with soot and fumes. Tanneries and soap-makers worked outside the main city, but their fumes still choked the lungs and burned the eyes for miles around. Sulfur, used in dozens of products, and a thousand other similar chemicals, made their contribution to the general aroma of the city.

But the strongest smell was simply that of a huge city with gutters instead of industrial sewers. Garbage and food-remains as well as actual sewage, were eventually dumped into the two large rivers that cut through the city proper, but they were moved there in carts, not underground pipes.

Shina's home city had used the same system, but she'd grown up in it and never noticed it before. Now, it was overwhelming, and her eyes were watering before they ever reached the main body of the city itself.

The masses of people were the second shock. Until she met Thag, she had never spent any time around the semi-human races of the world. She knew of dwarves, elves, orcs, and she'd even seen the king's orcs one time, but at a distance. Here, everywhere she looked, she saw not only the races she knew, but a dozen others besides, most of which she couldn't even name.

And they swarmed everywhere! A pocket of clear space appeared around Thag, people giving him a wide berth, and she tried to stay in that aura, but she was jostled, bumped into, and just plain crowded. Her ears became numb to the constant stream of "excuse me" and "beg your pardon", and the just as frequent "watch where you're going" or "hey!"

Never in her life had she been surrounded so closely by so many people! The royal district back home had wide streets and small numbers of people. Some parties had been crowded, but never like this! And never with this awful odor! Even the perfumes did more to burn her nose than to cover the stink!

The sound of the city was a tidal wave that smashed over her and pounded in her head. She felt it as if it were a solid thing, more than hearing the voices and the industry and the tens of thousands of animals in pens and boxes and cages, and birds on buildings and garbage heaps and filling the air itself till they seemed almost to block what little sun came through the yellow-brownish air.

Thag stopped a small boy and asked him where a good inn could be found. The boy sullenly asked what business it was of his, till Thag flashed a small gold coin, and suddenly the boy was all solicitous smiles and friendly help. Shina barely paid attention to it, too overwhelmed with the citiness of it all, till Koserana whispered in her ear, "Thag shouldn't be flashing money in a neighborhood like this. We need to get going. Worry about your nose later."

Thieves? Did that mean there might be thieves around? Shina had never been around criminals before. Even her kidnapper had been a nobleman, after all.

Goggle-eyed and staring at everyone and everything, Shina followed Thag and Koserana deeper into the throng, deeper into the smell, deeper into the city.

After a while, they reached wider streets and taller, nicer buildings. The people were less crowded and wore nicer clothing, but the overall stench of the city still filled Shina's nose, so she couldn't really tell if the people smelled any better.

Finally, they found themselves at the front porch of a large marble-fronted building, with potted plants on the steps and servants at the doorways. Thag thanked the boy, and told him there was another handful of silver available if he could check "all the inns like this one, and the taverns and brothels too if he needed, and find the half-orc Brad." The boy asked if he meant the one with the rose tattoo and Thag agreed that was the very one he needed.

But when they went up the stairs and tried to go in the front door of the inn, a well-dressed middle-aged woman stormed up to them and demanded to know what business they had there.

That's when Shina realized how they must look. Koserana and Shina were dressed in the use-stained deerskins the werewolves had given her almost two months ago, and Thag was in his usual tattered cloak and utilitarian leather shorts. Nicer clothes might have worked for Koserana and Shina, but Thag, no matter how he dressed, would always be Thag. Thag had insisted that Koserana must wear clothing before they came into the city – she had travelled nude most of the way, much to Kalco's constant embarrassment.

And while she had been overwhelmed by the stench of the city, when was the last time Shina herself had had a real bath? Not just a quick splash in a freezing river or stream, but an actual bath. She must stink horribly to this woman.

It felt like all the servants and the other customers of the inn were staring at her. People walking by on the street seemed to be looking at them. What must they all think, she worried.

Thag tried to press a handful of gold coins at the woman, but she was refusing to even look at the coins.

Shina urgently tapped Thag's arm till she got his attention and he leaned down to hear her. She whispered in his ear, "We can stay somewhere cheaper, Thag. You don't need to do this just for me."

Before Thag could respond, a tall, handsome young man, dressed in expensive clothing and with a charming smile on his face, rushed up the stairs to them. He was taller than usual for a human, and strongly built, with wide shoulders, narrow hips, and long, well-shaped legs. His broad face seemed made for smiling, and his eyes were a handsome light brown, under jet black hair and brows. His dark-brown skin looked smooth and warm in the sunlight.

He smiled at the proprietress of the inn, beamed at Thag, Shina and Koserana, and joined the conversation.

He … sparkled … was the only word Shina could think of. There was just something abundantly alive about him! His smile immediately made her feel better. Warm and welcome and safe. Like everything would be taken care of, just by him being there.

When he got to the porch of the inn, the proprietress smiled at him, and all unconsciously stuck her chest out to emphasize her breasts. The young man took this all in stride as he came straight up to Thag and his companions.

"Ah! You've finally arrived! Welcome! Welcome to Anytown!" His voice was deep and masculine and carried confidence and a sense of calm in every intonation. He bowed gracefully, one arm sweeping out in a courtly manner.

"Bradley, how wonderful of you to come by," the innkeeper gushed, before Thag or anyone else could respond. "I was just asking these people what their business is here. Let me get them on their way, and then I'm sure we can visit together for a bit."

"Oh! But, my dear," said the young man. "They're with me. They've come to our city across vast distances and through terrible adventures, and they positively must stay with me in the best inn in the whole town. We wouldn't want to give visiting royalty a bad impression, now would we? Just because they had to travel incognito is no reason to make them stay that way while they're here!"

"Oh, no! I didn't realize!" The innkeeper quickly sized them up, and decided Koserana must be the "royalty" Brad meant, just by process of elimination. She curtsied and smiled, "I'm so sorry I didn't recognize you, my lady. You must be tired from your journeys. We have an absolutely splendid suite on the third floor, with connected rooms for your maid and your …" she looked Thag up and down for a moment, "… and your guard."

With an imperious gesture, she called servants over and told them to prepare the "ivory suite", immediately.

Brad continued. "They'll need tailors, hairdressers, and all of that, of course. Send those over to the baths. We'll meet them there. Silk for the ladies, a satin cape for Thag, here, and enough tailors to have them dressed in time for a late dinner, if you please."

Brad turned to Koserana, taking his cue from the innkeeper's assumptions. "My lady, if you would follow me please. You positively must try our sauna baths. They're the best in the northlands!"

He kept up a steady stream of blather about the city and how wonderful it was till they were out of sight and earshot of the inn and the people gathering in front of it. Then he turned from Koserana to Thag and his manner changed instantly from buoyant charm to all-business. "Thag, what brings you to the septic tank of the world?"

Thag glanced around at the people on the street. "Saunas sound good right about now, Brad. Thanks for the rescue back there, but we need to speak in private."

Brad's face took on a serious look as he looked over the two women. He apparently couldn't decide which one was the center of Thag's reason for being in Anytown, so he gestured for them to follow and headed on up the street.

When they got to the baths, a wide granite building of only one story, with a grand and expensive look to it, Koserana got distracted by something across the street.

Shina couldn't tell what that building was. It looked warm and nice and had bright lights in the first floor windows, and there were an awful lot of scantily clad young women lounging around on the front porch, but there were no signs posted anywhere on it. But Koserana was staring at it like it was a kitchen and she hadn't eaten for a week!

"I'll be over there when the tailors get here, Thag," she said and pointed. Thag smiled and nodded. Brad's eyes got wide and he licked his lips, not quite nervously, but Shina couldn't quite tell what his expression was. "Good choice," Brad said after a slight pause, with a barely noticeable hitch in his voice. "We'll tell them where to find you."

As she crossed the street towards that odd building, Koserana … blurred. Her hair, which had grown out during the long trek, was suddenly groomed and styled in her preferred manner, shaved on the sides and long down her back. Gone were the deerskins, in their place was her old ankle-length dress of transparent green. Even the gold belt was back in place, emphasizing the sensual sway of her wide hips. The necklace that she used to cover her scars gleamed in the wan sunlight. And her tattoos were all of young women – beautiful faces, suggestive nudes, dozens all over, and all done with the highest artistry.

Shina stared. She had forgotten how incredibly sexual Koserana could be when she wanted. Just watching her walk away was a warm hand across her own groin. She watched, and Brad with her, till Koserana, surrounded by the young women of the porch, disappeared into the building.

"Damn!" Brad whispered. Shina agreed that that said it all.

Thag, unflappable as always, ushered the other two into the sauna building. Shina had never been in a sauna before, and wasn't even quite sure what it meant. But the word "bath" had been used, and she could smell steam from the entryway, and that was enough for her!

Enough, that is, until someone at the front desk asked her for her clothing. Right out in front of everyone, including Thag and Brad! "Wh… wh… what?" she stammered.

The attendant smiled, thinking her perhaps a bit slow. "Your clothing, madam. Please."

He mistook her continued hesitation. "We can have it cleaned and mended for you while you sauna, if you like," he suggested tentatively.

Not five feet away from her, Thag handed his cloak over to another attendant and skinned out of his shorts. Just the other side of Thag, Brad was carefully removing his expensive garments and handing them to another attendant, with careful instructions on how to clean and fold them. "My friend and the girl won't need their clothing back. Tailors should be arriving from the Gilded Swan Inn momentarily. They'll need to be fitted, so the tailors may need to wait while they clean up," Brad explained.

Thag corrected him, quietly telling the attendant that he would need the shorts repaired and returned, but that the cloak had seen too many miles and should probably be burned to get rid of vermin. He explained that the shorts could also be burned, but that he'd need them back afterwards. The attendant took that odd statement in stride as if he'd been asked such things every day of his life.

Shina was mortified. Everyone was looking at her, waiting for her to undress. In front of all of these strangers!

She nervously looked at Thag for approval, and then stared into his eyes, so she wouldn't accidentally make eye contact with anyone else, and fumbled her way out of her clothing.

Shivering, though the air was warm and comfortable, she directed the attendant to burn the clothing, without once looking at him, but asked that they return the knives when she was ready to leave. It was, she realized, almost all that she owned, other than a few ragged travel supplies left from Lisa's village in the woods, and now most of it would be burned. She stood there, wearing only the necklace Lisa had given her, blushing faintly, with her eyes locked on Thag's.

Anything was better than looking around at all the people she was sure were staring at her.

Another attendant, this one a young woman who was barely more dressed than Shina, led them back through several hallways, past many doorways that were blocked with heavy curtains, around which steam and a variety of pleasant smells curled. The halls were over-warm to Shina, and she wondered why they didn't open some windows or something.

Finally, the attendant led them into a medium-sized room, with a low ceiling that Thag had to duck to stand under. The walls were smooth, unvarnished wood, and there were wooden benches along them, built like wide steps so that there were low benches and high benches and some in between. This room had a heavy wooden door, with a slight gap beneath it to let in a tiny amount of air.

There was no bathtub in the room, and it was unbearably hot! Shina wasn't sure what was going on, but it was decidedly strange!

The young woman pointed them to a pool full of ice-cold water just outside their room, with three more wooden doors in the walls around it, and told them to pull the chain near the door if they wanted drinks or food or anything at all.

Brad asked her if a couple of the young women from across the way could be sent in, and the girl assured him they could. He looked around at Thag and Shina as if to ask them something with his eyes, but Thag shook his head "no" and Shina just stared at him with no faintest clue what he was suggesting. It was all so very confusing.

He shrugged as if to say, "to each his own", and told the attendant that "Two will be enough, thank you." He handed her some coins, she bowed, showing far more cleavage than was at all proper, and then walked away.

Shina finally got her courage up enough to ask, "Where are the baths?"

Thag just lay down on one of the top benches. The room was too short for him to sit up there, but he looked relaxed lying there. Brad muttered, "show off", then sat on the lowest bench and indicated Shina should sit there too.

She sat across from him, desperately trying to ignore his nudity and to pretend she wasn't just as naked as he was.

On the other hand, his nudity made it abundantly clear exactly how attractive he really was. He was fantastically muscular, but in a proportionate way, unlike Thag's odd and definitely inhuman bulk. Shina had grown used to Thag's looks over the months since they met, but Brad brought home how alien Thag truly was.

Much of Brad's strong chest was covered with a tattoo of a very beautiful rose bush, with vines extending out onto his upper arms and down onto his thighs. His body hair was sparse enough to leave it uncovered, though his heavy pubic curls did cover a bit of the tattoo. When she realized she was looking at his groin, pubic hair, and everything else in that area, she blushed again and tried desperately to avert her eyes.

"These are the baths," Brad explained, politely and gracefully ignoring Shina's stares. He was used to women being fascinated by him. He hated manipulating people, but exceptions like the innkeeper back there sometimes made it necessary – and women's reaction to him made it all too easy.

"You westerners don't know what real baths are. You sit in here and the sweat cleans out every pore in your skin, and relaxes your muscles like nothing you've ever tried before. Much better than soaking in a tub full of dirty water!

"If you get too hot, you can pour cold water over yourself at the pool out there. If you aren't too hot, that means you're dried out and need to get something to drink. It's important to drink while you're in here. They'll bring juice in a minute. We wait till after that before we talk about anything that matters.

"Till then, relax, sit back, and just let the heat take the miles off your body." So saying, he closed his eyes, spread his arms wide on the bench behind and above him, and leaned back. He did look relaxed, Shina realized. So did Thag, when she looked at him.

As predicted, a couple of minutes later servants arrived with three large pitchers of some ice-cold drink, with large blocks of ice floating right in it. The drink was colorful, so Shina assumed it was some sort of fruit juice, and hoped that it wouldn't be too sweet. Regardless, she knew Brad was right and she needed to drink something.

Shina couldn't help but continue comparing Brad to Thag. Brad's smooth, brown skin looked as healthy and vital as Thag's lumpy gray skin and rough black scales looked monstrous. Brad had brown eyes, closed now but she could see the memory of them in her mind, that sparkled with mirth and charm, where Thag had mysterious black spheres that shone like gems and swirled like oil on water. Brad had a warm smile with perfect teeth, while Thag had ragged, uneven rows of razor-sharp fangs, and dagger-sized tusks that projected from both top and bottom jaws into needle-sharp points.

Even Brad's perfect, healthy black hair was well groomed, compared to the armor-like scales and two large horns on Thag's head.

Shina was confused by what she felt, and her mind was going round and round in a whirl. She picked up one of the glasses of juice – maybe cooling off a bit would help her think.

Brad also took a glass, and began to sip at it. He smiled at her and started to say something as she took her first swallow.

Holy gods in the heavens! The juice burned her throat like liquid flame! She choked and sputtered the remains of a mouthful all over the sauna! Brad, sitting across from her, got a blast of "juice" – whatever the hell that stuff really was! – right in the face!

Then it hit her stomach, and she lit up like a firework. Shina had never drunk hard liquor before. She'd been raised on light wine, like most of the nobility, and had tasted beer a time or two when "slumming it" with her friends, but this was … it was … yeah, it was!

"What's in that stuff!" she finally managed to sputter out. Thag was laughing at Brad, as Brad sat there, drenched in "juice", a look of total shock and amazement on his soaking wet, and rather sticky, face.

She glared at the two men equally, then, in total defiance, picked up the glass and took another swallow. Brad flinched.

This time, she was braced for it, and the fire down her throat and into her belly felt good.

"Don't drink too much, Little One," rumbled Thag. "The orcs call it 'vodka', and humans like to mix it with fruit juice for some reason. A little goes a long ways."

Brad left the sauna to wash his face in the pool outside. When he came back, he admitted, "Okay, maybe I deserved that. I know you westerners aren't used to real drinks. I should have warned you."

Thag stopped him. "Enough fooling around. We'll have servants and tailors and prostitutes here in short order, so what has to be said must be said now."

Prostitutes? Shina thought to herself. Why would… and then it hit her. That building across the way, where Koserana was. Where Brad had asked "young women" to be sent over from. It was a bordello! She was shocked enough that she missed part of what Thag was telling Brad… something about a tower in the far east.

"We need to get there. But we need to stop at Xalax on the way. And we need you to come with us."

"Xalax? That's just a bunch of old ruins. Nobody even knows what used to be there. What do you need from that old place?"

"Sam said to take Shina there. There's something she needs. And I need your help to get her there. Can you do it?"

"Sure, yeah, anything for you and Sam, Thag. I owe you guys from way back, and even if I didn't, your project is worth the time. Are you taking the beauty with you, or is it just you?"

Shina was momentarily pleased, then realized from his gestures that he meant Koserana – of course.

"'The beauty', as you call her, is named Koserana. She's Lord Chalkos' property. Unless you want to anger him, you need to leave her strictly alone," Thag leaned up on an elbow and stared at Brad till he answered.

"Yeah. I understand loud and clear. Trust me, I don't want to mess around with Lord Chalkos any more than anyone else does."

Shina was confused, until she realized what Thag meant. *Brad doesn't know Koserana is Chalkos! It's a secret, and he's telling me to keep it that way!*

Thinking about Koserana again brought to mind what the young dragon was doing. In a brothel. With other women, from what Thag had told her. Images crowded into her mind and refused to go away! Damn this drink anyway, it was muddling her head and she couldn't stop thinking about Koserana, naked and beautiful, sex incarnate, and other women!

Brad was asking Thag, "Is it true what they say about him? That Lord Chalkos is the last of the battle-mages, and that he can't be killed because of being cursed by Gem himself?"

Thag smiled. "Let's just say I'm not at liberty to confirm that, okay."

Brad took a large swallow of his drink and looked a little nervous at the thought. "Got it. But that still doesn't answer the first question. Is she coming with us, or is it just the three of us?"

Thag replied, "Three of us."

Brad looked at Shina more closely than she was comfortable with. "Thag, she's just a young girl. Human women that age are too fragile for a trip across the eastern wastes. Are you sure she needs to go there?"

Before Thag could respond, Shina interrupted. "Too fragile! I just walked across the Northron Peninsula, I'll have you know! All the way from …" She paused. "Thag, what's the name of the castle I was in?"

"Sandy. Castle Sandy. Doesn't matter. Brad doesn't know where that is. But she's right, Brad. She walked over two-thousand miles of some of the roughest, coldest terrain in the world, during the winter. She's tough.

"And it doesn't matter anyway. She needs to go. Even if you have to carry her the whole way."

Brad shrugged his heavy shoulders. "Okay. Sorry. I'll watch what I say. Blame it on the vodka shower, please." His smile, so warm and genuine, calmed Shina right down.

"Sorry about that," she said, with a slight smile of her own. "But you should have warned me."

"Shoulda … coulda … didn't – my fault and I hope you can forgive me," and he gave a slight bow from where he was sitting, a charming gesture and mirth in his eyes.

Shina smiled. "Consider yourself forgiven," and tried to give a sort of sitting curtsey of her own, but blushingly remembered she was naked halfway through the gesture.

Why do I keep meeting men when I'm naked? She railed to herself. *First Thag, now this Brad person! Who next?*

Then there was a knock on the door. Brad said, "That'll be for me," and got up to get it, after getting a nod from Thag that it was okay.

There were two young women there, a blonde and a brunette, both completely naked. Shina could see that the blonde's groin was completely bald, though she was very obviously an adult woman, and wondered what could cause that.

Brad ushered them in, and Shina realized she was staring at both of them. Images of Koserana were still flashing behind her eyes. The flirting, the incredible nudity, that kiss when they first met! It just wouldn't go away, and she found herself feeling warm in a strange way.

Brad sat back down on the bench, with the blonde on one side and the brunette on the other. He offered them some of his juice, and they giggled and sipped at it. "Thag, you sure you don't mind?"

"Ooooh, he's a biiig one!" said the blonde, taking her first real look at Thag.

"Go right ahead, I'm just relaxing up here and won't bother or be bothered," replied Thag, ignoring the girl's comment the same way he'd ignored the flirts of the werewolf girls way back when.

Shina took a big gulp of her drink and tried to stop blushing and staring.

The two women began to rub Brad's shoulders, cooing over his muscles and what a big guy he was.

Shina saw that he was beginning to respond, and again found herself staring. He was huge! A quick, embarrassed glance at Thag told her that he hadn't noticed her staring at Brad, and also that he was even bigger, though his was still flat against his leg, unlike Brad's rapidly rising member.

She was blushing from the roots of her hair to the soles of her feet, but she just couldn't tear her eyes off the three people in front of her. Were they really going to make love right there? In front of her and Thag? Did people do that?

Brad looked at the blonde and asked, "So, gorgeous, what's your name?"

She smiled, rubbed her breasts against his biceps, leaned over and licked his ear lightly, and stage-whispered, loud enough for Shina to hear, "'Gorgeous' will do just fine. I like being Gorgeous."

Brad nodded. "Ah. In that case, you," he turned to the brunette and his eyes wandered appreciatively over her nude body, "…you must be Lovely, if she's to be Gorgeous. Will that do?"

The brunette kissed him on the neck and ran her hand lightly over the top of his thigh. "For tonight, I can certainly be Lovely."

Then she leaned down and took the rigid end of his erect manhood into her mouth, smoothly and gracefully swallowing him.

Shina gasped! She'd never even heard of such a thing!

Brad's head rolled back and he relaxed and looked like he was enjoying this immensely as Lovely began to bob up and down on him.

Gorgeous looked over at Shina and smiled at her. "Baby girl, you look hungry. Do you want us to share?" and she gestured at Brad. Then she licked her lips suggestively, "Or would you prefer that I come over there to you?"

Shina came to her senses a few seconds after she realized she'd just run, naked, out of the sauna and into the pool room. She was huddling on the floor in a corner, curled up around herself, and Thag was standing over her.

He gestured to Brad, who was standing in the door of the sauna, with the two girls looking over her shoulders from behind him, and the trio went back in and shut the door.

"Are you okay, Little One?" Thag squatted down next to her, his body blocking the view of servants who were staring at her odd behavior. At a wave from him, they dispersed out of the room.

She sobbed. "Oh Thag! I can't believe how stupid I am!"

"Stupid, Little One? You're not…"

She interrupted. "Yes, I am! I can't help how I feel. I'm jealous and anxious and all worked up and I'm stupid and I don't know what to do."

"What to do about what?" he asked, his voice soft and comforting.

She looked up at him. At the face she had once called monstrous but now thought was beautiful, at the eyes she was once thought blank and terrifying, but now could read every loving expression in.

"I'm scared, too. I'm scared … don't interrupt me! … I want what they're doing," she pointed back at the sauna, where she was sure Brad and

Gorgeous and Lovely had gone back to what she had interrupted.

Thag was a little surprised, and again he tried to speak, and again she stopped him. "But I don't want it with them. I want it with you!" Her voice dropped to a whisper. "With you."

She reached up and gently ran her soft hand along his jawline. The scales felt wonderful to her fingertips, and the leathery skin felt like safety and home and love.

She stared into his eyes. Those fantastic black gemstones that reflected every wise thought in his marvelous soul. She could see herself, crouching naked on the floor, mirrored in those swirling, magical eyes.

Thag didn't say a word. He just took her gently in his hands and effortlessly picked her up, and carried her to an empty sauna room across the pool.

Shina had long dreamed that it would be wonderful, and in a little while, it was.

***

Koserana came back to the inn when the horizon was just beginning to show the faintest light of the oncoming dawn.

The room smelled strongly of sex, and she could hear Thag's and Shina's heartbeats coming from a single room. *Ah,* she thought to herself. She was slightly jealous. She'd hoped to spend her lust on the women she'd been with all night, but, as always, it only blunted it, and didn't satisfy.

She heard a change in the heartbeats, and knew Shina was awake and coming out of Thag's room. *Well, let her. I'll say goodbye at least before I leave.*

Shina was naked and lovely. She smelled strongly of sex, and of Thag, on top of her own special smell that Koserana always found so enticing. Unlike any human she'd ever smelled before – or anything else for that matter. It was a magical scent, and she found it irresistible.

"Koserana," Shina whispered from across the room. Loud to her ears, quiet to the human. In the other room, Thag could certainly hear it too. He was pretending to sleep, she knew. Pretending for Shina's sake, to make her feel more comfortable. But Koserana knew better – he didn't sleep any more than she did.

Koserana walked silently over to where Shina stood, just outside

Thag's door. She smiled. She wished that Shina liked her the way she liked Shina, but she knew that few women actually felt that way. The ones she paid pretended they did, but she could always smell the difference, and hear it in their heartbeats and their voices. Some responded to her honestly, but it was rare. She tried to convince herself that it was okay anyway, and sometimes that self-lie worked.

"I was thinking about you last night, Koserana. Thinking about you, and about me."

Koserana knew what was next. Shina would tell her that she liked her, but only as a friend, not "that way", or words to that effect. She would be oh so nice, but it would be rejection. She'd been through this so many times before.

Expecting that, she was completely caught off guard when Shina took hold of her head and pulled her lips down into a passionate kiss!

It was electric and wonderful and the scents and the heartbeat were all exactly what she wanted! It was perfect, and Koserana leaned into it with all the passion she had!

After an eternity, Shina broke off, and looked deep into Koserana's eyes. She whispered breathily, "I love Thag. But I love you, too, and I want to do this. Even if it's just this one time. I want this as badly as you do."

Shina confidently took Koserana's hand in her own and led her to the suite's master bedroom.

Chapter 7: *Trouble Knocking*

About an hour later, Koserana came out of the bedroom and looked sullenly at Thag. He was sitting next to the fireplace in the main room, too big to use any of the chairs the inn provided. A large book that looked tiny in his monstrous hands rested on his knee – she knew that books of poetry and natural history were a habit of his and assumed this was one of those.

From under glowering brows, her lips in a tight line of resentment, she asked too loudly, "Am I in trouble?"

Thag smiled and calmly asked, "For what?"

Koserana's eyes and feet shifted uncomfortably. For all her bluster, she wanted Thag's approval, and definitely didn't want to fight him.

She abruptly pointed back at the bedroom she'd just emerged from. "For stealing her from you! I promise, I didn't mean to steal her from you! I just wanted her so badly! I …" Thag interrupted her by holding up a hand.

"Beautiful One, you can't 'steal' her. I don't 'own' her, so she certainly can't be stolen from me. She's her own person, and she can certainly make her own choices in life." He shrugged. "Neither of us owns her."

Koserana bit her lip and thought for a moment. "So… you're not even mad at me for taking her after you …?"

Thag shook his head "no". "Should I be? It's not like you forced her to do anything against her own will. She came to each of us and asked for what she wanted. We each care about her, so we gave. I might have been a little angry if you had refused her when she needed you, but how could I be angry that you and she made each other happy? It's a good thing for people to serve each other and care for each other's happiness. That's what love is about, isn't it?"

Koserana smiled radiantly, and ran lightly over to Thag, where she threw her arms around his neck in a friendly hug. "Oh Thag! I'm so glad you aren't angry! Even if you do lecture me!"

Thag chuckled and looked over Koserana's head at Shina, who had just stepped out of the room. She'd been hiding behind the door the whole time, not realizing Thag knew exactly where she was, since he could hear every breath and heartbeat even through the door and across the room.

She too had been worried – realizing after she had seduced Koserana that maybe Thag would be jealous. Now she just looked relieved.

Shina asked, just to be sure, "You don't mind me having sex with her?"

"Of course not."

Koserana got a wicked grin on her face, and looked him right in the eyes. "Wanna watch next time?"

Thag looked at the two of them for a moment before responding. "If you want to show off, make that offer to Brad. He'd definitely enjoy the show. Though …," Thag paused a moment again and thought, "… he might consider it an invitation to join in. Women have gone to greater lengths than that just to get him into their beds."

Shina blushed, but managed to reply. "After the show he put on in the sauna, maybe we should invite him. Just to get even."

Just as she finished saying it, Brad opened the door and walked into the room from the outer hallway. Thag laughed out loud, Shina blushed a deep crimson, and Koserana just kept smiling that mischievous grin.

Brad looked around, confused at the tableau in the room. Shina standing in front of Koserana's room, wrapped in a bed-sheet, blushing and looking mortified, Thag sitting on the floor near the fireplace, laughing his head off, and the gorgeous Koserana, nude as a newborn babe and standing practically in Thag's lap. He wasn't sure what he'd interrupted. The last he'd seen any of them, Thag and Shina had been in the pool room at the sauna baths, after Shina had abruptly run from the room in a blind panic. Now this.

No telling what was up, but Thag definitely found it hilariously funny!

"Um … am I interrupting something? Should I come back later?"

Thag couldn't stop laughing any more than Shina could stop blushing.

Koserana looked meaningfully at Shina, but spoke to Brad. "You can stay. But you might be coming later too." She nodded to herself as if that made sense.

Brad looked back and forth between the three. He had the keen feeling of being the outsider of an inside joke. When no explanation was forthcoming, he just decided to let it go.

"Ooookaaay," he drew out. "Well! Um … should I get us some breakfast so we can talk plans?"

Koserana grinned again. "Shina and I already ate this morning, but breakfast does sound good. Doesn't it?"

Shina went from red to a sort of purple. Thag laughed so hard he started beating his hand on the floor – the building was mostly solid stone and the floor was heavy, solid wooden planks massively reinforced, but Brad could swear the whole thing shook a bit.

"I'll just get us some breakfast then. I'll be right back, so don't do anything without me." Somehow, this innocuous statement pushed Thag even deeper into his paroxysms, and turned Shina an even darker shade of a dangerous-looking violet. Westerners were such strange people!

By the time Brad returned with several of the inn's servants loaded down with trays of food – Thag always liked to eat a lot – everyone had calmed down and regained their composure.

Shina was now dressed, wearing a simple robe provided by the inn, plain green with the symbols for "pleasant time away from home" in white on it. The tailors from the night before had provided a few simple things, and would be busy making more over the next few days, but Shina wasn't wearing her new clothing yet.

Thag, as usual, had shorts and a heavy belt on, and was sitting and reading a book.

Koserana, stunningly beautiful in just her skin and tattoos that mostly seemed to be of fae pixies and tricksters, was sitting next to Shina on one of the plush couches.

Everyone looked comfortable, and nobody was blushing or laughing, so Brad decided that whatever had been going on, must have been resolved.

Every servant that came into the room had to struggle to decide where to stare, but every single one of them ended up staring at Thag. Two muscular servants were struggling to carry a heavy table into the room, to set all the food on. When Thag stood up to go help them, everyone stopped moving and just goggled at him while he effortlessly took the table and put it where he wanted it.

These were people who lived in a city with a dozen semi-human races living shoulder-to-shoulder, even a few titanic half-ogres who served as longshoremen in the river district, but none of them had ever seen anything as monstrous as Thag before, and they unconsciously flinched from him every time he so much as shifted his weight.

Normally, a few would have stayed to make sure everything had been delivered acceptably. Normally, more than a few would have found excuses to stay and look at Koserana. This wasn't normally, and they all had to force themselves not to flee the room in open fear.

Brad was painfully aware of the servants' bad manners, and wished, not for the first time, that his friend could get a better reception from people who might otherwise like him, if they just got to know him at all.

Once all the servants were gone, Brad asked a few polite questions and made a suggestion about getting some of the finished clothing from the tailor later that afternoon. But he also pointed at his ears and looked questioningly at Thag.

To Brad's surprise, both Thag and Koserana pointed at a section of wall, and then Koserana pointed at the ceiling as well. He had expected Thag to respond, but he still thought of Koserana as just a woman – an incredibly sexy woman, but nothing beyond that. He understood she worked for Lord Chalkos, and he realized now that maybe that meant he needed to expect more.

Thag looked questioningly at Koserana and pointed at the spot on the ceiling she had indicated. She nodded emphatically. Then, to Brad's shock and amazement, her tattoos redrew themselves! Right before his eyes, the inks swirled across her skin and changed colors and outlines! Brad barely noticed that Shina was also staring, or that Thag wasn't.

In moments, the fae pixies and tricksters had all been replaced by arcane symbols and strange glyphs! As soon as Koserana knew Thag had clearly seen the pictures, she pointed at the ceiling again.

Thag peered at the indicated point, deep in thought. Everyone waited – they knew he had to work something out, and they all trusted him to come to the best decision if they let him.

Finally, after a minute or two, he spoke to Koserana. "Kill it." Then he stood up, walked over to the point on the wall that he had indicated initially, and waited. He pointed to the door and Brad firmly locked and barred it.

Brad gawped openly as Koserana stood up, stretched to her full height, pointed at the ceiling, and then glowed! Her eyes turned into balls of swirling copper, and a corona of light spread from her head and then down over her whole body!

Suddenly, the light arced from her outstretched hand! Where the spark of light met the ceiling, there was a silent, blinding flash!

At the same moment, Thag bunched his right hand into a fist and punched the wall! Stone shattered, and Thag's scaled fist smashed into the body of a man who had been standing on the other side of it! There was a sickening thud, and the man fell into the room, dead before he hit the floor.

"Any more?" Thag asked Koserana, and she shook her head in negation.

Shina stared at the dead man on the floor. She visibly swallowed and held back a retch in her throat. Pale, she walked over to the corpse and looked down at it.

"He was listening to us?" It was only nominally a question. Thag replied with a simple, "Yes."

Thag looked at Brad. "Whose?"

"Some duke in the west, most likely. He's put a bounty on her head," he pointed at Shina. "And he put a description of you into it. He's offering a lot of money for her, alive, and you, dead." He nodded at Koserana, "Describes you, but no price. Just says you might be with them. News hit town late this morning, so it was only a few hours behind you guys getting here. Good thing, too, or you'd have been arrested at the outer walls."

Thag looked more thoughtful than perturbed. "Any more to it?"

Brad smiled. "He does mention that you're 'potentially dangerous' and might be armed."

Thag nodded sagely and smiled slightly at that.

"So," Thag said. "We're known, we have assassins and sorcerers after us, and we're essentially out of time. No telling how quickly his sorcerers will recover from that," he pointed at burn marks on the ceiling. "Best we assume it'll only be a few minutes.

"Shina, Little One, you have an important decision to make."

Shina looked up from the body. Her eyes were wide, whites showing all around, and Brad knew she was close to panic.

Thag continued, "I would like to take you to meet Sam, far to the east from here. It will be a dangerous journey, far worse than what we've done so far. What she needs you for should be impossible, but the world needs it anyway.

"You can see world-shards. Nobody has done that for centuries. If we're right, it means you can do important things that nobody else can do.

"But it has to be your choice. We need you, but I'm not going to force you to do anything you don't want."

Thag's calm explanation soothed Shina away from incipient panic. Her voice was surprisingly steady, and her color was coming back already, as she answered, "What would I do if I don't want to go?"

"Stay here. Or go your own way. Make your way back to your father's house, if that's what you desire."

She didn't hesitate at all. "I'll go with you. Not just because I'm in love with you, but because I want to help."

Thag smiled widely, long fangs bared in an expression that would have intimidated her if she didn't know his moods and face so very, very well. Nodding his head, and with a touch of enthusiasm in his voice, he turned to Brad and said, "Then we have a real chance here! First time in centuries, but we have a real chance!"

Brad appraised Shina – maybe there was more to her as well. A spark lit in his eyes, Thag's enthusiasm spreading to him. "If that's the case, then this is definitely worth the risk."

Brad continued, "And that means we have fast planning to do. But not here. All that noise will definitely bring eavesdroppers, or worse," he thought for a moment then snapped his fingers. "I know just the place!

"Thag, the rest of us can get out through the passage here," he indicated the secret hallway revealed when Thag punched a hole in the wall, "but you won't fit. Can you get to the alleyway behind the inn without using the doors?"

"See you there," said Thag, and promptly leapt out the window. Even before the crash of shattering glass faded from their ears, Thag's shoulders sprouted gigantic wings and he was disappearing fast towards the back of the building.

Brad muttered under his breath, "Three floors up… I'll never get used to that."

Shina told him, "You should try it when you don't know he can do that and he just jumps – with you in a bag over his shoulder."

Brad did a mock cringe. "You'll have to tell me about that some time."

Koserana, with a look of confusion on her face, finally asked, "What's wrong with jumping out a third floor window?"

When Brad just looked at her, she asked Shina, who just shook her head and rolled her eyes a bit.

Shina took a quick minute to get dressed, throwing on pants and a shirt and her usual belt- and wrist-knives. It was all she had left of the outfits the werewolves had given her so long ago.

Koserana, as usual, just suddenly had the clothing she wanted – a skin-tight, black, leather catsuit that clung to every curve so suggestively that she was almost more naked in it than when she was actually undressed.

As soon as they were dressed, the three went into the dark secret passage and headed towards where Brad thought they needed to go.

It was obvious from how clean these passages were that they were used regularly, and Shina wondered how much the inn spied on its guests. When she asked Brad, he explained that the passages probably only went to the expensive guest suites, and were generally only used to spy on potentially dangerous or foreign guests. The city council paid most innkeepers plenty for use of spy-holes like this.

"After all," he explained, "those rooms are set up to be comfortable to westerners. Locals don't like that style of furniture, and think the plain ivory décor is boring. So they mainly use them for wealthy foreign merchants and lords – and spying on those would be worth good money."

"It can't be much good. How can they hear? The wall was half an inch of solid stone, even at the thin part. Or isn't it?" Shina asked quietly.

Koserana answered that question. "They put these little bell-shaped crystal things on the wall. You put your ear on the small end, and you can hear everything in the room, even through a thick door or a bit of wall."

Shina gave her a slightly startled look, wondering how she knew about something like that. Koserana shrugged and answered the unasked but obvious question, "My lord is a bounty hunter. It pays to know what your target is saying in private, and sometimes it pays to know what the people hiring you say behind closed doors when they don't think you're listening."

It only took a couple of minutes for the trio to find their way down to the ground floor. The first two exits they found, Koserana said there were people on the other side, but the third was into an empty back hallway, near the kitchens.

When Brad closed the door behind them, Shina couldn't even see the outline of it. If she didn't know they had just stepped out from that spot, she could easily have walked past it a dozen times without ever noticing.

Brad tiptoed to a back door that went the way they wanted. It was right next to a huge, open doorway into a busy kitchen, but they got out without raising any alarms.

The back alley, so far as they could see, was empty except for three drunks sleeping in a doorway, and a stray dog sniffing at a pile of garbage. Thag was nowhere to be seen.

The dog snarled at Koserana, put its ears back, head down, fangs showing, and slowly retreated from a threat it recognized and its masters ignored.

At that noise, faster than any of them could react, the three sleeping drunks suddenly stood up and drew weapons! Two of them had top-quality swords, while the third lifted up a huge arbalest that had been hidden behind him! All three had fine mail glinting under their filthy clothing.

The bigger of the two swordsmen addressed Brad in a deep, gravelly voice. "You're not as big as the descriptions led me to expect…"

Before he could say another word, Brad was startled to see a knife leap through the air past him and bury itself to the hilt in the neck of the crossbowman across the alley! The man gurgled on the pain and blood for a second, then fell lifeless to the floor of the alley!

Out of the corner of his eyes, Brad saw that Shina already had two more knives in her hands and had gone into a combat crouch!

Both swordsmen were startled. They had expected Brad to be the only threat. They recovered quickly, but not enough!

Faster than they could refocus their eyes on him, Brad lashed out! His powerful uppercut noisily shattered bones in the leader's face and neck.

Even before the first swordsman hit the ground, Brad was wheeling towards the second!

The assassin was fast and skilled! His sword flashed at Brad's chest. Blade met skin, and was deflected! Where the attacker had expected flesh, the blade instead found unyielding stone! The tip skipped off of what it should have pierced effortlessly, and the man lost his balance for the slightest moment from the unexpected impact.

Just as abruptly as it had started, it was over. Shina's second throwing knife slammed point first into the temple of the swordsman's unarmored head, piercing his brain and killing him instantly.

Chapter 8: *Taking Charge*

As Thag glided down from the roof of the building next door, seconds too late to join the fight, Brad was already confirming the three attackers were all dead.

Shina sprinted to the side of the alley, fell to her knees, and threw up violently. Her stomach just wouldn't stop! Long after everything in it had been sprayed on the ground, visions of the two men with her knives stuck in them were playing behind her eyes, alternating with horrific visions of that sword hitting Brad square in the middle of his chest and her moment of core-deep terror. Every vision triggered a mule kick inside her stomach.

Koserana scanned the nearby rooftops and all around with her eyes, and listened intently. Were there more of them? Had anyone seen? Was there any alarm being yelled nearby? Her hyper-keen senses stretched to their limits to be certain.

Brad collected Shina's knives from the corpses while Thag silently scooped the collapsed and exhausted young girl up into his arms. Without a word, Brad led Thag and Koserana out of the alley.

Already, as Brad had expected, a dense fog was forming all around them. He knew he could count on Thag for concealment as they crept silently through back alleys, on the way to a building he hoped was still safe.

It was only a couple of blocks, but a hue and cry had gone up over the killings at the Gilded Swan, and every moment was a nerve-wracking worry that they might be caught. When they finally got to Brad's destination, after an interminable few minutes, Brad felt a shiver of relief.

They gathered in a narrow alley outside the back door of the abandoned shop. Brad whispered to Koserana and Thag, "Anyone in there?"

Both shook their heads "no", so Brad carefully picked the lock and led them all in.

Shina, beginning to come out of her shock, looked around at the dark storage room he led them into. It was full of cobwebs and stank of some sort of animal musk. There were sagging shelves with a few boxes still on them, and a few crates stacked on the floor. An empty doorway, with the long-rotted wispy remains of a curtain in it, seemed to lead to the front of the shop, but she couldn't see clearly through the dark room.

Thag cleared a space on the floor and settled Shina there. She still felt too weak to stand, so she just sat, shivering at the memories of knives and spurting blood.

Koserana, concern on her face, squatted next to Shina, and waited patiently for her to talk.

Thag took Brad by the arm and led him through the doorway into the next room. When he spoke, it was quietly, but Shina was keyed up enough to hear every word.

"What the hell happened back there?" There was severely controlled rage in Thag's deep, quiet voice.

Brad sounded abashed when he replied. "I hesitated, Thag. They caught me flat-footed. I trusted my eyes instead of my instincts."

Shina's ears strained through a long silence. Finally, almost too low to hear, Thag rumbled, "You scared me, my friend. If it weren't for Shina, all three of you might be hurt or dead. I was too far away to protect you. Please don't scare me like that."

"I'll try not to. I'm kicking myself. I still can't see how I fell for a simple trick like that. I'm better than that."

"You and Koserana both. You both know better."

A door opened and closed somewhere, and in a moment Thag returned to the back room. He joined Koserana beside Shina. He looked so concerned, almost afraid.

"Are you okay, Little One? Did they hurt you?" He asked gently.

Shina lurched up into Thag's arms, her face pressed hard against the solid fortress of his massive chest. She gulped and then burst into tears as he softly embraced her.

Koserana leaned in to her from behind and Thag accommodated the dragon-woman into his arms. The shared warmth and kindness, love, spread a balm over Shina's hurt soul, and she just cried quietly for a while, held by the two people she loved the most.

Finally, after a few minutes, she spoke. "I killed them Thag. I didn't even think about it, I just … killed them! And the blood was everywhere!

And now they're dead!"

Thag knew that noblewomen in the western kingdoms were trained to defend themselves, traditionally with throwing knives and stilettos, but he also knew that Shina had never used her knives off the training floor – until now.

"I'm glad it was them and not you, Little One."

Koserana, quiet, her cheek lightly pressed to the back of Shina's head, whispered, "Me too."

Shina looked searchingly into Thag's face and eyes. "How do you do it, Thag? You killed that man in the wall, and you just looked at him lying there, dead on the floor, and … how do you not feel it?"

Thag looked sad. "But I do feel it. I feel every death I've ever caused, every hurt I've ever given. I'm not my father, who enjoyed causing pain. Nor am I my mother, who was insensate to it and killed abundantly simply because she was hungry. I *feel* every hurt I give.

"But, little Shina, this world is dying, and I'm fighting to bring it back to life. I wish I didn't have to hurt anyone, and I try to avoid it, but sometimes you have to fight for something bigger than yourself, and when you do, you have to fight to win.

"You killed to defend yourself and your friends. Sometimes you have to.

"Do you understand? Does that help?"

Shina had heard him speak of this before, when Koserana attacked Duke Antain – about fighting for a better world. But it hadn't been real to her that she might have to do some of the fighting herself – that she might have to take the training she'd had since barely after she could walk, and use it to end someone's life.

Now it was crashing in on her world.

"That's what growing up is, isn't it?" she asked Thag. "It means that you sometimes have to face some of the really ugly things in the world, and you sometimes have to make really hard decisions. I guess I never saw that before."

Thag just nodded.

Shina pulled back, wiping the tears from her face. Then she remembered the sound of a door. "Where'd Brad go? Is he okay?"

"He's fine." Thag smiled to see her spirits returning. "He's going to see if he can find out who that was in the secret alcove and in the alley. Maybe find out if there are more of them in the city, or if we can leave safely now."

Shina thought for a moment. It was hard to face the memories, but she needed to be sure she had seen what she thought she'd seen. The keen terror of watching that sword strike Brad's chest, while her knife seemed to move in slow motion, knowing it would be too late for the handsome young man – that had been as bad as the fountains of blood her own hand had caused.

But she was sure of what she'd seen. It was hard to face that memory, but face it she did.

"What is he, Thag? What is Brad? I saw a sword deflect from his chest." Koserana looked up at Thag, her curiosity also sparked. She had seen it too, but had ignored it in the shock of the ambush and of watching innocent little Shina kill two men.

"It's a bit complex, and he can tell you better than I can," started Thag. "He was born and raised in the wastes, and sometimes the spirits in that land pick out warriors or bards that they particularly like, and give them … special gifts. I guess that's the best way I can put it.

"It's kind of like how some of my stepfather's friends will help me when I ask them. They can make the weather help me, if they want to. It's stronger for him, and more … instinctive. Maybe even feral.

"As I said, he can explain it better than I can. That's how I understand it."

Koserana spoke up. "Spirits protected him, then? That makes sense."

"What do you mean, 'spirits', Thag? What are 'spirits'?" asked Shina.

"They're the workers the gods use to build worlds. The living essence of things like light, heat, air, water, and stone. They're what makes hot air rise in most worlds, and what makes rock stronger than water. Mostly, they just do what they're supposed to – the sun makes some air heat up, so it rises, and colder air comes in below it, making wind. The spirits are the living rules that make that happen. Every world is built by spirits and has rules of one sort or another.

"But for some people, mainly druids and similar people, they … 'speak' isn't really the right word, but it's the closest word there is – human language doesn't really have the vocabulary for it. That's what elvish and wizard-glyphs are for."

Both women looked like they were about to speak, but Thag cut them off. "Before you ask, yes, I do speak elvish. My stepfather taught it to me, since it was his birth-language. No, I don't know any wizard-glyphs. Only wizards knew those, and they're all dead."

"Except Gem," said Shina. "I know the myths, and they all say he's still around somewhere, right?"

Thag shook his head. "Sort of. I think Gem is still around somewhere – I'm not certain and my stepfather wasn't either – but he was dead for a long, long time. Even before the gnomish wars, before all the wizards were killed, Gem was somehow dead, but still alive, both at the same time. It's why they couldn't kill him when they were killing all the other wizards.

"And, no, I don't know what that means, or how he could be dead and alive at the same time. Wizards were strange folks, even by the standards of dragons and druids and spirits."

He paused and seemed to be looking at something. A memory or a thought, perhaps. When he continued, his voice was the barest whisper. "I would dearly love to find out, though."

A few hours later, Brad returned with what little news he'd been able to glean about their hunters and their situation.

Once they'd all gathered around him, and he'd been reassured that Shina was okay, he summarized what he'd found. "I can't learn much. The bounty is from the western lands, and the people who know the most about it are all westerners – my usual contacts don't know much yet since these are people who don't really gossip.

"What I do know is that they're offering a lot of money for you, Thag. They want you alive if possible, and delivered to some duke out west. Artis or something…"

Shina piped in with a correction, "Duke Antain of Klosia – he's rich enough to offer a pretty hefty bounty and he's got to be pretty upset with Thag. What about me? What do they say?"

Brad looked like he really didn't want to talk about it, but he looked her in the eyes and told her what he knew, "He's offering a hundred gold for you – and noted you must be kept alive at all cost. It's a fortune for some of these people. Sorry, didn't want to tell you all that, but you need to know."

He continued, "The bunch this morning were actually after you, Thag. They thought I was you when we came out into the alley. Since they want you alive, that's why they hesitated and didn't just jump us as we came out."

Thag smiled – not his usual close-lipped grin of pleasure, but a more predatory, fang-baring look. "Three men and a dog, with a crossbow and a couple of swords. If that's how they hope to take me, alive or otherwise …."

Brad chuckled and the two women both smiled.

"Ouch – for them," said Shina. Then she paused and thought for a moment. She cocked her head over the side and looked up at the barren ceiling of the ruined room. It was an idea, and maybe even a good one.

Brad was about to say more, but Thag held him up with a gesture at Shina. Koserana just looked on curiously.

Shina, eyes narrowed in concentration, looked at Koserana. *Yes, this might work,* she thought.

"Koserana – your lord, Chalkos, he's a bounty hunter, right?" Shina said, speaking a bit slowly as she continued to plot.

Koserana nodded in agreement.

"What if … what if you went to him, and had him ask around about the bounty."

Koserana smiled the same predatory grin that Thag had. "I can do better than that. I'm my master's agent in human lands. I do all his dealings for him. He does the work, but I negotiate the contracts and prices and all that. I can definitely ask around about this one." She had a sudden thought. "Also, lots of the other big-name hunters don't like to compete with my master. He's got a bit of a ruthless reputation, after all, and they don't like the idea of stealing from someone like him. That might work in your favor all by itself."

Shina, Brad and Thag all nodded at this. It was a good point.

Shina continued, "We need to travel east, right Thag?"

"Yes. For a long, long ways, and all of it rough going."

Shina thought again for a moment. "You can travel without much by way of supplies, and I expect Brad can too…" she looked her question at him and he nodded in agreement. "But I need more than I have if we're doing a long trip – clothing for different types of weather and terrain, new boots, a lighter hunting crossbow and some arrows for it, a good healer's kit, that kind of thing. And we'll need some money of some sort, so we can trade for more supplies along the way. Right?"

Brad replied, "If we want to do this right, we'll need all of that and more. Tents, tools, rope, food that we don't have to hunt along the way, in case hunting is bad or if we have to move faster than allows for it. A lot of stuff. I can get all of it, and I've done this before so I know what to get and who to get it from. Do we have money for all that?"

Koserana and Thag both had plenty of money, and handed it over to Brad. As he took it, he asked, "It'll take a few days to get all this. Maybe a week, tops. Can you two hide here that long?"

Shina shook her head. "It's not safe for Thag to hide in the city at all." She looked at him. "You're too conspicuous." There was no arguing with that.

Shina went on with her plan. "Thag, you'll need to head out of town. Tonight if possible. And you'll need to do it alone so you can move at full speed when you need to. Can't have you distracted by me." Thag was about to protest, but she stopped him with a gesture.

"I'll stay here with Brad. A little makeup, different clothing than people here have seen me in before, and color my hair – that kind of thing and nobody will notice me in a city like this. It's not like anyone here knows me or anything. Once we've got what we need, we can come out and meet you."

She asked Brad, "Is there a good place, a little bit east of here, for us to meet up like that?"

Brad didn't even have to think about it. "There's a butte, about ten miles east of town. It's about a quarter-mile wide, and maybe a hundred feet tall. Cliffs on all sides, but you can climb the north-east face if you know what you're doing. It's easy to find because it's mostly white chalk, and the rest of the hills around here are all black or dark gray."

Shina thought that would be a good landmark. "Will anyone likely be there?"

"Anyone up there is probably looking for us," Brad replied. "It's not a popular spot because there aren't any roads or rivers near it, and it's hard to get up onto. Plus, it's barren and there's nothing useful for miles around. Makes a good lookout point for that part of the wilds, so if there's anyone there, that's what they're doing."

Thag agreed. "And if there is anyone there looking for us, I can clear the area before you get there. I don't think they understand who they're trying to hunt. Not yet, anyway."

Thag turned to Shina. "It's a good plan, Little One. Any more to it?"

Shina thought of all the supplies Brad was proposing they take with them. "Will we need a cart, or mounts for me or Brad?"

Brad thought for a minute. "A cart, no. I've got that covered already. Can you ride a pony? Horses won't do well in the mountains, when we get there, but a pony might be good. Or maybe a couple of riding mules. If you can ride either, I'll see what I can get."

"I've never ridden ponies before, but I think I can learn how if you think it's a good idea."

Brad asked Koserana, "How about you? Will you need anything for your stay here, or for catching up with us. If that's even possible or desirable?"

Koserana replied, "I'll be staying here for a while, looking into the bounty and maybe misdirecting some of the hunters towards the south, or even back west. I can manage that myself. When I'm ready to catch up with you, my master can arrange that more easily than you can."

Shina thought to herself, *Yeah, you can fly a lot faster than any of us can walk, even Thag!*

"Then I think that's all of the plan," Shina concluded. "Unless anyone else has more or better?"

No one did.

"Well then," Shina said, her voice more firm and sure than it had been since her kidnapping. "Brad, you have a lot to do. You should probably get started on it right away."

He was about to tell her it should probably wait till tomorrow, but the way she looked at him told him that disagreeing wouldn't be in his best interest. He muttered something about getting an early start on all of it, and headed for the front door.

Shina turned to Koserana. "You should probably get started too. But come back tomorrow night, if you can, so you can tell me what you find. Okay?"

Koserana too felt like it was premature to start out right away, and was a little hurt to be dismissed so casually by her recent lover. Then she realized what Shina was actually doing, and bowed out gracefully.

"And me," Thag rumbled quietly. "I can't head out of town till it's dark, but should I give you some time alone?" He was still concerned about Shina's emotional shocks earlier in the day.

Shina grinned at him. "I'm feeling kind of … Lovely right now, Thag." She stepped over to him and put her hand against his chest, pushing lightly. It took him a moment to realize what she wanted, and then he sat.

Shina made sure Thag was watching, and then slowly undressed. She'd never deliberately undressed in front of anyone before – not like this. After a few tentative, hesitant motions, she realized what years of dance lessons and ballroom dances had been in preparation for, and her motions took on a slow, deliberate grace as she removed pieces of clothing one by one.

Thag, never taking his eyes off of the beautiful young woman, undid his cape and rapidly arranged it on the floor as a sheet for them to lie on, and then undid his belt and shorts and set them aside.

Shina, topless, instinctively ran her hands slowly over her breasts, and was pleased to see Thag's body responding, his member growing and hardening, even as her own sensitive nipples did the same. It was her first deliberate, planned seduction, and she wanted to do it right – even if she did have to ignore the run-down setting.

As she danced, she became more and more sure of herself. Her motions became more and more comfortable and natural. She took her time with each item of clothing, intuiting an erotic pace.

With a graceful move, she slid out of her panties and stood before Thag, marvelously nude. She had been naked around Thag many times – but never before had she felt this warm, this sensual, this radiantly erotic!

For a few minutes, she kept dancing for him. And then Shina made clear what she'd meant when she said she "felt Lovely". She knelt between his knees and smoothly took the end of his aroused manhood into her mouth.

Shina wanted it to be wonderful for him. After a long while, it was.

Chapter 9: *Dodge Out of Town*

The first day after Thag left town, Shina alternated between moping and acerbic upheavals so much that Brad and Koserana ended up avoiding her. Her father would have recognized this shadow of the girl he had raised.

Brad knew she was simply disconsolate from missing Thag, but he didn't have Thag's patience for Shina's tempers, so he just stayed away and let her work it out herself.

Koserana, upset that Shina seemed to be rejecting her, threw a bit of a temper tantrum herself, and spent the next two days alternating between madly working to convince everyone that Lord Chalkos didn't want anyone else poaching his hunt, and drowning her frustrations in a series of brothels. After a couple of barroom brawls that ended badly for both the participants and the furniture, she finally returned to Shina's hideout and tried to mend fences.

There was a lot of crying and I'm-sorrying and kissing by both of them.

Brad stopped by the next morning, and Shina's mood and temper had improved enough that he finally spent some time talking to her about their plans.

He told her that her plan looked like it was working. He still wasn't hearing as much on the grapevine as he would if it were an eastern affair, but what he was able to pick up said that Shina and Thag had disappeared, and that Lord Chalkos was hunting them off to the south.

Koserana stopped by one last time that evening. To keep the Lord Chalkos story believable, she would leave town and go south herself. She could even begin inquiries and rumors in some of the big cities to the southwest. Much of that territory was lawless enough that nobody would question the idea of two refugees fleeing there.

Shina's parting from Koserana was even more bittersweet than from Thag. She knew she'd be following Thag in a few days, but she wasn't sure she'd ever see Koserana again.

In a way, knowing she'd see Thag soon made her worry about him more, and miss him more. She wasn't sure why that was. Her last couple of days in Anytown gave her plenty of time to brood and not much more than that to do. Most of what she brooded about was Thag.

Without him there, she had time to think about their relationship. She spent hours debating with herself about it. Was she really in love with him, or was it just a crush brought on by his rescue and subsequent kindness? Even if it was love, how could it possibly work? He was not only a monster, only barely related to humanity by distant ancestors, but was also centuries old. She would age and wither in a few short years, dying in a handful of decades, while he would live; nobody knew how many long centuries or even millennia. Would he even remember her in a thousand years? How could he? How could anyone?

Surely he'd had other lovers before. He'd never said so, but he was so wise and wonderful and caring that someone must have loved him before. Did he remember them? He had never mentioned any of them. Did that mean he would forget her as the years and centuries flowed past? How could he not?

Or should she just be glad that she had him for whatever brief spell she had? After all, she realized, to her it would be a lifetime, no matter how ephemeral to him. Wouldn't that be enough? Could it be enough?

If she had a lifetime of love with him, her lifetime of love, shouldn't that be enough to be happy about? Her thoughts went round and round on the subject day after day.

Later, her thoughts turned to Koserana. That was even worse. Koserana was just a child by dragon standards. Her moods and passions swung with a child's impetuousness. Didn't it follow that her love would be just as fleeting?

How did I do this? I'm having affairs with immortals who will blink and I'll be gone.

When Brad came to her the next morning, he found her red-eyed and puffy-faced from crying all night. The news that they'd be leaving at first light the following day brought some of her composure back, but he still felt sorry enough for her to stay most of the day so she would have someone to talk to. The long hours of isolation and waiting, loneliness and loss, made her desperate for company, and he did his best to cheer her up.

Brad told her stories about his youth (she was thrilled to learn he was only twenty-four years old and not yet-another-immortal in her life) to pass the time.

"Where did you get your tattoo?" she asked.

He pointed at his chest and raised an eyebrow. Even though the tattoo was covered by a fine silk shirt, she could still picture it in her mind. She'd spent enough time staring at it in that fateful sauna, in a desperate attempt to avoid staring any lower. She nodded at his unspoken question.

"Well … it's not really a tattoo," he started.

Shina smiled – this was going to be quite a story, she guessed. She relaxed into the cushions he had provided for her small hideaway, and settled in for the tale.

His eyes got a dream-like look, focusing on memories only he could see, and he smiled.

"In the village I come from, everyone does a spirit vigil on the first dark moon after they start puberty. For most boys, it is when they get their first pubic hair. For girls, either that or their breasts grow enough to be noticed, whichever comes first.

"For most boys, their vision is hunting or war, sometimes both. A few have visions of talking to the spirits. For most girls, their visions are things like sex and family, but some end up hunting or other things.

"Whatever the vision is, the boy or girl gets a mark of one sort or another. The size, detail, and color of the marking tells you how strong your vigil spirit was. Some end up with predator marks. A paw means warrior, an eye means hunter. Wolves, bears, eagles, and griffons are the most common.

"Girls usually get flowers. Boys usually get animals."

When he paused there, Shina realized he was waiting for her to comment, so she did. "You have a rose. Is that a girl mark?"

He nodded. "Yep. Let me tell you about that."

"When I was eight, I got my first pubic hair, and the village elders and leaders sent me to the temple for my vigil. That's young, but it's normal for half-orcs. We age fast.

"Now, the way it usually starts is that the youth doing the vigil sleeps all day. You don't get to eat anything the day before, and you're supposed to rest and meditate on your destiny and your duty to the village and the tribe, but most kids just sleep. The vigil is all night, so sleeping the day before is smart.

"Me, I wasn't smart. Not by a long way. I spent the whole day pretending to be a great warrior and hunter. I thought I'd spend my whole life in glorious battle. A lot of imaginary orcs died horribly that day, let me tell you!" He had a humorous spark in his eyes, and Shina laughed at his jest.

"Of course, a few of those battlefields were my doom, but I died nobly and heroically, saving my whole village all by myself through my amazing sacrifices." He winked at her. "It was very, very noble, you see!" She grinned and nodded. Brad was pleased to see life and humor back in her eyes.

"Anyway, after a long day of fighting orcs in the woods and valleys near my home, it was finally time for my vigil. The sun was going down, so I went home and undressed – you do the whole thing naked.

"Then I went to the shrine.

"The shrine is mostly below-ground. It's got a roof over it, but you go down some stairs to get into the main room. That's this big circular pit, with a huge fireplace in the middle. Even though it's low like that, it doesn't just fill up with water or mud – old clan spirits keep it dry, you see.

"At the very back of the temple is a door into the side of the hill above the temple. Nobody goes in there except the priests, and kids on their vigil. It goes to a passage into the hill, with steps that go down and down into the bedrock.

"There are no lights in there when you do your vigil. There's a coal-pit at the bottom that makes it very, very hot – even hotter than a normal sauna – but it's closed up so no light comes out.

"The elders tell you to go in there and to seek your vision from the spirits. They tell you it's very important to stay awake the whole night. Those who don't – they go insane, and they don't get a mark either. They get driven out into the wilds and left there – their souls aren't strong enough for the spirits, so they can't be part of the clan or the village.

"The first thing I noticed was the darkness. I see really well in the dark – not like Thag, but much better than most people. But even to me it was totally dark. I had to feel my way down the stairs. Some kids panic or get disoriented in the dark and fall down the stairs, or accidentally touch the metal of the coal-pit and get burned. That doesn't get you kicked out of the village, but it's still seen as really, really bad luck.

"So I carefully felt my way down the stairs, and successfully found the bench I was supposed to sit on all night.

"They heat water on top of the coal, and put herbs and things in there that help you have your vision. I don't know how all of that works, but it sure smelled horrible to me! Wet and rotten and pretty nasty.

"Even with that smell, it was night and dark and I started to feel tired. I knew I had to stay awake till morning, but I started to feel so, so tired."

He paused for a moment, lost in the memory. His face lit up with a broad smile. He nearly whispered, his quiet voice filled with joy and reverence, "And that's when she came to me…"

"Who?" Shina asked when he paused again. He was a good storyteller, and knew how to get his audience to participate.

Brad shook himself, coming back to the present abruptly. When he continued, his voice had returned to normal. "My spirit, of course. It was still completely dark, but I could see her, clear as day."

His face and voice lit up again as he continued. "I couldn't see anything else in that pit, but she was bright and beautiful and full of color and life! I could see her bright green eyes and her pale golden hair. I could see every freckle on her face!

"I'd never seen anyone like this before in my life! The people I lived with were all dark-haired and brown-eyed. We have tanned skin all our lives, and get even darker in the sun. I'd never seen green eyes or blonde hair, and freckles were completely new to me.

"She was pretty small," he looked at Shina appraisingly. "Maybe your size or a little shorter."

"She was the most beautiful woman I've ever seen. Even more than your Koserana, and that's saying something!

"Anyway, she and I spent the night talking and joking with each other. I felt real joy for the first time in my life that night. She gave me a warmth that spread comfort through my whole body, starting deep in my stomach and spreading through every vein in me till it made my fingers and toes tingle.

"Before I knew it, it was morning. When the elders opened the curtain at the top of the stairs and let the first daylight in, my spirit disappeared. But she left the room filled with fresh, cool air that filled my nose and lungs with a sort of glow.

"I know that doesn't make sense, really, but it's what it felt like!"

Shina nodded. She told him, "It does make sense. The first time I saw you, I think I saw that glow too."

Brad was pleasantly surprised. "Really? Nobody's ever mentioned anything like that before." He smiled, and it was the innocent smile of a happy child. Shina thought that somehow suited this man's face. It was … appropriate for him.

"Anyway, the village elders were shocked when I came up the stairs. Since my father was an orc, they expected a war-marking, or at least a hunt-marking. All orcs get those. Instead, I had this."

He opened his shirt and gave Shina another look at it. She took her time and examined it minutely. The mark was amazing! Even Koserana's vivid tattoos couldn't compare in detail or depth. It really looked like a rose bush. It had every tiniest detail, and the thorns looked like they would pierce to touch. Fantastic!

"Yes, it's a feminine mark. But it's not one anyone has ever had before. First, roses aren't a thing out in the eastern wastes, nor the Mountains of the Sky, where I grew up. No one in the village had ever seen this before. All they could tell was it was a flower, and thus feminine. I didn't find out it was a 'rose' till a few years ago, when I came west.

"But it's also the most detailed, largest, most complex marking anyone has ever had. Elders came from miles around to see it.

"The next largest mark in the whole clan is a wolf – whole thing and pretty detailed – about this big." He held his fingers apart about three inches. "But even that is just black and light brown, no other colors.

"One woman I met once had a flower on her breast, only about as big as a fingernail, and kind of blurry and vague, but with four or five colors.

"What I have, mystifies everyone.

"And then I really hit puberty head-on when I was ten summers old. Grew and grew and grew, and my voice got deep and … well, and all the rest of that." He glanced knowingly down at his lap, mischief in his eyes and grin.

Shina giggled and Brad smiled.

"Anyway, that's when my spirit visited me again. I was out hunting.

Even though I didn't have a hunt-mark, I was still good at hunting, so I would go out alone into the woods and stalk whatever I could find. So I was alone in the woods, at night, and she came to me again. We spent the night together again.

"In the morning, I could … 'see' is a pale word compared to what it's really like, but I'll use it anyway. I could 'see' spirits all around me. And I could sort of talk to them with my soul. Not in words, not even in the words in the mind that most people mean when they say 'think'. It was just …" He stopped, at a loss for words.

"I always get bogged down at this part. It's impossible to explain to anyone who hasn't done it, and anyone who has doesn't need it explained at all. Thag does it with the spirits of storms and wind and knows what it's like. Maybe he can explain it better.

"The main thing is, the spirits are my family now. They travel with me. They protect me, and help me. I help them, just by being in the world and living – that's something they want and can't do on their own.

"And every year, this flower gets more lush, more colorful, and it grows a little more out over me. The vines are spreading onto my arms and legs now. The marks don't normally change after you get them, but mine does."

Shina looked, to be sure. "They're up onto your neck a little bit, too."

Brad smiled that pure smile again. "Really? I didn't know that!" He felt around his neck with his hand, as if he could find it there somehow. For a while, they sat in companionable silence.

After a spell, Brad asked, "By the way, I've been meaning to ask, how did you learn to fight like that? Back in the alley, I mean. If you don't mind me asking, that is."

Shina shuddered and had to pause to compose herself. She still had nightmares about killing those two men. Maybe it would help to talk about it a little bit.

"It's nothing as interesting as your story," she said. Her voice was quiet and the mirth had gone out of it.

She continued, "Every noble where I grew up learns to fight. Men learn swords and arbalests. Women learn knives, both poniards and throwing knives. It's mainly so that our slaves can't stand against us.

"I never realized how wrong that was until Thag talked to me about it. I understand it now, and I hate it. But, growing up, it was what I knew and I never questioned it.

"I used to hit…" she looked haunted, and Brad interrupted her before she could go on.

"Did you practice throwing a lot? You were very good at it."

Her eyes came back to the present. It took her a moment to realize he had asked a question, and a moment more to understand it. "Yes. Every week since I was five years old. Hours and hours every week, just throwing and recovering.

"You start with throwing at a piece of heavy cloth. That way, if the hilt hits, the knife doesn't bounce back at you.

"Then you throw at a wooden wall, till you can make the blade stick every time.

"Then targets. Then smaller targets. Then slow-moving targets.

"Most women can hit a small, fast target almost every time by their fifteenth birthday. That's when most get married, and then they're usually too busy having babies and raising families and helping their husbands with business and politics.

Words rushed out of her. "But I didn't do that. Get married I mean. I didn't get married. I got kidnapped instead, and now I'm in love with Thag, so I'll probably never get married."

She looked up at Brad. "Do you think I should be?"

He blinked in surprise a few times. "Married? I … I don't … I mean …"

She shook her head "no". "I mean: Should I be in love with Thag? Do you think I should be? Because I am, but I'm not sure I should be. I'm not sure what's right, and I'm confused and unhappy and just confused and …" she trailed off, not realizing she was repeating herself, but not sure what else to say.

Brad became totally serious. "I can't tell you what you should or shouldn't do, or who you should or shouldn't love. Only you can do that. But I can say you're happier when you're with Thag than when you're not. Everyone can see that."

Shina thought back to the werewolves assuming the same thing.

And Koserana, when they first met. Maybe he was right. She nodded silently in hesitant agreement.

Brad waited. He could see she was thinking it through. Not that thinking it through was necessarily the best thing to do when it comes to love, but at least it was better than wallowing in morbid doubt and confusion.

"Maybe you're right," she finally said. Her voice was back to normal for the first time all day, and she seemed to relax a bit. After a moment, she gave him a genuine, comfortable smile. "Maybe you're right. And … and that's good enough."

She was surprised to realize it was. Just the idea that it might be right, might be okay, was a comfort and solace. A tight pain deep inside her released, and a wash of peace spread from where it had once been.

"Thank you, Brad. You're a good friend. I think your spirit chose well."

***

The next morning, while the sky was light but the sun wasn't quite up yet, Brad and Shina set out to leave Anytown.

First, they dressed Shina up in a bit of a disguise.

There was no disguising her height – platform shoes or anything comparable would just make her less short, and if anyone was looking for "short", "less short" wouldn't accomplish anything useful. So they skipped that step entirely.

Coloring her hair a bland light brown was the first step they did take. Red hair, especially outside the western kingdom, was rare enough to be noticeable.

Then some drops in her eyes to change the dark blue to dark brown. The drops were expensive, illegal, and made her eyes water for a while, but anyone looking for a redhead with dark blue eyes would overlook her now.

Next, they strapped down her breasts. It was uncomfortable, but flattening her chest combined with her small stature made her look almost like a child. She was also to carry a large pack on her back, which would de-emphasize her hips and modify her feminine gait. There was no disguising her gender, but by making her look even younger, they hoped to get past anyone who didn't know her and was just going by the duke's published descriptions of her.

Common clothing, made of undyed wool, well-used and slightly dirty, would complete their attempt to hide her in plain sight. Anyone who had seen her arrive to Anytown would have seen her in the were's doeskins. Anyone from the inn would have seen her in fine silks (which were packed away – Shina liked them too much to just throw them away). Nobody in her life had ever seen her in the comfortable, functional garb of a midlands peasant.

It would have been remarkable to anyone who knew her before that she comfortably undressed in front of Brad, and just as casually changed to the new clothing. She never even thought about it, and felt neither embarrassment nor anything else about being nude in front of him. It wasn't even "I've done this before", she simply gave no thought to it at all. Being both an easterner and a gentleman, Brad paid no attention. It would never have occurred to him to do so.

In a few minutes, Brad left the building by the front and made sure no one was watching. When he was sure, he gestured for Shina to join him.

"Follow me a bit behind. You're not with me, we just happen to be going the same direction on the same street. Right?"

She nodded. She knew, first-hand, how crowded these streets would be in a little bit. It would be easy to "be on the same street" without being "with". She was more concerned about getting separated from him entirely, but knew that going east would be easy enough, especially in the early morning. If they got separated and she got lost, she would just have to go east till she found the edge of town, and then keep going east till she found the plateau where Thag would meet them.

Fortunately, she didn't lose sight of him, even as the crowds grew thicker after the sun came up.

They walked at a casual pace down first one street and then another. Always trending east, but if she hadn't had Brad to guide her, she would have been lost inside of two blocks.

Her hometown, where she barely spent any time on the streets except in coaches with expert drivers, was laid out in a series of concentric circles, with short radial streets at fixed, regular intervals. Everything was planned and the whole city was laid out as precisely as the kingdom's best engineers could manage.

Anytown, on the other hand, was a labyrinth. Streets ended abruptly at houses, or took crooked twists and turns, or doubled back on themselves. Intersections were entirely haphazard, and rarely at anything resembling right-angles.

The neighborhoods and districts of her home were clearly delineated with boundaries, many of them in the form of tall defensive walls with fortified towers. Wealth stayed with wealth, commerce with commerce, poverty with poverty.

In Anytown, a walled manse of obvious (even tacky) expense might have ramshackle huts built against the outside of its fences. Stinking tanneries might be right across the street from taverns – Shina wondered how anyone could possibly eat or drink in that thick air. She even saw a bakery right next to a smithy, and wondered if they considered all the soot just another ingredient in the bread.

And the crowds! She had been overwhelmed by them when they first arrived. Two days later, making a hasty exit from "the septic tank of the world", the crowds were still overwhelming, but a bit less so. By the time she and Brad reached the outer walls of the town (*Why walls on the east side but not on the west?* she wondered), the sun had only been up for an hour or so, and the crowds were already so thick that she almost had to walk on Brad's heels to avoid being separated from him.

But in those thick clots of people of all shapes and colors and sizes, nobody seemed to notice a small, adolescent, peasant girl with a huge pack on her back, walking behind a tall, handsome young man. If anyone did notice her, they certainly didn't seem to pay any attention at all.

A few months ago, her father's daughter would have been scandalized to not be the center of attention – and would have taken steps to correct that! Now, she was just glad to be anonymous, unnoticed, and hopefully unremarked and unremembered too.

Just as they reached the gates, Brad stopped so suddenly she almost bumped into him. He was looking at someone who was very carefully not looking back at him. It was a man, taller than usual though shorter than Brad, with long, muscular legs and arms, wide shoulders, a thickly muscled chest over narrow hips. His black hair hung in long, narrow braids almost to his slender waist. His eyes, like most easterners, were pale brown, almost golden. He was wearing heavy leather leggings, knee-high boots with thick soles and studded seams, a heavy black vest that left his upper arms bare, and had large leather bracers with metal backings on his wrists.

To Shina, it was strange to see a man wearing a knife on his belt instead of a longsword, but the knife he had was masculine enough to make up for it. It was almost as long as her forearm, and had a thick, obelisk-shaped blade on a large hilt with a plain ball-pommel.

He also had the tattoo of a wolf-head on his right bicep, and Shina wondered about that – was it one of the spirit-markings Brad had told her about? She had to resist an impulse to walk up closer and take a look at it.

Brad only took a moment to regain his composure and start walking again, but he kept glancing at the man. Shina, distracted by the whole thing and not very adept at subterfuge, followed closely behind him, trotting to catch up as he started walking faster towards the city gates.

Brad looked back at her, realized she was confused, and then openly gestured for her to come to him. He took the pack from her and gestured for her to follow.

He led her to a small corral and set the pack down.

Quietly, he told her, "We're in trouble. The fellow back there, he's a spirit-hunter. I don't know him, but I know his type. He's dangerous, has spirits that help him hunt and kill, and they don't come into town unless they're hunting someone in there.

"I don't think he's looking for you. I don't think he even noticed you. I think he was hunting me. What I don't know is why. His tribe and mine are too distant to have a feud.

"Regardless, we need to get moving, and fast. He'll be able to track us, but if we can get to Thag before the hunter catches up to us, we should be okay."

Brad then touched the large pack, just touched it, and it disappeared! Suddenly, without warning or sound or anything, it was just gone!

Shina gave Brad a startled look. "How?"

He grinned widely. "Magic!"

The exasperated look she responded with was worth it to him.

"It's in here," he said, gesturing at one of the wide bracelets he always wore. "These have room in them. That's why we don't need a cart."

Shina looked closely at the bracelets for the first time. They were bronze, wide and thick, and had no decorations or markings at all. Just metal circles around his wrists, with a sort of half-twist in each band. But then something … her eyes felt kind of … she wasn't sure – but she could sort of see a place around the bracelets. Large spheres, maybe ten feet wide, with a wide variety of things in there. There weren't walls to the spheres, they just sort of stopped existing at a certain distance from the bracelets.

She nodded. "I can see it. Like rooms around them. Sort of there but not at the same time."

Brad gawped! His mouth fell open and his eyes went wide! "You … you … you can _see_ it?"

Now that she'd noticed it, she couldn't stop seeing it. She nodded emphatically and said, "Yes, it's kind of obvious. I'm really not sure how I didn't notice it before."

Brad took a deep breath and tried to get his composure back. "Well … okay. That's … different." Then he quickly looked around. "But we don't have time to talk about it! We need to get moving."

It only took a minute to get a horse for her. "I would have gotten a pony, but I think speed matters more than durability in the mountains right now," he explained as she stared up at the mountain of animal she was expected to climb up on. It was a wall of pale white fur, its shoulders easily higher than her head.

She tried twice to mount it on her own, but it was just too high! So Brad and the owner of the corral, a dour-faced man who was all too eager to help lift her, put her up on the saddle on its back.

The ground was a mile below her, and the saddle rocked with every breath of the monstrous mount and every tiny shift of her weight!

When Brad paid with gold, the man suddenly became solicitous. "And a remount for her? And a pair for you as well, sir?"

"Neither," said Brad curtly, and took the reins to lead Shina's new nightmare out to the road.

At first, Brad just walked. That was bad enough. The whole thing swayed like a ship in a storm, and Shina was sure she'd fall to her death at any moment. She gripped the saddle tightly with her knees and took a death-grip with her hands on the saddle-horn.

Then Brad sped up. He was jogging, and the horse turned into a jackhammer! Every pounding step rattled Shina's bones. Her teeth felt like they were being shaken out of her head!

"Stand up on the stirrups!" Brad shouted back at her.

"The what?" she barely managed to get out of her shaken mouth.

"The stirrups! The foot things!"

It was terrifying, but she tried it. In moments, she had settled into a knees-bent stance, her body leaning slightly forward.

And then Brad sped up again. Now he was running flat out! Shina only had a moment to wonder how long he could possibly keep that up, and then she realized she was flying!

The horse! The wonderful, amazing, beautiful horse! It was running smoothly and beautifully beneath her, and she was flying over the ground!

The wind whipped her hair out behind her!

The lush grassland was a blur beneath them!

The power!

The rush!

The thrill!

The land opened up around them and the sky was a giant bowl of cerulean perfection.

Her pulse raced in rhythm to the pounding feet of the marvelous creature she rode!

Too soon, Brad slowed to a walk. When Shina looked back, she was amazed to see the city was just a smudge of brown air in the distance. It had seemed like mere moments, but they were already several miles away!

This horse was truly amazing!

The horse was breathing heavily, and had a foam of sweat on its chest. It's legs were dripping, and the rest of it was damp. Steam was coming out of its mouth. She'd seen her own breath do that in cold weather before, but never on a mild day like this.

Bewildered, she asked Brad, "Will she be okay?"

"He. He'll be fine. We just need a drink," he indicated the small stream they were stopping next to.

"You should climb down and walk around a bit," he advised her. "If you don't, your legs will cramp up."

When she tried to climb down on her own, she discovered that her legs had turned to damp noodles, and Brad had to lift her down to the ground.

All three drank briefly from the cold, fresh stream, and then Brad said, "Time to move on."

She didn't feel like she could move an inch away from the stream!

Then Brad put his hands on the back of her neck, and warmth flooded through her in an irresistible rush! Her legs felt strong and sure. Nascent pain in her calves, hands, back and neck didn't fade, it just vanished.

Brad put his hands on the horse's neck, and the animal threw back its head and made a strange, high noise that she'd never heard before, but instinctively recognized as a challenge against the whole universe. It stood straight and proud and pranced a bit, just for the fun of moving.

For the first time, Shina realized that Brad himself wasn't sweating or breathing heavily, and hadn't been for even a moment.

He realized her question and replied, "This is my spirit's gift. Life! For me and for me to gift to my friends.

"Sure, I can fight and kill and bounce swords off my chest. But this," and he gestured at all three of them, "... this is the good part. This is what makes all the rest worth it."

Shina couldn't resist Brad's infectious enthusiasm and agreed wholeheartedly: That *was* the best part.

When Shina got back up on the horse, she looked around. Back towards the city, there was ... someone? Yes, someone was coming towards them. Still far off, but coming straight towards them, fast.

"Brad. I don't know if you can see them from down there, but there are people coming towards us from back there," she said and pointed.

Brad looked, but without the higher perspective of being on horseback, he couldn't see them yet.

"How many? Can you tell?" he asked.

"Three, I think."

Brad thought a moment. "Shina, if we get separated, you go to that hill over there," he pointed almost due east, at a small hill about a mile away. "From the top of that, you'll be able to see the butte. Go straight to it. Thag will see you coming and will come to you."

Shina tried to protest. "We should stay together..."

Brad interrupted her. "Let's go. Just remember what I said. Ride like the wind, and don't stop for anything except Thag himself." Before she could say another word, he handed her the reins and took off running.

She had no idea what to do with the reins except hold onto them, but apparently that was all she had to do. In moments, they were running again – the grasslands flying past under her horse's hooves. Again, Brad had no difficulty keeping up. She began to think he might even be holding back to stay with her.

They were about halfway to the hill he'd pointed out when Brad signaled to stop. Fortunately, the horse understood his signal, or just stopped because Brad had stopped, since Shina had no clue how to stop the horse herself.

They turned and looked back the way they'd just come. Shina was surprised to see that the trio following them were gaining rapidly. She was about to point them out to Brad when he suddenly swore.

She didn't know the oath or curse he used, it was in a coarse, guttural language she'd never heard before, but the tone was unmistakable!

"Run, Shina! Run!" he yelled. With a push and smack, he sent the horse galloping away.

Cursing under his breath, Brad made sure Shina was on the way, and then turned to face their pursuers.

The wolf from earlier had been joined by a pair of damn bear-warrior orcs! This was going to get ugly fast!

He put his hand on his shirt, over the rose. "Ends here, my love. Let's just give them one last story to tell about us!" he said.

Brad knew he had one chance to save Shina. Without the wolf, the two bears would be too slow to catch the horse before she found Thag. There was no way he could stop a pair of berserkers, but the wolf was going down!

It would only be a minute or two till they caught up. Pray gods that Shina had time to get away.

He braced himself, and let them come to him. Damn but the wolf was fast! Brad smiled. Fast, sure, but dumb enough to race ahead of the bears when it saw him standing there, ready for it.

To his eyes, it was a man and two orcs rushing towards him. But his other senses saw the truth as the three carnivores, one small and fast, the other two huge, powerful and almost unkillable, raced towards him.

Brad stomped. The wolf, only a dozen yards away, sped up! It started to leap at him, its mouth wide to rip out his throat!

The ground under it erupted! Green and brown vines shot out of the soil, writhing like mad snakes!

In moments, the wolf was wrapped in a cocoon of rose vines, the heavy thorns tearing at his flesh! Blood began to pour out of him as his struggles made them rip him even more violently!

And then the bears were charging past their tangled companion. A few vines lashed at them, but their thick hide shrugged off the thorns and their mighty muscles ripped the vines effortlessly.

Brad's skin was armor, his muscles pushed to limits no mortal human could match, his bones had the strength of stone in them. But he was no match for the avalanche of enchanted predator that slammed into him!

On the first impact, Brad felt his bones bend and break. Muscles tore. Something inside him sent a shock of incomprehensible pain through his whole being.

In a second, he was lying on the ground with the bear towering over him. His eyes saw it raise up a heavy axe, his other senses saw it rear up and raise its claws in the air, ready to tear him in half.

He made half a motion as it paused there, about to bring the weight of death down on his supine form. At his desperate last urging, a few last vines wrapped around the bear's feet. He knew it would never hold the monster warrior, but he hoped it would give Shina a few extra seconds.

And then something dark and huge happened to the berserker!

With a crash, something titanic slammed into the ground on either side of Brad's head!

Claws like daggers on a hand the size of a dinner plate slammed into the bear's head! Bone shattered, flesh tore, a blast of hot blood sprayed across Brad as the bear's head was ripped off!

The second bear saw her mate fall lifeless as this huge thing suddenly appeared out of the sky and slammed into them.

She was already in battle frenzy, but a wall of red flowed across her vision and her eyes tunneled till all she could see was the titan that had killed her mate.

She hadn't lost a fight since she was six years old. She'd been blessed by the bear spirit when she was only eight. Now, twenty years later, she had all the battle-experience in the world on top of a fully mature orcish body, a body built by ancient wizards to win wars on strength, blind tenacity and unrelenting ferocity!

With the fury of a maddened she-bear, the orc spirit-warrior waded into the fight with no thought of mercy or sense.

Brad saw Thag crouch over him. Thag's head came down as he stared into the berserker's eyes. Brad knew Thag would rather intimidate than fight, but knew also that it was hopeless – no berserker ever backs down once the fight has started, and no orc knows the meaning of fear.

The she-bear slammed into Thag with all the power of her spirit-amplified muscles. In her decades of battle, she had smashed down doors and flattened shield-walls held by strong men. Thag's legs shook a little at the gigantic impact, barely rocked by a blow that would have felled an ox.

The bear was fast and strong. She was tough and brutal.

The titanomachy was over a fraction of a second after she slammed full-force into Thag.

Thag, unhurt, was standing over Brad when Shina finally got back. She had seen Thag's desperate flight over her and had finally worked out how to use the reins enough to turn the running horse around.

The horse shied at all the blood and slaughter, and at the scent of the monster standing in the middle of it all. Shina jumped off its back and raced to where Brad was lying on the ground.

Brad was covered in blood, and she could see bits of bone sticking out through his chest and one of his arms. He was lying so still!

"Oh no!" she cried out.

Thag looked up at her, startled. "What?" he asked.

How could he be so cold and uncaring? "Brad's dead, Thag! Look at him, he's dead!"

Thag, a puzzled look on his face, looked down at Brad. "What do you mean, dead? His heart's still beating. I can hear it just fine."

Shina just stared at him. "Your friend is lying there dying, and you're just listening to his heart!" She was shocked.

Thag sighed. "He'll be fine, Shina. He just needs to rest a bit."

Brad's eyes opened to the tiniest slits. Shina raced over to him and knelt down by his head. He looked right through her, and then put his hands flat on the ground.

And the ground moved!

Shina was startled, and then saw clearly that it wasn't the ground moving, it was the grass. Somehow it was growing! As she gawped at it, inches of grass grew in seconds. Flowers sprang up out of the ground and bloomed in mere moments. In a minute, the blood and the three corpses had disappeared into the dirt, nourishing the rampant plants.

The smell of fresh grass and thousands of blooming flowers filled the air with a heady perfume. The air itself took on the fresh, clean feel of a cool mountain breeze, but filled with a scent more wonderful than anything Shina could ever have imagined.

She turned her wondering gaze back to Brad himself, and was amazed to see his wounds disappearing. Bones sank back into flesh. His arm writhed as it straightened itself and the tear made by the protruding bones vanished, leaving not even the faintest scar.

It only took a few minutes, and then Brad was lying in front of her, deeply asleep with a peaceful look on his face and not a sign of injury anywhere on him.

The grass was a couple of feet high and the profuse flowers covered the ground in a carpet of fantastic colors.

And Brad started to snore.

"He'll sleep the rest of the day. Probably tonight too," announced Thag.

Shina looked up at Thag. "He's amazing," she said, wonder in her voice.

Thag nodded. "Definitely," he said, like it was the most normal thing in the world. Then he casually picked Brad up and slung him over his shoulder. "Get your horse and let's get going."

Five minutes later, Shina wished it were that easy. First, simply catching the horse proved impossible for her. Shina hadn't thought to tie it to anything when she dismounted, and she didn't have Brad's charisma with animals.

Finally, Thag set Brad back down and simply chased the poor animal down. It was too exhausted with fear from that for her to ride, but at least they got it back.

Shina had imagined a lot of ways that her reunion with Thag would go. Many of her nights alone in the abandoned shop, she had fantasized herself to sleep, planning how they'd make love once she got out of the city and met back up with him.

But now that the moment was finally here, she was too physically exhausted from her wild first ride on a galloping horse, with her legs in burning pain from the unaccustomed exertion, and too emotionally exhausted from the pursuit, battle, and the shock when she thought Brad was dead. Instead of a wild seduction, she walked along in a sort of painful fugue for a short while, and then Thag caught her as she collapsed and just picked her up and carried her.

It was kind of awkward for him, carrying Brad over his left shoulder and Shina in his right arm, and the horse's reins tied to his belt with the frightened, worn-out beast following him as best it could.

It could smell the kind of ultimate predator Thag was, and wanted nothing to do with him, but it followed numbly where its reins led it.

As he walked, Thag mused that at least leading it was better than carrying it. That would have been even more awkward, and probably would have injured the animal.

Thag spent most of the walk trying to figure out what exactly was going on. He theorized that the three spirit warriors had been hunting them for something other than Duke Antain's cash bounty. He thought to himself, *"What can a western duke offer three eastern tribesmen that they would value in the slightest? They don't need gold, and can't carry much anyway. They certainly don't need his political favors. So why were they chasing these two?"* So, while he was pretty sure he knew what they *weren't* after, he didn't have any good ideas on what they were up to. That bothered him.

He didn't get far that day. The horse began to stagger, and he decided that was far enough. He'd just have to camp, even though it was barely mid-day.

Chapter 10: *Castle*

During The Empire times, when the battle mages ruled the world with iron fists powered by the last of the wizardly magic, Herztad was founded as a simple army camp on a strategic island. The island, a mile-wide shelf of hard rock in the middle of a shallow lake, was inhospitable and barren till imperial engineers built a couple of simple wooden docks and established a supply dump for the army's river patrols.

After a few raids by bandits and river-pirates, the original camp was fortified and a permanent garrison was established.

Over the millennia of The Empire's rule, the simple fortifications were expanded into first a keep and towers and later a castle with high walls and a mighty army, ruled by the dukes of Klosia from their capital in Mezurg.

During the world-wide wars that finally overthrew the battle mages after millennia of nightmarish domination, Mezurg was burned and magically desecrated over and over again. First, the dukes evacuated their families to Herztad for protection from the wars, then finally moved their own court and capital to the heavily fortified island.

By the time of Duke Antain's rule, three generations after the death of the last battle mage and the fall of The Empire, medium-sized cities had grown up on the north and west shores of the lake, and the original fortified island was one of the mightiest castles in the Westlands.

Where the fortress he'd kept Shina in was a simple border-garrison with walls and towers, his capital was a colossal citadel.

Its outermost walls were built up from the bedrock below the lake itself, enclosing a stretch of water that housed dozens of military ships in an artificially protected harbor. The passages through that wall were protected against large ships by heavy chains which could be raised and lowered from fortified towers that flanked the gateways. High towers with thick stone walls guarded either side of each passage, with spouts that could spray flaming oil on boats that approached too close, and ballistae and trebuchet emplacements that could fling rocks or metal spikes as far as the shores of the lake itself.

The edge of the original island had been rebuilt into the foundation of another set of mighty walls, with even higher towers. From these, arbalesters could rain down arrows on anyone who managed to gain the top of the outer walls, or anyone in the inner harbor. Heavy stone bridges, arched and buttressed, crossed far above the waters from inner walls to outer, and defenders on these could rain arrows, rocks and flaming oil on invaders below them in the harbor. Many times in the violent history of Herztad, small numbers of defenders had held those bridges against armies of invaders.

Inside the inner walls were the towers and keeps and fortified barracks of the duke's most loyal officers and armies. Thousands of dedicated, even fanatical, soldiers were garrisoned between the island-wall and the innermost keep. Those soldiers were the trained and experienced veterans of a dozen wars, equipped with the best arms and armor the duke's treasuries could afford. One man in a hundred even had empowered weapons crafted by the battle mages – only the king's own bodyguards could boast a better percentage of those frightful armaments!

Here also were the towers that housed the duke's war-wyverns and trained battle griffons. The dog-sized griffons were superb aerial hunters, able to pick out enemy knights and attack them from on high. The wyverns, able to carry an armored man for miles through the air at far better speed than the fastest horses, flew patrols around the fortress at all times of day and night, only excepting winter blizzards or the worst of the frequent summer thunderstorms.

Messages had arrived to the ducal sorcerers in the palace at Herztad. The duke was on his way back home, and he was furious!

A disturbed beehive dropped suddenly on an angry anthill would have been less of a madhouse than the frightened citizens and soldiers – all desperately, vainly, and counterproductively trying to make sure the duke's arrival would be as orderly and unvexing as possible.

Everyone in the palace, even the most menial of slaves, knew the duke had lost something important. Most didn't know what. Even amongst those few who knew whom (not what) he had lost, only one knew why it mattered to him. There were six rumors for every five people, and all of them agreed only that the duke had been balked in some plan, and was in a murderous rage.

One of Antain's knight-generals abandoned the city on the fastest wyvern he could steal. Nobody knew why, but that didn't stop anyone from having a firm conviction for which rumor "must be true".

Finally, as tensions mounted and rumors bred like minks, the duke's wyverns swept in over the horizon. *Calamity* was the message everyone saw in the brutal speed the duke was forcing the beasts to. He didn't land on one of the wyvern-towers in the inner fortress, instead leaping from his mount's reptilian back as it hovered over a balcony on the innermost keep. Household guards, the best and most loyal of the duke's elite soldiers, caught him as he landed, and he brushed them aside without a word and stormed into the innermost sanctum.

As cold and forbidding as the castle appeared from the outside, all black and gray stone barely relieved by harsh steel, the inner sanctum of the ducal family was the diametric opposite. The duke, dressed in chainmail and field-leathers, was drab indeed compared to the luxurious halls he stomped through. Gilded wizard-torches, eternally burning nothing, spread a warm, steady, amber glow on finely crafted and polished wood. Marble statues, bronze-framed paintings, marvelous tapestries with bright pictures, plush rugs, these were the things of the ducal quarters.

Guards and servants dove out of his way, unnoticed by Duke Antain in the rage that swept him towards the women's quarters. Wide-eyed stares followed his back. Every man, woman, and child he passed went from terror at his approach to profound relief as he passed them by.

At the fortified door to the women's quarters, the four orcs that guarded the doors were the only people who didn't fear him. The duke only employed a dozen orcs, and they were the sole gatekeepers to the domain of his wives and concubines. Everyone in the castle knew, of course, that those twelve could hold this sole entryway against a horde of human soldiers. Could and would, without fear or hesitation or any possibility of bribery or corruption.

The guards, covered head to foot in heavy plate armor and armed with the black metal of battle-mage spears and swords, towered over the duke. The door they stood guard over was veneered to look like beautifully crafted wood, but was actually foot-thick steel braced by a dozen heavy bars, mounted in thick stone walls. In the thousands of years since the keep was built, only two armies had ever taken enough of the castle to reach this door. None had ever broken through it.

As the duke approached the door, one of the guards signaled the day's password to guards on the inside. They could see him through a magical gem on the door – one that some said dated back to the old wizards, from before the shard-wars. The door slid silently open on heavy hinges, and the duke didn't even have to break his stride to enter this inner sanctum.

And then he stopped, rocked back on his heels, and wildly stared around! Where were the guards? Who had opened the door? What was going on? There should be more guards – highly skilled women-warriors loyal enough to die protecting his wives and concubines. He stood in the middle of a beautifully decorated guardroom, a simpler door ahead of him, and he was alone where there should have been a dozen armed amazons.

Empty halls led past empty rooms. His heavy boots clanked echoingly in spaces that should have rung with the lovely voices of dozens of his women and scores of slaves.

He slowed, listening carefully, and silently drew his mage-steel sword into his hand.

The duke crept silently past rooms that his keen eyes told him had been neglected for days if not weeks.

He sniffed at the air, seeking past the faded perfumes for anything that might tell him what had happened here. There was a smell of blood, but it was faint, and he saw no stains on carpets or furniture. And the smell of some blood in the women's quarters didn't necessarily mean anything – during moon-times, that smell was strong enough to overpower the incense and perfume.

At the end of the hall he had to choose. Up to the wives' quarters or down to the slaves' plain rooms? As he paused, he even considered violating millennia of tradition by calling for guards. He would have to pay the orcs extra to do something that was technically not part of their existing contract, but it might be the smart thing to do.

A faint sound came from above, maybe a whisper of a feminine voice. He made his decision and crept silently up the stairs.

He peered into the large common room at the heart of the wives' quarters, his eyes barely above the level of the last steps, his body hidden behind the column at the center of the spiral staircase.

"What in all the hells…", he muttered, shock and fear filling his voice as his face blanched and his eyes widened.

Bright green eyes stared back at him.

Chapter 11: *Hard Work*

After about a week, Shina no longer needed Brad to heal her after a few hours on horseback, and their daily progress increased significantly. Brad said it was almost two-thousand miles to the pass they wanted to use over the eastern mountains. They needed to avoid the few rare communities, and had to circle far around them to avoid being seen on the mostly flat terrain. Thag estimated that they would take a little over a month to get there at their best pace, bolstered considerably by Brad's healing and shared stamina.

Brad tended to call the horse "the horse", and Thag made jokes about naming it "Brunch", but Shina determined he needed a name and decided to call him "Sachem". Brad had mentioned that it was the orcish word for a type of spirit-talker, and she liked the sound of it.

It turned out that Brad could not only run all day, while also feeding fresh strength to her and horse, but could talk while doing so. More precisely, Shina found that Brad apparently couldn't *stop* talking, even while running next to Sachem. And during the frequent brief stops for water, his chatter ran as constantly as the numerous small streams that crisscrossed the plains.

Thag spent his days scouting the lands around and ahead. Shina missed him during the day, but Sachem was always spooky when Thag was around so it did make travel much easier to have him over the next hill or flanking them widely.

The bountiful plains provided abundant food for all of them. It quickly became tradition for Brad and Shina to end the day's travel when they found Thag with a campfire and something already cooking for them.

Nights, they camped. Brad, Shina, and Sachem would sleep while Thag watched over them. Some nights, he and Shina would make love while Brad slept, but most nights Shina was too tired from the day's travel.

Day after day of travel over rolling plains dotted by the occasional rocky outcropping and networked with shallow streams and ponds. There were numerous small hills that Thag said were all that remained of towns and villages that had been empty since the shard-wars when the gnomes invaded their world.

Vast herds of wild animals shared the land with them. Millions of big cow-like things Brad told her were called "aurochs", vast swarms of sundry varieties of deer and elk, antelopes, uncountable rabbits and ground squirrels, all filled this land. Every stretch of trees swarmed with birds, and there were even some huge flightless birds that strode across the plains and hills on long legs instead of flying. They frequently came across wild horses in herds so vast she couldn't see the far side, even from atop Sachem.

Of course, with that bounty, predators abounded. Hardly a day went by that they didn't see wolves or bears, or wild griffons and wyverns. She fell in love with the sightings of leopards and cheetahs and was enchanted by her one sighting of a plains tiger, with its huge fangs and deadly grace. The predators steered clear of Thag, but had no knowledge or fear of humans.

The sky seemed bigger and more full of the "stars" that Thag told her were actually worlds apart from their own. He told her the wizards used to call them shard-worlds, and said that their own world was just one of thousands, maybe millions, floating in the void, waiting for the gods to finish whatever it was they started when they made all the worlds.

"The gnomes came from one of those. So did dwarves and elves." He told her one night when they talked about her "islands in the sky".

Shina looked up at the myriad of floating worlds. She couldn't see any details on most, just specks in the distance. But there were hundreds that were close enough to see terrain on them – what looked like mountains and seas to her. Some, she realized she was seeing just the rocky "bottom" of the world, and the top would be where any features were. A couple were close enough to see the green of giant forests or maybe plains like the one they were crossing. She wondered what it all looked like through Thag's dragon-eyes, with his vastly superior vision.

She pointed at one that looked like a pool of flame. "What about that one? The one that's on fire?"

Thag looked. "If I understand the old lore correctly, there are worlds made of fire. That's probably one of those. Some others are made of water, or even wind.

"Humanity occupies ones that are made mainly of stone, but the other elements rule a few.

"I read once that dragons found numerous huge worlds made entirely of wind, or of toxic storms even. The lore and the old books aren't very clear on all of it, and there aren't any elder dragons left to ask about it."

Shina looked at the sky and wondered what it would be like to travel to a world made of storms or flames. Dragons and wizards used to travel those worlds, till the gnomish shard-wars killed all the wizards and almost all the dragons. It sounded wonderful to her – seeing other worlds. Before meeting Thag, she had never even considered travel or adventure. Now, it was her life.

Adventure – it had taken her from her home and made her a prisoner. And then it led to Thag! Without that, she would never have made friends with a werewolf, met the most beautiful dragon in all the shards, or learned that the "stars in the sky" were other worlds that, maybe, someday, she might find a way to visit.

Brad told her that orcs and primitive humans used to hunt these lands, but that they were slowly abandoning them as tribes shrank over the generations. "Too few children are born each year, and the tribes get smaller and smaller all the time. Nobody knows why, but everyone knows it's true," he said.

"He's trying to reverse that trend himself, you know," pointed out Thag.

Brad laughed and then explained to Shina that every woman he made love to got pregnant. Even ones who were too old for that, or who had been barren their whole lives till him.

"How many women have you had children with?" Shina naturally asked.

Brad muttered something unintelligible, but Thag answered for him. "At least three-hundred, the last time anyone counted. Probably close to a thousand by now."

Shina laughed at Brad as he sputtered a string of half-excuses. "How can you possibly make love to a thousand women?" she asked him.

"I was in love." He shrugged, smiling.

Shina just stared at him.

Finally, he commented, "I fall in love a lot. Women are … wonderful. I don't know what else to say."

Shina thought for a minute. "Hold on. You're like twenty-five years old, right?"

"Yeah."

"A thousand women? How many is that per year? How is that even possible?"

Thag interjected, "It's really hard work, but he's good at rising to the challenge…"

Brad avoided conversation for a few days after that.

***

To the north, a band of twenty orc spirit-warriors sped south and east. Their leader knew exactly where the object of their hunt was, and where she was going. They would catch their prey before the pass.

Far to the south, an army of men and orcs, mounted on horses bred for speed, endurance, and courage in battle, raced northward. Every day, some were lost to exhaustion and left behind for the wolves and predators of the plains, but their barbarian king pushed the survivors mercilessly. The spirits of his ancestors told him what was at stake, and he knew he must not fail.

Chapter 12: *Green Eyes*

Duke Antain, his mind in shock, stumbled his way up the stairs and into the common room of his wives' quarters.

The room was covered in splashed blood! Some days-dry, some sticky-congealed, some bright and fresh. It was all over the walls, the floor, the rich and fancy furnishing! It even dripped from the high ceiling in a few spots!

The bodies of his wives and concubines and their small army of slaves, even the amazon-guards, were strewn in heaps all over the room!

In the middle of the carnage stood a girl, appearing no more than thirteen or fourteen years of age, nude, and covered head-to-foot with a wash of blood. In her left hand, she held a long knife with a saw-toothed blade. Her eyes seemed to glow emerald green, and had no whites or pupil in them at all.

Antain's favorite wife, Saisha, knelt on the floor next to the girl, in profile to the duke. Her body and head were upright, and her arms and hands rested peacefully at her sides. He saw that her eyes had been burned out. Blood from Saisha's mouth dripped over the right hand of the green-eyed girl, which held Saisha's throat lightly.

Before Antain could speak or do anything but desperately try to make sense out of this scene of macabre horror, the girl raged at him. "You lost her! I told you that you would be punished if you failed!"

Her voice was ice-cold venom, and far too adult for her young body. "I told you to get the girl. With her, I can make you king of the world. You failed, and now some of my rivals have caught her scent and are hunting her."

With a savage thrust, she drove the knife into Saisha's chest. A spray of blood hit the girl right in the face, and she licked her lips.

"You are mine, My Lord Duke. Mine! And the girl will be too! Do not fail me again, or I will unleash a plague on you and your people that will make this seem like a pleasant dream!

"Go!"

Duke Antain, a man afraid of no army, fled the room in terror.

Chapter 13: *Making a Pass*

Shina's first sight of the mountains they were to cross was a faint, purple-looking line across the eastern horizon. Day by day they grew until they dominated the land as far as she could see to the north and south.

The last week of travel had been through increasingly hilly and rocky lands, and their pace had dropped considerably as they climbed higher and higher into the foothills.

When they were close enough, Brad pointed out the pass they would use.

"There's a fortress at the top of the pass. It's been fought over by so many tribes throughout the years that I don't know who rules it these days. Not many people cross the mountains here, but enough do that the tolls pay for solid walls and a strong garrison.

"It probably got a lot of traffic in the old days when the plains held cities and towns instead of ruins and nomadic tribes, but we'll almost certainly be the only ones going through when we get there.

"We'll get to the base of the pass late tomorrow. I think Thag will want to camp there so we can go up during the day. The path is a bit tricky at places and we'll be slow going up. I'm not sure the horse will be able to go faster than a walk through most of it. Regardless, we should get to the top by late afternoon the day after tomorrow."

Shina asked, "What do people call these mountains, anyway. You and Thag keep saying 'the mountains' or 'the eastern mountains', but don't they have a name? Like the Argent Crowns to the north."

Brad shrugged. "I don't know. I grew up in mountains far to the south and east of here. *Real* mountains – at least twice the size of these, and far more mountainy. If that's even a word. The ones I grew up in were called the 'Halais Altain'. That means 'roof of the world' in my native language."

He smiled and continued, "But names are a deceptive thing, you know. The name of my language simply means 'talking', in that language. Just like the name of my tribe translates best as 'people'. Most languages work that way. Ask Thag – he speaks and reads hundreds of them."

Shina thought for a while. "I think we should name them. We'll call them the 'East Rock Mountains', in honor of a language called 'Talking'."

Brad laughed. "East Rock Mountains it is, then! We'll have to tell Thag so he can write it on a map or something and make it official."

A few hours later, Thag caught up to them. As soon as he was close enough, he signaled for them to stop, which was very unusual.

"We've got trouble," he announced. "There's a large group ahead of us, camped at the foot of the pass. Men and orcs. And there's another group north of us and coming our way. Might be a small band, or might be scouts for a bigger army."

Brad and Shina craned their necks and looked east and north, but saw nothing except more foothills, more rocks, more grass and scrub-trees.

"You can't see them from here," Thag pointed out.

"Twenty to the north. How many to the east?" asked Brad.

" I counted a hundred and seventy-two men and twenty-six orcs. I didn't get very close, so I may have missed a few."

"Is that too many?"

"We have the same problem as always," said Thag. "If I attack, enough can get past me to attack you two. I'd eventually kill them all or chase them off, but not before they could kill both of you."

"Any spirit-warriors?"

Thag shrugged. "I can't tell that the way you can. I saw some markings, but nothing strong enough to matter."

He continued, "The group to the north is another matter. Most are wearing leathers, so I couldn't see markings. I couldn't get close enough to smell more details without being spotted by them. They're moving fast enough that there have to be some wolves in the group. The leader is the biggest orc I've ever seen. And ...," Thag paused. ".... And you'll have to see it for the rest to make sense. You might understand it better than I do."

Shina spoke up. "Maybe we should go north. Brad and I should see that group, then maybe we can make some decisions about what to do."

Thag and Brad both nodded.

They had only gone north for about an hour when Thag again came back and reported the group ahead of them had turned due south and was heading straight towards them. Before, the orcs had been going south by east to intercept the group's eastward path. Somehow, they had known to turn straight south as soon as Shina and crew turned north.

Brad looked around. "I don't see any scout-griffons or any hawks. How can they know where we are?"

"I've been looking too. I'd see either one before they saw me, and I haven't seen any yet today," replied Thag.

Shina quickly looked up and around. She had never even thought of looking for griffons to see if they were being tracked. They had seen quite a few wild ones over the weeks leading up to the mountains, but she hadn't been paying attention to the skies as a threat.

Thag took up a position on top of a low ridge, and had Shina and Brad wait below the ridgeline, out of sight. They tied Sachem to a scraggly bush at the foot of the ridge, next to a runnel of water, and Brad caused some succulent greens and dark grass to sprout around him. The horse was overjoyed to take a rest and have food and drink nearby and Thag not.

Atop the ridge, Thag stood with his feet planted at shoulder-width, his hands on his hips, and his head held high, facing the oncoming group of orcs. Not a belligerent pose, but a solid one. It might not intimidate, but it would say clearly, "This is my place and you will have to go through me to pass it".

The orcs came over the land openly, at the fast lope of the wolf-blessed. The ground passed rapidly beneath their feet and, in minutes, they came over the slight rise due north of Thag's position.

Twenty of them, and all heavily armed. All but one wore heavy leather and hide armor that covered their bodies from neck to foot. The one exception was naked from the waist up and wore only plaid woolen pants on its legs.

Thag knew the pattern of the plaid would tell other orcs what clan and tribe the orc belonged to, but he didn't recognize it. He had only ever dealt with a few of the tribes in this land and all he could be sure of was that the pattern was neither that of the Bloodfangs nor of the Redhands.

The orcs paused at the top of their small hill, a hundred or so yards away from Thag. He knew they had seen him from miles away, but he was inwardly amused when he saw them finally size him up and realize that what they were facing wasn't a big man in some fanciful armor and helm. Orcs don't really know fear, but they do know confusion and concern for the unknown, and he saw both in them.

The orcs stopped and three of them engaged in a quick discussion. After a moment, one turned its spear upside down and tied a ribbon to the end of the haft. Thag gestured for that one to approach.

He turned his head enough to speak to Shina and Brad, but never took his eyes off of the orcs. "You should come up and see this. Stay below the ridgeline, but watch. If anyone draws a bow, I want you two to run straight south and not stop till I catch up and say so."

Shina whispered to Brad as they crawled up to the top of the ridge and peeked over it. "What's a 'bow'?"

"It's like an arbalest without the stock. Shoots arrows, but you have to pull it back by hand. Not as much power as western arbalests, but you can fire them really rapidly."

She looked for anything like that, but all she saw were spears and axes and some strangely curved staves. Several of the orcs had quivers of arrows on their hips, but she didn't see anything to shoot them with.

Thag walked down the hill to where the orc with the reversed spear had stopped, not quite halfway between the two parties.

The top of the orc's head barely reached the height of Thag's impossibly huge shoulders. Shina knew that made the orc slightly taller than Brad, maybe seven feet or a tiny bit more. Its heavily muscled arms were barely thicker than Thag's wrists. She got the idea the orc wasn't used to looking up at anyone, but it had to crane its neck a bit to talk to Thag.

After a minute, the orc went back to its … Shina realized she wasn't sure what you called a group of orcs like this. Its tribe? She knew from Brad that orcs lived in tribes and clans, but she didn't really understand the complex relationships of those things. Orcs were heavily militant, so maybe the right word was something like squad or platoon.

"Brad," she whispered. "What do you call a group of orcs? Like this one?"

"Too damn many orcs."

Shina was shocked by the raw hatred in Brad's voice. She glanced over at him and saw murderous anger in every line of his face and every tense muscle in his body.

The orcs talked for a minute, then the biggest one, the one that was bare-chested, walked over to Thag and he led it up the ridge towards Brad and Shina.

Shina kept glancing at Brad. Normally, he was urbane, charming, confident. Not now. A vein was throbbing on the edge of his forehead. His lips were compressed into a thin, bitter line under his flaring nostrils. His eyes glared. Tendons on the back of hands stood out starkly, where he was gripping the rocks of the ridge.

Thag stopped a few yards from the top of the ridge and Shina heard him say something like, "Wait here," to the orc.

Thag continued up to them, and Brad and Shina stood as he reached them.

Thag took one look at Brad and asked, "Can you promise not to start any fights with them? They're friendly."

Brad's head jerked as he suddenly looked away from the orc and glared at Thag. "What?"

"Brad, can you promise not to start any fights with them?" Thag's deep voice carried all the patience in the world.

Brad simply glared at Thag.

"They're here to help us. But if you can't make that promise, I'll send them on their way. We could use the help, but I won't impose them on you."

Brad's breath was coming in short bursts, and his skin darkened for a moment. Then he grimaced and shook himself briefly.

A curt sound escaped his lips. Shina was pretty sure he was cursing in his native tongue, but didn't quite catch the word.

"Tell them I promise I won't start any fights. But if they start anything, anything at all ..."

Thag nodded that he understood, and gestured for the orc to join them.

Shina finally got her first good look at a living orc.

The first feature she noted was that his large arms had heavy chains running down them. The chains wove in and out of the skin, each link half-embedded. From behind his neck, the chains followed the contours of massive muscles down to the wrists, where they met lighter chains that continued across the back of the hands almost to the first knuckles. Shina wasn't sure from this angle, but it looked like the chains joined together behind a heavy leather collar that covered his thick neck.

Gods! That must have hurt to have all that put in! Shina thought. She had had her ears pierced when she was quite young, like most women of her class, and that was bad enough. This must have been infinitely more painful!

He was big! Not Thag's size, but even so, much bigger than any man she'd ever seen.

Thick cables of muscle stood out in stark relief under grayish-bronze skin. Unlike Thag, his muscles had a human-like shape and contour to them. His bones were put together the way a human's are, though noticeably larger and heavier. His thick-fingered hands were large, but they had human proportions. It was only the chains across the back of them that made his hands look dangerously inhuman.

His face was broader and more angular than normal for a man, with a heavy, almost chinless jaw that stuck slightly forward. The one truly alien feature was a pair of small fangs that stuck up from the lower jaw and protruded slightly out past the lips. Human-looking dark-brown eyes, topped by a heavy brow and thick black eyebrows, looked at her from above a wide, flat nose. He had no other hair anywhere that she could see, but she'd known plenty of men who shaved all their hair off for when they had to be in battle armor.

His chest was bare, and looked almost human, except for two rows of nipples running from low on his chest, about where a human male's would be, down to his waist. It reminded Shina of a dog or cat.

The orc bowed gracefully to Brad and greeted him in a guttural language. She thought she heard him say "Ang Brad", and wondered if that were some sort of title for Brad. He turned, bowed to her and said something in that same language.

She curtseyed and greeted him in turn. "A pleasure meeting you, sir."

Thag got a look on his face like he wanted to say something, but then thought better of it.

The orc looked at Brad expectantly, and Brad muttered something. Shina thought it might be a translation of what she'd said, but wasn't entirely sure.

Shina smiled at the orc and asked Brad and Thag, "I didn't catch his name."

Thag again looked like he was trying to swallow something unpleasant, but Brad answered, "Varlad – it means 'leader'. Not like 'general' or 'king', but like someone who goes first because they know the way. It also means 'the one who attacks first' and 'the one who dies first', too." The sound at the end of the name was halfway between a "d" and a "th", and Shina wasn't sure she'd be able to pronounce it correctly, but she'd do her best.

Brad pointed at Shina and said her name for Varlad.

"Zey-nah," said the orc, trying to get it right.

"Shy-na", she corrected, as politely as she could.

Brad shook his head. "They can't quite do the 'sh' noise. Mouths aren't shaped right for it. 'Z' is about as close as any of them will get."

Thag gestured for the other orcs to join them.

Brad pulled a bottle of vodka out of his bracelet and downed the whole thing in one go, and then tried to be gracious or at least polite to all of them.

There were introductions all around, and Shina was again amazed that Thag got every name right on the first try, and never forgot one or even needed prompting for it.

The orcs couldn't manage her name, with all of them settling on 'Zey-nah', but they had no trouble with Thag's. And they insisted on calling Brad "Angbarad".

It only took a few minutes for everyone to be introduced, and then Thag had a long conversation with the orcs. Shina couldn't understand any of it, but they all kept gesturing east and south, so she assumed it was about where they were going.

Then she saw Varlad's back! She knew from Brad's story that what she was looking at was a spirit-mark, not a tattoo, and the image shocked her.

Brad had told her about wolves and bears, flowers, and even birds. They'd talked about semi-legendary heroes marked by wyverns or griffons, even tigers. She knew trees were common with certain people destined to be craftsmen, and mountains or views of the plains, even streams or rocks, with travelers.

The mark wasn't quite so large or vivid as Brad's, but it wasn't far from it.

To Sachem's consternation and Shina's pleasure, Thag ran alongside her when they finished their conference and started travelling again. Shina didn't know what had been decided, but they were going towards the pass again.

Varlad was running ahead of her, the marking brightly visible in the early afternoon sunlight.

Shina whispered. She knew Thag's keen ears would hear her clearly, even as they travelled. "Thag, is that marking what I think it is?"

Thag nodded and smiled. "It's a dragon. The first dragon-blessing I've ever seen. She's unique."

Shina was puzzled. "Who's unique?"

"Varlad. Who are you talking about?"

"Varlad? But ... but ... 'she?'"

Thag nodded again. "Except when they're pregnant or nursing, the only way for you to tell a female orc from a male is to look inside their pants." He paused. "I don't recommend trying that without an invitation, of course."

Shina thought for a moment. "And you can tell by what? Smell or something?"

"Yes. The scent is clear. Male perspiration has a different signature to it than female in almost all species. It's blatant to me. There just isn't a visible clue, like you humans have, except the actual genitalia. No visible secondary sexual characteristics."

'You humans', Shina thought to herself. Sometimes it was easy to forget how alien Thag truly was.

"Thag, where do orcs come from? Are they from another shard, like elves and dwarves?"

"No. Hmmm ... you know about trolls, right? Like my mother?"

"Yes. What about them?"

"Well, trolls were made by wizards. They wanted something better than guard dogs, so they turned some people into trolls. Made them bigger, tougher, and much, much stronger. Gave them claws and fangs and skin as tough as leather armor. They also made them so they could heal almost instantly from most wounds. During the shard-wars, the trolls fought against the gnomes very effectively. But when the last of the wizards were killed, the remaining trolls went insane and lost most of their intelligence. They turned into monsters that eat whole villages and always crave more.

"Orcs were also made from humans through magic, but it was the battle-mages this time. They were trying to make their own trolls, but they couldn't work magic strongly enough to get the full result. So they got bigger and stronger and tougher, and nearly fearless, and loyal to a fault. But they didn't get armor or healing or the hunting senses that trolls have."

Shina understood. "Did wizards make the dragons, too? They seem to have made just about every other fantastic thing around."

"No. Dragons are older than wizards. And just as powerful. Just in a different way. Wizards use magic on the world around them. Dragons used magic on themselves. Wizards *do* magic, while dragons *are* magic. Does that help?"

Shina nodded. She needed some time to think.

Her lover was half a troll – something made by magic to defend wizards. And he was half a dragon – something made by ancient magic to travel the void and explore hostile worlds.

Her other lover was fully a dragon. Though she wondered, not for the first time, if she would ever see Koserana again.

They had just met up with a product of battle-mage magic that had been marked and blessed by some sort of dragon-spirit.

On her other side was Brad, another half-breed. He was blessed with spirit-powers and senses that allowed him to heal horrific wounds or simple saddle-blisters and strained muscles, and he could call up plants from the earth in profusion and abundance at speeds that dazzled the eye. He carried a wizard-bracelet that could hold a whole storage room worth of stuff in it. …. And he could get barren old women pregnant, though somehow that seemed more like an "ewwww" item than something out of old legends. She had forgotten he could also deflect swords off his skin, but she would never forget him killing that wolf-warrior by growing thorny vines all over him.

It seemed sometimes that the only normal person in her life was herself. Even her father was one of the most powerful sorcerers in the world. But Shina? She was just a human woman who saw stars as worlds instead of points of light.

And yet, somehow *she* was the one that Thag thought was important.

She wondered what Varlad would think of that. Would she still help if she knew that she was helping Thag protect the most normal person for a hundred miles in any direction?

Maybe Thag had made a mistake. She hoped not, since she really wanted him to be happy, but a little knot of doubt was stuck deep within her, and she could only ignore it when she was distracted.

Thag briefed her on the plan as they travelled. They would meet up with the other army, the southern barbarian horsemen, late in the afternoon. If, as seemed most likely, that army intended to stop them, Brad and the orcs were to defend her while Thag would do what he could drive the enemy away.

Shina wasn't too sure about all that. Thag was tough, sure, but enough to defeat a whole army?

Thag seemed confident, and she trusted him enough to keep her worries to herself, so she chatted with him about inconsequentials while the miles rolled by beneath them.

"Can orcs always travel this fast?" she asked.

"No," Thag replied. As always, he expatiated, "But we have five wolf-blessed warriors with us. That means fast and far. Brad will have to refresh them before any battle. They'll exhaust themselves if they keep up this pace much longer.

"Five wolves, six bears, two leopards, one tiger, four aurochs, one hawk, and the only dragon in the world. It's a pretty formidable force. Add in Brad for healing and defense, and we've got an army even without me."

Though Thag probably didn't mean to leave her out of that list, the omission rang in her ears. But he was right – all she had were some knives. What good were knives compared to the kind of people she was surrounded by?

They stopped several times for water and for Brad to refresh everyone's exhausted bones and muscles, and then they were there. The base of the pass over the East Rock Mountains. And between them and the pass were two-hundred men and orcs on horseback.

As soon as they came into sight, three of the men galloped straight towards them.

Thag had everyone halt near a large rock.

The trio arrived swiftly, their horses blowing and sweating slightly from the run. The men, all human, had long black hair and elaborately braided beards on their pale, round faces. Sky blue eyes, aquiline noses, jet black hair, and similar sneers on all three faces – Shina almost felt she could assume they were brothers, or at least cousins. They wore black leather armor reinforced with bronze scales and rivets, carried slender, curved swords, and had round shields on their left arms. Each wore a peaked helm with flaps over the cheeks.

The leader, or at least the one out front, spoke to Thag in a language she hadn't ever heard before. He kept his distance, but his voice carried.

Shina leaned towards Brad. "What are they saying?"

He shook his head. "I don't know."

The words were alien to her, but when he pointed his sword at her and glared in open anger, the message was clear enough.

A few more unintelligible words, and then suddenly Thag reared up to his full height, shoulders spread wide and back, legs braced, hands and claws spread and held low. He snarled something back at the man.

Thag yelled something at the men, and they wheeled suddenly-panicked horses and flew back towards their companions!

But Thag didn't let them run! He grabbed a spear from one of the orcs and hurled it with such force that it smashed the man off his horse and flung him head-over-heels right over the horse's neck and head.

"They want Shina!" Thag snarled. Shina had never seen him angry before and it was terrifying! Rage wrote itself across his face and sparked in his inky eyes!

"You," he pointed at Shina. "Stay here. Stay with Brad. He'll protect you!"

To Brad he growled, "You can prepare this time. The orcs will buy you some time. Use it!"

He spat orders to the orcs, and they fanned out in front of Shina and Brad and braced themselves for the inevitable cavalry charge.

Brad, incongruously, sat down next to her and closed his eyes. He curled up his legs in an odd position, with his feet twisted up on top of his thighs. His relaxed hands rested lightly on his knees. His breathing slowed and deepened. Shina wasn't sure what she was seeing, but it looked a lot like Brad was going to sleep sitting up!

Thag turned and charged straight at the barbarian army!

Shina wanted to scream! Thag was going to die to protect her, and she wasn't even worth it!

Before the scream could leave her throat, black clouds raced across the sky, blotting out the sun and all the shards.

When Thag was half-way to the enemy, the rain hit so hard it knocked her off Sachem and she landed hard on the rocky ground, her breath knocked out.

Seconds after the rain, screaming winds tore over them. A small tree snapped and was torn away into the sudden dark!

Lightning! Bolt after bolt of molten fury tore through the storm – spears of elemental fury tearing into the enemy army!

The thunder drowned out even the sound of the blasting wind.

And then the broken little tree began to grow! In the flashing strobe of lightning strikes, she saw trees all around them, their trunks burgeoning in seconds from tiny saplings to mighty oaks.

In moments, they were surrounded by giant trees, a roof of heavy branches sheltering them from the frigid rain and thick boles blocking the worst of the howling winds.

Two men on horses charged into their clearing amidst the trees. Orcish spears ripped them from their horses and slaughtered them in seconds.

Four more charged in from one side, and three from another. Battle raged through the clearing, and she couldn't even hear the clash of swords over the constant pounding of the thunder!

She didn't hear the horseman behind her. She felt the shock of his lance piercing her back and knocking her again to the ground! Pain tore through her as she saw the spearpoint spring out from her chest in a fountain of blood. For a fraction of a horrible second, the bottom half of her body went cold and numb as her spine was severed. And then the spear was ripped out and the pain and numbness vanished as suddenly as they had come. Strange warmth spread into her body, and the wound vanished as if it had never been there.

All around, she saw orcish allies taking horrific wounds that healed so fast they barely had time to bleed. Sword cuts vanishing before the blade even finished moving. Arrows and spears dropping out of wounds that disappeared faster than her eyes could follow.

The battle was quickly concluded. In the end, the orcs killed only a dozen men. Another sixty died in the grasp of thick vines covered in daggerlike thorns, men and horses crushed and pierced as they tried to ride through the trees. Thag killed another eighty, some by storm, some by claw, fang, or fist. Four were injured but not killed. The rest fled back south, so terrified most never even tried to rejoin their clans, but just kept running.

With the battle over, Brad fell deeply asleep and Thag had to carry him out of the ancient-looking grove of trees and bushes and into the pass. He took barely enough time to question the four prisoners before sending them on their way.

Thag insisted the group move immediately into the mountain pass. Shina led Sachem in brooding silence, the poor horse too physically and emotionally exhausted by the storm and the battle to carry her. She was soaked through, and getting cold as they moved up into the mountains. With Brad unconscious, and Thag preoccupied with getting them into the pass, she had no one to talk to. The orcs, excited by the day's ferocious battle, chattered enthusiastically with each other, but she couldn't understand any of it and they couldn't understand anything she said.

Thag kept going long after it got dark. One of the orcs took over leading Sachem, and another helped Shina keep up. After a time, even the orcs got tired and they had to stop and rest. Thag seemed to resent the delay, but he recognized that the rest of the party didn't have his ability to go on day and night after day and night, and bowed to the inevitability of the break.

Finally, Shina got her spirits up enough to ask what they were running from.

"The warriors I questioned back there: They told me what's pursuing us. It appears that they were one of dozens of scouting parties. What's following behind them is the whole Wyvern Clan."

"Thag, I don't know what that means," Shina started, but she was interrupted when Brad groaned and tried to sit up.

"Oooh, I hate this part!" Brad grunted. Then he rolled over onto his side and looked up at her. "It means ten or fifteen *thousand* men, and another two or three thousand orcs, are hunting us. Maybe a hundred spirit-blessed warriors and hunters. And Wyvern Clan is the craziest bunch of war-fanatics this side of the continent."

He grimaced for a moment. "Help me up, Big Guy. We need to keep moving."

Shina's legs and muscles sent shocks of exhaustion-pain through her as they began the steepest part of the ascent, but she gritted her teeth and refused to complain.

Just how powerful is Brad? She wondered silently. What he had done at that battle made the earlier fights in the alleyway and against those three orcs look like child's play. He plodded along in front of her, obviously totally exhausted. Hours of running as fast as a horse hadn't worn him out in the slightest, but this had drained him. When he looked around, she saw that his eyes were bloodshot and sunken, and there were bruises around them that made them look even worse. His hands shook with the palsy of total exhaustion. But they had to get out of danger, and he walked on his own two feet.

Seeing him this way, she felt ashamed of all the times Thag had carried her. All the times she'd been "tired" and made others do the work for her.

The orcs, except Varlad and the ones Brad said were aurochs-blessed, staggered along. They had marched long and then fought, and now they were climbing a steep pass through rugged mountains. Shina couldn't understand what Varlad was saying to them, but the tone was jocular and they smiled when she addressed them. It seemed to keep their spirits up and their bodies going.

She wished someone would joke with her. Brad, usually handy with a quip or double-entendre for any situation, was silent. Thag followed at the back of the party, helping those who stumbled, herding them towards what she hoped would be the safety of the keep at the peak of the pass. He had no time for her grumbling, as she saw it.

The setting sun covered the peaks around them with a wash of blood as they finally reached the top of the pass and saw the high walls and cliffs ahead of them. Shina shuddered at the omen of it all.

The pass was less than a hundred yards wide, walled in by high cliffs on each side, and the keep's fortified walls easily blocked the whole passage. There were no towers on the walls, but there were three tiers of arrow-slots in the walls of the cliffs around them. Tunnels into the canyon walls, Shina realized. There would undoubtedly be men positioned on the tops of the cliffs themselves, to protect against mountaineers sent to assault the keep from above.

Twenty feet of solid stone wall, pierced by a narrow gate at one point. A steel pipe led under the wall, allowing a small stream to keep the moat full before flowing off down the pass. It was thoroughly intimidating, and it blocked them completely.

Thag motioned for everyone else to stay out of arbalest-range. Alone, he advanced to within a dozen yards of the gate and yelled that travelers needed refuge from enemies and the night.

On top of the walls, the commander of the keep's guards, Sheriff Rock Little, conferred with his men.

"Our orders are to keep them from passing here," he told the men. "We don't have to do anything, just let the clans capture them. There's something special about the girl back there, and we just have to make sure we don't hurt her. Bart Ridge Keep holds firm tonight, but there will be ten thousand Wyvern Clan warriors here by morning, and we don't want them to ride through here and kill us all."

One of the guardsmen asked, "Should I put an arrow in the monster?" gesturing at Thag.

"Oh no, don't do that. If you shoot him, you'll just piss him off. I know about this guy. Heard about him when I was out west a few years ago."

"We hold firm. Let Wyvern take the losses when they fight the monster."

Thag, a dozen yards away and below the wall, turned and walked away. He'd heard enough.

"Brad, we need to get into there. Any ideas?" Thag asked when he got back to the group huddled out of range of the walls.

"If I had a couple of days, I could grow vines over the walls and get us up there. But I'm guessing we don't have that long."

"Wyvern will be here in the morning," Thag confirmed.

"Can you break down the gate?" Brad asked.

Thag shrugged, "Not a chance. I'm not a battering ram, you know."

Brad barely heard Shina mutter to herself, "That's what *you* think."

Brad's tired face ached from his almost futile attempt to not laugh, but he just couldn't stop a major smirk.

Shina couldn't follow as Brad and Thag spoke with the orcs in their guttural tongue, but they didn't speak long.

Then Varlad suddenly charged straight at the wall!

Guards gathered along the top of the wall, pointing and exclaiming excitedly. Shina could hear their shouts of amazement at a single orc charging towards their fort. She couldn't understand what was being shouted, but the voices rang out clearly in the confined pass and clear mountain air.

Shina was very tired of not knowing what was going on. Varlad was charging a castle. Thag was watching expectantly. Brad was staring at his own feet, too tired to raise his head and watch the big orc get herself killed. Shina felt like she was the only one who didn't know what was going on, and maybe the only one who cared about it at all.

Even the guards on top of the wall didn't seem to care. Why should they? The wall was twenty feet of smooth stone, topped by a corbel-supported parapet with crenellations and merlons along the top and downward-pointing metal spikes along the bottom. Varlad was sprinting at them with a large axe in her hands, but what could she possibly *do* to them?

Varlad was twenty feet from the moat when she leapt. Shina's eyes went wide as the huge orc soared through the air – no leap could take her that high! She flew upwards as if something were lifting her with terrible speed into the air!

In a second, she was atop the wall! She caught herself with her right hand on one of the merlons and swung her axe left-handed into the face of one of the stunned guardsmen!

A whirlwind of death and steel tore into the men atop the wall! Varlad's axe chopped and hacked, while her other hand and her feet struck and kicked at amazing speed!

An arrow launched at point-blank range tried to find her heart, but she blocked it with the axe!

Shina had never seen fighting like this! Blood and severed body parts flew everywhere! Even a few whole men were thrown from the wall and smashed to the stone of the cliffs or the floor of the pass. The flickering light of torches and lanterns added a macabre layer to the chilling horror of spraying blood and gore.

Screaming voices and clashing metal filled the narrow passage with unbearable din.

And all through it was the bloody flash of the heavy orcish axe swung by arms impaled with terrible chains.

Varlad leapt into the keep, behind the wall, disappearing from view. The screams of her victims spoke of more unbearable violence It was impossible for Shina to think of those men as "enemies", not when they had been scattered like rag-dolls before a cyclone. This wasn't battle, it was slaughter!

"Thag! Make her stop!" Shina screamed.

Thag turned to her, sadness in every line of his face. "I cannot, Little One. If I make her stop, you die here, or I have to kill a whole clan of men whose only offense against me is that they would kill me to stop me from killing them."

Shina wept.

"Why, Thag? Why all this? Why?"

Thag looked reluctant, but then decided to answer anyway. "Fear, Little One. Our world is dying. It has only a few years left. You have the power within you to heal it, and the power to dominate it. They fear you, and they fear the alternative to you. It's a harsh thing."

Shina wanted to ask "What power?", but Brad spoke first. "How many years?"

"Maybe ten or twelve, my friend. It could be much less, it won't be much more."

Brad merely nodded his acceptance and lapsed back into exhausted silence.

Shina, overwhelmed by the harsh day and the bitter hopelessness in Thag's voice, knew he was holding back something dire, but she couldn't bear to ask any more, to hear what he might answer if she questioned.

The gate in the wall swung open and Varlad stepped quietly through, covered head to foot in dripping gore.

Thag led them all into the fortress. Blood was everywhere! The scent of it filled her nose and her throat. As soon as Shina saw it up close, she ran to a corner of the courtyard and threw up over and over till all her body could do was spasm on a hard, painful lump of knotted muscle in her stomach.

Someone touched her gently on the back of her shoulder. She turned and looked up, expecting it to be Thag, but it was Varlad! The orc had a concerned look on her face, under a mask of drying blood. Shina screamed and batted feebly at the nightmare standing over her!

Varlad looked confused and concerned, but turned away when Thag called out something to her. With one last worried look, Varlad walked away, leaving Shina quivering in shock and revulsion in her little corner of the courtyard.

Thag squatted down next to Shina, towering over her as always. *Did he look like that after the battle at the bottom of the pass?* Shina wondered. *Or at least, would he have if it weren't for the rainstorm he used to strike terror into his enemies?*

"Thag," she finally managed to say, her voice broken and quiet. "What are we doing? What am I doing? Why do all these people have to die? Why would people be afraid of me?"

"They say people fear what they don't understand," he replied, his deep voice quiet and calm and soothing in the midst of all this wreckage. "Sam, the druid I told you about, my stepfather's teacher, she told me to get you. She told me that you have the blood of wizards in you. That you might be able to heal the world."

"What does that even mean, Thag? 'Heal the world'?"

"Our world has been dying for a long time, Little One. The shard-wars, when the gnomes came here with their electromagical soul-stealers — they didn't just kill the wizards and dragons. They also wounded the world itself. It was part of what they did to every shard-world they attacked.

"They went from shard to shard, stealing the souls of everyone who could do magic. Wizards and dragons were their favorite, but sorcerers, druids, even the spirit-blessed, these too they hunted. Somehow, they used magical souls to fuel their machines.

"At the heart of every shard is a soul. The druids call them 'titans' — the spirits that *are* worlds. The gnomes left behind dead worlds when they killed those souls and used them for power.

"Sam thinks a wizard could heal the world. She thinks you have the blood of wizards in you and that you or your children could possibly save our whole shard.

"She wants me to take you to the ruins of Xalax. That's the fortress-city where Ariel and Gem handed the gnomes their first-ever defeat. There, she says we'll find some answers about you. And either refuge or proof that we don't need refuge.

"The messenger she sent wasn't able to answer any of my questions. Just told me to get you to Xalax at any cost and to find refuge there.

"Does that help?"

Shina thought for a moment. "Yes. Yes it does help. Why didn't you tell me this before?"

"Too many others around in Anytown and since. I didn't want to put anyone in more danger than necessary," he replied.

"But all the way here, it was just Brad. Don't you trust him?"

"Of course I trust him," he said. "But if Brad became separated from us and was captured, they would torture him endlessly to force him to answer questions about you. What he doesn't know, he can't be forced to reveal. Any competent sorcerer would be able to tell whether he was telling the truth about knowing anything useful about you. What he doesn't know, he doesn't have to lie about, and a sorcerer would know he wasn't lying.

"It keeps him safer this way. And you, too, of course. But we're past that point. They know who you are. I don't know how, but they know. There's no safety in ignorance, not for you or me, not anymore."

"I'm tired of people making decisions for me," she said. "I'm tired of being manipulated. My father tried to use sorcery to force me to do what he wanted. Duke Antain used force to push me the way he wanted. I love you, Thag, but please let me make my own decisions. Or at least convince me instead of pushing me around."

Thag looked at her silently for a bit. "Of course, dearest.

"But," he continued. "Right now, I think I'm going to push you around a bit more." He smiled broadly, fangs sticking out all over the place. "Towards a bath." He feigned pinching his nose shut.

Shina smiled. He knew her so well, even when to change the subject to keep her from dwelling on things. She asked, "Do we have time? Will Wyvern Clan get here that fast?"

"We have time. We'll be able to tell when they enter the pass. There are alarms in the fort. Alarms that work for us now. They haven't hit the pass yet. Even when they do, we can still get a few hours head start."

Thag called something out to one of the orcs and the orc gestured to follow him. "Bath and sauna are this way," Thag told Shina and helped her to stand up.

There, they found Varlad pouring buckets of water over her head and scrubbing herself with a brush. Thag hefted a large barrel of water up onto his shoulder and told the two women to stand where he could pour it on them.

For Shina, it had been a while since she'd had a barrel of ice-cold water poured all over her. The shock left her blue and her teeth chattering, but she felt clean when it was all done.

Varlad seemed to like the clean feeling too. She smiled and handed a stiff-bristle cleaning brush to Shina, gesturing at her own back and chattering incomprehensibly.

Shina worried about bumping the chains on Varlad's arms and shoulders, but she gamely attacked the big orc's back with the brush while Thag poured another barrel of rainwater over the two of them.

Shivering and frantically rubbing herself with her hands for warmth, Shina dodged into the sauna. Someone, probably one of the orcs, already had the fireplace in it running, and it was wonderful after the freezing shower-bath.

The sauna was too small for Thag, so it was just Shina and Varlad. She wished they could talk, but quickly settled into companionable silence. Shina wanted to apologize for her behavior back in the courtyard. Varlad had been a sight out of a nightmare, covered in blood after killing a whole garrison of men, but she'd been doing it to protect Shina, and she knew she owed her for that.

When they got out of the sauna and put on fresh clothing from their packs, one of the orcs rushed up to them and said something. Shina caught the word "wyvern", so she ran to the front gate looking for Thag.

He was standing atop the wall, looking west into the night sky. She quickly joined him and looked where he was looking, but she couldn't see anything but stars and the moon out there. "What are you looking at, Thag? If Wyvern are in the pass, even you won't see them through all the rock of the mountains. Not till they come into the passage there and are right in front of the gates. Like we were."

"Wyverns, not Wyverns," said Thag, as if that clarified anything. "Sixteen men on western hunting wyverns, flying in from the west. They'll be here in a few minutes. They look like kingdom men, but even I can't see their lord's insignia from here."

"Get inside," he told her. "I need to get orcs with bows up here. If the riders attack us, we can kill the wyverns underneath them pretty easily. You don't attack a fortress with wyverns."

Shina ran into one of the towers. She started to tell the orcs that Thag needed them, then realized they wouldn't understand anything she said, and left it up to Thag to figure out what to do.

Shina took over the viewpoint from one of the cross-shaped windows that archers use, where she could see Thag and the wall. Several of the orcs joined him, and they had their curved staves with them.

She realized that those must be "bows" and realized they did sort of resemble the spring-arms on arbalests, if you looked at them the right way. Wood instead of metal, and without the pulleys and gears she was used to, but the same sort of wavy-curve shape and with a cable across the ends. Either the orcs must be very, very strong to pull "bows" without pulleys and gears, or these must not have anywhere near the power that western arbalests had. Maybe both.

It was ten long minutes before Shina could see the flying wyverns coming in from the west. The sky was long-since dark, but the diffuse starlight and moonlight were enough to finally see the flying beasts as they approached the fortress. She couldn't see the coats-of-arms on them, so couldn't tell what lord they belonged to, but the men on their backs were the usual western soldiers she'd been around all her life.

Thag jumped off of the wall after telling the orcs something and gesturing west at the incoming wyverns. He opened the gate and walked out onto the short bridge over the moat, leaving Varlad guarding the gateway and the rest of the orcs on top of the wall with their bows in-hand.

Thag's plan to shoot them out of the air if they flew over the fortress and tried to attack it proved unnecessary. The wyverns flew into the canyon in front of the main gate and landed there. Sixteen men, all but one dressed in the warm but light armor of flying scouts, and armed with the darts and shortswords favored by that profession. The last one was armed with a longsword and wore heavier leather-and-plates armor.

When they dismounted and strode forward into the light spread by lanterns atop the wall, Shina gasped in shock and anger. It was Duke Antain himself!

Chapter 14: *The Duke Redux*

Duke Antain looked at the fortification in front of him. It was formidable, but he assessed that, were it held by mortal men, the force he had with him would be more than enough to overwhelm it. The assessment was pure habit, he had no intention to attack this place, regardless of who the girl had defending it for her.

He decided to land well clear of the front gate. It would give the people inside time to look him over. He wanted to avoid any rash actions on anyone's part, and he knew that these people would be inclined towards hostility towards him. Better if they had a minute to make cooler-headed decisions.

The gate opened briefly, and he saw what he thought was a large orc in ornate armor silhouetted against the lights inside. He approached it carefully, and as he got close, he realized it was no orc. It was something … different. Something he had never seen before.

It was huge, over eight feet tall and easily four feet wide at the shoulders, maybe more. It was just standing there, but he could only imagine what it would be like in a fight. *It's forearms are thicker than my thighs!* It had heavy, wicked-looking claws on its fingers and toes. Heavy horns curled forward from the sides of its head, curving out and down parallel to its malformed jaw-line. The face was vaguely reptilian, but not quite like any lizard the duke had ever seen. Fangs lined the sides of its jaws, protruding raggedly up and down past its scaled lips.

At first he thought the eyes were merely obscured by the back-lighting it had from the lanterns behind it, but as he got closer he realized its eyes were truly alien. Shiny black orbs with no pupils, no whites, no features he could see at all.

The … "monster" was the only word that seemed to fit it … waited patiently for him to approach. Its stance spoke of relaxed readiness to spring into battle. The kind of patient but explosive pose the duke had seen before on the very best sword masters and the deadliest knife fighters.

Antain prayed briefly that it wouldn't come to violence. He was a master of it, and was armed with the best mage-steel blade in the kingdoms

– recorded as having been made by the battle-mage emperor himself – but he was intimidated by this gigantic *thing* that waited for him.

He briefly wondered if it could speak any language he knew, or could even understand human speech at all. Then he dismissed the idea – it wouldn't have been sent out to meet him if there was no hope of communication. It was waiting for him, not attacking, and that meant it wanted to talk.

The duke swallowed a lump of nervous trepidation that was growing in his throat and finished approaching it. Just out of what he judged would be its reach, he stopped.

It took a moment to clear his throat, then he addressed it in formal Western Imperial. "I am Duke Antain of Klosia, here to speak to Lady Shina of Berdonia. You may take me to her."

The duke's men spread out behind him into a battle line. They knew the range the orcish bows on the walls would have, and were prepared to rush through that to take the walls if they had to. They were trained for this and knew exactly the odds they faced with orcs on the walls. But none of them knew what to make of the monster facing their lord.

They assumed the greater threat was the orcish bows, knowing that their lord would be able to strike the monster with deadly effect.

They didn't know why they were here. They just knew that they would die gladly and expensively if their lord asked it of them.

Thag had recognized the duke before the wyverns even landed. He had decided that it would be better to meet him out here, beyond the walls, where conversation could be more private. And, if it came to a fight, he'd rather not expose any of the orcs to unnecessary danger.

He knew by sight the mage-steel blades these men carried. He'd fought those before. Like all sharp objects, they could cause him pain. But that was all.

Thag decided that Formal Imperial was the right language to reply in when the duke addressed him. "Warlord Antain of Klosia of Berdonia, son of Warlord Kilanta of Klosia, ruler of the island-castle Herztad, named Hearts-Home by the Emperor's Captain Thullandinian II of Kerandria when given it as his charge, I greet thee. Lady Shina, Descended of Dragons and Wizards, has not granted thee audience and hath reason to suspect thy motives. On Her behalf, I bid thee reveal thy purpose in asking the boon of her presence."

The duke was floored. He'd expected some faint ability to speak, not the convoluted grammar and pronunciation of the old imperial court! The king's scholars and priests didn't speak the old language with this fluency! He stumbled through his reply, "I … I … um … I haven't … speak good the old language. I asking for Lady Shina … talk me."

He felt like a total fool. This *thing* had forced him into a level of formality that he hadn't used since he was a squire in the king's army. He was blushing and it had put him squarely on the defensive.

He rushed on, "I need talk her. I … um … you talk Kingdom West? Is more better I talk this."

He couldn't quite tell if the monster was smiling, snarling, or smirking. It struggled to say, "We no talk the Kingdom West. You come, they stay."

Some creation of the battle-mages. Left over from the old wars. Antain thought about the monster. *The fluent old-language gives that away. Means it's as dangerous as it looks.* His confidence came back as the creature turned to lead him into the fort. If it was a battle-mage artifact, that meant it was probably a little more dangerous than an orc. He was experienced enough against orcs to know how to fight them. Something slightly more dangerous was hardly a threat to him.

As they passed through the gate, he saw the biggest orc he'd ever come across. It was bare from the waist up, and had done something painful looking with chains run through the skin on its arms and shoulders. Those would hamper it in a real fight, but these wild orcs liked to do dumb things to show off how tough they thought they were.

On the walls and in the yards, he saw twelve orcs, including the big one. He assumed that was half of them, maybe more. It could be less, but better safe than sorry. He still had hope this wouldn't turn into a fight – but if it did, he fully intended to win, and assessing a potential enemy was as natural and automatic to him as breathing. More, since he could hold his breath if he wanted to.

The monster – he belatedly realized it hadn't introduced itself and idly wondered if it even had a name – led him into the fort and into one of the inner towers, right up against the wall of the northern cliff. Two orcs, the really big one and another, both with crude steel axes and the smaller in light leather armor, stayed with him while the monster signaled for him to wait there.

The orcs closed the outer door and latched it. Most likely to keep his men out if they managed to successfully assault the outer wall. What it really did was lock them in the tower with the duke. Now he felt confident again. Two orcs and a mage-creation, plus a little girl, against him in mage-armor and with a mage-blade – he had faced similar challenges dozens of times and had always won. That they hadn't disarmed him spoke poorly of their ability to assess him. They were overconfident. Orcs often were.

Shina watched Thag lead the duke into the fort and then into the ground floor of the tower she was in. She was furious, of course, but curiosity was taking over. *What could he possibly hope for, coming here to talk to them?* Shina knew Thag would let the duke have a chance to explain himself – Thag always preferred talking over fighting. After the bloodbath today, Shina was coming around to Thag's point of view on the subject.

She wasn't at all surprised when Thag came straight to the room she was in, nor that he'd left the duke in another room. He could always tell where she was, and she suspected it was some power of his superhuman senses of sight, hearing, and scent. Given his history, though, she wouldn't have been surprised to find there was something magical about it all.

As soon as Thag opened the door, Shina joined him in the stairwell. "What does he want, Thag? Why's he here?"

"He wants to talk to you, Little One. He didn't say what about," Thag replied.

"I left him in some doubt as to my nature and status," Thag continued. "Don't say anything about me to him, and don't talk to me where he can hear us. I'll keep you safe around him, but we want him to underestimate us for now. Okay?"

Shina nodded. Intrigues were very familiar ground to the young woman who'd grown up in her father's household.

"Are you ready?" he asked her.

She simply nodded and went back into the tower room. She picked out a heavy chair and set it so it faced the door. She'd keep the duke standing while she sat. It would set the tone she thought Thag wanted for this.

When Thag returned, he came in first, turning sideways to get through the narrow door. Shina was reminded of when he first rescued her.

Here they were in a tower, Thag stooping and twisting to get into a room she was in. The presence of Duke Antain solidified the memory, though last time he hadn't been physically present, but it had been his tower.

Varlad and another orc, one Shina didn't know the name of, followed the duke into the room. They were there to make sure he didn't cause any trouble, but his proud manner, soldierly stance, and arrogant walk made them appear to be an honor guard for him.

Another memory came to her – the duke dancing with her at the ball. Whose manor had that been at? Ah, yes! The Gaurdon family estate. They'd both been in expensive finery that night, and he had seemed so charming and graceful. She'd read once that a good swordsman had to be able to dance, and she guessed that explained the duke's fluid skill on the ballroom floor.

Thag stopped him when he was about ten feet away from her, and she nodded that the duke could address her.

Duke Antain looked at her for a moment. She wasn't quite the young woman he had met at court. Months of living in the wild, and thousands of miles of travel, had weathered her. She was still attractive, but in a very different way. Before, she'd had the courtly beauty of soft skin, expensive makeup and dresses, and the feminine roundness given by a rich diet to the young and healthy. Now, her skin was darkened and roughened by harsh cold, wind, and bright sun, and any remaining baby fat had long since been replaced with lean muscle – giving her an athletic strength and vitality, accompanied by experience and intelligence behind eyes that had finally seen some of what real life had to offer. It was not the beauty of noble youth, but it was still undeniable beauty.

Shina, Thag and both orcs were totally taken off-guard when the duke dropped to his knees and lowered his head in a deep, subservient bow!

"Lady Shina, I surrender completely to your mercy and beg your forgiveness."

Chapter 15: *A Pregnant Pause*

"He told us about how his oldest daughter slaughtered everyone in the women's quarters and sent him to re-capture Shina," Thag told Brad. It had been a fascinating and somewhat horrifying hour, with the duke telling his whole story to Shina.

Brad, still not fully rested from the huge outpouring of power he'd expended in the battle at the base of the pass, was lying on a cot in the guard captain's quarters.

"Have you ever heard anything like it?" Thag asked.

Brad thought for a moment. His voice was distant and his eyes were focused on some thought, when he replied. "Did he mention her eyes?"

"Yes. Bright green. He mentioned they were bright green. Does that matter?"

Brad threw off the blankets and tried to stand up. When he wavered, Thag helped him to his feet. "Take me to him," Brad said.

Brad was staggering so badly he would never have made it to the tower on his own, much less up the stairs to the top floor, where Shina was still questioning Antain. They were seated across a large table from each other, with Varlad and the other orc standing behind the duke, silent and alert.

Shina took one look at the dark rings around Brad's eyes and how he couldn't stand without Thag holding him up. "Brad! You should be in bed! What are you doing here?"

Brad ignored her and looked straight at Antain. The duke didn't know what to make of this strange, possibly sick, young man, but he noted that Shina obviously cared about him. *Her lover, perhaps?* He thought to himself.

"Her eyes. They're green. Can you see them in the dark?"

Antain gasped and his eyes widened abruptly. Brad was already cursing under his breath by the time the startled duke could respond with a shocked, "Yes."

"Damn! Damn! Damn!" Brad was growling. He looked up at Thag.

"This is bad. Really bad. I know who she is, and it's worse than anything anyone thought before."

Antain started to interject that the big uber-orc didn't speak Kingdom West, but Thag interrupted. "Who?"

"Her name's Kamaia. She's a very powerful demon. She might even be the one who made you," Brad told Thag.

Thag paused to think. Silent, he took a moment to settle Brad into a chair. Shina, seeing the look on Thag's face, knew not to distract him, and just watched silently.

Antain, however, had no such compunction. "A demon?!" he interjected loudly. "A demon! My daughter can't be a demon! How can you say that?" He was half-way through jumping to his feet, but Thag, moving faster than the duke's eyes could even follow, was suddenly standing over him and pushing him back down into his chair. The duke was a strong man, and was shocked when Thag effortlessly pushed him back down with a single hand.

"Stay seated! I don't trust you, so you will sit still and speak when you are spoken to," he told Antain.

He turned back to Brad. "Do you think it's true? Do you think a demon has crossed into the physical realm? Full-on possession?"

"It's the only thing that makes sense. How do they always know where we are? Sorcerers don't have that kind of range, and can't track you two anyway. If they could, her dad would have known where she was. If any demon could come into the world that way, it would be Kamaia.

"Also, the Wyvern Clan does engage in pretty heavy demon-worship. It makes sense they'd be the first ones in this part of the world to chase after her, if a demon wants her.

"But it's worse than that, Thag. If one demon wants her, more do too. And you want to go east, into the wastes. The orcs over there, they aren't like the ones you know here in the west. They're dark. They openly worship blood-demons. They don't even try to hide it behind fake honor, like these ones." Brad pointed at Varlad and her soldier.

Shina looked nervously at the two orcs, but they apparently hadn't understood what Brad said. For once, she was glad of the language barrier between them.

Duke Antain was glowering. His face grew more and more flushed. He wasn't intimidated by the beast standing over him, but he knew he needed to be diplomatic with young Shina, so he held his tongue. It had him grinding his teeth in frustration, but he held himself silent. *No one treats a blooded Duke of the kingdom this way! The beast will pay for this! But not now. Not now...* the refrain ran through his head.

The look Thag gave him was opaque to Antain, but Shina read the silent speculation in it. She realized Thag was hatching a plan. She didn't follow all this about demons – she wasn't quite sure what made one spirit a "totem" and another spirit a "demon". But she knew demons were bad, and Brad and Thag were obviously taking this quite seriously.

After a moment, Thag addressed the duke. "Your wyverns – are they trained to follow only you, or will they obey other guides?"

"My wyverns?" The question struck the duke as totally non sequitur. It took him a moment to gather his thoughts. "They follow me, or their rider. Why does that matter?"

Thag turned back to Brad. "Can you keep wyverns in the air?"

Brad sighed. "Not tonight. If I can sleep the night, then yes. But not tonight."

Thag addressed the orc soldier in their language. For a brief moment, Brad looked daggers at Thag and the orc, then he sighed and surrendered to the inevitable. The soldier helped him stand up from his chair and leave the room. Despite his antagonism, he leaned heavily on the orc's support as he limped out of the room.

Shina watched him leave, then asked Thag, "I've been meaning to ask. Why does he hate orcs so much?"

"Orcs raped his mother and killed her husband. That's how he was born. He's half an orc himself, you know. They raided his mother's village. She was the only survivor, but she was rescued by warriors from another village before the orcs could kill her. When he was four or five years old, more orc raiders killed his mother. There is constant raiding and warfare in that part of the world."

Thag kept talking, but changed the subject. "Shina, you and Antain and Brad are going to fly to Xalax on the wyverns. You can't fly on your own, so Antain is going to have to guide your wyvern there. Brad will keep you flying further and faster than anyone else can keep up with."

Before Shina could object that she didn't want to travel with Antain, Thag continued. With a gesture at Varlad, he said, "You, you're going with them. Brad will be distracted, and you need to guard Shina."

The duke interrupted. "None of my wyverns can carry an orc that size! It'll be hard enough having one carry your friend, Brad. He's a large man, or whatever he is." He'd been listening when Thag explained Brad's ancestry. He'd never known that orc men could impregnate human women, but he believed it easily enough. "The orc is simply too large for any western hunter. If I had one of the large work-wyverns, the ones that carry armor and supplies for armies, that would be another thing. But those are big and slow. What I've got here is hunters – fast and agile, but not strong enough for this!"

"She won't need a wyvern. You'll find out why when she's ready."

Varlad interrupted. In the language of the west, she said, "No, it's okay for them to know now." There was a blurring of their eyes, like mist but more like a spot they just couldn't see, and Duke Antain was suddenly looking at the most beautiful woman he'd ever seen! She was tall, well-built, with rounded hips and heavy breasts. Her golden hair was shaved off the sides of her head, what wasn't shaved hung down past her hips. She was wearing a metallic collar, a partially see-through green dress, and a golden belt. The most amazing set of tattoos he'd ever seen covered her arms, shoulders and a line down onto her perfect thighs. Realistic, highly detailed battle scenes rendered in vivid color – he had never seen body-art like it before in his life!

Shina shrieked in joy! "Koserana! How... where ... why?" She couldn't finish her question.

The beautiful blonde simply smiled. "Told you I'd see you again!"

Varlad/Koserana turned to the duke, who was staring at her, stunned. "We've met before. I don't like you. But if Thag says I shouldn't kill you and eat you, I won't. Not this time, anyway."

Again there was the vision of fog or a strange limited blindness, and what stood there was the thing from the village! The creature he thought he had killed with his arbalest all those months ago! It had survived! And it was standing so close that its face was mere inches away from his!

He hadn't had the best look at it before, in the night and the press of battle. Now he was closer than he wanted to be, and he got a *good* look.

It was somewhat reptilian, and about the size of a small pony. Its skin was covered in scales of burnished copper and bronze. It had long legs with sharp-looking claws, a long, almost serpentine neck, a thick tail, and large bat-like wings. Its face was oddly familiar, until he realized it looked like a healthier version of Thag — the same semi-reptilian, predatory look, but without the mottles and the ragged fangs. And where Thag had horns curving forward, this creature had a ridge of small horns that started above the brows and swept elegantly back into a crest behind its head.

The eyes had that same shiny, smooth look, like polished metal or gemstones, but with a swirling inside them like oil on water. In contrast, Thag's were blacker than midnight, and this creature's were coppery. They were opaque, but the swirl seemed to extend deep into them, deeper than was even possible.

"What are you?" the confused duke finally asked, after staring in a mix of fear and fascination for several seconds.

He was surprised when it spoke. "A dragon, of course!" Its voice was deep, but hadn't the sepulchral rumble that Thag spoke with. Somehow, the voice sounded feminine, despite its depth and resonance. "Lord Chalkos is the name I most often go by. Very not pleased to meet you!"

As it finished answering, it blurred again, back into the form of the beautiful blonde woman.

"You shot me once. It hurt. But Thag told me I can't kill you unless you try to hurt me again. Or Shina. So I won't. But I really want to!" Though this woman looked like she was in her early twenties, a full adult in Antain's eyes, her petulant voice reminded him of an unruly child. He was deeply confused, and, he realized, actually somewhat afraid of this strange creature.

She shifted her gaze over to Shina. "Hi!"

With that, she strutted over to the younger woman, grabbed her into a passionate hug, and kissed her warmly and thoroughly. Shina melted into the kiss and ran her hands over Koserana passionately.

"Ladies," rumbled Thag after a reasonable delay. They broke off their embrace and faced him. "Later, if you please. We have planning to do."

Duke Antain was staring at all of them with his mouth hanging open. He blinked rapidly a few times and tried desperately to make sense of all of this.

It also struck him that the big monster, the one they called "Thag" was speaking perfectly fluent Kingdom West – it had been mocking him!

Thag looked at him intently. Antain wondered if, along with everything else, Thag was some sort of sorcerer that could read his thoughts.

"Antain," Thag said. No "My Lord Duke" or any other honorific. "You're angry, and that's understandable. But please try to understand, there is more going on here than you know. We're not making fun of you – we're trying to protect our whole world from the kind of thing that killed your family. If we offend, it's because there are few we can trust, and keeping potential foes off-balance is a tactic we need to use to have any chance at all. We need every lever we can find just to have any slight hope of success."

A stratagem? The calculated insults, the lies, the manipulation, these were a stratagem? From *this* creature? It looked …

"Who are you?!" the duke asked, his voice shocked to barely a whisper.

"I am First Counselor Thag Ulak, Officer of the Imperial Court, Agha Vizier of the Southern Continent, Adopted of the Sovereign of the Wilds, Third Voice of the Emperors, Ambassador to Dragons." Thag bowed with a courtly flourish.

"This," he pointed at Chalkos/Koserana/Varlad, "is Queen Chalkos, Inheritor of Ariel's Blood and Domain, Highest-born of the Dragons." Koserana nodded gracefully, and then ruined it by giggling quietly.

"And she," he pointed at Shina, "is the heir to Gem, his direct descendant, and rightful empress of our world." Shina's jaw dropped.

He continued, ignoring her for a moment, "But we usually dispense with all the formal titles and all the court etiquette, and just call each other Thag, Shina, and Koserana. It's more friendly that way."

Duke Antain wasn't accustomed to being the lowest-ranked person in the room. If this was true, his ancestors had been vassals to vassals to vassals to servants of their ancestors. The battle-mages had been imperial regents for the Blood of Gem, and the Highest-born of the dragons had been co-equal to the original emperors of the whole world.

Thag, if he truly was a Third Voice to the Emperors, outranked King Yonind himself by three or four tiers, and the two women outranked

Thag!

Then it struck him! This might be the exact opportunity he had been searching for his whole life! A way to break his lands away from the bloody tyrant on the royal throne!

"My liege!" he exclaimed and dropped from his chair. Facing Shina, he knelt on the floor again, and bowed so low his forehead touched the floor.

Thag addressed him, since Shina was still trying to stop gawping at the absurdity of it all. "Antain, you need to go prepare your men and wyverns for a long trip far to the east. You'll leave at first light. Angbarad will lead your flight, and Chalkos will guard it. You will be personally responsible for Shina's safety. Prepare and then rest. You have a long trip ahead."

The duke stood, bowed once more towards Shina, and backed out of the room. As soon as he was gone, Thag shut the door and then turned to Shina.

"What in the world was that all about, Thag?" she exclaimed! "I'm no heir to Gem!"

Thag smiled and shrugged. "Of course you are. Gem had two children we know about, and probably several more that aren't in the records, before he embraced undeath. Statistically, after this much time, just about everyone alive is descended from him. And also from innumerable farmers, craftsmen, storekeeps, shepherds, kings, soldiers, prostitutes. You name it, you've got it in your ancestry, if you look back far enough. Family trees work that way, you know."

"But… but … you told him I'm the rightful empress of this world. A 'direct descendant of Gem'."

"Little One, what would an 'indirect descendant' even be? Either someone was your ancestor, or they weren't. 'Direct descendant' is the only kind there is. Humans with a vested interest in land-inheritance make laws that pretend otherwise, but it is a pretense and nothing more."

Before she could argue more, he interrupted. "The duke needs to believe in you. He's hated King Yonind for decades. To be blunt, King Yonind is a terrible ruler. He rules by violence and blackmail, and uses your father as a cudgel against people's minds where those two things fail. Duke Antain isn't much better, of course. But he could be, if we guide him towards it.

"Imagine if you had been a queen or empress, the way you were in your father's house. Now imagine if you had that power, but with what you've learned since. Should Antain be denied a chance at that same kind of lesson?"

He paused while she digested that, then continued, quietly. "Or should I believe that he can't change? That people can't change? I have faith in you. Can you have faith in others? At least enough to give them the chance?"

In the quiet after his question, Koserana whispered to Shina, "Thag's always right, you know. Listen to him."

Shina took a deep breath. When she spoke, it was to ask, "You mentioned plans. What do we need to plan?"

"Little One, you need to go to Xalax. It's where you need to go to earn your heritage."

"What if I don't have a heritage, Thag? What if I'm not who you think I am? What if I don't deserve all … this!"

"Then you won't be able to enter Xalax and we'll have failed."

Shina's imagination filled that failure with dire portent. "What happens if I fail? What happens if I can't go in?"

Thag looked puzzled. "What do you mean?"

"I mean if I fail, what happens. Don't magical tests usually mean that you either get some boon or you die … or worse?"

Thag shrugged. "No. If you fail, you simply won't be able to enter the sanctum in Xalax. If you can go in, you'll find your heritage inside. If you can't, you can't. We'll need to find another potential wizard and start over."

"But Thag, you told Brad we only have a few years before our world dies. Or was that another …" she stopped herself from using the word "lie". "… another deception?"

"No. Our world has approximately ten or twelve years left. Every potential we've tested over the last three-hundred years has failed. And people like you are very, very rare. It's hard to find humans who can see the world-shards for what they really are, instead of seeing 'stars'. If we don't find a wizard soon, it will be too late. Our world and everyone and everything in it will die and fade back into the void.

"Even Chalkos," he continued, glancing at Koserana. "She's not old enough to escape our world on her own. Not for a few more centuries."

Shina sat down, her legs collapsing under her. "But … that means … if I fail, everyone will die and it will be my fault."

Thag put a huge hand on her shoulder. "No, Little One. It will be the fault of the gnomes and the battle-mages. It's not your fault the world is dying. It just may be your opportunity to undo the harm done by others."

She looked up at him, desperate for hope. After a moment, she squared her shoulders, took another deep breath, and asked, "What do I need to do?"

"You'll go with Koserana, Brad, and Antain…"

Shina interrupted. "Thag, you call him 'Brad' when you talk about him with me. You called him 'Angbarad' with the duke. And I think I heard the orcs call him that. Why does he have two names? Is 'Brad' a nickname for 'Angbarad'?

"'Angbarad' is the name he was given by the chief of his tribe when he passed his rites of adulthood. It's his formal name. Brad is what he prefers – it's a sort of nickname."

Shina sensed Thag wasn't telling her everything. "What does 'Angbarad' mean and why doesn't he like it?"

Thag smirked. "It means 'tower of iron' in an elvish language from another world-shard."

"'Tower of iron'? That doesn't sound so bad. Is it because he's tall and strong?"

"No, dear, it's not because of his … height."

A few months before, Shina would have blushed as she realized what "tower of iron" must refer to in Brad's case. The new Shina, the one who had just taken the life of the world onto her shoulders and accepted it, smiled wickedly. "Hundreds of children, eh? I guess he earned his name!"

Koserana looked lost. "I don't get it. What's it mean? I know the orcs all call him 'Angbarad', but I thought it was because he's a warrior. Why are you two laughing at me?"

Thag and Shina gave each other a look, and then stopped laughing and apologized to Koserana.

Shina took control of the conversation again. "Thag, I understand that I'll be travelling with Chalkos," she nodded at Koserana, "and Brad, and that Antain and his men will be along to protect me. And, to keep them out of trouble if I know how you think. But I think the duke was right when he said wyverns won't be able to fly with you on their back. Where will you be?"

"I'll follow along as best I can. I'll get Brad to explain the route to me, and I'll catch up to you as quickly as I'm able."

"Oh no! Thag, I don't think I can handle this without you! How will I? I …." Thag put a finger on her lips and quieted her.

"Little One, right now you need to get to Xalax as soon as possible. There are armies behind us, and doubtless there are more armies between us and Xalax. We can't fight our way through all of them. I can't keep you safe through that. But if you fly over them, Brad can keep you flying longer and faster than any other wyverns in the sky. That makes you safe from anyone pursuing. And the duke knows how to avoid trouble ahead of you.

"Chalkos will protect you from anything that can catch you or intercept you. Chalkos and Brad can fight anything less than an army. And Antain and his men are a small army in themselves. You'll be better protected than you have ever been."

"Thag, that's not true! I'm safe when I'm with you! I want to be with you!"

"Shina, my love, you need to do this. For our world, for yourself, and for our son! You have to!"

Shina was about to respond when Thag's words suddenly registered. "Our … son?"

Koserana was nodding. Thag nodded "yes". "Our son, Little One. He's only five days old, and you need to be safe to keep him safe."

"Five days … I'm pregnant!?"

"Yes. What did you expect, with all the love-making we've been doing?"

Shina felt like she needed to sit down, even though she was already in a chair.

"I thought…," she started. "I didn't … I guess … Are you sure?"

Thag and Koserana both nodded emphatically. Koserana was the one who replied first. "It's the smell, Shina. We can smell things like that. And when I'm Chalkos, I can see the aura. Thag can probably see it, too."

Thag nodded confirmation. "Definitely pregnant. Smells healthy, and smells like the kind that actually gets born." He sniffed and, looking at Koserana, said, "Smells male to me…"

Koserana shifted to Chalkos and sniffed closely at Shina. "Definitely male. And definitely yours, Thag." She seemed to have no idea how offensive that statement would have been to humans. "Think it'll be an egg, like you were, or a baby, like humans have?"

Shina stared at her dragon-friend in no slight horror.

Thag simply shrugged. "No way to tell yet. Either way, if we keep Brad around, he should be born healthy. Brad has that effect, even on women he's just around and doesn't actually sleep with."

Shina was pale and shaking just a little. "Thag. A baby? Our world is dying and I'm pregnant and how can I possibly be the person who's supposed to save the world? I'm scared, and you say I have to go ahead and leave you behind and travel with the duke who kidnapped me, and I'm supposed to somehow save the world? Just because I see islands in the sky instead of 'stars'? Whatever 'stars' are?"

Thag picked her up and held her, his gigantic arms clasping her to his broad chest. She could feel his warmth and the slow, powerful beat of his heart. After a minute, he set her down on her feet. Looking directly into her eyes, his own swirling with love and concern and confidence, he simply said, "You can do this."

Shina swallowed her fear – a small ball that settled somewhere in her stomach like a lump of lead. She closed her eyes and took a deep breath through her nose. As she exhaled heavily, her muscles relaxed and she pushed the fear out of herself with a gesture of her hands. When she opened her eyes again, she felt calm enough. She knew the fear was still somewhere, and that it could come back stronger than ever before. But it was gone for now, and that would just have to suffice. When it came back, that would be the time to deal with it. Right now, for this second, everything was okay.

"You *will* follow, right?" she asked Thag.

"Anywhere. Always."

Chapter 16: *Wyverns, Wyverns Everywhere*

Shina and Thag plotted and planned late into the night. He explained that he was going to see if he could get some help for them, but she didn't know any of the places or people he said he would ask. She just had to accept that they were people he knew, and that he hoped they could meet at the ruins of Xalax and help.

"I won't go straight to Xalax. I may get there quite a while after you, but I will get there," he assured her. "And hopefully with allies. Some of them may even arrive before I do."

He cautioned, "I'll tell any I send your way to use your horse's name as a password. Beware of enemies pretending to be friendly. Keep a guard at all times – Chalkos can help with that, but her judgement is poor, so keep yourself alert for betrayal.

"Only trust Antain so far as you have to. He's using this for his political games. He only listens to his own interests and needs, and has little regard for anything beyond blind ambition. Even the 'freedom' he seeks is the freedom to inflict his own will on others."

In the morning, Shina was sad to leave Sachem behind. One of the duke's men promised to take good care of him. He was going to ride east through the pass, then go south and try to work his way back west eventually.

Thag suggested that they should spread the news of Shina's mission to as much of the world as possible. "After all," he said, "our enemies know about us, so it will be best to inform any potential allies as well."

Two of the soldiers, who were giving up their wyverns for Shina and Brad, and all nineteen of the orcs, would try to spread the word. There was no point in trying to hold the fortress at Bart Ridge, since they already knew Wyvern Clan was on its way up the pass.

Thag saw her off, waving as the wyvern she was tied to rose into the air and eventually flew out of sight. She flew ahead to where everyone else was waiting for her, their wyverns hovering on slow wing beats. She wanted so badly to look back for one last glimpse of Thag, but knew that if she looked she would never have the courage to leave him.

Thag called up a rather nasty rainstorm on the western side of the pass. He knew a disciplined army would barely be slowed by it. A barely-organized barbarian mob, on the other hand, would be delayed for hours, maybe a day or more. It would be enough.

He made sure the gate was barred, and that there were plenty of supplies available in the fort. No need to have thousands of men suffer. Not when Shina was already far out of their reach. Wyvern Clan would be well-fed for a short while when they breached the fortress. They would stop to eat and drink, and that would delay their pursuit just that much longer.

Then he climbed the long stair to the top of the high cliffs above the fort. It was time to attempt something he'd always wanted to try. From a castle wall, with the help of the winds, he could glide a few hundred yards. From a plateau in the plains, a mile or more. What about from the top of a mountain…?

***

Earlier, Duke Antain had patiently described wyvern-riding to Shina in the hour before dawn. "What you'll be doing is simpler than riding a horse, your highness, since your wyvern will just be following me. It's also more physically demanding. And if you fall off, you will die." It seemed to be a speech he had given before, and Shina readily imagined the dozens of young soldiers who had been trained by Antain and his masters-at-arms. Her eyes burned from lack of sleep, but she tried to focus on the droning voice of the duke.

"Falling off a horse can be dangerous, but lots of people survive it every day," he continued, apparently missing her woolgathering.

"Fall off a wyvern in flight, and you just get a long look at the piece of ground that's going to shatter you. But you won't fall if you do what I say, highness."

"First," he explained, "with your permission, you will be tied to its back with these leather straps." He held up some straps that were attached to a wyvern's back. "Second, your wyvern is trained to keep you on its back. If you don't fight it, it will keep you there."

Shina took her first good look at a wyvern that morning. By lantern-light, she inspected the harness and the animal itself. It's thick, smooth skin was covered with snake-like scales, some so fine they almost couldn't be seen. The wings were huge, and the chest muscles that powered them were immensely thick and heavy.

The harness itself was attached to the wyvern's back by means of stainless-steel rings embedded into the creature's skin. She wondered briefly if that was painful to the animal, but the scars were long-healed.

The straps seemed secure, though she felt badly for the animal if she yanked on them – how would that feel, she wondered. Her mind flashed to the chains in Varlad's skin and muscles, and wondered how those felt to the big orc.

The wyvern was larger than a horse. One of the riders had his wyvern spread its wings so she could get a good look. She had never realized just how huge those wings were! The span must be fifty or sixty feet, she estimated.

These wyverns, she was told, were light, fast hunters – racing animals bred for speed and endurance. One of the duke's men, a flyer named Nicman, bragged to her this breed could sprint a dozen miles in as few minutes! Or they could soar for almost a hundred miles a day. In the long haul, he explained, they weren't really faster than a good horse, they just didn't have to go around things like rivers and lakes and hills.

His enthusiasm for the animals was contagious, and Shina found herself excited to see what it was like to soar through the skies!

Two of the duke's younger men, Nicman and his friend Kidolch, showed her how to ride. She casually deflected their fumbling flirtations as they tied her to a wyvern's back and had it walk around the yard. They showed her how to wear the goggled leather helms all wyvern-riders wear to keep wind out of their eyes and to keep their noses and ears from freezing at high altitude.

When they lifted her onto the animal's back, she was flattered and amused by the occasional "pardon, highness" as hands "accidentally" brushed her breasts or buttocks. The young men would smile charmingly, then glance apprehensively at Thag and promptly switch to all-business behavior for a few minutes before forgetting themselves again.

In short order, they had her kneeling on its back in the position they said was best for long flights, and had her strapped securely to it.

Once she was comfortable with just being on the wyvern and had settled into the straps and handholds, they had her fly a short circle around the fortress.

It was amazing! She saw the fort shrink beneath her, and the cliffs soaring past as the wyvern pumped its wings to climb. Raw excitement flooded through her and her face felt like it would split in two from smiling so hard!

She knew that long-flight would wear on her legs and back horribly if it weren't for Brad's healing, but the sheer excitement of flight and the amazing vista of the fort spread out below her overwhelmed any apprehension she might have felt!

She laughed silently at herself when she realized that she'd actually been "exercising" for this every time she knelt on top of Thag for sex. But that thought led back to her as-yet-unfelt pregnancy, and a tiny bit in the back of her mind was still panicking about that! Better – much better – to focus on the sights and thrills of flying!

All too soon, Kidolch led her back to the ground, where it was still dark despite the brightening eastern horizon.

Nicman helped her get into the heavy leather long-coat used for high-altitude flight, with its form-fitting cap and panels that would cover her legs when she knelt. He also helped her smear a black cream on her eyelids. "We'll be flying east, into the sun, and this helps with the glare," he explained.

It was all strange and new, but she had learned to accept such. *I wonder how bored I would be by a "normal" day*, she thought ironically.

The sky was lit, that pale, magical blue that precedes actual sunrise, when they were finally ready for the first day's flight. The pass itself, surrounded by mountains and cliffs, was still dark, but the fleeting clouds and snowy mountain peaks were graced by a thousand colors of the coming dawn.

Wings beat powerfully and the wyverns leapt into the sky!

Up! Up! Up! Cliffs racing past them!

Suddenly they were in the clear, cold air of the high mountains, and the sunlight broke over them in a flood of brilliance!

Shina gasped in wonder at the scene spread below her! She could see *forever!*

The land below her was a fantastic vista of hills and valleys! The down-slope of the mountains spread before her, fading in the distance into the distant plains of the eastern wastes.

Behind and to the sides spread a wall of black peaks with snow-white mantles of glacial ice.

Below and ahead, the blacks and grays of the mountains gave way to dark-green carpets of primeval forest, scattered with rivers and lakes and streams, and then finally to the infinite grasslands and limitless forests of the boreal tundra!

Everywhere she looked, there were a million shades of every color she could imagine! As sunlight spread below them, the dusky hues and shadows were lifted to reveal a polychrome of life and land below, set on a canvas of stone and water.

Above, uncountable world-shards filled the ice-blue sky, lit by the golden glory of the rising sun.

Shina had expected fear at the view and the height. Instead, fear was left rapidly behind, lost in the land behind and below by the thrill of being alive for something as awesome as this.

She quickly grew accustomed to the powerful, slow beats of the wyvern's majestic wings. As she settled in to the rhythm of it, her legs and hips found the circular rising-and-falling motion that made it comfortable.

Shina knew now why Nicman and Kidolch loved flying their wyverns so much!

Chalkos flitted through the air around them. When she saw Shina was watching her, the young dragon went through a silly series of complex aerobatic maneuvers – loops and spirals and even flying upside down for a short distance. Shina laughed at the show-off, happy that her friend was having fun.

Shina spent some time admiring how Chalkos looked in the bright sunlight, flying gracefully through the thin air. The metal scales and glittering eyes were as beautiful in their own way as Koserana was in hers. Shina wondered idly if Varlad was "beautiful" to other orcs, or if that was even a thing.

She realized she'd been avoiding thinking about Varlad's slaughter at the fort. That thought brought her admiration and wandering thoughts to a screeching halt.

As Chalkos, her lover was an alien thing, her thoughts far from human. She had slaughtered dozens of the duke's men back in the werewolf village, mostly out of petty spite. Yes, some of the villagers needed rescuing, and Antain needed to be first distracted and then sent packing back home. But Thag would have figured out a way to do it without killing indiscriminately.

As Varlad, she reveled in a gore-fest that left the walls of the fort dripping in blood, and bodies and body parts piled in the courtyard. That fight, at least, had been necessary, but the manner of it had been … not just grotesque, but overdone.

Thag had killed, she knew. The battle at the foot of the pass, and who knows how many other times over the centuries. But he did the minimum necessary and used shock and magic to drive as many as possible away in fear, rather than killing them wholesale.

Chalkos/Varlad left no survivors if given the chance.

Shina realized she'd been thinking of Koserana as a person, a human woman, who could turn into a dragon. The truth was, Chalkos was a dragon who could disguise herself as a human, or an orc, and perhaps as other things as well. That was the critical distinction.

Thag fought against his dark heritage, the gluttony of his troll mother and the larceny and greed of his dragon father, and the casual wrath and violence of both. Chalkos was slowly learning such restraint from Thag, as Thag had learned it from Llwddan, his stepfather.

But it was clear that Chalkos was, indeed, truly a dragon, in a way that Thag wasn't. Powerful, dangerous, proud, greedy, and with little self-restraint and only the faintest reasons to ever learn it.

She remembered Koserana telling Antain that "…Thag told me I can't kill you and eat you…", and finally confronted the factuality of that statement. It took an admonition from someone Chalkos both loved and feared to keep her from killing and *eating* a man.

Such thoughts were uncomfortable, and Shina was enjoying the morning and the flight too much to dwell on them for long. One day, she would have to deal with her relationship with Koserana, and decide what it really meant. But not today. Not this morning. Not while the sun shone and the land below was graced with glory!

After a day of wonders unveiling themselves at every mile, the duke picked a camping spot on a fortified hillside. Chalkos scouted the ruins while the others hovered above, out of bowshot. When she reported it suitable, they landed.

The duke and his men were pleasantly surprised when they climbed down from their mounts and found that muscles were not cramped or even tired! The men, braced for the usual tingles and pains from blood returning to long-strained limbs, smiled and nodded in appreciation.

Shina, accustomed to the effects of Brad's magic, knew how they felt, but was expecting it. Nevertheless, their obvious joy at this discovery was infectious and she found herself smiling along with them.

Most of the men soon set out to hunt for deer or whatever else was available, to feed their wyverns. The two who stayed behind quickly had a camp set up for everyone.

Shina looked around at the old ruins they had picked to camp amidst.

"Thag could probably tell me the name of the castle. Right, Brad?" Shina asked when Brad joined her.

"I don't know. He never spent a lot of time in this part of the world. The empire of the battle mages had outposts here, but he spent most of his time closer to their capital. That was far to the southwest from here, on the other side of a large sea.

"At least, that's what I think. He hasn't told me much about his time in the empire," Brad said.

"The empire? Is this an imperial ruin, then?" asked Shina.

Koserana, having just joined them, replied at the same time as Brad. "Yes. Definitely," they said.

Shina looked at what was left. Partial remains of thick stone walls still stood, but were falling to vines and weather. Roofs were long-gone. Everything was built in circles and ovals – the walls, the towers, the courtyard they were camping in, everything she could see had been round when it was still standing. Only the fallen stones, large rectangular bricks of worked granite, were squared. Even those had lost their sharp corners and edges to time and weather.

The outer walls still stood. At least ten feet thick, and easily twenty feet high, they were sagging, but remained formidable. A lone archway, its gate long-since fallen without trace, was the only opening to the rest of the world.

Towers that looked like they had once been quite solid stood on either side of the gate. Shina couldn't tell how tall they had been, since the upper levels had fallen into a pile of rubble at their base.

She imagined the people who had once lived here. Emissaries of the empire, they were assuredly a military group. Like the ancestors of the duke. She wondered what their days had been like.

Maybe Thag could tell her, one day.

"It must be ancient," Shina said after a while. "To have fallen so thoroughly."

Brad pondered a moment. "Maybe. Weather in this part of the world is harsh. The empire abandoned the eastern wastes almost two-hundred years before the last emperor fell. This can't be much older than that.

"You want really old," he continued, "wait till we get to the ruins around Xalax. Those are from the gnome-wars. Tens of thousands of years old, and still enough to scare any sane man. You'll see!"

Shina shuddered at the thought of it.

Even with her friends, the ruins in the night felt lonely without Thag, and she soon returned to the campsite for comfort and warmth.

When she approached, Antain and his men stood and bowed to her. "Highness," the duke said, and gestured an invitation to join him at the campfire.

Shina was embarrassed by this. She decided she couldn't keep up a charade. "Lord Antain, you must know that I'm not really…."

The duke interrupted her with a raised hand. "Don't say it, Majesty. It matters not whether you are truly the one rightful heir to Gem's title. What matters is that we have decided to believe you. And when we return to civilized lands, we will convince others. It's what we need. And what you need."

He obviously considered the subject closed. "Now, if Your Highness would please join us for dinner."

For a while, conversation was limited to dinner and food. "Would Your Highness care for some wine?", "Pass a loaf of bread, please," and, "This venison is so gamey!"

When Brad pulled a barrel of fresh apples out of his bracelet and shared them around, everyone was openly impressed. Again, Shina realized she had grown accustomed to things that others treated as nearly miraculous.

When dinner was over and everyone was settling in around the campfire, Antain had a few questions about plans and schedules.

"Lord Angbarad," the duke began.

"Brad," the half-orc interrupted.

"Excuse me?" asked the duke.

"It's just 'Brad'. Just call me 'Brad', please."

"Lord Brad," Antain started again. He was growing accustomed to these people and their regular lèse-majesté, but interruptions while he was speaking were still a strain. "I've seen what you can do with the wyverns. Never have I even dreamed such stamina was possible! And we ourselves arrived as fresh and ready for action as if after a good day of rest. Is that something all of your people can do, or is it unique?"

"It's pretty rare," replied Brad. "I've never met anyone else who can do it, but I've heard of a few throughout our history."

One of the duke's men whispered something to the man next him and both smirked. They were looking at Koserana, across the campfire from them.

"I heard you," Koserana said quietly but firmly. "'Stamina so we can be "fresh and ready for action",' sounds pretty good to you, doesn't it?" She glared and her eyes took on a coppery sheen. A wave of fear washed over everyone in the camp. Shina reflexively blocked it, but she could feel the emotion pushing on her, trying to get to her. It was only a second or two, and then Koserana's eyes returned to their normal beautiful bright blue and the tide of fear receded. "I don't play with my food," she finished abruptly.

The two men swallowed convulsively as the blood drained from their faces and cold sweat formed pale droplets on their brows.

After an awkward silence, Duke Antain cleared his throat and got everyone's attention back onto him.

"How soon do you expect Thag to catch up to us, after we get to the ruins?" he asked.

Brad answered, "He won't really 'catch up to us'. If he's not ahead of us already, he will be by morning."

Antain looked doubtful. "We must have come over 200 miles today. Maybe more. He can't possibly …"

Brad interrupted him again. "Yes, he can." He thought for a moment. "Antain, if a horse could gallop at full speed all day, without having to rest at all. If it had to stop briefly to drink every few miles, and maybe to eat once a day or so. How far could it go in a day? At a full gallop all day."

Antain shook his head. "I don't know. Nobody knows. It's not something that can be done. I could speculate that hundreds of miles would be possible, but it would be a guess."

Brad nodded. "That horse is slower than Thag. He can eat on the run if he has to. He can glide across terrain that would stop or slow a horse, like cliffs or ravines. And he can outrun any horse ever born, without even pushing himself.

"Weather won't slow him down, either. It won't rain on him unless he wants it to. Hot and cold aren't really a thing for him.

"And he can swim if he has to cross a lake or river. Far better than any horse. Plus, Thag doesn't have to go around to avoid lions and tigers and bears. They avoid him."

Brad nodded to confirm his own words. "Yeah. If he's not ahead of us already, he will be by morning. Did I mention he doesn't sleep? Ever? He can run all day and all night, all week if he has to. For as long as he needs to."

Brad nodded at Koserana. "She's the same way. No sleep, not ever. But she's probably even faster than Thag, since she can fly and he can't." He looked at her for confirmation.

Koserana nodded. "I'm not as tough as Thag. But I am faster."

Brad smiled and nodded, then looked back at the duke.

"Me? I need to sleep. I'll be busy keeping you guys going all day tomorrow, and this stuff is exhausting!" With that, he settled down onto a blanket, folded it over himself, and promptly fell asleep.

Duke Antain wasn't sure he believed all of that. *But,* he thought to himself, *if it is true, the martial possibilities are astonishing! What I could do with a scout who can fly faster and further, see and hear better, and never needs to sleep! What I could do with a soldier like Thag in the middle of my battle-line!* He was still plotting and imagining when he finally drifted off to sleep a long while later.

Shina quickly and easily fell asleep. She was long-accustomed to Thag and Koserana keeping watch all night and not having to concern herself about it. After most of a year, she'd become very comfortable sleeping easily on even colder, harder ground than this. It felt nice to be in a camp with a good fire and lots of company.

One of the men kept a watch. He would trade with another in an hour or so. They knew Koserana would stay up and guard them, but they weren't comfortable trusting their lives to her. Not before her little display of temper and definitely not after.

The fire slowly burned down and its light faded from the ruined walls of the old castle.

One pair of human eyes watched the night sky from atop the old wall, seeing a huge expanse of snowy-white stars twinkling their pale light on the dark world below them.

One pair of draconic eyes watched too. What they saw no human can truly understand. The first dragons were born as men, but they had left that heritage far behind long before Chalkos was ever hatched.

Hundreds of miles to the east, huge feet with giant claws pounded over the ground as a dark thing ran relentlessly through the night.

Chapter 17: *Ruined*

Shina looked down on a line drawn across the land. On one side, forest and grass and bushes and all the abundant life of the taiga. On the other, barren rock and lifeless dust.

Brad had warned her that Xalax was surrounded by a wasteland, still toxic from the battles of the gnome wars thousands of years before. So she had known to expect … something. But not this knife-slash across the land, and the dead desolation that she now saw.

Plumes of dust and grit blew into the air below her wherever a breeze stirred against the land.

There were no hints of green. Even where she saw streams cross the border, the grass and trees stopped abruptly.

The early-morning sunlight cast long shadows of every hill and rock in the lifeless wastes. The harsh lines and strong contrasts made it even worse.

They had hundreds of miles left to go. Without Brad keeping the wyverns aloft, their expedition would have been doomed to failure. Brad said nothing living could cross the wastes around Xalax without carrying supplies with it. Seeing how lifeless this land really was, she didn't doubt that at all. If the waters were poisoned, as they must be, how could anything cross such lands?

And what would they find at Xalax? They had supplies only for a couple of days – these light, fast wyverns couldn't carry more than that, and the contents of Brad's bracelet weren't enough for this many men and beasts for any length of time. And what about Chalkos' and the wyverns' needs to hunt and eat fresh meat?

They had camped early the day before, on a plateau that Chalkos said was inaccessible to the clan-armies that were following them. They needed an early start and would spend the whole day crossing the wastelands. If they didn't find Xalax by nightfall, they would have nowhere safe to land, and might not make it out of here alive. Even Brad couldn't keep the wyverns flying if they couldn't find food for them.

Pursuit was a few days behind. Hundreds of thousands of men and orcs, wyverns and griffons and thousands of warhorses and all the rest that went along with the largest army seen in these lands since the rebellion against the battle-mages.

Duke Antain was certain that the barbarians had emptied whole cities to hunt them. He had a fevered look in his eyes these days – he had no hope against that army, but his drive for revenge against the demoness Kamaia burned hot deep inside him and kept despair balanced with determination.

Desolation lay ahead of them. Certain death lay behind. And Shina missed Thag. She was sure he had some plan for all of this – but she hadn't any slightest hint of what that plan might be.

He's pinned his hopes on me. The whole world and all of Thag's plans and aspirations rest on me, she thought. A dark lump of despair filled her nightmares and threatened her every waking minute. She was going to fail. Going to disappoint Thag. Their son was doomed. She was going to let the whole world die. And there was nothing she could do about any of it!

She looked around herself again, taking stock of her companions.

Duke Antain was a brutal man, and he had hurt her and terrified her when he kidnapped her, but he was also one of the best military men in the world. Brilliant in his victories, and his few defeats had cost his enemies so dearly they gained nothing even by winning a few battles.

The duke's men were elite soldiers. Tough, smart, strong, with battle-trained reflexes, and were totally loyal to their duke. They liked her, but she knew if the duke turned on her that his men wouldn't hesitate a second to kill her if he ordered it.

Brad was her friend. But he was also a deadly warrior who could deflect sword thrusts off his skin, heal people's wounds as fast they were received, and could summon strength and stamina for his allies out of thin air. He had immense power.

Chalkos was a dragon! She was young, immature, rash, and petty, but she was also deadly, swift, clever, and potentially immortal.

Herself? She was just good at manipulating her father – who was a powerful man, but was also thousands of miles away. She was young, inexperienced, and fragile. The one time she'd had to defend herself in a fight, she'd ended up throwing up from the fear and horror at killing a man. A man who had at the very least meant to kill her friends and kidnap her.

She had only survived this long because others kept her alive. Sometimes with dire consequences for themselves, like her werewolf friend Lisa who had lost her whole village, or Brad, who had nearly died protecting her from barbarian spirit-warriors.

Even Thag! She knew it pained him every time he had to use violence, and he'd been forced to do so over and over again ever since he first rescued her from Antain's tower.

All because she was weak and couldn't protect herself. Others had to do it for her, and the costs to them were horrific.

Hours went by, and the only change to the land below them was the angle of the sunlight on it. Everywhere Shina could see, the land was broken and dead from horizon to horizon.

As the sun rose above them, she watched their shadows on the land far below. Over the grassy plains and lakes of healthier lands, she had found the shadows fascinating. Here, they just highlighted the emptiness.

She saw dust-devils and even a small sandstorm below them as the day wore on. But never once did she see green or the motion of animal-life. Streams and even a few rivers crossed these lands, mostly through heavily eroded gorges, but even those looked dead.

As afternoon wore into early evening, she started to see glints from the land below, as if the soil and rocks contained hints of metal or glass. At first there were only a few and they were rare and far-between. But as they flew further in, these became more and more common.

The day was growing old when, unbelievably, she saw a dark patch on the horizon, directly ahead of them. It looked almost like… it was! It was trees! Some sort of oasis in the middle of the dead lands!

As they approached that promise of life, she saw more and more metal in the ground. And strange hills and lumps in the ground. Rocks with angles that seemed too straight for nature, too square.

Finally, as the sun approached the horizon, they passed over a ring of metal fragments and what was obviously wreckage of some sort. Inside it was the ruins of once-mighty walls and towers of worked stone.

And what wreckage! She saw towers made of blocks the size of

had found no clues towards what they were looking for. A river, most likely an old canal or moat since it was inside the ruins of the city, bounded the area on three sides, with the cliffs to the south as the fourth boundary.

If what they were looking for was outside of that, they might never find it. The ruins went on for miles in every direction, and they could search for lifetimes without finding anything in there. So they limited their search to inside the boundary defined by the river and the forest, on the assumption or faint hope that they might find it if they did that.

On the second day, Antain had his men kill one of the wyverns and feed it to the others. Men can't eat wyvern meat, but they can cannibalize, he explained. The beasts were starving, and they'd all be dead soon if they didn't make sacrifices like this. Since they didn't have the supplies to make a successful sortie from the wastelands, it didn't seem to matter anyway.

Of course, they all knew that they had only a limited time before they'd run out of supplies themselves. They had plenty of water, since there was a clean spring or fountain in the living part of the ruins, but they only had a few days left of food. Without Brad and his storage-bracelet, they had less than that.

Brad and Drew re-appeared late on the second day. Nobody asked where they'd been, since they all assumed they knew. But they were glad to get the supplies from Brad. That gave them about an additional week to survey the place most of them were now convinced they would die in.

Some tried to keep good spirits, but their dwindling supplies, the unending death all around them, the dust devils and the occasional rain-of-dirt from out in the wastes, coupled with the omnipresent knowledge that they didn't know what they were looking for, pushed most to a state of fake smiles and false good-cheer.

"Of course, we'll find it tomorrow. We just need to figure out where we haven't checked yet," was the common phrase, spoken with the confidence of men who were trying to keep each other from giving up.

Drew seemed confused by the whole "lack of supplies thing". Shina asked her about that, and her reply was, "Here are soil, water, and sunlight. What else you need?"

"We're not trees, Drew," Shina said. "We're people. We need food."

Drew looked at her intently. "What food?"

"It doesn't matter what kind. Just food."

Drew shook her head 'no'. "No, what food? What means food?"

Shina stared. "Brad," she called to him. "Can you understand her?"

Brad and Drew started talking rapidly in some language Shina didn't know. How could she not know what food is? It must be a language thing.

Then suddenly Drew stood up, standing with her arms raised high above her head. She raised her face towards the sun and stared straight at it! Before Shina could even think to warn her that staring at the sun is dangerous, Drew transformed!

Her skin suddenly became rough. Her arms and legs stretched, and her fingers spread wide and grew long and thin. Hair-fine threads sprang from her feet and burrowed into the dirt.

Taller and taller she grew! Her legs fused together while her arms branched into a million writhing strands!

Her feet were covered completely by the thickening threads that were spreading from them all through the soil.

In moments, where Drew had stood, was instead a rapidly growing young oak tree!

With amazing speed, the trunk thickened and the branches spread! In seconds, green buds sprouted all over what had been her arms and turned into a million-million growing leaves.

It only took a few minutes for there to be no sign Drew had ever stood there. Instead, a gigantic oak, easily sixty feet tall and eighty feet across, dominated the whole campground.

One of the soldiers was the first to recover from the shock of the metamorphosis. "Too bad," he mused sardonically, "that she turns into an oak instead of an apple tree. Then at least we could eat." A few near him chuckled appreciatively.

Brad turned to the man. "What was that?"

The soldier was immediately apologetic. "Sorry, I didn't mean to be rude or anything. I was just wishing we had an apple tree or something. You know, like … well … an apple tree or something."

Brad put his hands on the sides of his head and looked pained for a moment. "Sometimes I am actually dumb enough to deserve some of Thag's jokes about what body part I do my thinking with!"

Everybody was quiet. There were a lot of "do you know what he's talking about" glances from each to the others, but even Shina wasn't sure what Brad meant. Was he upset about the comment about Drew and apples? If so, why? It didn't make much sense.

Brad turned to Shina. "I'm going to be exhausted after this. Like last time. You know how it'll be."

Before Shina could point out that she had no idea how it would be and hadn't the faintest clue why he'd be exhausted, Brad sat down. He twisted his legs into a pretzel shape and rested his hands, palm-up, on his knees. His eyes closed and he took a deep, slow breath and let it out very, very slowly.

She had seen this before! Right before a major battle. Right before he killed people by crushing them with trees and vines! What was he going to do?

"Brad!" she screamed. The apples comment didn't mean …

And then bushes and trees sprouted from the ground all around him! They grew at unnatural speed, towering over him. An impenetrable mass of wood and thorns and bushes spreading rapidly over the ground!

People scrambled to avoid trees sprouting where they'd been standing.

A few of the natural trees of the forest toppled, their roots irresistibly pushed from the ground by Brad's burgeoning thicket.

Just as Shina was about to panic and run from the onrushing growth, she realized what she was seeing!

Apple trees!

And cherries!

And thorny bushes covered in giant masses of dark berries!

A pear tree, the fruit already ripening in front of her eyes, had sprung from the ground not ten feet from where she was standing!

As others realized what was going on, cheers rang out.

The oak, surrounded on all sides by growing fruit trees and bushes, shrank and disappeared as rapidly as it had appeared in the first place. Shina couldn't see what was going on in the middle of the new orchard, the trees and bushes were far too thick to see where Brad was.

It took almost an hour for the growth to stop and the plants to settle into shapes and forms that were normal for them. Shina knew that Brad was somewhere in there, exhausted and desperately in need of succor and help, but she couldn't get to him! She couldn't even try! The thorns were too thick, the bushes too dense!

Then a path appeared, and Drew was carrying Brad's limp body in her arms.

Shina rushed to them, afraid that her friend had pushed too hard. But he was still breathing, his heartbeat under her fingertips was shallow and fast but definite.

As before, he had huge bruises around his eyes. His skin was a deathly shade of pale white. And he drooped in Drew's arms, his muscles gone to mush and his limbs hanging like a puppet with cut strings.

One of the soldiers approached fearfully. "Can we eat? Is it safe?"

Shina nodded. "Yes. And please bring me some water for Brad. Right away, please."

The soldier rushed off to do her bidding. The look on his face was unmitigated awe as he ran for the spring.

Drew set Brad down on the grass and got Shina's attention.

"He do this. He make trees. Yes?" She said.

"Yes. He made the trees. I've seen him do it before. Last time, it was oaks and poison ivy and thorn-vines as weapons. This time, it's …" she pointed at the splendor of fruits and berries where before had only been scrub pines and a few scraggly bushes.

Drew smiled broadly!

"I am dryad, Shina. I and he, we do better together than he alone!" She looked like she expected Shina to understand what that meant, so Shina smiled and nodded at her as if she got it. Maybe it was some odd way of saying she liked having sex with him, but she wasn't sure how that had anything to do with the trees and such.

"He'll need to sleep for a day," Shina told Drew. "You guard him. You keep him safe while he sleeps. Okay? He'll need water, and when he wakes up he'll need food. Lots of it."

"I keep he safe! In trees, I keep he total safe!"

Again, Shina just let the confusing part roll over and past her. "Good," was all she said.

The fresh fruit didn't solve the problem for the wyverns. Shina knew the duke would keep as many alive as possible, as long as possible, but everyone knew the clock was ticking for them. With no source of fresh meat, they were doomed.

And that also meant that only Chalkos had a reliable means of escaping this place. Even if the armies of Kamaia didn't follow them over the wastelands – something Duke Antain assured her a large army would do slowly but surely if they knew anything at all about supply chains – some of them were going to die here.

Day after day crept by. Search parties swept tentatively into the ruins of the city proper. They couldn't go far, and they didn't have time to search thoroughly. Still, they couldn't find anything that seemed to fit Thag's "threshold". The few intact doorways they did find were easy for everyone to pass, which Thag had assured Shina only a wizard could do if they found the correct place. And when Shina passed through any of them, nothing seemed to happen.

There was one piece of hope, in all the ruins and destruction. Brad and Drew were able to start growing trees and plants together along the dead verge of the river. It was difficult for them, and Brad was constantly on the verge of collapse, but it was important to them for reasons Shina couldn't quite take the time to understand.

Shina knew it might not matter. If the world died in just a few years, their immense effort to restore life to this wasteland was all for nothing. But it gave them hope that even the old damage of the gnome wars could be alleviated, even if only slightly and with great effort.

Chalkos reported that the army-horde had started into the wastes on the fifth day of their explorations. The horde was ruining the land for miles around their camp on the edge of the wastes, gathering supplies and killing every game animal for dozens of miles around. The advance part of that army was traveling along a stream into the desolation, and it ran foul with the waste and filth of the whole horde. Even if the waters hadn't been undrinkable because of the curses of the wastelands, they would have become so as that army moved along them.

By the seventh day, she had a good gauge of their progress, and said it would be a month or maybe six weeks for them to reach the ruins. Scouts might get there a few days before that.

Shina, Brad, Drew, Koserana, and Duke Antain were gathered near the foot of the cliffs. A council session of sorts, trying to work out a way to find what they needed and then escape while they still could.

Duke Antain was saying something about caves. "If we had a defensible cave, or something similar, in these cliffs, we could hold off an army for a long time. Not forever, but every hour might count.

"Thag said he'd send reinforcements if he could. I don't see how that's possible, unless he meant just Drew here, and, no offense, I don't see how just one dryad can make a difference against an army. But if we are to die here, I'd like to take as many of them with us as possible, and give Thag as much time as possible to deliver his reinforcements. We may fail, but he may succeed after us."

Antain shrugged as if resigned to his fate. "Who knows? Perhaps we are but a diversion, meant to draw this army here where it will be trapped if he cuts their supply lines behind them. We may be pawns being sacrificed in some larger game."

Shina had had thoughts along similar lines. What if she were being used that way? If so, she could forgive Thag his subterfuge. He was trying to save the world from a demon, after all. But she was determined to go down fighting, like the duke.

She pointed at the cliff face. "There's a cave in there. Just up around that outcropping, I think. I saw it when we were flying in. Is it big enough for what you want?"

Antain looked at her quizzically. "What cave? My men haven't reported any caves."

Shina shrugged. "Maybe it was just a shadow on the cliff face, but it looked like a cave to me when I saw it."

Koserana chimed in, "I've been looking for fortifications, or even a good ledge on these cliffs, that we could defend from. I haven't seen any caves either."

Shina stood up and started walking briskly along the cliff's base. "I could have sworn…." She muttered.

The outcropping she had referred to was only a few yards away, and it didn't take much to walk around it.

There! Right where she had said it was! "This cave! Right here!" She pointed into it.

The cave was wide enough for a couple of men to stand side-by-side in it, and seemed to penetrate deep into the cliffs. The opening looked like it had been smashed by the gnomish weapons, like most of the ruins, but it looked stable enough to be safe to go in. She couldn't tell how deep it was, because it was pitch-dark inside, but it looked deep enough to hold at least most of them at one time.

The rest of the group caught up with her.

Duke Antain looked confused. Koserana gave Shina an odd look, glanced right at the cave entrance, and then looked back at Shina, the question "What?" written all over her face.

Brad looked at the cliff face intently. He was the first to speak. "There's a cave there?"

Shina stared at them. "What's wrong with you guys? It's plain as day! That cave!" She pointed again.

The others all looked where she was pointing. Antain shook his head. Koserana muttered something about "stupid practical jokes" and rolled her eyes at Shina.

"No! Wait!" said Brad.

"Shina, you see a cave there? A cave that goes into the face of the cliff?" He actually sounded excited.

Shina nodded. Now she was the one who felt confused, again.

"Can you go into it?" Brad asked.

Shina shrugged, and took the necessary two steps to cross into the opening.

Antain gasped! Koserana's eyes went wide with surprise! Drew and Brad stared right at Shina as if something had happened!

"What?" she asked. Nobody replied, but Brad looked immensely satisfied, with a huge smile splitting his face.

Antain approached, stopped a pace or so in front of her, and reached out. His hand stopped right in front of her, as if he were pushing against the outside of a window.

Shina could actually see the flesh of his palm flattening against some irregular surface mere inches in front of her face! A surface she couldn't even see!

A sense of awe came over her! Her skin prickled and hairs stood up on the back of her neck and all down her arms! A chill swept through her as she realized exactly what this meant!

Something made a noise behind her in the cave.

Chapter 19: *Ferry Land*

Deep in a sound on the eastern edge of the Great Ocean, dozens of miles from the mainland, ink-dark eyes peered from the calm waters. The night-dark waters and wind-ripples concealed the tiny part of Thag's head that barely came out of the water.

His ears, still submerged, tracked a pod of Orcas to his north. They were a dozen miles away, and appeared to be deliberately avoiding him.

He could still smell the blood of the shark that had attacked him a mile or so away. The attack had been very timely – the shark's flesh nicely filled Thag's stomach and would keep him from hunger for a few hours yet.

He didn't like what he was seeing.

The island he was inspecting had five traps that he could see on the only approach to the inside of the island. The beach, merely a tiny strip of rock at the base of a forty-foot cliff that otherwise rose straight from the waters, had two traps on it – a hidden pit right where it met the path up the cliff, and a fine wire right at neck-height for a human. In the dark, human eyes would miss the thin, black wire.

The beach was the local ferry landing, but the ferryman would know the traps and how to avoid them. He would know the traps on all of the islands, not just this one, of course. But Thag needed people from this one. The rest had no kin-tie to his stepfather, and would never listen to him at all, just as the ferry men had refused him passage – as he had expected.

On the path, there were another three traps. A trip-wire that went under a rock and would probably trigger a spring-driven spear, a false hand-hold along a steep part of the path – it would give away under weight and drop anyone holding onto it off the cliff onto rocks, and what looked like a simple rock-trap that would roll a boulder down the path.

But his stepfather's people almost always did things in sixes. Where was the sixth trap?

He could see a way across the beach that would avoid those traps. He could see a way that an agile man could pass the traps on the path up the cliff.

These people were nothing if not agile, so all of that made sense.

Could there be something at the top that he couldn't see from here? Thag doubted it – an elf would stop here and expect to find six visible to him. Anything Thag couldn't see, an elf also couldn't see. So that meant guests, even invited ones, would never start the path.

It wasn't just about actually defending the path, it was also a message that spelled out who lived here and who they would welcome as guests. A message as old as the elves themselves.

Patience! He counseled himself. Elves are patient to a fault, at least with each other.

Perhaps…? He ducked back under the water and swam a little closer to the beach-shelf. Yes! There, right off the shore, a forest of spikes right below the surface of the water, hidden in seaweed! An unsuspecting swimmer would be gutted by them, and a boat would either ground itself or have its hull ripped open!

He surfaced again. Less of his head above the water than an alligator would reveal. In the dark, with the light waves of this calm weather, no human eye would ever have seen him. But he knew that those guarding this place had more than human eyes! So he called to the spirits of the air and sea for help.

Fog rolled in over the water, and in minutes was so thick that eyes less than his wouldn't have even been able to see the island, much less the slow approach of a black creature below the surface! The fog would have to do for announcing himself. He hoped they would recognize it for what it was – having to use a trumpet would be inconvenient!

He swam around the spikes, then leapt easily over the pit and ducked, with some difficulty, under the wire.

At the base of the path, he stepped over the trip-wire, climbed past the fake handhold, and deftly avoided the trigger for the boulder.

He knew he could have bulled his way through the whole thing. There was nothing in these traps that could kill or even seriously hurt him. But that wasn't the point. Elves could survive most of these things almost as easily as he could – avoiding the traps was as much of a statement as the traps themselves were.

By avoiding them, he was saying "I belong here. I am a guest and should be treated as such." If he had instead smashed his way through them or just climbed some part of the cliff that bypassed them entirely, he would have been declaring himself an intruder and unwelcome.

He wasn't at all surprised when he was greeted at the top of the cliff by at least a hundred elvish warriors. They knew who he was, and, all things considered, being greeted by a hundred immortal soldiers armed with longbows, spears and swords was about as friendly as he could hope for.

"I must speak with the ruler of my father's noble people," he announced in their ancient, formal language.

A perfect woman, ageless and beautiful, gracefully stepped forward from the mass of soldiery. She was nearly six feet tall, athletically built, with slender hips and firm breasts. Her golden hair, fine and silk-smooth, hung past her waist. Her face was slender, with generous lips and large, well-shaped eyes. Despite the darkness of the night, Thag could easily see that her eyes were the pale green that is almost universal amongst elves. Delicate ears, crested with a definite point, completed the look.

"Your father was an abomination. But your stepfather's petition is one we will hear. Come." Her voice was a soft and perfectly modulated mezzo soprano that made even this simple statement nearly musical.

Thag knew that most of the men would be tenors, of course, and every woman would be somewhere in the soprano range. They all had blonde hair, whether golden or pale, healthy skin that ranged from almost-albino to nearly jet-black depending on how much sun they were getting, and pale green eyes with a few violet or golden exceptions just for what little variety these people could stand.

Ages ago, near the birth of the world-shards, some people with just enough magical talent to craft their own bodies, but not nearly enough to become dragons, and no skill for wizardry, had decided to make themselves "perfect" – and they had stuck to it long enough to end up really pretty, very physically competent (at sport or war), essentially immortal, and neurotically narcissistic. Vanity didn't even begin to cover the depth of their self-love!

Ignoring her insult, Thag followed the woman to their village at the center of the island. Their leader's log cabin, a large, crudely built structure that tried to hide it's primitive construction behind layer after layer of decorations, carvings, inlays, and just plain paint, was situated on top of a small hill that gave it a good view of the island and the surrounding waters.

The structure was a bit over a hundred feet long and half that wide. It was easily twenty feet tall, but much of the height was the steeply-sloped roof of split logs and wooden shakes. There were a number of large wooden poles standing up around it, with torches mounted on them. The walls had numerous unglazed windows with wooden shutters to keep out the weather.

Thag mused to himself that it had the best view, and the most exposure to the common seasonal storms of this region. A few miles to the south, where the rain was constant through the year, and this place would be a soggy lump instead of a building.

His escort, all one-hundred of them, bowed low as they approached the lights around the structure. Simple torches with wrought iron covers to keep the rain off cast unreliable light all around the area. Though elves have excellent night vision, they still have the human tendency to be more comfortable in the light than in the dark. Thag followed suit and bowed at the building.

The animal-hide curtain in the front doorway was pushed aside, and the light of the large bonfire in the middle of the single room cast shadows out to where they waited. Thag saw yet another young-looking elf, knew full well that they were all agelessly young, but this one had even fancier furs and leathers with even more decorations sewn onto them. Might be their king, he thought.

A musical voice called out to them, "Come in! Come in! We saw you coming and have been waiting for you."

Just saying they saw him coming was meant to be insulting. It implied a lack of stealth on his part – a skill that the elves excelled at and thus considered highly important.

Thag and the girl who had first greeted him stepped inside. The rest would wait outside. The guards would pretend they had a chance of stopping him if he wanted to make trouble. He would pretend along with them. But it was all about posturing, and everyone knew it.

Inside was a single, large room, with a small back section partially isolated by woolen curtains. The front half was lit by a large central fire. Most of the heat and some of the smoke dissipated through a vent in the roof, which also let in a steady drizzle of wind-blown rain.

The furniture was mostly carved wooden blocks. They made up for their primitive utilitarian crafting by being covered with gaudy carvings and bright paint. Most of the pictures in this house seemed to be sexual in nature, and some were quite explicit. Thag wondered whether sitting on the chair with a bas-relief of male genitalia carved in the upper surface was a punishment, a reward, or just plain sophomoric humor.

Regardless, it would be awkward, so he assumed that was the chair they'd ask him to sit on. If they ever got around to such.

The king sat on a carved throne that might once have been grand, but was fading with age, at the far end of the room. His clothing might have been splendid ages ago, but now looked like more than a few moths had benefited from it.

Thag's escort announced Thag herself, rather than waiting for one of the courtiers to do it. Clearly, but not loudly, she proclaimed, "The abomination-spawn known as Thag the Terrible Monster wishes to speak with the immortal king of the Perfect People. It has asked the boon of an audience with the royalty that spurns all lesser races."

The king gestured for one of his servants and whispered to her. Thag pretended he couldn't hear him from across the room. "Get me something to eat," was the gist of it.

A courtier standing halfway to the king, near the bonfire, responded to the announcement. "Royalty is busy and should not be disturbed by crude things seeking the wisdom and might of the Most Perfect. What business does Llwddan's pet have with the Exalted?"

The woman, who still hadn't even given Thag her name, turned to Thag and asked, in a quiet voice, "What business could you possibly have with our king?"

Thag didn't modulate his voice at all. Everyone with ears in a hundred yards heard him easily. "You're all going to die in a few years if you don't help me right now. Every ... single ... one ... of ... you!" he emphasized carefully.

From across the room, the king shouted, "How dare you threaten us!" He was going to continue, but Thag yelled back, and everyone was too busy trying to get their ears to stop ringing to do much else.

"SILENCE!" Thag shouted, thoroughly fed up with the whole thing!

The heavy wool curtains at the other end of the building shook to his enormous voice! Elves, with their fine hearing and subtle senses, cringed and cowered from him.

He strode over to the royal throne, roughly shoving several guards out of the way, and stood defiantly in front of the king – a living tower overbearing a gilded child!

"I will NOT coerce your help!" said Thag. "But I will demand that you either help *immediately,*" the roof shook from his voice, "with soldiers and arms, or that you let me be on my way and stop wasting my time! Our *world* is at stake, and *you know it!* And you cowards would play childish games with me while brave people die to save a world you are as tied to as they?

"My father would disown all of you!"

"If you won't lift a finger to save your own hide, and the hides of your people, because you're too busy playing little games for children, then give your people permission to make their own choice!" He lectured the king, his voice still full of fury.

He turned his back on the king and looked at the rest of the elves in the room, and a few who were just barely brave enough to be looking in through the curtained doorway or the open windows. "Any of you who wish to live, who are willing to fight for your own lives, meet me at the dryad oak on the west cliff. Bring weapons if you have them. Bring courage and valor if you have those. Leave childhood and petty games behind. You have one hour!"

Without a glance at the king cringing in fear behind him, Thag strode from the room. In his rush and fury, he ripped the hide from the doorway and threw it to the ground. Elves dodged from his path, sure he would crush them if they stood their ground.

A few of the armed guards and soldiers looked around at their companions, and then set out to follow Thag.

A few fathers and mothers looked at their children, and then went to their huts for weapons and followed Thag.

A trickle of armed men and women, all of them graceful in their ageless beauty, swept silently onto Thag's path, their feet light and their hearts heavy. They knew what he was talking about. They knew there was small or no chance of success. But they looked at their friends, their lovers, or their young children, and they knew they had no choice at all.

It was a somber gathering at the dryad tree. Thag was still fuming, and none dared approach him or incur his wrath. The dryad stood silently, her branches ruffling slightly in the sea-breeze. The elves, still in shock, whispered greetings when they saw friends they had hoped for or had not expected. Their mood was dark and their voices subdued.

The light of the rising moon silvered the forms of almost two-hundred elves when Thag decided it was time.

His voice quiet but firm, Thag told them, "You know the way of it. Accept the dryad's gift and we will all see each other when we meet her sister. It is bright day there, so cover your eyes when you step through. Trust."

The elves closed their eyes and stepped to the tree, reaching silently and blindly but surely to touch the bark.

Thag reached over an elf's head and rested his hand on the trunk. "It is time," he said simply.

Silver moonlight shone down on an empty cliff-top on an island in a faraway sea, lighting the view for an ancient dryad tree that stood alone.

Chapter 20: *War and Wizardry*

Brad and Drew were making love when she suddenly pushed him off of her. "Again?" he asked, not expecting a reply.

Because giant oak trees don't talk, and Drew was busy being one of those.

Brad knew what to expect, or thought he did. Thag's recruits had been trickling in for the last couple of weeks. A pair of druids were first, followed by a small family of some sort of giants – they didn't speak any languages anyone else did, so they stayed by themselves in the camp. A small troupe of orc warriors showed up, but nobody seemed to trust them and they made their own camp.

By ones and twos and small groups, the camp had grown till it was nearly a small village.

All had arrived by means of dryad passages, whatever those should be called. The way Brad understood it, someone who trusted a dryad completely, who was willing to sign their whole life over to the dryad and do whatever was asked of them, could somehow be transported from one dryad to another, across any distance in the world. It wasn't immediate, if he understood Drew correctly. Sometimes it would take days to cross even short distances. Distance apparently didn't matter, just trust.

But that meant that Drew periodically had to drop whatever she was doing and turn into a tree so people could "step through her" and arrive.

Most of his own time was spent growing trees and bushes. They had the whole length of the river covered in light forest by this time! A feat he could never have done alone, but Drew was able to amplify what he did with plants. Their groves and berry bushes and a whole garden of vegetables, was feeding everyone.

The trees also made up a fairly good defensive wall, per Duke Antain. With Drew animating and guiding them, the trees themselves were a formidable army – no mobility, but they could crush armored men in the grasp of their strong branches and twisting roots. Not enough to stop the horde that crept closer to them every day, but enough to make taking this place bloody costly!

As they all reasoned, if that was all they could do, they could at least do that!

So Brad was braced for a few arrivals. He speculated to himself about who they would be this time, and whether it would be more than the prior record of ten people at once.

And he was caught completely by surprise when he was suddenly surrounded by dozens of the most amazing people he had ever seen! Hundreds of them!

Towering over their heads was a sight he hadn't even dared hope would be there! "Thag! Over here!" he shouted in joy, waving his arms above his head even though he knew Thag could easily see him over the height of all these short people!

Brad had a tendency to think of anyone less than his own six-foot-four as "short".

"Brad! Hello!" Thag rumbled, pleased to see his friend.

Elves stepped out of his way as he strode over. "I knew from the dryads that you were here, but I don't know much else. Where is everyone? How is it all going?"

Brad knew what Thag really meant. "She's in some sort of cave, over in the cliffs. I can show you where, even if I can't see it myself." He knew he didn't have to say who he meant.

Thag smiled and his eyes gleamed. "She's in the cave! That's wonderful!"

Before Brad could say another word, Thag took off running straight for the cliff. It was less than a mile, but Brad was huffing as he arrived, just in time to see Thag disappear right into the face of the cliff! Just like Shina kept doing!

He crouched over, hands on knees, trying to catch his breath. "How the hell do they do that?" he muttered to himself, between gasps of air.

He was in good shape, but trying to keep up with a sprinting Thag was too much for even an athlete like Brad.

Once again, Brad wondered if his friend really understood what it was like for the rest of the world. How could he? Brad could keep up with a running horse and be fresh at the end of the day. Thag could leave him so far in his dust that Brad had no idea how much faster the half-dragon could really go. There was no point in racing against him!

He wandered to the particular piece of cliff, and pushed against it one more time. Even from inches away, he couldn't see any difference between the cliff face here and all of the rest of it. Touch and smell discerned no difference either.

He was almost surprised Thag could see it. He had half expected that he wouldn't. Since Koserana couldn't see the cave, and she was a full-on dragon, Brad had half-expected that Thag, a half-dragon, would no more see the cave than he himself did.

But, honestly, it was hard to be surprised when Thag could do something, or when he knew some obscure fact. It was more astonishing when he couldn't, or when he didn't know.

Shina was deep in the library, trying to understand the history of how the world-shards came to be, when a pale blue light appeared in mid-air a few feet from her, and a whispering, disembodied voice said, "A visitor has arrived at the main gate."

Who could that possibly be? She wondered as she set down the lesson and started for the "cave" entrance.

When she got there, the tunnel was filled with a horrifying silhouette. It was gigantic and inhuman and had glistening eyes and huge horns and claws!

Shina's shriek of "Thag!" barely got there faster than she did! She leapt into his arms and was cradled to his chest.

For a minute, they just held each other. The feel of his massive chest and overpowering arms, the texture of his skin, the scent that meant safety and love and home to her! These filled her senses and reveling in it was enough without words.

She felt the fear, the self-doubt, the omnipresent apprehension and uncertainty melt out of her, and realized she was crying on his shoulder from relief!

"I'm here, Little One," he rumbled as he held her. "I'm here."

She wiped her eyes with her hand and told him to set her down. "I must look like a mess," she commented.

Thag smiled at her. She was wearing worn-out travel clothing, covered in dust, and had streaks on her face from her tears. Her eyes were red and her hair was mussed. "You look beautiful," he pronounced, and meant it with perfect sincerity.

Suddenly she perked up. "You can come in here!" she exclaimed.

"Of course. I'm enough of a dragon to do that."

"But Koserana can't even see the gate!" she insisted. "And definitely can't come in. To all of them," she gestured towards the door and the people outside it, "this is solid rock. Including Koserana, and she's more of a dragon than you are!"

Thag shook his head "no". "She's too young. This is actually a different shard in here. She can't travel through the Void yet, so she can't come in. In a century or two, she'll be able to. I'm older than she. If I could fly, I'm old enough that I could travel to other shard-worlds. This one, I just have to step into – no flying necessary."

He continued, "You should be able to carry other people in here through the gate. They wouldn't be able to leave without your help, but you should be able to help someone step through the door if you want to. Wizards can do that, even without learning their craft. Or so I've read.

"That's one of the differences between wizards and dragons. Dragons can only use that magic on themselves, wizards can affect others. So you can carry others across the Void, while I can't."

Shina thought for a moment. "What about sorcerers? Like my dad? They use magic on other people. Does that make them wizards?" She paused. "But Koserana can do that, too. I've seen her, and I've felt the emotions. Isn't that magic?"

"No, Little One. Magic uses the power that created the shards – the energy in the Void that the gods used to create the worlds themselves. It's about creating and changing and building rules, or breaking them. Sorcery is different. It follows the rules of the world, it doesn't break them.

"Eating isn't magic, but it changes things. Sorcery is no more magic than eating is. Does that help clarify it?"

"I think so. It wouldn't have before I started studying in the library here. Have you seen that? It's got more books than anywhere!" replied Shina.

She grabbed his hand and led him down the tunnel excitedly. "You'll love it in here, Thag! More books than … tons of books! You'll love it!" She was so excited she didn't realize she was repeating herself.

Thag let her pull him to the main room of the old school – the library. Along the way, they passed several of the crystal servants that still worked to keep the place orderly and clean. Vaguely humanoid collections of floating crystals, animated long-since by the apprentice wizards of the school, they were what had alarmed Shina in the entry-hall the first time she came in. They walked about, cleaning, polishing, tidying up, and every step made a faint chiming, clattering, clacking noise.

There were several of them around. Thag had never learned how many, despite having spent several decades in the school's library when he was growing up. He still wasn't sure if there was any means of communicating with them or directing them in any way. Over time, he'd learned to step around or ignore them, just like the rest of the furniture in this enchanted place.

Once they were out of the entry-tunnel, and the damage caused by gnomish weapons during the ancient war, the school was as marvelous as it had ever been.

It was all cut directly into solid rock, which had been carved on every surface with a thousand bas-relief images of exquisite detail. Nature-scenes where the trees and grass had every detail of every leaf were interspersed with thousands of scenes of the peoples of hundreds of shard-worlds. Some of the scenes were cut so deeply into the surface of the walls that they formed mini-alcoves filled with detailed statuary. Some were barely scratched into the hard, stone surface.

Thag knew many were historical or legendary images from various worlds, but he was also sure that many were fanciful imaginings of the many artists who had been attracted to the school over the millennia it had been open. Wizards, he knew, tended to be creative folks. It was part of what made them who they were.

Nowhere did the halls feel like cold stone. The stone felt alive and warm and evoked feelings of beauty and sanctuary and safety. Despite the century-of-centuries since it had been abandoned, the school was still a living place, and it welcomed those strangelings who could cross its bizarre threshold.

The many rooms, both the instruction halls and the quarterings, were mostly paneled in ancient wood, preserved through the ages by the tireless crystal servants. A light wood, beautifully polished to a golden-brown sheen, covered much of the walls in those spaces.

The abundant furniture – hundreds of chairs, chaises, Roman couches, tables, bookshelves, podiums, and so on – was mostly made of a darker wood, much of it with polished bronze fittings or details. Thag was unsure how the soft cloth coverings and padding on some of it had survived the ages, but assumed it was some magical effect of this place. He'd also found that the delicate-seeming chairs and such could easily support his immense weight, and had concluded that wizards must like to make things durable.

The lighting was provided by small sparks that floated through the air and followed people around. They would settle at a perfect angle for reading, or above the head for conversations – so they would light up both faces without glaring in either person's eyes. Thag wasn't sure what they did when someone wanted to sleep, but maybe he could ask Shina if she'd been in here overnight. He had observed often enough that most people like it to be dark when they try to sleep.

The lights followed him around even though he had no need of them. For Shina, of course, they were crucial.

Many of the rooms had illusionary windows – squares or rectangles on the walls that showed outdoor scenes from dozens of worlds. Thag had read once how to make them change scenes, and had spent whole days just playing with them that way.

So far as he could tell, the views from them were of present time, not the world of long-ago when the school was built. Fortunately or unfortunately, all one could do was pick which world to see, and the scene would then wander randomly around – he couldn't use these to do anything as useful as spy on what Kamaia was up to.

So, while the whole school could be called a "cave" technically, it was actually more comfortable and friendly than many homes.

As always, Thag wondered what it had been like when it was full of students and instructors. Had it been a quiet, studious place? A bustling chaos of magical wonders? Had the students been serious or prankish or playful? Had it been friendly or aloof or even hostile? Was the school discipline lax or iron-fisted?

From the few history books he could partially parse out, he gleaned that it had been in operation for thousands of years before the gnome wars, so he suspected that its character had changed over time as the people in it changed. But wizards were immortal, so perhaps the culture had been as slow-changing as that of elves or dragons.

He wondered about these things every time he went there.

Shina, tugging his hand impatiently, led him into the main library. He assumed she would take him to one of the bookshelves, but instead she pulled him to one of the displays.

A shelf, chest-high to a normal man, with hundreds of gems set on velvet padding. There were emeralds and rubies by the dozen, a few large diamonds, and the top shelf had a half-dozen large sapphires.

It was pretty, but Thag had seen it before and found it merely pleasant. Not like the wealth of ancient books on hundreds of shelves all around him.

"Thag," Shina said almost breathlessly, her eyes wide with a kind of awe. "Look at these!"

He looked at them. They were pretty enough, he guessed. Some were large enough for ornate pendants, some so tiny they would be best in clusters on a ring or brooch. They were all cut as angle-edged squares or rectangles, flat on top and bottom, with octagonal surfaces. He presumed that a jeweler would have a name for such a cut, but he didn't know what it would be. Despite his draconic heritage, he personally found shiny things at most mildly distracting, instead of fascinating as Chalkos found them.

Shina saw that he was trying to be polite, rather than fascinated. "Pick one up!" she told him, pointing at the shelf.

So Thag picked one up. He picked one of the large rubies, since even those were tiny in his hands and he didn't want to drop one that was too small.

He looked at it closely. He wondered, as always, what it must look like to human eyes. To his, it was a colored rock that someone had put a large effort into cutting into a geometric shape that, so he was told, made it more sparkly when people looked at it.

He knew these were important to Shina, but he couldn't fathom how or why. Trying not to disappoint her, he looked closely and tried to be interested in it.

"Can't you hear it, Thag?"

"Hear what?" He tried holding it next to one of his ears. Nothing. He could hear Shina's beating heart, and that of the child she was bearing. This close to her, he could hear the sound of air in her lungs and the noises made by blood passing through her veins. But the stone was silent.

"Here! Give that one to me," she said.

Thag handed it to her.

Shina held it up. "This one's a ruby, or at least it's red. The red ones have knowledge about magic in them." She closed her eyes and looked like she was listening intently. "This one is about fire. Making air into fire. Lots of things about fire. I don't understand most of it. I think I could spend my whole life studying this one gem. It has that much in it!"

Thag suddenly understood. If that one gem had a lifetime of material, this shelf … it had hundreds of gems on it! Dozens were as big as that ruby! There might be more in these than in all the books in the world!

And they didn't depend on being able to read languages that were dead millennia ago! Not if Shina could understand even part of it!

Now he was excited! *This* was treasure!

"What about the other colors?" he asked…

Brad waited a few minutes, then decided they were too busy to come out and say hello or whatever.

In their shoes, he'd be in there quite a while himself, he knew. Just the I-can't-believe-it's-only-been-a-couple-of-months kissing would take quite a while, if Brad knew anything about anything. So he went back to where Drew was surrounded by the incoming crowd.

These new people were milling around, looking a bit lost. By the gods they were all so beautiful! They were dressed like a primitive tribe, but their weapons all looked top-quality to him. It gave a weird juxtaposition of art, function, beauty and crudity. He'd never seen a more ornate or deadly-looking longsword than the one a woman was carrying, but she herself was dressed in coarsely-crafted doehide that looked like it had seen better days and a few too many moths besides.

From their universal beauty and grace, Brad knew these were elves. He wondered if they spoke any languages in common with him.

"Hey there," he said to the first one he came to. He was just under six feet tall, and looked so similar to everyone around him that Brad would have had a terrible time picking him out of a crowd. The elf ignored him completely and walked away.

A dozen attempts later, Brad was pretty sure they all disliked him for some reason. He was used to that from men – even the ones who didn't know he was a half-orc usually instinctively recognized him as a competitor. But even the women were treating him like something they had found on the bottom of their shoes, and that was new to him!

Finally, Drew found him in the crowd. She looked just as she always did, and was as nude as she always was. While that usually enticed him, she actually looked plain compared to the elves.

He knew he'd seen someone like them before, but he couldn't remember who or where.

Drew took his arm in her hand and started to pull him out of the clearing. "I no like elvishes. They are rude. We are going."

Just then, a ripple of attention spread through the elvish crowd. Something on the other side of the clearing, towards the camp, had their attention. And they did not look pleased.

Brad had a brief glimpse of golden hair cut short on the sides, and suddenly knew exactly where he'd seen elf-like looks before. He was already nodding to himself before he got a better look at Koserana as she strutted through the crowd of elves.

Every one of them, man or woman, looked daggers at her. Even in this crowd of stunning beauty and superhuman sexiness, she stood out like a bonfire in a dark night.

The elves' motions were fluidly graceful, but Koserana's strut made them look like they were stumbling around blind and drunk. And she did it effortlessly!

She was back in her translucent green dress and golden jewelry that was her "best look". Her hair was perfect. Her makeup was somehow subtle and stunning at the same time. The elves looked like pale imitations, or maybe like children playing dress-up in their parents' clothing.

He could almost hear her purring as she sashayed through the crowd.

And all of her tattoos were of elves being tortured or killed.

"Hellfire!" Brad ground out under his breath. Was she trying to start a war right here? He leapt into action, throwing a cloak around Koserana's shoulders and then grabbing her forcefully.

She was strong enough to break his grip, but she went along with him as he dragged her back towards the invisible cave.

"Damn it, Koserana! You can't provoke them like that! Thag brought them. He needs them for something. Don't anger them and chase them off!"

Koserana's eyes went wide! "Thag? Thag is here?" She sniffed as they got to the cave entrance area.

"He *is* here!" She turned to Brad, desperation in her eyes. "Please don't tell him what I did! Please!"

Brad felt an almost overwhelming sense of need and pity thrown at him. His totem blocked most of it, but he could feel her trying to force him to help her.

"Koserana! Knock it off! Or I will tell Thag! Stop trying to control me!"

The pressure cut off suddenly, and it was just a superhumanly-beautiful, almost-naked young woman holding onto him desperately and begging him with her eyes.

The trials the spirits sent his way!

He deliberately let go of her and stepped away. His voice was softer as he said, "I won't tell Thag. But I can't guarantee none of them will," he gestured vaguely in the direction of the elves. "Did you think of that?"

Her shoulders slumped and the life went out of her face. Her voice was tiny, childlike, "No."

"What's the history there? You didn't act like that for any of the other people Thag sent."

Koserana looked up at him. She still looked like she was about to cry, but maybe he could help her if he got her to talk about it.

"They made me their pet," she said.

Brad nodded for her to continue.

"Elves killed my mother and father while I was still an egg. They stole me and my brothers and sisters. Everyone else died before they were born, because they didn't treat us very well. It was so very, very cold!"

Brad wasn't sure if she meant it was cold when she was in her egg. He wasn't sure even dragons could remember that early in their lives. But it sure sounded like it. And he knew enough to doubt his doubts.

Koserana continued. "When I was born, they put a collar on me. It made me do what they wanted.

"The elves were bandits in the desert. They used me to help them raid caravans and camps.

"At first, when I was really small, they just made me fly around and describe what I had seen. Later, they made me fight for them.

"I killed people! I can smell them burning and hear their screams. I can taste a woman I bit to death with my fangs." She looked horrified. Brad had seen her kill on several occasions in their travels, and she had never seemed reserved about it. More excited by the thrill than anything else. Which one was the subterfuge? Maybe Thag would know.

"Thag says I was about sixty years old when a king killed off the bandits and I escaped.

"I ripped the collar off, and it burned my skin and almost killed me. But it's gone now!"

Brad remembered the scars he'd seen the few times Koserana didn't cover her neck, and again when she was Chalkos he'd seen those. And the chains that covered Varlad's neck when she was disguised as an orc made sense now too.

"The elves never knew I could change shapes. If they had, I'm sure they would have made me do that too," she shuddered at the idea. Brad wasn't sure if she was assuming they would have raped her, or something else, but he knew that she was upset by whatever she was imagining them doing. He knew what humans or orcs would have done, and assumed elves would be similar enough.

Brad took her into his arms and comforted her. He wouldn't tell Thag about her provoking the elves. But if was any judge of character, he would bet the elves would complain. A lot.

He'd always heard about how wonderful and amazing and perfect elves are. How they were beautiful beyond compare and immortal. He'd never wondered what that would do to their heads and hearts.

For the moment, he took Koserana into his arms and just held her.

Duke Antain saw the new arrivals and was impressed. He'd heard of elves, of course, but he'd never seen one before. His teachers had told him they lived in the Eastlands, past the Great Ocean, and that they were extremely insular, even xenophobic, about dealing with humans.

They looked well-armed at least. A couple of hundred armed people would make a welcome addition to his tiny army, of course, but he wasn't sure what Thag thought even this number would be able to do against the giant horde that was coming for them.

Chalkos scouted a couple of times a day, and reported to Shina, who forwarded the information to him. He knew the oncoming army was at almost a quarter of a million soldiers. Their approach was slowing every mile, as their supply lines got longer and longer, but, inevitably, it would be a battle of hundreds against hundreds-of-thousands.

They'd be outnumbered a thousand to one, and there was nothing they could do about that. The more people Thag added to their side of the equation, just meant more would die in a hopeless battle in this desolate place.

The forest-line that Brad and Drew had been growing at the river-moat would help a little. It was too long a line for this small an army to hold for any meaningful amount of time, but every bit of cover and defense was welcome.

They had grown a miraculous line of large oaks with heavy thorn-bushes under them. The enemy would have to burn it to get through. Till they did that, it would provide excellent cover for his archers to annoy the attackers.

Unfortunately, he knew that "annoy" was the best they'd be able to do. His men were armed with mage-forged arbalests, but even those would only do so much. If they killed a hundred men each, they'd still be overwhelmed in a matter of minutes.

After the enemy fired the forest, he'd have to retreat with any survivors. After that, it was just light woods and then the cliff face. He estimated it would take less than a day for the attackers to burn their way through Brad's forest-line, and then the battle and war would be over almost as soon as it was joined. Maybe an hour at most, depending on how much running they did versus how much fighting.

Even running wouldn't help much if the enemy had wolf-totem spirit-warriors, and he knew they did.

Chalkos might escape, since she could fly away and didn't need supplies to survive crossing the wastelands.

A few clever and lucky people might escape by stealing the horde's supplies and following their line to the living lands around. But the odds were against that by huge margins.

He knew enough about Kamaia and her horde to be certain that he himself was doomed no matter how he tried to cut it. They'd see to that, since he had not only failed her but had even betrayed her.

All his ambitions and plans would come to nothing out here in the most ancient battleground in the world. It was a good place to die! And he'd make them pay as much as he possibly could before they took him! It was an empty gesture, he knew, but it was all he had left, so he'd make it grandly and with as much style and poise as he could muster.

The elves explored the area of the ruins and the defensive line Brad and Drew had been growing, and then settled themselves into the campsite.

Their way of settling in was to simply push other people's tents or bedrolls out of the way and take over wherever they felt like it.

The first trouble came when an elf took food one of Antain's men had been preparing, and started eating it. The elf didn't ask, didn't speak, didn't even seem to notice that the soldier had been about to eat it himself. He just walked up, took the food, and sat down to eat it.

The duke had to have his men restrain their offended comrade to avoid a fight.

"Different people, different customs, Milvich! He probably doesn't speak any language we know, and maybe he thought you were a cook or something!"

Within an hour, it was plain to everyone there that the elves didn't care about anyone but themselves, and they were willing to ignore anyone they didn't feel like pushing out of their way. A dozen fights were narrowly avoided.

The duke moved his camp, and everyone who wasn't an elf, away from the spring at the center of the woods, over to where Shina's "cave" seemed to be. Trips to get water were fraught with risks of being pushed, bumped into, or brushed aside, but it did minimize opportunities for fights.

Finally, as it was beginning to get dark at the end of the day, Thag and Shina came out of the cave.

Antain hadn't known Thag was back! That might help with the elves at least.

The duke jumped up from where he'd been sitting, and then bowed gracefully. "Your Highness. My lord Thag. A minute of your time, if it pleases you."

He led them a little aside, so they could speak with some privacy.

"We've got a problem, my lord," he addressed himself to Thag. Shina was officially in charge, but Antain knew who really called the shots and solved the problems. "While I appreciate the additions you have sent to reinforce my few men, some of them may not integrate well into our command structure. We'll need discipline to survive even the few minutes we should be able to buy with these forces. I'm afraid that may not be easy with some of the recent arrivals."

The duke couldn't really read Thag's inhuman face, but he got the idea the giant monster was amused.

"The elves, right?" Thag cut straight to the chase.

"Yes, my lord. The elves. They seem ...." He wasn't sure how to continue without questioning Thag's judgement in sending the elves to join them in the first place.

"Fight their leader," suggested Thag, in a voice that conveyed this was an obvious, simple solution, and an everyday thing. He might as well have said, "The sun is up during the day" was what his tone carried.

Duke Antain paused. Then, slowly, "Fight their leader?"

Thag explained. "Elves are arrogant and vain. It takes a special sort of obsessive narcissism to become one.

"They aren't born elvish. They have the look, but not the indwelt magic that makes an elf an elf. When they reach adulthood, they have to be able and willing to use magic to turn themselves into elves. If they fail, they are exiled, and die in a normal human-span of years.

"Their particular magic requires a level of obsessive self-worship that most people can't even begin to approach. Those who succeed at the transformation are affirmed in their belief that they are creation's own perfect people.

"To them, everyone else is a failure. They believe everyone would be an elf if they could. Thus, anyone who isn't an elf 'just isn't good enough', by that logic.

"What they respect is perfection. If you can beat their leader in a fight, then you must be an even more perfect warrior than she is. They won't *like* you, but they *will* follow you in war if you can do that.

"If you lose, you'll be dead and your men will be expected to serve the elvish leader.

"Can you accept that, or will you bow to them and let their leader take the reins?"

The duke, always a proud man, didn't hesitate. "A duel to the death? With the winner taking the loser's right-of-command? I can accept that." He thought for a moment. "What's the etiquette for this? Do I send an emissary to deliver a challenge? Are there limits on the fight or rules they will expect me to follow? Will I have to use mortal weaponry?"

Thag shook his head. "Use your mage-forged weapons and armor. Anything else would just be suicide for you. As far as etiquette and rules go, just go over there armed and ready and start a fight with her. They know who you are. They'll be expecting it and will accept it.

"The only rule is that you have to fight alone. If your men help you, hers will help her. That makes it a war instead of a dominance duel.

"The first to deliver a killing blow wins. But keep in mind, you probably can't actually kill her. Decapitation might do it, but stabbing her through the heart won't. It would count as winning, though. They enjoy that kind of thing."

Shina interrupted. "The elf would enjoy being stabbed through the heart?"

Thag looked at her. "Yes. She'd survive it, but it would be memorable. That matters to them." When he saw that Shina and Antain didn't understand him, he continued.

"Can you remember the last time you were really bored? When maybe a whole day, or worse a week, went by without anything interesting happening?" They both nodded.

"Now imagine that day or week being a century. And then a thousand years of nothing interesting.

"Imagine being so physically perfect that sports and games are almost meaningless. They all run about the same speed, and it's very, very fast. They're all about as strong as each other. And they have thousands of years to perfect athletic skills, so no-one is much better than anyone else at anything.

"Imagine hearing the same songs and poems and stories for thousands of years.

"Imagine there is nothing new in the world that you haven't seen a hundred times before. You've done things that nobody but an elf can do. You've explored every possible variation on sex, art, violence, food, and everything else you can think of.

"And imagine that combined with a personality that sees itself as inherently perfect. When you're perfect, any change makes you worse, not better.

"That's how bored the average elf is. How frustrated with worlds that pass by – years turning to ages to epochs, and nothing is new enough to be interesting.

"Most of them turn to violence and cruelty and arrogance after a while. A few, like my stepfather, try to do impossible things – like raising a half-dragon, half-troll to make it anything but a monster. Many end up suiciding from sheer boredom and ennui.

"Losing a fight and taking a mortal wound is extremely rare for them. They can survive most injuries, and they don't get sick. It takes extreme violence to kill an elf." Thag looked sad as he said the last piece.

Shina had almost forgotten that Thag was raised by an elf, that he was talking about people he viewed as near-kin. She wondered what horrible violence had killed the man he thought of as a father. She wasn't used to comforting him, it was usually the other way around, but she reached out and took his hand in hers. He gave her a grateful glance.

Antain pondered for a minute. "It would be better if I didn't actually kill her, right? She's their best warrior, by some tiny margin. If I understood you correctly. That means she'll be useful in the battle we face. Am I correct, my lord?"

Thag nodded agreement.

"What about their weapons?" he asked. "I've never seen anything quite like those. Do they make them? Are they similar to the mage-forged steel I use?"

Thag shook his head "no". "Wizard-work. Their weapons are from the gnome wars. They can cut normal steel like butter, and they never break or rust or get dull. But no elf would let a weapon do any of his fighting for him."

The duke nodded his understanding. Shina was confused. "What does that mean? 'Let a weapon do his fighting for him?'"

Shina expected Thag to answer, but it was the duke instead. "Mage-forged weapons are from the battle-mages. The weapon is an extension of the warrior's will, but it does some of the fighting for you.

"A normal sword requires great skill to use successfully. That takes training. Like your own training with the knives you wear.

"A mage-forged sword can be deadly in the hands of an untrained peasant or a raw recruit."

He took a wicked-looking poniard from a sheath on his belt and handed the weapon to Shina, hilt first. She took the knife. It felt like a quality knife to her. As good as some her father had given her when she was learning the blade as a young woman. But it didn't feel like anything more than that.

Then she looked at it the way she looked at magic, and saw a strand of force woven into the blade. It made a complex pattern through the whole weapon – too complex to follow without some study. The little bit she had learned from the gems in the school made her think it was battle-magic, rather than elemental, but she couldn't tell much more than that.

The duke drew another knife and gestured for her to stand and face him. "Decide to spar with me, your highness. If you please."

Shina did. And found her body being directed by something outside herself! The knife pushed her arms, legs, spine and head into a fighting stance with a perfection of balance and form! It was subtly building on her years of training and practice, making her better than she'd ever be on her own.

Her eyes widened as she glanced at the duke, who was also in a fighting stance. One of the masculine ones she'd been trained to identify and face.

"Now, if it please you, cross blades with me for a few practice forms."

She flowed through a few of the forms her instructors had trained her in. The blade gently guided them into a more perfect motion! She could feel it adding to her expertise!

It was fun! She could tell it would be deadly serious in a real fight, but for this sparring, it was thrilling to move just a little faster, just a little more smoothly, just a little … more!

She looked at the duke's weapon and realized it too had a weave of battle-force imbued into it. While her knife and years of muscle-memory continued the spar, she reached out with her will to look at his weapon.

The strand pulsed with intricate power as it guided him in countering her every move. It was almost like the two knives were dancing with each other, and she and duke were just parts in a magical machine.

Something she saw, or felt, a sensation she couldn't put words to, came to her and she realized that it was a two-way thing. The knife could guide her, but she could also feed her will to it.

Under the guidance of the knife and her will behind it, she became a blur of motion. Her practice thrust accelerated! Her feints and parries blazed to a pitch of speed the eye couldn't follow!

The duke, one of the best fighting men in the world, was sweating! She was besting him!

A feather-touch of her will reached out and brushed the strand of power in his blade.

Duke Antain staggered as the knife stopped supporting him, directing him! He felt the exact moment when it became simply a high-quality steel blade and lost that special edge that had made it mage-forged.

His trained reflexes, forged in a thousand battles, recovered superbly, switching gears in the blink of an eye from mage-blade-fighting to simple-fighting. But his mind whirled with confusion that staggered him. How? No mage-blade had ever failed anyone ever before!

Shina realized immediately that she was at an overwhelming advantage, and stopped the spar almost mid-form. She stepped back from the duke and gave him the formal bow of a spar well-played.

He was pale and had a desperate look on his face as he stepped back from her. She could have killed him effortlessly! He knew it, and it horrified him!

"W… what did you do?" he stammered.

Shina looked concerned and then realized how shaken he really was. "I'm so sorry, Antain. I got caught up in the magic of the knives and I didn't realize … I'm sorry."

Antain wiped cold sweat from his forehead and swallowed convulsively. He looked for a moment, perplexed, at the inert weapon in his hand. "What did you do?" He asked again, fear slowly being replaced by simple confusion.

Shina looked at Thag for guidance, but he shook his head that he couldn't help with this. So she tried to explain what she'd done. "I saw the magic in the knives, and I wondered what made it work. I realized I could make it work better if I did one thing with it. And I saw that I could affect it another way, and that way … made it go away."

Thag nodded his understanding. The duke simply looked more confused.

So Thag stepped in. "Antain, you know history and warfare. Suppose for a moment that a battle-mage, any of them, not necessarily one of the emperors, showed up here and decided to join the battle. Which side would win?"

The duke didn't have to think about that one at all. "Whichever side he joined. The other side would be wheat before a reaper in the face of a battle-mage." There was no hesitation or doubt in his mind.

Thag nodded agreement. "Yes. Now, which side would win if a great dragon joined the battle?"

The duke had seen what Chalkos could do to a small army. He imagined for a moment that she was no longer an infant and almost shuddered at the image it brought to his mind. "The dragon. Even if it fought alone against both armies and the battle-mage, I think the dragon would win."

Again, Thag agreed. "Wizards are more dangerous than dragons, Antain. And Shina is a wizard."

Shina's jaw dropped. The duke turned pale again.

"She can stop that whole army?"

"Not yet," Thag replied. "It takes centuries for a wizard to master their magic. Right now, she's a rank novice. A few hours of study, and no real practice. And no master to apprentice her.

"But magic is her birthright. All of creation is powered by magic, my good duke. She can do things, already, purely on instinct and native talent, that no battle-mage, no elf, no dragon, can imitate."

He paused for a second, to drive the point home. "Like disenchanting your blade in the middle of a fight." The duke glanced down at the weapon again, still shocked at all of this.

"Your weapons are battle-mage magic. As powerful as battle-mage workings seem to you, they're child's-play to a wizard. Any wizard. The battle-mages were made by apprentice wizards, not even by masters. Gem's undead creations could smash battle-mages as easily as you could crush a fly.

"If we can buy her the time, Shina will grow in skill and knowledge and power. She can, by herself, save our world. If we can keep her alive long enough to learn how to do it!"

He towered over the duke, driving the argument by sheer presence. "*That!* is the only thing that matters here. Shina *must* survive and must learn. She's got years before she'll be able to heal our world. We have to give her those years.

"And Kamaia will do *anything* to stop that from happening."

Thag directed the duke. "Go. Prepare for your duel with Captain Evendes. Think on what you learned here."

The duke, dismissed, started to walk away. When he'd only gone a few steps, Shina suddenly remembered his other knife. "Antain! This is yours," she said, holding the knife by the blade, hilt towards him.

He turned and looked back at her. A look crossed his face that Shina couldn't quite place. "Keep it, your majesty, please. Every time I see it on your belt, it will remind me of this. Remind me of what we're fighting for." He bowed to her, and then turned and strode away.

Shina put the mage-forged knife in her belt. Something was different about the duke, but she wasn't sure what.

"Thag," she said. "He looked … different just now. What do you think…?"

"Respect, Little One. For the first time, he respects you. Before, you were a pawn, or a figurehead. He obeyed you because it fit his plans, and because he feared me. Now, he is changing how he thinks of you.

"He's begun to see you for who you are, instead of what he can use you for. He'll fear you for a while, but it's already turning to respect. The duke is a brave man, and fear is short-lived for him."

Shina looked towards where the duke had disappeared into the trees.

"Is that good?" she asked.

"It's very good, Little One. The duke has never respected anyone but himself before now. He despises King Yonind. He fears me. You, he will learn to respect. That's an excellent thing."

Shina realized that Thag didn't mean it was good for her. It was, but her wise Thag was more concerned for the duke's well-being than for how he thought of her. She thought about what he'd said about elves and their self-worship, and what he'd just said about the duke.

But she also had other things on her mind. "Thag, we need to stop Kamaia, right?"

"Yes, of course."

"How?" she asked.

Thag shrugged and gave a little sigh. "I don't know. I honestly don't know. We can kill the body she's possessing, but that just drives her elsewhere. She'll show up again, and perhaps even worse. It may be our only option, though. Kill her over and over and over in order to buy you time to study.

"Even if we run away – have Drew pass us through the trees to the eastern continent – that will only delay her briefly. She can travel from body to body more easily and rapidly than we can travel from dryad to dryad. There are so very few dryads in this world, for one thing.

He shrugged again. "At least she can't harm you in the school. It's another shard, and she can't cross the Void. If you could spend the next ten years in there, we could send Antain and the elves and everyone on their way and you could study undisturbed. But you need to travel to see Sam so she can guide your studies. We can't stay in the school. Can't even afford to stay in Xalax much longer."

Shina thought for a minute. But she couldn't come up with any ideas either.

Chapter 21: *Trapped!*

The duke's duel with the elvish captain was an incredible thing!

Thag gave the duke one final tip, "She's faster than you, and she's been doing this since before the gnome wars." And then Antain simply walked up behind Evendes and tried to stab her in the back with his sword.

She was quietly sitting down, eating some fruit she'd actually bothered to pick for herself.

With no warning, no slightest twitch, she was suddenly a blur of motion! The duke's sword thrust hard right through where her spine had been a fraction of a second before, and hit only air!

A lesser swordsman than Duke Antain would have stumbled. Would have been thrown off by not meeting the resistance of a solid body. The duke, counting on feints within feints within tricks within misdirections, never paused!

Evendes was on the attack! Her sword appeared in her hand as if by magic, and she was weaving through the most complex patterns Shina had ever seen!

Shina had spent most of her life around master swordsmen. She had seen duels and fights and even a small battle once. She knew master-footwork, and the precision of the fighting stances and the deadly elegance of the moves and counter-moves of the practiced forms.

These two were beyond anything she'd ever seen before!

Weapons blurred and glinted in the waning sunlight and the flickering firelight of the many campfires.

Feet danced in intricate speed!

A few elves stopped what they were doing to watch. A few showed a glint of interest in their eyes. One perked his head up and gazed intently at the fight.

Attacks and counters blazed so fast even her trained eye couldn't keep up!

And then she saw what the duke was doing, and saw that the elf wasn't prepared for it!

He left his defenses open the slightest bit. Just a hint of a parry off by the slightest angle. His light chainmail presenting the tiniest of gaps.

Evendes' blade flicked like a lightning bolt and pierced soft flesh! Blood spilled! And for the barest moment, the tip of the blade caught in the bone of one of Antain's ribs!

It was enough! His mage-guided steel shot into the elf's groin, piercing arteries and muscles! Hot, bright arterial blood sprayed and Evendes staggered, losing control of her left leg.

The fight was over.

The watching elves went back to what they'd been doing. None even came over to help their champion as she fell to the ground with a wound that would kill most men horribly and painfully.

The duke, sweating and bleeding, but still standing under his own power, stepped away.

A dagger flashed through the air, thrown as Evendes collapsed! The throw was perfect. The blade sped, true and deadly, straight at the duke's eyes.

His hand was too fast to follow as he caught the blade an inch away from his face.

Evendes smiled and sat. She looked uncomfortable, but had back all the grace and beauty of an elf. Sitting on the ground, one hand holding her own intestines inside her body and pressing against her rapid blood-loss, she bowed to the duke. And fainted into an honest collapse. She would heal, given time.

Thag stepped between the combatants and gestured for Shina to attend to Antain.

The wound was smooth, cut by a blade that was more than razor-sharp. The nick in the ribs was minor. So Shina got out her medical kit and started treating him.

Then she suddenly looked at it and laughed.

"What's funny?" asked Antain. He was in some pain, and didn't like being laughed at.

"Do you know," she asked, "where I got this kit?"

He looked at her blankly.

"We stole it from you and your men after you injured Chalkos. I refilled it a few times since, but it's the same kit that your man – I don't remember his name – had for treating you."

The duke smiled at the irony and chuckled. "I would bet the whole kingdom you never expected to be healing me."

Shina smiled back. She realized that the kidnapping and escape were forgiven by both of them. It felt good to have this man's respect. She felt better about the war with him on her side and with them as friends and allies of each other.

"That should heal up in a few minutes," she told him as she finished applying the kit.

"That was a seriously stupid way to fight," said Thag from behind her. "You two were so closely matched that it worked. But you're a heavy soldier, duke. Why leave yourself in light chain, when you could have had the fight easily in the plate-armor you favor? Why that level of unnecessary guile?"

Antain looked puzzled. Shina was about to come to his defense, but he gestured for her not to.

"I don't understand, my lord. I don't have any heavy armor here. What those orcs brought with them wouldn't fit me, and wouldn't be as good as my mage-forged chain anyway. Mage-forged chain is better than a few simple metal plates."

It was Thag's turn to look confused. "What do you mean you don't have heavy armor here? Why not use your mage-forged? Why leave it as a chain when it would serve you better as plate, or even half-plate?"

When all he got was a blank look, Thag suddenly understood.

"You don't know how to shift the armor?" Thag asked.

"Shift the armor?" was all the reply he got. Antain looked very, very confused.

"Give me your gauntlet," instructed Thag, holding out his hand.

Shina wondered what was going to happen. Thag's giant hand and claws could never fit in a glove made for a man like Antain. But, of course, with magic involved, the studded-leather glove easily fit itself to Thag's hand, leaving his claws exposed even though the fingertips had been closed when Antain was wearing it.

"Now, watch," Thag directed. And the glove, formerly heavy leather with metal bands riveted to it, was suddenly a plate-steel gauntlet, with spikes over the knuckles and metal protection over the whole outside of the hand.

"And again," Thag said, and the glove was simple leather and fingerless. And then it was back to how it had been when the duke first gave it to him.

Thag took it off and handed it back to the duke.

He explained, "The trick is to practice putting your will into the armor. Demand that it take the form you want. It takes some practice, but imperial soldiers usually learned the basics in a few hours of hard work."

He stood there, the duke looking at him in awe. "You really did live in the Empire, didn't you?" asked Antain.

Thag nodded. And then suddenly looked like he'd had an idea. "Oh! You can do the same with weapons, if you like. Here I've been wondering why you carry all those extra weapons — knives and arbalests and swords and spears and all that. I guess you didn't know you can make those shift too, right?"

"You can?" asked the duke, looking at the arsenal on his belt with perplexity. "How does nobody know this?"

Thag shrugged. "The civil war against the Empire was pretty bloody and killed most of the professional soldiers of the day. Maybe none of the survivors ever knew. But …" he trailed off, staring into the distance.

"But I've seen some of Yonind's personal guards shift their weapons and armor. So they must know."

The duke cursed! Shina mentally noted some of the terms and phrases as he paced up and down, swearing and cursing in the most fluent and eloquent stream of profanity she had ever heard.

He finally wound down enough to turn to Thag. "That bastard kept this secret from his own armies! We lost good men because he didn't let them know that they could have heavier armor or better weapons if they needed them!

"Thag! Can you imagine what a properly-trained cadre of men could do with arms and armor like this! Light cloth while maneuvering for position, then medium armor and shields for the exchange of heavy-arbalest fire. Then shields and pikes to set for a charging enemy, or spears and light armor if charging them! In a set battle, shields and swords and heavy plate for the front rank, and a back-rank of men with spears or bows as needed, and light armor to move from position to position to shore up the line wherever needed. And, if the line broke, heavy armor to reform it, or light cloth for a fast retreat!"

He was pacing and excited, a light in his eyes and a spring in his step. Shina realized this was the duke in his best element, planning battles and wars.

Thag rumbled, "I don't have to imagine it, Lord Antain. I've seen armies like that. I've fought with and against them. When both sides have that flexibility, it's the better general who wins. When only one has it, it's hardly even a battle."

The duke, more animated and excited than Shina had ever seen him before, simply said, "Teach us!"

Shina left Thag showing Antain's men how to do tricks with their armor and weapons. A lot of very excited men playing with their shiny new toys, with one adult teaching them the rules of the deadly-serious game of mage-war.

She wandered into the school and decided to look a few things up. Taking one of the diamond index-gems, she found what she was looking for and got the two relevant gemstones for what she wanted.

Rather than sit alone in the library, she wanted to be around Thag, so she went outside and sat near the newly appointed training grounds and studied.

An hour later, his young students making progress in learning new ways to make themselves clank and clatter, Thag came over and sat down beside her, leaning up against the tree she was sitting under.

"What are you up to, Little One? You look a little alarmed about something."

"Thag, how were you planning on leaving here?" Shina asked.

"Same way most of us arrived, dryad paths. Why?"

Shina got a pained look on her face. "Because, according to this gemstone, wizards can't use dryad paths. I looked it up."

He looked confused. "What do you mean, 'can't use dryad paths?' All you have to do is trust the dryad with your life and any two dryads can move you around."

"Gem theorized that it was because wizards' wills work differently than other people. Something about conduits and the Void, but I don't really understand that part yet. It blocks those paths. And a few other things, too. But those aren't relevant right now."

"Gem? You have some of his theories there?" Thag was very excited. Fragments of bits of books written on Gem were all he'd ever been able to find. One of the two most powerful wizards ever to live, and they didn't even know what his real name was, just the nickname "Gem".

Shina nodded. "These sapphires," she indicated the one she was holding. "They're his. Like a diary. He talks about lots of things in them."

Thag sat and thought for a few minutes. Shina knew that look, and didn't disturb him. Koserana, curious about the noises from the clanking armor, came over and joined them, but she too knew Thag's pensive look, so she sat next to Shina and just held hands with her silently.

He was still looking inwards when he started to speak again. "I'm still not sure how we'll escape Kamaia and her army. If we can disable her, the army will fall apart. Too many clans with too many feuds in too great a proximity to each other. She's all that's holding that together. But I don't know what we can do about it.

"However, assuming we figure something out, or get lucky, or whatever, I think we'll be able to get out of here without too much difficulty.

"We can send the duke and his men on their way. The elves will leave for their homeland, or might go with the duke now that he's their war-leader. Either way, they can all travel through the dryad paths.

"We three, and maybe Brad if he wants to, or maybe not if he wants to stay with Drew, can travel through the wastes without too much difficulty. I still have my soup-bowl, and that will work for food and drink. And if there aren't armies involved, Chalkos and I can protect you as much as needed till we get to the eastern lands.

"It appears you can take the most important part of the library with you," he nodded at the gem Shina was holding. "So that works better than I hoped. It will definitely be needed when we get to Sam.

"I was worried about that part. If we had to travel to her, and then come back here, and keep traveling back and forth as she directs your studies, that would be rough, if not impossible. But if you can take the gems with you, you can study in her tower and that will be the best of all options."

Shina interrupted. "Thag, you keep mentioning Sam. You say she can help me study. Is she a wizard? If so, why do you need me?"

"She's not a wizard. She's … well … you'll have to meet her to really get what she is. But she's not a wizard. But the first wizard-school in this world is her home, and she's been around thousands of wizards going through their apprenticeships, and masters doing their own studies.

"She doesn't do wizard-magic herself. But she knows the sequence of training, and can answer questions that come up, if another apprentice ever asked something similar or anything like that. She knows the practices and training-drills you'll need to do, and what the old masters looked for to make sure apprentices were doing them right.

"But she doesn't travel. So she can't come here. So we have to go to her."

Shina realized that Thag probably had no idea how mysterious and convoluted that sounded. She wasn't sure what most of that meant, but it sounded like another immortal, and that was about right for how things seemed to be working out in her life.

She was mortal, surrounded by immortals, and somehow she was still the important one. She was beginning to believe some of it – she had wrecked the duke's knife after all, and gone into the school, and she could learn from the gems when nobody else could. But it was still overwhelming enough that she tried to leave the bigger concept alone to avoid being crushed by it.

She knew she'd never be a master wizard. Thag had said several times that it took centuries, if not millennia, of study and practice to get to that point. But she hoped that she could somehow learn enough in the few years they had. Enough to heal the world.

And maybe she'd be able to learn some more before she died – she was young and, fate-allowing, might have enough decades left to learn adequate magic to be able to do some good with it.

Thag continued from where she'd interrupted him. "So, if we can somehow deal with Kamaia, we might be able to travel overland, and over the straights, to get to the eastern continent. From there, it'll be more dangerous than over here, but we have a chance. The three of us crossed the northlands well enough, and the eastern continent isn't that much more dangerous."

Shina wasn't exactly sure how Thag measured "more dangerous". There weren't many things that threatened him. But she had faith in him. If they could survive Kamaia, and delay her enough to get away with the gems, she was happy to assume they might be able to get to Sam's place. And to hope that she might have time to do something for the world.

One step at a time, she reminded herself. Thag had told her a long time ago, "If you have to walk a long journey or a short journey, you do them both one step at a time. The most important thing is to actually take the steps." Thinking that seemed to help.

The first step was to try to figure out how to defeat Kamaia.

But that seemed like the first step off the edge of a very high cliff…

The weeks crawled by.

Duke Antain was forging his men, the elves, and the sundry individuals Thag had called on for help, into a cohesive military unit. As he discovered the abilities of each, he actually got excited about the upcoming battle.

"It will still be a massacre, my lord Thag," he said at dinner one day. "But we'll bloody their noses badly before we all die!" He was genuinely smiling, and some of the elves laughed joyously as he said it.

The spare mage-forged weapons, from when Antain and his men thought they needed to carry one of each, they distributed to those who felt they could put them to use. One of the elves, out of purest ennui, decided to use one. He said it felt strange, and some of the other elves decided to try it.

In the end, only the one decided to keep using it. "It's not so good a sword as what the wizards gave me when we fought the gnomes, but it's a far better dagger than my sword will ever be!" he quipped.

Shina studied. She woke early and studied while she broke her fast and bathed. She studied through the day, eating again only when Thag reminded her to, and stayed awake nights till her head drooped and her eyes burned.

Thag, alert to her condition, held her back. "Our son needs you to sleep, Little One," he gently reminded her a few times. She almost grew to resent the unborn child for forcing her to cut back from what would otherwise have been self-destructive behavior. But she couldn't hate Thag's child. She loved Thag too much for that, and was so very proud that he loved her.

Koserana, with no role but flying scout a few times a day, took to comforting Shina as much as possible. Shina would study, and then spend hours trying to sort her new knowledge out by discussing it with the young dragon. Koserana didn't know much about magic, but she was at least a sympathetic ear, and didn't have Thag's duties as de-facto ruler of a tiny kingdom. Thag had to mediate disputes, translate a dozen languages between strange people, and help with the battle-planning and the training, and had few hours every day for her.

He tried to spend time with her. But every time there was any slightest emergency, everyone came looking for him to sort it out. At all hours of the day and night, he had to be available for a million and one details of their lives.

Shina accepted that. His ability to sort things out and help people resolve their disputes and problems was a large part of what she loved about him. But she was very grateful for Koserana's constant company nonetheless.

"Just when I think I understand something in this," she complained one time to her friend about the gem-books, "right then, I always find something on top of it that doesn't make sense!"

Koserana, more thoughtful than usual that day, replied, "Maybe you're studying it out of order or something. Don't try to understand the most advanced stuff. Just understand what you can for right now. Thag says Sam will be able to help sort out the rest of it."

She added, "If we get to Sam and she can help, then you'll understand it the way it's meant to be understood. If we all die in the battle with Kamaia, it won't matter that magic is too complicated. If we survive, it won't be too complicated after you understand it. Right?"

While it wasn't the most coherent method for study ever suggested, and while the description was far from Thag's carefully thought out lectures, it at least put the subject in perspective. Shina laughed for the first time in days. "Yes. Okay. If we're all dead in a week, it won't matter that the guy who wrote this gem is a bad teacher. I can live with that. Well, or not, I guess, if we're all dead."

Koserana laughed, and Shina felt better after that. She still studied as if her life depended on it, since she was pretty sure it did, but she relaxed a little and just focused on the things that seemed to make at least a little sense to her.

Two days before Kamaia's horde was expected to arrive, Shina came running up to Thag shouting excitedly, "I can make fire!"

Thag smiled broadly. "Show me."

So she did. It was a pale flickering thing, about what a small candle would make. But it was clear and real and burned at the end of her fingertip without wick or fuel. She lit and doused it by will and skill alone, demonstrating her new ability to all who watched.

"That's wonderful!" exclaimed Thag.

Brad chimed in, "I knew you were hot, but that's ...." Shina laughed and threw the tiny flame at him. It disappeared before it had gone a yard from her hand, but Brad dropped to the ground shouting about "magefire" and laughing.

Duke Antain, when he saw them, asked, "Could you? Make magefire, I mean."

Shina, the thrill of discovery doused instantly, shook her head "no". She still couldn't do anything that would even affect the tides of battle, far from winning it for them. She knew Gem and other mages had won whole wars by their craft, but she was a novice and had not the art of those old masters.

Finally, the day arrived when the horde appeared on the horizon.

Shina had seen armies before. She expected organized ranks of marching men, maybe some light cavalry at the flanks to pincer the defenders. She expected griffons to lead the charge, and wyverns to hover overhead and drop rocks or arrows or fire-pots.

Antain had warned them all that their line of defense in the trees protected them from arrows and dropped rocks, and even from flying griffons, but made them vulnerable to fire. Drew disagreed with him for some reason, but was so incoherent about it with her stilted speech that nobody, not even Brad or Thag, could understand what she had tried to say.

What they saw instead was a charging mass of bodies! It covered the horizon, raising a gigantic cloud of dust that caught the morning sunlight like fire in the sky. Thousands and thousands of people charging towards them at full speed, single-minded in their bloodlust!

"I can see her," muttered Koserana.

"Who?" asked Shina. She couldn't see any details at this distance, but knew that dragon-vision could easily see people even with miles between them.

"Kamaia. Brad and The Jerk said she has glowing green eyes. I see a human girl who has glowing green eyes. Looks enough like The Jerk to be his daughter. Gotta be Kamaia, right?" Shina didn't try to get her friend to stop calling Duke Antain "The Jerk". Everyone, even Thag, had given up on that long ago.

Shina looked where Koserana was looking, but the closest enemies were still miles away. Even at a dead run, even if they could keep up their speed over the distance, it would be a long time before they were close enough for her to see individual faces. And Kamaia could already see the color of their eyes!

The duke's horn called out a signal. All along the front, fleet elvish warriors leapt to action.

Shina knew from councils what was going to happen next. The hordes could charge like that because of wolf-totem spirit-warriors in their ranks. She remembered his lectures on the coming battle.

"First, they'll charge at us. With wolves in their ranks, they'll be moving fast and they won't tire or slow down. So elvish archers will need to close with them while they're still a long ways away. Spot the wolves – it won't be hard to tell them apart. Kill those. Then run back to our lines.

"If you get into a melee, avoid the bear-warriors. Leave those to Thag and Chalkos. Same for aurochs-warriors. You won't be able to hurt those. They probably only have a couple, but you'll need to stay away from them.

"If you have to fight a bear, tire it out. Small wounds that bleed a lot are your best bet. You won't have time to wear them down, not with the odds we're facing, but it's the only thing that works.

"If you have to fight an aurochs, you're dead anyway, so go out in a blaze of glory. Try to hurt it so the next person has a tiny chance against it.

"If they have a mammoth and you can't avoid it, and Thag doesn't rescue your sorry ass, enjoy the show. You won't have a better option!" Everyone had laughed at that. Somehow, the humor made their hopelessness less dire.

The running elves were fast. Faster by far than anyone Shina had ever seen. Even faster, she thought, than Thag. They leapt as one and cleared the sixty-foot-wide river as if it were a tiny stream. Not a stride was lost in landing on the dead earth on the far shore, and the elves blurred into man-sized missiles racing across the land.

Unlike the horde charging at them, the elves ran silently, and didn't raise a single puff of dust from the dry, loose earth they were crossing. Even racing into battle and almost sure death, the elves were things of deadly grace and beauty.

Someone in the oncoming horde saw the elves racing towards them and accelerated out of the pack.

Gods those were fast! In seconds, they were closing on the elves!

She saw elves fire arrows at the attackers. Where they fired at the main horde, even though they didn't pause in their run and even though the horde was a smear of moving targets at extreme range, Shina saw they must be hitting their targets with deadly precision – whole sections of the charge slowed suddenly!

But the blurs were moving at the elves with deadly speed!

Koserana muttered one word, "Cheetahs!" and leapt up from the tree they were hiding under. Only she could carry this fight!

There was a blur and Chalkos winged toward the miles-distant battle.

Shina couldn't see the details. It was too far for her human eyes. But it was easy to track the burnished form of her flying friend as she swept to the help of the elves.

Wolves down, the elves were fleeing for their lives. As fast as they were, the blurred warriors were faster by far!

One elf went down under a pursuer!

Another was seconds from being caught when suddenly Chalkos

darted over him and a gout of magical flame blasted where the blur had been.

Chalkos swept wide and sprinted towards the next cheetah-warrior, while the prior one floundered in a pall of smoke and toxic flames on the dead earth of the wastes.

Shina couldn't watch. It was too horrible! Those were people dying out there!

A beautiful, immortal elf, who might have helped defend their world against the gnomes, whose only sin was more-than-slightly-justifiable pride, had just died to defend her against horrible odds. Unbeatable odds.

Her beautiful friend was killing more people by breathing toxic, flaming acid on them!

Others were dying with elvish arrows stabbed into their fragile bodies.

She wept as she watched the battle unfold in front of her.

If only there were some way to remove Kamaia from the field. To give some of these people a chance. To save at least a few of her friends from certain doom.

And suddenly she had a plan!

"Thag!" she yelled. She didn't know where he was, but she needed him, and she knew he would hear her from wherever he might be.

In moments, she heard him crashing through the brush below her. She climbed down the tree so fast she almost fell, and then jumped into his arms as he arrived below her.

"Take me to the duke, Thag! I have a plan!"

He didn't hesitate or question her once, he just held her in his arms and smashed his way through the dense thorny bushes. She knew it hurt when the thorns tore at his legs, but he was healing as fast as they cut him, and this was urgent!

"Duke!" she called as they arrived. "I have a plan!"

Everyone listened to her. Thag frowned at the risk. Elves laughed and smiled and even cheered. The duke looked serious and considered, then started giving orders briskly and decisively. She had given him the strategy, and he knew the tactics that would give them their only slightest, faintest hope of success.

In minutes, they had all the defenders gathered and instructed. They formed up as the duke had directed, and then he gave the final command. "We attack," he announced simply, and everyone started into motion.

They used one of the burnable wooden bridges they had placed for crossing the river. Originally intended to tempt the horde into traps, the bridge now served their sortie.

Across, their enemy still a mile away, Thag and the duke's men formed up into a wedge and began the slow charge of heavy infantry. Elvish swordsmen and their other allies formed the flanks of the wedge.

Elvish archers followed behind. They would fire over the heads of their allies, to give their charge a softer target when they needed it.

And they began their slow, steady charge.

The enemy lines began to bow towards the small wedge that attacked where it should have cowered behind fortifications and defenses.

The elvish arches began their fire first. At ranges nobody else could hope to do anything useful, their arrows found every mark. Thag knew that enemies were dying with arrows unerringly placed through eyes or throats. He wished the elves would fire for legs or feet – it would help as much but without killing. But he knew their boredom-fueled bloodthirst wouldn't accept that.

When they reached the right range, the duke's men turned their enchanted weapons into heavy arbalests and loosed a few arrows into the front ranks of their enemies. A few fell, injured or killed, but it wasn't even a drop in that ocean of warriors.

But it convinced the enemy this was exactly what it looked like. Desperate people trying something hopeless.

So the horde charged!

It took seconds to cross the remaining yards. Thag surged ahead of the men following him. He brushed foes aside, ignoring anyone he could, his eyes on exactly what he wanted.

The bear-warriors, berserk but tired from their long charge, their minds muddled by exhaustion they weren't used to feeling, all swept towards Thag. They knew one thing, kill the strongest foe for the most glory!

A gigantic warrior, his skin covered with thick red hair, charged out of his surging allies straight at the giant that was running past. Aurochs-warriors were never known for anything but their toughness and strength, and this one was bone-tired from charging without support from wolves, so his mind was even duller than its usual haze.

When Thag simply ran right over him, knocking him to the ground and breaking his arms by the simple expedient of stomping on them as he passed over, the aurochs-warrior just lay there, trying desperately to figure out what the hell had just happened.

Thag grabbed his target and didn't even slow down. The impact knocked Kamaia's wind out of her and she was stunned for a few seconds. He picked her up and took a wide curve through the enemy ranks till he was running straight back towards the duke and his men, who were just engaging the front ranks of the enemy. Thag's massive body shielded Kamaia from a numberless multitude of spears and arrows.

As Thag leapt over his allies, the duke and his men shifted to full plate and heavy shields, and their weapons flickered into a hedgehog of long pikes. They set their spears and took the brunt of a tidal wave of enraged clansmen!

Thag's kidnapee beat her fists futilely against his thick skin. She kicked. She tried biting till her teeth hurt themselves against his armor-hard shoulder-scales. Her powerful will reached out and tried to take over his mind, but hit hard against a wall stronger than adamantine-steel and smoother than polished glass! She could crush the wills of powerful sorcerers, given time, but no power shorter than the gods themselves can mind-dominate a dragon!

She reached back to her horde and commanded them to rescue her!

And hundreds of thousands of warriors abandoned all thoughts except chasing the monster carrying their mistress!

The horde broke like a river around a rock and charged straight past the duke and his bruised men.

They ignored everyone except Thag, running right around his allies!

Elves stood in their midst and watched, amused and laughing at the hilarity of it all, thrilled for the first time in millennia by something so new that it took a wizard to think of it!

Thousands, intent only on catching Thag, raced past all of Shina's allies who stood on the battlefield, leaving untouched the enemies they had been prepared to crush mere moments before.

Had there been wolves or cheetahs left in the onrushing horde, Thag wouldn't have stood a chance. The wolves would have hindered him till too many even for him could catch up. Cheetahs would have stolen his prize by killing the young woman he carried so carefully.

She must not die! That was the most important thing of all!

His colossal legs ate up the few miles to the river, and he rushed over the bridge at breakneck speed.

The fastest of the horde, leopards and tigers, maybe a lion or two, were only a hundred or more yards behind him as he crashed into the forest.

Drew cleared a path before him and closed it behind as rapidly as she could.

A trickle of the most agile, fastest members of the horde made it through quickly enough to keep pursuing him. This was going to be insanely close!

And then he was there!

Varlad, ready to defend Shina to the death if she needed to, stood before the cliff-face/cave-mouth. Right behind her, barely inside the cave, stood Shina, ready for this split-second plan.

Kamaia saw the orc waiting for them and slammed her will into its brain, only to bounce back just as hard as with the thing that was carrying her! She raged!

And then a clever thought came to her and she bit down hard on her own tongue! Her body would be dead in a few seconds as blood poured from her mouth! Nobody could treat her this way!

A hand shot out of the face of the cliff and grabbed her ankle. The monster carrying her, the progeny of her old experiment in dragon-breeding, threw her at the cliff. She had a brief moment of hope that the impact would kill her even faster than the bleeding!

Her revenge would be irresistible! She would have a new body out of her horde in mere seconds! She would torture these things for defying her! And when she found the wizard she would turn her against them! Possessing a young wizard was simplicity itself to a demon as powerful as she, and she would wreak such havoc on this world as it had never seen when she had the only wizard in the world as her slave!

Shina grabbed the ankle of Thag's baggage, and yanked with all her might, hurling the two of them into the tunnel entrance. Blood was fountaining out of Kamaia's mouth.

Shina had a brief glimpse of a feral face dominated by crystal-green eyes, with the tunnel into the school as its dramatic backdrop, and then a will of irresistible potency slammed into the sorcerous shields she had learned from her father. Her mental shields were mighty. She had defended herself successfully against the most powerful sorcerer in the world, and against the rage of a pain-maddened dragon. Against this, they might as well have been a wall of spun sugar.

In moments, the onslaught was piercing needles into her raw mind.

Thag yanked Shina out of the cave.

The attack ended as abruptly as if it had been cut off by an axe.

She was lying on the ground, Thag was looking down at her, into her eyes. She tried to sit up, but her whole body felt like one big bruise!

She tried to talk, but all that came out was a sort of gargling, hacking noise.

And Thag looked into her eyes and saw no demon there.

Chapter 22: *Waste Not*

Shina's world was pain.

Her bloodshot eyes contrasted horribly with the dark purple bruises all around them. The whole world had a faint red tinge from the blood leaking inside them.

Every joint and every muscle burned. She'd sprained her ankle once, and this felt like that, but for her whole body.

Breathing hurt. Her heart was beating like a trip hammer, and she felt every beat in her head as a lance of pain and force.

She was vaguely aware that Thag was holding her. He was sitting, she thought, with her in his lap. She curled up around her pain, trying to hold it in. Trying to contain it. But it contained her, wrapping around every thought, every feeling. Every tiniest motion sent screaming agony along nerves that were already overwhelmed.

She longed for Brad to arrive, to sooth her pain and heal her ravaged flesh. A small part of her knew that he was busy saving lives near the battle-line, but most of her screamed that it was unfair and wanted to tell the world that he needed to help *her!*

If only she could speak! She would tell Thag to get Brad. That nothing else mattered. That she needed him.

Thag sat with Shina curled up in his lap, wishing he could do more for her. He'd sent for Brad, but the half-orc was busy and would be for a while. He didn't dare take Shina near the battlefront, where Brad was. She was too fragile, too important to risk that way. Not if he could help it.

He'd seen humans hurt this way before. Without magical healing, they would take months to recover. He knew some humans envied the fact that, for him, wounds like this would heal almost as fast as they were inflicted. He'd feel a brief sting of pain, but nothing like what poor Shina was going through right then.

Of course, no human would voluntarily take the baggage that went along with that. They wanted to heal fast, but not to be monsters.

Chalkos landed gracefully next to him. She didn't bother shapeshifting, just spoke with that juvenile-dragon voice that sounded so oddly deep from such a feminine source. "Thag, they need you up front. Antain says he needs you."

Thag didn't miss that Chalkos called the duke by name. That meant she was taking this seriously.

He glanced down at Shina, curled up in a ball in his lap.

Chalkos followed his glance. "She'll be fine. Bring her with you. She'll be as safe there as she is here."

With a fluid motion, the young dragon leapt into the air and flitted off towards Antain's command post.

Thag stood up, carefully cradling Shina in his arms, and walked as smoothly and softly as he could.

The first thing he noticed as he caught sight of Antain's position was that Brad looked worse than Shina. *"He's pushing himself too hard!"* Thag realized.

"My lord Thag!" bustled Antain. "We need your advice!"

Thag looked past the encampment and stopped, stunned at what he was seeing! Kamaia's army was tearing itself apart!

He had known they would fall into rival factions. The tribes she'd called together hated each other only slightly less than they worshipped her, and only the demon's steel command had made them cooperate at all. But this was a catastrophe!

All over the battle-plains, tribes were massing for all-out war!

Hundreds, soon to be thousands, of fights were already raging over the wasted lands!

Antain followed Thag's gaze. "Is it what it looks like? Are they about to start a war? We can't possibly survive if they all start fighting! It will all inevitably spill over to our side of the river, and we'll be just as dead as if we'd never captured the demon!"

Thag didn't hesitate. "Antain, bring a bodyguard. We're going over there."

He glanced at Brad. "Brad, we'll need you to translate. I'm sorry, but I only know a few of the languages out here."

He continued, "Chalkos, get the elves! Catch up with us as soon as you have them!"

Thag gave Chalkos a stern look. "And be nice with them! No teasing, no tricks, no taunting!"

Chalkos somehow managed to look contrite and conciliatory, despite her armor-plated draconic face.

As she gathered up the elves, two of them began arguing about what medicines they could use to help. They were far enough away that Shina probably couldn't hear them, but Koserana could hear every word. "We've got fleshmend brew!" retorted by, "It would kill her unborn child!" followed by, "If only we had some bloodwarmth powder!" and "But we haven't, have we?" On and on, round and round it went.

Koserana didn't really pay attention to it, but she couldn't help but hear every word.

As Thag carried Shina towards the battlefield, she finally accepted, deep inside, that Brad would not, could not, heal her this time.

For a moment, a blackness of despair tried to rise up and cover her. But she was stronger than that! For her child, for herself, for Thag, she pushed the blackness back.

Her mind wandered through the pain, and she vaguely remembered something she had read in Gem's crystals, something about ways for the mind to command the body.

Thag's jogging steps barely shook her, but each slightest jar shot spikes of pain into her sensitive nerves.

She wondered, briefly, what it felt like to the people Kamaia successfully possessed. Did it hurt like this? Worse? Was it numbing? Was this pain the key to demonic possession, like a slaver's whips but on the inside?

Shina felt it when they got to the river. The world around her felt dead! It was as if a sound that had been around her all her life had suddenly been silenced!

The pain faded as a deep sense of doom crushed into her. As if all the darkness in the world was pouring into her very soul!

A tiny spark, deep inside, woke up and blazed a wordless defiance at the dark!

And Shina knew, for the first time, knew in her deepest being, that she was indeed a wizard, and could do something about this!

By sheer force of will, she focused on her love of Thag and their unborn child, pushed the pain down out of her consciousness, and stood firm against the dark doom of the blasted lands around her.

Time froze. The moment became forever.

She perceived her body as a fractured container for her self and her will, and she dug into the knowledge from Gem's crystals and crafted the runes that would channel the life needed to mend the cracks in it.

Some things became obvious to her. Reality and the creative fuel behind it were things she could perceive. Not see, not touch, or hear, or any other human-body sense, but perceive. She didn't have the words for it, but knew they were in the crystals. Other wizards, more experienced than she, had codified this strange sense in ancient days.

Mysterious references in the material she had studied before grew clear in her mind as she grasped this new way of experiencing the worlds around her. Notes and concepts and descriptions that had evaded her every attempt at understanding stood out clearly and became instructions for things she now knew she would one day be able to do.

She knew she still had a long way to go on this journey to become a wizard who could heal a world. But she also knew she had just taken the first step out the door of merely human experience onto a strange and dangerous path that led away from everything she had ever thought of as real.

The moment ended. Time became a stream of motion.

Shina heard noises around her, slowly realized they were voices and that they were speaking words she could make herself understand.

Speech! It was so slow and so inefficient and so easily garbled compared to the speed and clarity of wizard-thought! But she needed words to reach the people around her.

Her eyes felt blind, so she painstakingly built vision into them, struggling with the wizard-concepts. Slowly, painfully, she healed her own sight, and saw that a large group of people were sitting near her, gathered around a small campfire.

Touch became an overwhelmingly fascinating thing as she returned her senses to her body. She could feel every slightest feature of the leather clothing she was dressed in, every tiniest bump and ridge in Thag's skin against her hands and face, even the dance of air on every inch of her body.

Thag was speaking, mainly through Brad as a translator, to dozens of tribal chieftains. It had taken hours to gather them all together, even with the help of fast-moving elves to spread the word of the gathering.

He wasn't sure what he'd be able to do. Stopping them from slaughtering each other was his main goal, but he hoped for more. He wasn't even sure he'd be able to stop the oncoming war, but at least he delayed it while they talked.

Shina was curled up in his lap. He didn't dare leave her alone, unguarded, so he put up with the awkwardness of having her there. He knew it made him look less imposing to the chiefs, but it was worth it.

Mid-sentence, Thag sensed the change in Shina and stopped speaking.

Everyone stared as pale blue light wormed over Shina's body, erasing every slightest bruise!

Even her hair took on a healthier glow as the light crawled over her.

Perhaps strangest of all, it didn't stop there, but also erased worn spots, mends, and patches from her clothing, leaving behind a bright newness to all of it.

After a moment, the lights faded, then Shina uncurled out of Thag's lap. She stood with her head held high, her back and neck ramrod straight, her feet slightly apart and her hands clasped together at her waist. Thag, seeing the pride and certainty in her, smiled.

As the chieftains stared at her, she announced in a loud, clear voice, "I have defeated the demon-queen Kamaia. You will bow to me!"

Before translators could even start, the chieftains stood and, as one, bowed deeply to their new wizard-queen.

Brad stared, goggle-eyed, his mouth hanging open.

Koserana giggled.

Thag beamed.

One of the elves jumped to his feet and shouted. "How did you learn our language? How can you …." He trailed off.

Shina stared him straight in the eyes, an open challenge on her proud young face.

The elf blinked first, and then looked down and could no longer meet her gaze. Some of the chiefs nodded, looks of satisfaction on their faces. A few scowled.

One of the scowling malcontents, a huge orc with half his face covered in scars and the other half in swirling tattoos, rumbled, "Kamaia was our queen.

And you bested her. So that makes you the new queen."

Shina started to speak, but the chief held up a finger in caution, so she paused.

"But!" he said. "But! That doesn't mean you'll stay that way. We honor your conquest, but," his voice rose to almost a shout, "we don't have to obey you! How dare a tiny little girl try to command the warriors of the Plains Lion Clan!"

He would have continued his ranting, but Thag stood up, stepped over to him, and punched him straight in the gut.

The chief was a strong man. Powerfully muscled. An experienced veteran of dozens of wars. His every muscle had the strength of a steel cord.

He folded around Thag's fist, the air rushing out of his suddenly compressed lungs in a loud "wumph", and dropped to the ground, gagging and gasping.

Thag wrapped his fingers in the downed chieftain's hair and pulled his head up so he stared straight into the black pit of Thag's draconic eyes. "Insult her again, and it won't be a light tap next time."

With a bow to Shina, Thag sat back down next to her.

Translators, still unsure what was going on when Shina had spoken simultaneously to each in their every native tongue, suddenly realized they were needed and caught up with Thag's comment.

When they did, another chief bowed to Shina and then approached Thag.

He was a huge man with dark reddish-brown hair down to his waist, dark eyes, and enough curly hair on his bare chest that it almost looked like he was wearing a sweater. Shina belatedly realized the man was wearing boots up to mid-thigh, leather gloves up past his elbows, some jewelry, and nothing else! His almost-fur could fool the eye at a glance, but he was almost naked and his genitals were hanging out in plain view!

With a definite effort of will, she stopped herself from blushing and staring, and forced her eyes to look up at the man's smiling face.

As he spoke, she knew that he was using a language she had never heard before, but she was beyond that now. With what she had finally grasped of the lore in the gems, she held onto the "Core of Babel", as Gem had named it, and understood every word. Not just as it was spoken, but as it was meant by the speaker.

"You're strong, whatever you are," he said to Thag, and glanced at the felled chieftain still struggling to breathe on the ground. He smiled. "I want to know how strong. Hit me, please. Do not hold back."

A young woman acted as translator. "What you are is strong," she said, struggling for words and phrases. "He want you hit him."

Before Thag could respond, Shina interjected. "It's not precisely what he said. He complimented you on your strength. He wants to know how strong, so he asked you to hit him, too. I think he wants to make sure it's real. He asked you not to hold back. But I ask, please don't really hurt him."

Thag nodded. He looked around briefly, then got up and walked over to one of the multitudinous ruins sticking up out of the barren ground. He pointed at a block of stone, about a foot thick and twice that wide and tall.

"You see this?" Thag asked.

The redhead chieftain looked puzzled when it was translated, but nodded his agreement.

Thag pointed at the stone again. "Feel it. Determine how solid it is. How heavy. How strong."

Several of the chieftains joined in. Shina took over the translations, since she could speak once and everyone would understand her, instead of having a large number of questionable translators to handle the multitude of languages represented by this gathering.

At Thag's prompting, each of the chiefs touched and prodded the rock. They felt how heavy, how solid, how durable it was.

When they were done, they stood watching, curious about what he was leading up to. Some looked bemused, some cheerfully interested. Only a couple looked belligerent about the whole thing.

Finally satisfied, Thag stood next to the stone block. Shina was interested in how much of a ritual he had made of the whole thing. She realized he was leading them, getting them used to the idea of following his directions, but she knew there would be more to it.

Thag gestured for everyone to step back.

Suddenly, without telegraphing his move at all, Thag struck! His fist smashed into solid stone and blasted it to fragments and rock-dust!

Everyone ducked as gravel and fist-sized chunks of blasted rock flew everywhere!

When they recovered, they looked in awe at Thag. He held up his hand – bleeding and with every bone in the hand and wrist shattered. Barbarian eyes, already wide from the display of brute strength, bugged wider yet as they watched the bones and flesh heal.

In seconds, his hand was unmarred.

Wide-eyed and drop-jawed, the dozens of overawed warriors looked back and forth between the shattered remnants of a once-solid stone, and the cleanly healed hand that had smashed it.

After a brief moment of resounding silence, Thag pointed at Shina and said, simply, "She's the boss."

No translators were needed.

Thag asked the redhead chief, "Do you still want to get hit?"

With a loud laugh, a wide smile, and a shake of his head, the chief declined.

Shina thought for a moment. She, too, looked at the hand and fragments of rock. But she was familiar with Thag's incredible strength and healing. They weren't new to her. But the idea she'd just had was....

She opened the pouch of wizard-gems that she'd brought out of the school with her, and pulled out one of the stones she thought of as the indexes. While Thag talked to excited barbarians about how broken that stone was and how not-broken he was, she searched for what she needed.

It took a couple of minutes, but the mood and conversation were still very much focused on the broken stone, so she thought her idea would probably work.

It was difficult. Without her father's training on controlling and focusing her own mind, she wouldn't have been able to concentrate on all of the complex things she had to hold in her mind at the same time.

One of Gem's commentaries said that destruction was always the easiest magic. She was trying one of the more difficult things.

Things kept trying to fade out of her mind! Or they'd shift when she put her attention on the next step. She knew she had to have it exactly right!

And then it clicked! Everything she'd been studying since she first went into the school, all the practice and reading and trying small things – it all came together!

Eyes glanced her way, then stuck.

Blue flame surrounded her hands and crept up her forearms slowly.

She raised her arms and pointed rigid hands at one of the fragments of the stone.

Pale blue light played over the fragment, then spread slowly around to other pieces. The faintest aura caressed the dirt where rock-dust had blasted over many square yards of the ground.

The light, so pale it was almost inferred rather than actually seen, grew stronger.

Bits of rock-dust and small fragments in people's hair, on their clothing, even clinging to their skin, picked up the glow.

People all around were holding their breath in anticipation of they knew not what!

The light grew and grew. Just as it seemed on the verge of waxing to pain, it shrank from all around into the spot the stone had been in when Thag hit it.

Everything had been slow and gradual till that moment, but suddenly it moved at dazzling speed! In a moment, the light had faded from everything except the illusion of the broken stone.

Too fast to follow, illusion was replaced by reality and the stone once more stood where it had been!

But it wasn't merely as if Thag hadn't hit it! It was smooth and polished, worked and perfect as it had been when first put in place in the old city. Thousands of years of wind and rain, even the battle-scars of the war with the gnomes, all faded and the stone stood as if the ages had never touched it!

Shina slumped, exhausted physically, emotionally and mentally. Koserana barely caught her as she suddenly fell down..

Thag smiled broadly, baring scraggly fangs in his mouth and a glint of dragon-fire in his eyes.

One-by-one, he met the eyes of the chiefs, holding each gaze for the barest moment.

Last of all, he caught Antain's eyes.

"She's the boss," he repeated. His voice was soft, but it was the only sound present, and nobody there missed any tiniest bit of exactly what he meant.

Chapter 23: *On the Road Again*

Shina came to a minute or two later. Thag was holding her, and she looked up from his lap, deep into his beautiful eyes.

She pursed her lips and exhaled a deep sigh.

"Wow!" she said, her eyes going a bit wide, and then took another deep breath.

Thag looked down at her, patient curiosity written clearly for her in every line of his face.

"Oh, Thag! That was amazing!" Shina half spoke, half sighed.

Thag nodded. He knew that repairing the rock wasn't what she meant. "Amazing" was too weak a word for that, but he knew her well enough to be certain she had something else on her mind.

She stared past and through him for a moment, gathering her wits.

"It was like sex, but … not 'better' … maybe … I don't know the word!" She smiled and looked into his eyes. "It was hot and cold and light and dark and it … yeah … it … wow!

She started talking fast. "It felt almost like sex. Like really good sex. Like the times when I just can't take any more but still want it, you know?" Before he could begin to respond, she continued. "Like that time when we … but not really like that either! It was different! Like my whole body was having sex! It felt like I was glowing and full of light and like the warmth when you come in out of icy cold and like it shot through my whole body!

"It was like when Brad gave me that 'vodka' juice! Like I was on fire inside! But in a good way!

"It was like the first time I had sex with Koserana and she …." Her voice faded for a moment and her eyes looked elsewhere again.

"But it also wasn't like that at all! It was butterflies in my stomach at the same time as I felt totally in control. Like I was in water over my head, but totally safe at the same time!

"Everything was crazy and everything was totally sane," she said in a fast breath. She looked at him again, and smiled.

"It was like you and like Koserana. It was amazing!"

She sprang up and put her arms around his huge neck. She couldn't reach all the way around, and he always had to hold her up when she hugged him this way. He loved that.

Thag hadn't said a word. He didn't have to.

"Oh, Thag! I love you so much! I knew you would understand!" She muttered into his chest.

The next few days were spent on conferences with the chiefs, speeches to the tribes, breaking up not a few fights, keeping the elves from egging people into fights (most of them got bored and had Drew transport them back to their islands), and repeatedly telling people that Antain was Shina's seneschal, and then explaining what that meant.

"His title is 'duke', which means 'in charge during war'," Thag explained over and over.

Several of the warriors realized this meant that challenging Antain was how they should settle precedence and authority. The few who survived their duels against him, and the ones who witnessed the blood-soaked carnage of the one attempt to ambush the duke, quickly realized that there was a reason he was in charge. Word spread rapidly after that, and people started walking quietly around him and bowing deeply whenever he looked their way.

Duke Antain was immensely pleased. Here was an army he could use to forge a kingdom!

Then Thag explained to him, very briefly but very clearly, that using this army to attack west of the Argent Crown Mountains was absolutely forbidden, and the duke's ambitions dimmed a little…till he realized that east of the mountains was a far, far larger land. With that, he settled into the role comfortably.

Brad discovered that half of the barbarian horde was female. And the female half of the barbarian horde discovered Brad. Thag and Shina didn't hear a lot from him after that. They knew he'd be ready to march east when they were, and that was enough.

Drew discovered that, not only was the other half of the horde male, but that none of them had ever seen a dryad before, and that they knew about forests that hadn't had a dryad's touch in millennia. She spent a lot of time with them communicating about life and forests and trees. Some of it may even have been spent talking. Shina didn't ask.

Shina spent her days studying with renewed interest and certainty. And with the growing effects of her pregnancy on her body. Morning sickness was mild for her, but she still found her mood doing strange acrobatics and her body reacting to things in ways she had not expected in the slightest.

Thag and Chalkos assured her that she and the baby smelled perfectly healthy, no matter how many times she felt compelled to ask them. Of course, it was fortunate that she didn't have to wake either of them up when she would suddenly awake mid-worrying about it and go looking for reassurance in the middle of the night.

Once the chiefs found out that Shina was pregnant, she quickly got very tired of being asked if she was up for the trek she and Thag were planning.

Some of them were actually interested in her well-being. Those she answered politely and assured them that Thag's child could take a little bit of a walk in the countryside, so they shouldn't worry.

Most simply wanted her to winter in their villages and give birth there, since it would be an item of inestimable prestige to have her, The Stone Wizard, in their villages. All of those quickly found out that there may still have been a little of her father's daughter left in her temper after all.

Finally, after what seemed like lifetimes, but was really only a couple of weeks, the army set off to leave the wastelands. They would have to go out the way they had come in, following their supply lines and caches. It would be easier this time, since the lines would get shorter every day rather than longer, but it would still take far too long for Thag and Shina to wait for them.

Instead, the small band – Shina, Thag, Koserana and Brad – would head east and a little bit north. They had a long way to go, would have to travel by foot, and Thag knew they needed to get to Sam's tower as quickly as they could. It would be horrifically difficult, but they had to do it.

Brad stocked up his bracelet with quite a supply of food and drink. The chiefs wanted to know where they could get bracelets like that, and

Thag told them they'd have to earn them from Shina.

When Shina pointed out she didn't have any, he countered that the bracelet was made by a wizard in the first place, and maybe she would learn how to make more. If she could, it would give her even more exaltation in the eyes of the warriors, and that was worthwhile. It was true, he elucidated, that the only way more would ever be made was if she learned to do so, and thus true that the only way to get those would be to earn them from her.

Experimentation had shown that Brad couldn't grow anything at all beyond the river that marked the last line of the battle at the foot of the cliffs. Even with Drew's help, there simply wasn't any life in the earth for him to call out to and speed up. It meant, till they left the wastelands, he wouldn't be able to do any of his more powerful magics — no thorn-bushes or trees to protect them in a battle, no berry bushes to eat from.

He even had to limit how much healing he could do, since that seemed to dull and become weak in the wastelands.

Thag hoped, reasonably, that they wouldn't need any of that till they got out of the wastelands on the eastern side. Nothing lived there to attack them, after all.

It was a somber group that gathered for one last meal at Brad's fruit trees, one last drink at the old magical fountain outside the school.

Shina and Thag could see the cave entrance, and knew that Kamaia was still inside there. Insane, deadly, immortal, and trapped. There was no way to safely find out what was going on in there. Only Thag could go in without being possessed immediately, and he wouldn't be able to tell what she was up to. The very immunity he had to her also made it impossible for him to communicate with her.

Brad couldn't see the cave, but knew it was there and had been warned about it. Unnecessarily, since he couldn't go in even if he wanted to. But it was sobering nonetheless. Finding the limits of life itself in the wastes around them, where his spirit magic was so mortally constrained, put a further damper on his usually good spirits.

Koserana picked up the mood of the adults around her and stayed quiet. She alone of the four was in no danger at all in the wastelands. She could fly the whole distance in a few hours, so leaving was a triviality to her. The main threats for most, the absolute lack of food and drinkable water, weren't at all life-threatening to her.

Draconic hunger, gluttonous as it may be, is an extension of greed and hedonism, not a necessity of life. Like all children, she needed food to grow, but she didn't need it to live. In the short term, it wasn't any more important to her than scratching itches or looking pretty. Less important, by far, than looking pretty, in fact.

No dragon ever got itself killed for hunger. Many have died for vanity.

Thag, of course, could no more die in the wastes than Koserana could. Hunger was a very real thing for him, from his troll mother's heritage. A constant, gnawing aching in his gut, never satisfied no matter how much he ate, was something he had lived with for centuries. Too long without food, and his temper would fray. He had, many times in his youth, become quite dangerous to be around because of that. But it couldn't kill him. Torment him, always. Kill him, never.

The wastelands stretched ahead of them for hundreds of miles. Thag could run that in a day or less. The only real danger to him would be the many pits in the ground. If he fell into the wrong one, he might not be able to climb, or even dig, his way out. It was a threat he was accustomed to avoiding.

But Thag also carried the weight of the full responsibility for saving the world of his birth. He'd had his chance to escape and had turned it down. Save or die trying, he had sworn, and he'd be damned if he was going to die trying!

Even more, he loved the young woman who travelled with him. The wastelands could snuff out her life as easily as a gale could put out a candle. He knew he'd have to be clever, wise and alert to keep her alive. This was almost as dangerous as their original trip through the Argent Crown Mountains. He couldn't bear the thought that a failure of his might hurt or kill her in the wastes.

That she carried his son, his first child, merely added to the burden.

Mainly because of how cautiously they travelled, it took them almost a week to get to the eastern edge of the wastes.

One day, about halfway through their trek, they came upon the gigantic ruins of an ancient gnomish war machine. Recent rain had washed away thousands of years of accumulated dust and sand from the thing. The ruins had once been a bipedal walker of some sort, easily forty or fifty feet tall, with armor several feet thick. The crew spaces inside it were tiny. From the ancient legends, they knew machines like this had slain countless dragons and wizards, destroyed whole cities, and smashed worlds into ruin. Seeing one, even one long-dead and ruined, was sobering and horrific.

The mood lightened over time after that. They would never forget that sight, but they would also never forget that this wasteland, this horrific place of death, was also the first place where the ancient wizard Gem and the dragon Ariel had turned the tide of war against the gnomes and brought hope back to the world.

After a few days, Koserana realized that Brad was actually pretty witty, for a mortal. She soon warmed up to the charismatic and charming half-orc. She loved his jokes and puns and clever observations. And it didn't hurt that he played up to her vanity at every chance.

Thag and Shina chuckled when Brad and Koserana started flirt-tormenting each other. They all knew it wasn't going anywhere, but they enjoyed the show.

After one of Brad's particularly amusing anecdote about watching stars at night with a pretty girl, Koserana even accused Thag of being boring for not having stories like that. When he barely responded to her tease, she pouted till he told a story about the battle-mages and their empire. It took him three days to tell it, and Shina wished she were able to stay awake for all of it. Koserana forgave Thag his "epic boringness" (her words) when she realized the story was about her and included the hunt for the elf bandits who had held her captive when she was a baby.

Koserana, her eyes aglow with self-admiration, was fascinated by the whole account.

Thag later admitted to Shina that, when he first met Koserana decades ago, he'd learned to couch his morality stories in ways that fed her vanity, humor and curiosity. He also admitted that he liked the fact that, with Koserana, he could tell a story "the right way" – meaning he could spend days, or even weeks, on it, and didn't have to summarize it down to a few hours or minutes.

As he put it, "The really important stories require a lot of details. That's why they get written down in long books for most people. You can put anything in a book, if you tell the story right."

Shina didn't hear the whole story, but she gathered that the moral of it was something like, "Don't eat people who might be nice to you if you let them live".

The night after the story was over, when Shina asked him about that, Thag told her, "It was one of the hardest things my step-father ever had to teach me. Passing the lesson on is something I owe him, and owe Koserana too."

Shina thought about it. "Thag? Did you ever eat anyone? A person, I mean."

Thag smiled wickedly, licked his lips, and replied, "No one other than you."

Later, lying exhausted on his chest, Shina thought to herself, "And Koserana thinks he's boring and doesn't have a sense of humor!"

Chapter 24: *Lying*

The first day out of the wastelands, the four travelers were stalked by a huge thunderstorm all morning.

Thag suggested taking shelter under one of the giant oaks in a nearby forest. "Lightning likes oak, but I can convince it to leave our tree alone. It won't be much shelter, but it's better than being out in the rain."

He explained that the forest needed the rain, and it wouldn't hurt to have a storm erase some of their own tracks, so they may as well shelter for the day instead of traveling on.

It was just beginning to sprinkle when they got to the tree.

Brad looked up at the tree. "I can get this to grow a few extra branches above us, without hurting the tree. Not a roof, but it'll help." He stood next to the tree, his head bowed and his right hand extended, the palm flat on the rough bark of the thick trunk, fingers spread wide. Shina expected him to close his eyes, but he didn't.

She looked up at the increasing flow of drops through the branches, and knew that they'd have a few dry minutes, but not much more than that. Her eyes abruptly narrowed in thought. *Maybe if I...* she thought, a plan forming.

Shina went to Brad and whispered his name, afraid to disturb him but curious enough about her idea to risk it. He looked up at her and smiled. She took that as an invitation to say more. "Brad, if you grow a bunch of small branches right near the trunk, I think I can make them rain-proof."

Brad nodded. "Up high or down here?" he asked.

Shina pointed a few feet over their heads. Moments later, small branches with tiny, bright green leaves sprouted from the trunk where she'd indicated. When they'd grown to about six feet long and made a roundish roof-like shape, she nodded her satisfaction. It was porous, but it would work if her idea was valid.

Shina began drawing power into herself, and forming it into the complex runes and patterns of magic. Then she began changing the way water works in the small area of the branches over their heads: A narrow, focused effect in the branches Brad had grown for her, and a wider, more diffuse effect over the whole tree.

As the storm fully broke over them, she watched as the rain falling through the tree met her rules and deflected to the paths she wanted.

All around, the wind howled and buckets of water poured down. Even under other trees, the ground was quickly soaked. Under their tree, the travelers and the ground stayed comfortably dry.

Thag smiled with pride.

Brad and Shina looked into each other's eyes and smiled brightly. They had done something together that neither could do alone, and it had been fun!

Koserana watched them for a minute, and then made a joke about "I love work, I could watch it all day!" She stretched out languorously and pretended to take a nap. Brad found himself speaking softly and trying not to disturb her. Intellectually, he knew she didn't sleep, just like Thag. Instinctively, his eyes saw a sleeping person and he walked and talked quietly and tried to avoid waking her.

Thag muttered, "It doesn't count as 'watching' if you have your eyes closed." Koserana tried not to grin, but couldn't completely stop her lips from curling the tiniest bit.

"We need to plan," said Thag. He gestured for Shina and Brad to sit against the bole of the tree. Once they were seated, he crouched in front of them and drew a quick sketch of a map on the ground, cutting the outlines with his sharp claws.

"I don't know this area very well. I've been through it a couple of times, but I've never spent any real time in this part of the world. I know the geography from books, but that's not the same as actually knowing a place.

"Before the gnomes, this part of the world used to be heavily populated. Lots of cities, and farms of some sort from horizon to horizon wherever you stood. After the gnome war, it was ruled by battle mages, the Emperor Am'het'o-nan and his general and rival, En'cal-ras.

"The constant warfare between those two, and with their neighbors, split the region up into a few major coastal fortress-cities — similar to

Antain's capital at Herztad – and lots of little farming communities with small castles to protect them.

"When the battle-mages were still alive, this area was in constant warfare. I don't know what it's been like since then.

"Brad, do your people have any contact with this part of the world?"

Brad shook his head "no". "The wastelands are between us and them," he pointed out.

Thag nodded. "The route I've taken before to cross here won't work for us. It would kill both of you. I've got a couple of ideas, and I want your opinion on them. Or any other ideas."

"I usually follow the edge of the Arctic glaciers. It takes me to a narrow sea that leads to some islands off the shore of the eastern continent. The weather is brutal, and doesn't know me – we'd definitely end up travelling through blizzards and storms in some of the most unforgiving land in the world. Thousands of miles of freezing cold. No ready supply of food for much of it. Mountains and glaciers on the land, rip-tides and storms at sea. I can swim through that, and she," he pointed at Koserana, "can fly over it, but not you two. So that route is out of the question." He looked at them for agreement and they both nodded.

"There used to be shipping lanes from west to east across the ocean here. It's the widest ocean in the world, by far, but there were those who sailed it. I don't know if anyone still does. If they do, it'll be from the old coastal cities of the battle-mage empire. Even if they don't, there might be charts and such that would make it possible for us to try it ourselves.

"We're not sailors, but if we can get a whaling boat or a deep-water fisher to help us, we might be able to try the crossing even if we can't find someone who has done the trip before."

Shina and Brad both nodded in agreement. It sounded like a plan.

"Last recourse, if we can't find anything better, we get some wyverns and you two fly on them. You'd have to go north till you can cross in one flight, and I can help with that. It would mean splitting up again, and I don't like that idea. But if we have to, we try it. Okay?"

Shina asked, "Will they have wyverns?"

Brad answered. "The battle-mages all kept wyverns and griffons at all of their fortresses. Unless they've been killed off since, they'll have some there."

Thag, who had been about to launch into a long discourse on the history, habits, and the reasons for omnipresence of wyverns, realized Brad's answer had been enough and left it at that.

Shina looked at the bracer on Brad's wrist and said, "We have plenty of dry supplies, but we're short on just about everything else." She addressed Brad, "You should set some of those water barrels out to collect some of this rain. A couple are a little low."

Brad shook his head. "Still amazes me that you can see inside this thing," he pointed at the bracer. "I have to pull things out and eyeball them out here." He walked to the edge of the tree and pulled two medium-sized barrels out, then wrestled them out into the rain.

He was drenched when he stepped back under the tree, till Shina gestured at him. Something smooth, completely invisible, rock-hard, and perfectly contoured to every texture of his skin, clothing and hair, slid across his body. It took only a moment, and then he was comfortably dry – and cleaned of every slightest speck of dust or anything else. She'd been doing that ever since she learned how a couple of weeks before, and Brad had to admit it was both incredibly convenient and more than slightly creepy. She was getting better at it – the first time, it had swept his eyes dry and cleaned out his nose, mouth and sinuses in a very unpleasant manner. After a few days' practice, she'd worked out how to make it avoid those areas.

Thag commented, "You're getting more comfortable with magic. That is excellent."

"Per the records from the school, most students spend a couple of years studying on their own to get comfortable with basics like this, before they even start their apprenticeship. So I'm trying to do that," replied Shina.

Koserana, her draconic senses able to pierce even heavy rain, suddenly sat up and looked alarmed. "Thag, something big is coming towards us!" She pointed out into the storm.

Thag listened for a moment, but all he could hear out there was rain and wind and thunder. The dragon's senses were sharper than his, so he had to just trust her.

"Aggressive?" he asked, just as a huge thing burst out of the rain and charged into the shelter under the tree.

It was incredibly fast! Shina only had a moment to see a gigantic blur, and then it was onto Thag!

It was taller than Thag, and heavier. And uglier, she realized. Its damp skin was a mottle of gray, various shades of brown and green, and speckles of sickly black. It had the same basically human outline that Thag had, but even more exaggerated into massive bones and muscles.

Thag met it head-on in a crash of titanic power, mere feet from where Shina sat against the tree.

And then she saw something she had never expected to ever see! It pushed Thag back towards her, overpowering him with sheer brute strength!

The thing howled briefly, and then viciously bit into the side of Thag's neck. It's huge fangs pierced the armored scales easily. Blood sprayed from the huge wound it tore in Thag!

Brad grabbed Shina and pushed her behind him. Where his hand touched her, she could feel the stone-hard enchantment on his skin.

"Troll!" Brad growled.

The troll was winning! Thag was being overwhelmed by its immense fury and power. It was stronger than Thag, and his inhuman healing couldn't keep up with the savage damage its fangs were wreaking on his throat!

A rumbling voice roared, "Stand back!" from the side, and Brad pushed Shina to the ground, covering her vulnerable body with his.

Glistening copper flashed and suddenly Shina's eyes were blinded by a flash of flame so bright it made the lightning look pale!

Squinting, she saw Chalkos darting around the two titans. Thag held on and hindered the troll with mass, power and claws, while the young dragon bathed the two in blasts of toxic flaming acid!

Shina could barely see the heart of the inferno, where Thag and the troll were covered in clinging hell.

The troll was trying to escape Thag's grasp!

It tried to smash his head, but the blow was deflected by Thag's draconic horns.

It let go of his neck and desperately tried to struggle out of his grip, but their roles had reversed and Thag pinned it with his claws and bit deeply into one of its arms.

Even soaking wet, branches of the tree burst into flame wherever they were too close to the dragon-fire. Brad, spotting the danger, picked up Shina and dragged her back towards the sheet of rain still pouring down.

The troll finally dragged Thag into the rain, seeking water to douse the horrible fire. Chalkos kept blasting away at it, and the troll's weak mind finally realized, in its final moments, that water can't mitigate the fire born of creation itself.

Finally Thag extricated himself from the blackened skeleton of the monster. His body ached and felt horribly weak for a minute. And then even the horrible wounds his neck had taken were healed as if they'd never been.

"Burn it to ash, please. Anything less, it'll come back from," he directed Chalkos.

She complied, covering the scorched corpse with controlled blasts of flame, till nothing was left.

Weeds and underbrush burned away around it, but the rain kept the fire from spreading. Where dragon-flame touched directly, no amount of rain could slow it, but beyond the direct flame, no natural fire could last in that downpour.

Soon enough, with some help from Brad, their tree was also doused and its burned branches were healing and regrowing rapidly.

Shina ran to hold Thag. She quickly regained her composure when she saw he was essentially unhurt. She knew he felt the pain from his wounds, but even that was short-lived.

"Why did it attack us, Thag?" she asked. "Is someone sending things like that for us now?"

It wasn't an unreasonable question, but Thag thought not. "Trolls kill and eat everything. They were created by wizards, I think. But they were driven mad by the gnomes. They're always hungry, and it hurts.

"I didn't know there were any left in the world, outside of the southern continent's deeper swamps and mountains. The battle-mages hunted them down whenever they heard of them."

He turned to Brad. "You knew what it was. How?"

"There have been a few seen in the mountains south of my home. I thought you knew that? My people mostly try to avoid them, but sometimes we have to fight them."

Chalkos stood near Thag and said, in her strangely deep voice, "I know about them too. I've met a few over the years. I usually just fly out of their reach and burn them from above. They're really dumb, so it's usually pretty easy."

Shina had finally gotten used to the merciless way her friend fought, but this seemed a little extreme. "You burn them down, where they can't fight back and they can't hurt you?"

Chalkos just looked at her.

Thag answered. "Little One, I know it seems harsh, but my mother's kin are best slain whenever possible. They are a plague on the world. If a wizard could restore their sanity, that would be one thing. But without that, there are some illnesses that can only be cured by excising the diseased flesh. Left unchecked, the trolls would devour all animal life in the world. They consume flesh, and it matters not to them whether it is still living when they start eating.

"My mother slaughtered whole villages before my step-father killed her and burned the corpse to ash. She ate children while they still struggled in her hands. And, because of trollish madness, she only resorted to eating animals when every human in reach had been consumed."

Shina looked at the place where rain was already washing the troll's ashes away. Another victim of the gnomish armies, she realized. Like everything and everyone slain by the battle-mages. Like every victim of Kamaia – a world-spirit driven insane by the gnomes' horrific weapons. Everything seemed to rest on how to undo the damage they had done.

With strengthened resolve and a promise to somehow perform that healing, however it could be done and whatever it would cost, Shina shuddered and pulled her gaze away from the tragic sight.

"Across the ocean, will it be like this?" she asked. Thag took it as hopeful. It meant she was thinking ahead and planning towards success.

He talked about the lands across the ocean. Once, they were the seat of the empire, when High Emperor Ka'then-arad had been at the peak of his power. The lands were filled with wondrous cities and civilizations. Ranches with herds that covered miles of land, farms that rivaled the output of the amazing civilizations from before the gnomes. Craft-masters even the elves admired.

But the unending civil wars and plots and sieges of the battle-mage empires turned most of the continent into ruins over the millennia. Nothing as blasted as the wastelands around Xalax, but many lands ruined only slightly less. Whole cities burned to the ground, and even the ground salted so they couldn't be re-settled.

The herds went feral. The farms and gardens and orchards became forests and wildlands. All that was left were broken towers standing in the midst of miles of waste and desolation.

"It's harsh like nothing on this side of the ocean, but it can be crossed. There's plenty of game, and there are routes that avoid the worst of the blasted areas. There are only three mountain ranges to cross, and only one of them is as harsh as things we've already successfully navigated. Nothing that compares to Brad's homelands. Not where we're going.

"The middle of the continent is amazingly flat and wide, and is hunted by a wizard-monstrosity. We'll have to avoid that somehow, but we can figure that out when we get there.

"There are elves in a few places, and dwarves in some of the mountains. Neither is friendly to outsiders, so we'll avoid most of them unless we need something from them. I have friends in a dwarvish town on the near coast, and we'll hopefully be able to ask them for help. There may be humans, but if there are, they live far to the south, and we're not going there.

"Then, finally, on the far coast, we'll find Sam's tower. Before we get to it, we'll enter her protectorate, and there we'll be safer than anywhere else in this world."

"Thag," Shina asked, "why did the battle-mages build those civilizations and then tear them down so viciously?"

"They didn't build anything, Little One, except armies and weapons. People, many of them either refugees fleeing other worlds from the gnomes, or descended from such, built things. When Gem and Ariel left our world to pursue the gnomes, they left behind a world that was hurt. It had scars like Xalax. But it was healing when they left.

"Some apprentice wizards, charged by Gem with making sure the world would be defended when they were gone, created the battle-mages and left them in charge. But they made them too aggressive, too battle-hungry. Like the trolls, they were perverted from their original purpose into something harmful.

"Most of the histories agree that there were originally ten-thousand battle-mages. They agree that, within a thousand years there were fewer than a hundred left. It's not clear in the records, but demons like Kamaia may have driven the destruction.

"Battle-mages were creations. They didn't age or die of disease. But they were killable. Mostly by each other.

"Antain was correct that a normal battle-mage could turn the tide of any normal battlefield. They were brilliant at strategy and tactics, at subterfuge and stratagem, and almost unmatched in fighting. A battle-mage could take on a dozen elves single-handedly and expect to win.

"The emperors were the twelve strongest, smartest, most cunning and skilled of the battle-mages. They rose to rulership over almost the whole world. But they didn't rule wisely and fought each other constantly.

"In all the thousands of years that they ruled, only two things ever killed an imperial battle-mage. Ten were killed by others of their own kind, and two died at my hands. Nothing else ever succeeded."

Thag pointed at Chalkos. "They killed young dragons as a matter of policy. They mostly ignored the southern continent, so they didn't know about my father. Once my step-father led them to my actual father, they killed him. It took six of them working together, and an army of elves and druids.

"But he wasn't a full dragon. The gnomes ignored him because he lacked the spark that makes a real dragon. The battle-mages destroyed the ones the gnomes missed, because they knew that a full-grown dragon would overpower their armies and themselves as easily as a lion overpowers a lamb. Even an imperial battle-mage is no match for a real dragon, once it's grown up.

"They didn't set out to set you free," he addressed Chalkos. "They intended to destroy you as well as your elvish masters."

Chalkos nodded her long neck. She'd know that for years.

Thag looked at Shina. "And they killed wizard-children as soon as they were discovered. The laws about children who see worlds instead of stars were set aside by the kings of men because my step-father made them feel foolish for believing in an outdated superstition. For millennia, children like you were slain as soon as they were discovered. But, finally, generations after the last battle-mage was finally overthrown and the empire brought low, you were born, and the world gained a tiny candle of hope.

"When the word reached Sam that a human child saw 'islands in the sky' where most people saw stars, she sent me to find you. It was a desperate hope, but the only one we had: A rumor from a comment made in the presence of servants when your father got a painting made. But the rumor made it to the right ears.

"And I found you locked up in a tower, embroiled in a political fight between Antain and his king. The whole world risked because two men learned too well from the battle-mage traditions of power, jealousy and fighting."

Brad knew a little of battle-mage history. They were long enough ago, more than a hundred years now, that much of it had faded to almost-legend, but millennia of presence doesn't fade to total ignorance quite that fast. He'd never heard such a negative view of them before. But, then, he'd also been assured dragons were a myth, and had believed it until he met Thag a few years ago.

Shina knew the official history of the battle-mages. That they'd been glorious and powerful and had ruled an empire that spanned the world – the heirs left behind by Gem when he pursued the evil gnomes across the void to other worlds in an unimaginably distant past. She knew they had gradually lost their empire, and had been overthrown finally by an alliance of men and "dark powers", in order to free mankind from what had become an oppressive rule.

She realized that the "dark powers" mentioned in the stories and songs of her own kingdom had probably been Thag and his step-father. Maybe Kamaia had figured into those tales somewhere. But the "demon" summoned by "an ancient wizard" to kill the last of the emperor battle-mages, was almost certainly her very own Thag, his story twisted by power-hungry men into a figure of evil and darkness.

Maybe this Sam, whoever she was, also counted as a "dark power" in the stories. None of them were named.

"You've mentioned Sam before, Thag. What is she?" asked Shina.

Thag thought a moment, then finally responded. "I'm really not sure. She used to work with actual wizards. She knew Gem personally. And she usually looks like a little girl or a young woman, when she looks like anything at all. But she's no more a little girl than I am. Less of one, really.

"You really will have to meet her and see what you think for yourself. I'm not even sure what she'll look like to you, since your vision is different from mine. She's hard to explain.

"But she's almost as old as the world. She remembers when the titans were still shaping the land and seas. She remembers the first dragons and the first wizards. At least, the first ones in our world – she says dragons were born somewhere else, and wizards were born everywhere. Whatever that means.

"And she'll help us. She wants to save this world, since it's the only one she lives in. She's neither dragon nor wizard, and can't escape to other worlds.

"She lives near a wizard-tower on an island on the far coast of the eastern continent. I've never been to the tower, but I've known her most of my life. My step-father introduced us when I was still a child, only a few years old. Maybe fifty or sixty, if I remember correctly."

They talked long into the stormy night. First light saw the woods dripping wet, but the sky was clear enough that they decided to move on. At Thag's insistence, Shina removed her magic from the tree. "We don't need it any further, and there's no way to tell what it might unbalance in the world if left in place."

Days of travel turned into weeks and then months. Shina was showing real signs of her pregnancy now, though it hardly slowed them down yet. They discussed delaying the ocean-crossing if they felt she was near her term before they left, and everyone agreed that would probably be best.

As they went further east, they found more and more villages and farms. Nothing so dense as the large western kingdoms, but enough that efforts to avoid them took them more and more out of their way. Some nights, Shina, Brad and Koserana would seek shelter in a farm or small village while Thag spent the night circumventing it, but most they avoided because they didn't want to separate the group.

A few times, they had to run from angry villagers who had spotted them in the country. From rumors they caught, a monster with two beautiful women as prisoners had been seen in a few places, and the local lords were all set on freeing the women.

Brad usually wasn't mentioned, which made him question a few stories he'd learned growing up. "If they can get us so wrong, and leave me out entirely, from eye-witness sightings, how mangled are the 'histories' we all know? These people can't even get a story straight two days later!"

He argued, "What if Gem wasn't the undead abomination everyone says he was? Maybe he was just a wizard who got distorted in the telling? And maybe even Ariel isn't told right? What if she wasn't a dragon at all?"

He dropped that line of questioning when Chalkos hissed at him for suggesting her personal hero, Ariel, might not be a direct relative, and when Shina pointed out that she had Gem's diaries "right here in this pouch", and that they confirmed both Ariel's draconic nature and Gem's undeath.

"But I can't read the gem with the descriptions of undeath. It won't let me and all I get is fog from it." She couldn't explain the sensation any better than that, and even Thag eventually let it drop despite all his curiosity about the gemstone "books".

***

Chalkos soared.

Her wings gripped the wind two miles above the mountain tops that spread from horizon to horizon beneath her as she drifted across the sky.

Chalkos always loved flying. Adults exercise for reasons, but she was still child enough to fly just for the joy of it. The effort in her muscles radiated that pleasant feeling of young athleticism at its peak. The bitter-cold, thin air would have killed a human, but for her it was a thrill across her skin. Bright sunlight glinted on coppery scales and she gleamed in it.

Perhaps someone at just the right angle, with the sun at just the right spot, would see a speck of glare in the sky, but she was too high for most people to see even if they looked. And most people don't look up anyway – they focus on where their feet will be next and glance no higher than the terrain around them. But for her draconic eyes, the land below and the sky above were full of rich details.

Miles below and more than a dozen miles behind her, she could see her friends climbing over the shoulder of a mountain. She saw Thag help Shina over a small ledge in their path, his strength never failing her. Brad, born and raised in mountains far steeper than these, walked and climbed easily.

Even at that distance, she could see the details of Shina's beautiful face. If Chalkos' scaly features had allowed it, she would have smiled as she watched that amazing young woman.

Mostly, Chalkos looked at the land ahead of her friends. They needed paths that didn't dead-end in cliffs, that didn't pass too near the many hazards of the terrain, and that avoided most habitations.

This was a lawless land, much given to banditry even before the battle-mages lost their empire over it, and worse since. It also had remnants of the old wizardry left insane and dangerous by the slow dying of the world. It was up to Chalkos to steer her friends away from things like that.

It had been bad enough when they ran into that troll! They certainly didn't need anything really dangerous to get near Shina and her soon-to-be-born child.

She saw that the best route for them would mean crossing a small lake. Brad and Shina had worked out how they could quickly grow a tree and magically craft it into a simple bridge or raft, so the lake might be okay.

The young dragon darted out of the sky and dove head-first into the icy water. For her, there was no shock of cold, and flight became swimming in an instant.

The water was deep and the depths were shrouded in stygian blackness, but she scouted easily and rapidly. She snapped a few fish out of the water for a snack, avoided a few crocodiles near the shore because she thought they looked cute, and determined there was nothing that would threaten her friends.

A fountain of water roared off her back as she surfaced and sprang back into the sky. Her wings beat quickly and her speed through the air dried her before the last ripples of her passage had faded from the surface of the lake.

Flying barely above the ground, she darted across hills and over trails, taking a close look at things she had seen from miles away.

She didn't really need to do this part, but it was fun!

It never came up that Chalkos could help with chores other than flying scouts, so it never came up that Chalkos didn't have the patience for them.

Months and thousands of miles sped past, and they finally reached the cities of the coast.

Chalkos said that there were some very large islands a couple of hundred miles off the coast, east of the cities. The sea would be hard to cross, but grew much narrower both far to the north and closer to the south. Chalkos also reported that there were many sea-going vessels "of a strange design" that mainly engaged in fishing around the cities. None seemed to travel out into the larger ocean, which was just past the islands, but she thought they could probably sail to the islands if they wanted to.

Thag explained and they all agreed, though reluctantly, that the three who looked human enough would go into one of the coastal cities and get a ship. Thag would have to go around. The fear he engendered in most people would make booking passage impossible.

Thag decided he would meet them on the southern edge of the islands. From there, they would have to sail as far north as was safe, and then attempt the risky eastern passage to the west coast of that continent. He set off at his usual tireless sprint, heading south and east along a course Chalkos described to him.

Shina missed him before she even lost sight of him. She did her best to hide the anxiety she was constantly filled with over her pregnancy. Constantly worrying about whether she was suitable for raising a son, worrying about the future of a child in a doomed world, worrying over how she would deal with it if their son were truly inhuman, and worrying that her pregnancy itself made her too much of a burden on her friends.

Not least of her worries was that Thag had required the wisdom and patience of an elf to be raised into anything other than a monster. He had told her of the hunger and rage he had to overcome. She knew he had grown up jealous of the beauty of the elves around him, till he had finally matured enough to see their narcissism and pride as the flaws they truly were.

But she was no elf-druid! She remembered vividly how she had treated her father's household slaves and servants, and the young suitors who had begged her attention. How could someone like that possibly raise a child of Thag's? Was she even suitable to raise a merely human child, given her own upbringing?

Months of worry and anxiety had worn her down almost as much as the harsh conditions of their trek. If she had realized how much the others all went out of their way to care for and comfort her, to protect her, she would have crumbled.

She tried to hide how she felt, and was falsely certain she had succeeded only because she had never had friends before and was unaccustomed to dealing with people who could be socially discreet, like Thag and Brad, or who were oblivious to the whole situation, like Koserana.

As Shina, Brad, and Koserana approached the western boundaries of the city they had picked, the setting sun sent their shadows scouting the road ahead of them.

Chalkos had only flown over the city once, during the day, so they weren't sure what to expect as they arrived in the evening, with the light crepuscular and the city falling into shadow.

As with all cities left over from the battle-mage empire, it was heavily fortified and extensively guarded. Chalkos had never before seen the material the walls and fortifications were made of – a strangely smooth stone that had no seams or cutting-marks on it. Though the smooth, gray stone was new to her, the buildings made of it had the familiar thick walls, crenelated battlements, round towers, and appurtenances of buildings in a permanent warzone.

The total lack of the usual farming villages and large farms, ranches, orchards and other sources of food they were accustomed to in the far west was very strange. Inland communities had been surrounded by such, but Chalkos had found that the nearby coastal cities seemed to rely almost exclusively on their huge fleets for food. This city alone had thousands of fishing and whaling vessels sailing in and out of it at all times of the day, and others had similar fleets.

The outskirts of the city were a few sparse buildings. From the air, they had looked unoccupied, but they were well-kept enough that they must fulfill some useful purpose and must be maintained by someone. Most large cities in the west had huge outskirts of warehouses, smithies, tanneries, soapworks, ramshackle dwellings, stables, and the like. The coastal cities of this land only had a few small outbuildings, and then the sheer walls rose starkly from empty grounds after a wide, deep moat.

Shina and Brad had been told all about what Chalkos had seen in her overflights, and knew what to expect. They just hoped they could find shelter before the night – they had hoped to arrive earlier in the day, but there had been a few unexpected delays and they were later than they wanted to be.

Shina's steps were heavy as she approached the western edge of the city. Her belly felt odd, and she knew that the baby would be born very soon. Perhaps even that very night. She was exhausted, emotionally burned out, and trepidation filled her stomach with acid-anticipation.

Vivid pictures filled her mind of what would happen if the baby were born with horns or claws like Thag had. She imagined the terrible damage it would do to her if that were to happen. She didn't know that babies are born without these things all the time in the animal world. It never occurred to her that the baby's frequent stirrings and healthy kickings would have already harmed her if he had Thag-like claws, proving thereby that she was safer than she feared.

She had been told repeatedly that having Brad nearby always seemed to guarantee healthy births, but she dismissed that and thought to herself that Thag was only trying to comfort her when he said it.

Koserana glanced up from the road when she heard someone coming towards them. His pace was a hurried walk, almost a jog, and soon she saw him come around the corner of a building a few hundred yards away.

The man was tall and had the well-padded build of someone who is strong but who eats more than he should. A layer of fat over an inner layer of strong muscle gave him the barrel-chested look common to many successful, older craftsmen.

He stopped, squinted towards them and the setting sun behind them, and then, catching sight of them after a moment, hurried towards them while gesturing for them to come to him.

Shina, now long-practiced at the translation spell she had learned from Gem's gems, cast silently and felt the energies engulf herself and her two friends.

As soon as the man was close enough to see her clearly, he stopped suddenly and, wide-eyed, muttered something to himself. Shina didn't catch it, but Koserana clearly heard, "By the emperors, she's as close as he said she'd be!"

In a louder voice, he greeted them. "My ladies! My lord! I've been sent to fetch you into Xi'chant'iros before nightfall! Come swiftly, please. There are hazards inland during the dark!"

When they caught up to him, Brad asked, "How'd you know we were coming? And who are you?" His voice wasn't threatening, but it wasn't friendly either.

"My lord! My name is Qagillera. I did not myself know you were coming," he rushed through his words. "I was told. I am but a humble slave of my master. It is he who wishes to provide you shelter for the birth. That's what I was told. There is danger in these lands in the dark. We must hurry!"

Koserana appraised Qagillera. He was telling the truth as far as he knew it, but that left a lot of room for his master to lie to him. "What did he tell you about how far along she is?" she asked, putting her arm protectively and possessively over Shina's shoulders.

Qagillera's eyes went wide with surprise and his posture was honestly startled. "He said she would give birth tonight, and that it must be under stone shelter or catastrophe will befall the whole world. Come, we must hurry! Even without my master's invitation, you must be in shelter before the dark." Fear added urgency to his voice and his manner, and Koserana could smell it on his skin and breath.

He turned, gesturing for them to follow, and started towards the city.

When they stood still, not following, he paused and turned back towards them. "Should I fetch a cart? Will it be easier that way? Does she need help? Or slaves to carry her?"

"Brad," Koserana addressed the big half-orc. "We should trust him for now. But keep your eyes open."

Shina just wanted to sit down. To stop and rest. When Koserana and Brad started to follow the man, she reluctantly took a step, and then another. She had walked almost half a huge continent easily, but the next few feet felt endless.

Brad looked at her, then turned to their host. "Get a cart. Or some strong slaves and a palanquin. She needs to lie down."

Qagillera immediately turned around and took off at a fast jog back into the city.

Brad muttered to himself, "I'm not Thag, but I can carry you a little ways." His instincts warned him that the night was dangerous out here. He easily scooped Shina up into his arms and started to carry her towards the city. As soon as he picked her up, Shina fainted away, too exhausted to carry on.

Koserana caught up with him in a few steps. "I'm stronger. Give her to me."

Brad replied, "You are stronger. That's why you guard us while I carry her. There's something that wants to hunt us out here."

Koserana didn't see anything or hear anything, but she had learned over the miles and months to trust Brad's instincts.

As the sun touched the mountains behind them, a small group of men appeared at the gates. They were large men, and they carried a seat mounted on poles between them. Qagillera was right behind them and directed them to hurry and take Shina from Brad.

It only took a moment to seat her properly, and then they were off at a fast trot. Brad noticed that the men all looked nervous. Their eyes darted at every shadow and every slightest hint of motion, and their bodies were full of twitches and sudden starts.

As the last fingernail of sun disappeared behind the mountains, Koserana heard the first whisperings of a strange noise in the distance.

"We must hurry!" said Qagillera. The bearers broke into a run, heedless of the hazards of tripping or stumbling in the dark.

In moments, they passed the gates, and huge chains pulled the massive doors and bars shut right behind them.

Brad and Koserana slowed their pace for the merest moment, but Qagillera urged them on. "The walls only keep out some of the dangers of our nights. We must be inside, under stone, before the true dark!" He glanced upwards at the evening sky, still lit by the hidden sun. It wouldn't last long, but there was still some slight, crepuscular light from it.

They raced through strangely dark streets. Unlike any other city in their experience, it had no external lights, none of the amenities meant to make being outside at night easier and more convenient. Some slight light leaked around shutters on sealed windows.

After a minute, Qagillera noticed that nobody was tiring or even breathing hard from the run, and looked around at the three travelers, trying to determine who might be behind this strangeness. He couldn't tell, but that didn't stop him from pushing for ever more speed.

Koserana heard something coming up fast from behind them! She looked, and saw a black shape against the growing darkness. A beast of some sort? Maybe, but it looked like nothing she had ever seen before, and something about it frightened her.

One of the bearers shrieked! "The stalkers! They are upon us!" Foam came from his mouth.

The darkness was full, and everywhere Koserana looked, her dragon-eyes saw nightmares closing in on them. They couldn't outrun them!

She could have flown! She could escape. But she would never abandon her friends!

She prepared to transform. She would take the fight to their enemies! She knew it would be her death, but a dragon would certainly take a few with her!

Suddenly, intense white light blazed over them! The creatures howled, a soundless wave of overwhelming terror and anguish, and fled back to the dark!

Shina, her right arm upraised from where she sat in the carry-seat, held a mote of pure radiance in her hand! It shone clearly even through the flesh and bone that held it. Koserana stared at it for a moment, stunned. The very essence of light and vision was in that glow! Despite its awesome brilliance, it didn't even hurt eyes that turned straight to it — more pure in its purpose of lighting than even the rays of the sun.

The bearers and Qagillera stood frozen, staring at Shina in a weird mix of worship and terror. Brad crouched, combat ready, waiting on a hair-trigger if they moved against her.

Koserana almost changed to Chalkos right in front of them. Secrecy and trickery be damned if they attacked her lover!

Qagillera recovered enough poise quickly enough to tell the bearers to get moving and gestured the way to go. After a moment's pause, they were all running through the streets again.

Despite Brad's magic, Shina's arm quickly grew tired, and her hand fell to her lap, the glow fading to a faint glimmer. It barely lit the street around them. Despite the dimming, the night-creatures seemed to fear her still and paced the party at a safe distance.

Soon, they approached a large, fortified mansion. The main building was a full three stories tall, and surrounded by additions and wings and smaller buildings of various sorts. The grounds, several acres, were protected by a ten-foot stone wall topped by another fifteen feet of crossed steel poles with sharpened ends. Wealth, and the force necessary to protect it.

In other cities, there would have been guards out and about. Patrols would have paced the wall outside and in, and doors would have strong men outside them. Here, the entrance had a small stone building next to it, with thick walls and steel doors. Metal shutters covered the windows tightly, letting only the slightest light escape.

The mansion itself presented just such a formidable façade. A few beams of light escaped narrow cracks in strong shutters and sealed doorways.

As they approached, the outer gate swung open for them, opened from within the guard-hut by chains and levers without exposing the men to the dangers of the night.

In a minute, they stood outside the sealed main doors.

Night creatures, sensing their prey was about to escape them, dared close in on Shina's fading light.

"Shina," whispered Brad. "We need light so they can open the door for us."

Shina's drooping head came up a bit. Her tired, bloodshot eyes cracked the slightest opening, but seemed blind as they sought Brad's face. After a moment, she nodded almost imperceptibly and strained to raise her hand in the air again.

Brad held her wrist and lifted her hand above her head. She looked grateful for a moment, and then shuddered as she drew magical power into herself and re-lit the shard of wizard-light.

For a moment, her hand blazed back the night. For a moment, the creatures fled in all directions.

In that moment, the door swung open and they all surged inside the open hallway presented to them.

And then the light faded to nothing and Shina collapsed. Her body started shaking with the effort and a grimace of shock twisted her face into an ugly snarl.

Brad stared for a moment and then realized exactly what was going on!

"Someone help! She's giving birth!" he yelled.

He grabbed Qagillera by the front of his shirt and lifted him off the ground. "She's giving birth!" he repeated, loudly. "She needs a bed and a midwife! Now!"

It didn't really occur to him that the man couldn't help with these things while being held off the ground and yelled at.

But Brad's yelling had the intended consequences. In moments, servants and guards surrounded them, trying to help but afraid to approach the angry half-orc.

"Brad!" Koserana shouted. Brad looked at her, his eyes half-berserk. "Let him go! They need to help Shina!" She gestured at the young woman curled up in the middle of the floor.

Brad took a deep breath.

Intelligence came back into his eyes.

He set Qagillera down and half-heartedly patted the man's shirt flat where he had crushed it.

With a sweeping gesture, he invited the servants to take Shina, and stepped back from her to make it clear it was safe.

A few rushed to her, picked her up and began to carry her deeper into the mansion. One, a statuesque matron, gestured for Brad and Shina to follow.

"There are couches in the living room down the hall. I don't think we have time to get her to a real bed. Will that suffice, my lord?" she asked Brad as they hurried down the entry-hall.

Brad nodded. "Yes. She needs to lie down. And she needs a midwife!"

The woman grabbed an excited young boy by the arm. "Get Xiona! Hurry, lad!" she snapped at him, and the boy ran off at a full sprint after giving her the briefest nod of acknowledgement.

When they arrived to the living room, down a bewildering labyrinth of halls and doors and doors and halls, the servants laid Shina down on a large couch and then most were shooed out of the room by the tall matron.

Koserana took Shina's hand in hers, and suffered the crushing grip of desperation without flinching.

Servants quickly undressed Shina. More arrived with hot water, towels, food and drink for Koserana and Brad, and a dizzying array of all the civilized things they had missed for most of a year since leaving Anytown.

A ripple spread down Shina's naked belly.

Koserana asked Brad, "You have many children, right? You must have done this before, right? What do we do now? What if the midwife doesn't arrive in time?"

Brad, his eyes wide and a little wild, looked at her for a moment. Finally, he managed to get out the words, "I make them, but I don't know anything about them after that. I always get chased away from town before this part!"

Koserana looked puzzled, so Brad forced himself to regain a bit of his usual composure and clarified. "I usually get exiled from villages long before my children are born. The men don't usually like me much by that time. And in cities, I hire a midwife who knows what she's doing. So I just don't know!"

The boy and an old woman arrived at a run, puffing and blowing into the room, and Brad's face took on a look of profound relief. He'd been around enough midwives to know a good one when he saw her.

As the midwife set up shop next to Shina's couch, the noble owner of the mansion showed up, accompanied by a young boy with an odd look to his eyes.

The noble looked down at the boy, and the boy said, "She's got another couple of hours. Her son will be born at midnight of the new year."

Brad and Koserana were confused. It was late-summer, the new year was months away.

The nobleman nodded, then approached Brad.

"I am Baron Motaku," he introduced himself. To Brad, he said,

"My lord Angbarad," with a slight bow. "Welcome to my home. Tomanus, here," he indicated the boy, "told me of your coming and how important the infant is going to be."

Brad looked at the boy, Tomanus. He couldn't have been more than six or seven years old, and was boringly normal except for something in his gaze.

Brad's totem suddenly spoke to him in his mind! She had only done this twice before in his whole life! His face lit up with joy as her voice sounded as though in his ears. "My love! The boy speaks for the mightiest of us. As we are joined, thee and me, he is joined to the world itself. Respect him, and fear him, but trust him."

At the manifestation of Brad's totem within him, everyone in the house took in a deep breath that filled their bodies with life and vigor! Brad stood straight and tall, his head high and his shoulders back. Joy filled almost everyone around, but most of all him. Only Koserana was untouched, for her magic, dragon-born and dragon-bred, was senior to the magic of world-spirits.

From that moment, the birth transformed. All difficulty and exhaustion disappeared from it, and Shina gave birth easily and smoothly, exactly at midnight.

As the baby gasped its first breath, Tomanus spoke. "Exactly at the start of the year, as I pronounced."

He looked at Brad and answered his unspoken question. "Not the new year as reckoned by mortals or mortal-born. The exact anniversary of when I took on physical form and became the world. One-hundred and twenty-seven thousand, six-hundred and two years ago at the very moment of midnight, our world was born. Your queen's child shares the same birth-minute as our world does. As it must be."

He continued, "Thank your wife for me, Lord Angbarad. She is one of my favorite children. She has been sorrowful ever since her sister, Kamaia, went mad, and grieves for her even more now that she is trapped beyond our world. Our gratitude for what your wife has helped with tonight will comfort her."

Shina listened to all of this while staring at the perfect baby boy she held in her arms. So tiny! So perfect! She made her decision and announced it. "His name is Mornu."

Koserana, totally fascinated by the infant, beamed a wide smile. "I like him."

Lord Motaku glanced at the child. A faint hint of pale green flashed in his brown eyes. His voice was unnaturally serene as he quietly ordered his guards, "Kill the man and his slaves. The infant must be unharmed!"

Even before he had finished speaking, Brad leapt into battle!

"Guard her!" he ordered Koserana, without taking his eyes off of the Baron.

His leap carried him to the first of the Baron's guards, and a light tap of his bracelet filled each of his hands with a long steel sword.

Two short-spears glanced off of Brad's bare chest, deflected by skin hard and strong as granite. Two swords flashed in unison and the guards fell back, their armor and the flesh under it slashed to ribbons!

Brad worried for a brief moment, but his spirit-vision showed he faced only mortal soldiers. Twelve armed men became twelve corpses in mere seconds.

And then he faced Baron Motaku as the man, panicked, tried to escape the room. One hand fumbled at the door, the other tried to drag Tomanus between him and the raging half-orc.

Blood-covered steel flashed over Tomanus' head into the Baron's neck. Blood gushed and the corpse fell, still shuddering, to the floor.

Brad whirled to face another group of guards! His eyes searched for that hint of green – demon-sign – but saw none of it.

Before he could react, the guards dropped to their knees and set their weapons on the floor.

Every man and woman in the room suddenly knelt and bowed their heads.

Brad stood, quivering with battle-lust, confused.

Koserana, her eyes swirling, liquid copper, stood over Shina, ready to transform if she needed to, and looked to Brad for guidance.

Shina, holding Mornu protectively, had a faint yellow glow around her right hand, and looked poised to thrust … something … at whoever threatened her child, but everyone was motionless and she paused.

Tomanus lightly touched Brad from behind. Brad whirled, swords ready, but the young boy simply started talking calmly and quietly, as if nothing important were taking place. He was dripping with the dead baron's blood, and he simply ignored it.

"You own them now. You killed their master, and you own this place and all in it now."

Brad tried to understand, but didn't even have time to ask a question.

"It's their way here. You own this house now. They are waiting for you to tell them what to do."

Shina, raised as a noble in a land of slave-owners, understood first. She explained to Brad, "They're slaves, Brad. While the Baron was alive, he owned them and they obeyed him. You killed him in combat. You're the new Baron. Tell them to stand up and get back to their work. Tell the soldiers and guards to protect us and the house. Tell them we all need baths and a clean room. Tell them we'll sleep the night in a safe room with comfortable beds, and will make more decisions in the morning. And tell them we're hungry and need food and wine."

Brad started to just tell them, "Do what she said", but realized it needed to be more formal. He took a few deep breaths to calm himself, and then gave the orders Shina had suggested. At each order, people rushed to do his bidding, and they very shortly were brought to a richly appointed bedroom with a couple of beds and a nice couch. Golden platters of hot food were brought, along with crystalline glasses full of an ice-cold drink Brad couldn't quite place, but which was soothing and pleasant when he tasted it.

In short order, the three were quickly and efficiently settled, Brad and Shina into hot baths and Koserana on a large floor-pillow. Attendants bathed them carefully while others fed them dainty dishes. Some of the food was strange to them, but hot, tasty and filling, and anything was a huge improvement over the camp-fare and dry-stores they had been living off of for months.

Brad felt slightly uncomfortable. He was accustomed to sauna-baths, not wallowing in a tub of hot water. The attendants were slaves, not the paid professionals he was comfortable with from Anytown. It was all very strange to him, but Shina was able to guide him through the experience.

Brad tried to spend some time questioning Tomanus, but one of the other slaves explained that Tomanus could barely speak, and couldn't even dress himself or feed himself, when the titan wasn't "with him". Apparently, the effort of even a few minutes was immense for the dying world-spirit, and it only possessed the boy briefly and when it had something important to say.

Shina and Koserana spent most of their time oohing and cooing over little Mornu. Brad, following the traditions of his birth-tribe, introduced himself to Mornu as if to another adult man. He told the infant, "Well-traveled and well-arrived," and lightly touched his finger to his tiny face.

He explained to Shina, "Where I grew up, we know the soul has travelled to arrive in the body, and we give first-greeting to the soul as if it were the adult it will become and had walked far to come and stay with us. It's the same greeting we give to friends who have been away on long trips."

Shina smiled. "I like that. Welcome home, Mornu," she said.

For a while, if Mornu did anything, even just giving a milk-laden burp, the two women treated it with a round of giggles and bright smiles.

The pampering didn't end with the baths, but Brad finally herded most of the servants out of the room, doused most of the candles and all of the lanterns and tried to sleep. Shina was too excited to sleep, but too exhausted to really stay awake. Koserana, as always, was wide awake. She finally took Mornu into her arms and gave Shina a chance to rest.

Mornu, it seemed, was no more inclined to sleep than Koserana. As Brad relaxed for the night, he briefly wondered if the baby would inherit his father's draconic immunity to the need for rest.

Koserana finally set Mornu down in a pile of blankets near Shina, and tiptoed over to the couch Brad was lying on. He sat up just enough to give her room to sit, then lay back down with his head resting on one of her legs. As pillows go, she was one of the nicest he'd ever used, and, as always, the close-up sight of her perfect body was more than easy on his eyes.

"Brad," Koserana whispered. "You like me, don't you?"

He was suddenly very, very awake.

"Yes. You're a good friend," he replied. It was the safest wording he could think of.

She looked down at him and met his gaze. "You know that's not what I mean. You're not really my type," she said. "But if you want to make love to me, I'll let you."

Brad replied slowly. "Koserana, if it were just a physical thing, I'd love to. But you're special, and I don't want to ruin our friendship by making it physical. First, you have to more than 'let me' – it would have to be something you wanted, not just something you'd allow. Second, I'd get you pregnant, and you're too young for that, even if Thag wouldn't hunt me down and kill me slowly for doing it."

She smiled and his heart beat a little faster, despite his every attempt at self-discipline. "First, maybe I do want to more than just 'let you'. Second, there are ways to avoid getting pregnant, even with you. You can't get me pregnant in my mouth, or my hand, or my …"

Brad interrupted fast. "Okay. Yes. True. That's all true. But I'm still just a half-orc, and you're a dragon. My kind almost never live even thirty years. You could live forever. It can't work. And Thag would find out, and he'd spank you and boil me slowly."

He paused for a moment. "Wait! How do you know all that about sex? About things like … well, like hands and mouths and … all that?"

She laughed quietly. "Mr. Tower of Iron, I've probably spent more time in more brothels around more prostitutes than you've spent breathing. You just think different because you've only known me for a little while. Remember Anytown? You hired two prostitutes for your sauna? I had sex with a dozen women that night! And I'm almost seven times as old as you, so I've had that much more time to learn about sex and 'things'."

Her laugh was light music, joyous and sexy. "I just haven't been doing that much recently because of Shina and Thag. I like Shina, and she likes me. But she's in love with Thag, and totally loyal to him, and I'm just a sex-friend. Like she is for me. It's fun and wonderful and I love it, but it's not like Thag and her. That's love."

Brad realized he'd had no idea Koserana even noticed things like that. It was frequently hard to remember that this beautiful young woman was more than a hundred years old before he was even born, but she sometimes reminded him of it. Sometimes forcefully.

She continued after a moment. "I like you, Brad. And if you ever want to teach me how men do it with women – with hands and mouths and everything else – you just let me know. But, we'll be sure to get Thag's permission first. I wouldn't want to steal you from him!"

Brad sputtered for a moment, then just smiled and shook his head. She was really, really good at teasing people. Especially him.

He relaxed back onto her leg, closed his eyes, and muttered, "Who knew a mere pillow could talk so much?"

Koserana just smiled. She'd won, and she knew it.

Brad's last thought as he faded away into sleep was to wonder what Thag was up to on the night his firstborn came into the world.

Chapter 25: *Midnight Death in the Darkness*

Thag was sitting on a beach, talking to the local wind and sky spirits. He had some idle time, and they had come to him begging for stories of far-off lands. Air spirits always liked stories about travels and strange places, even though they themselves tend to roam vast distances. Thag's step-father had taught him that air spirits are the world's greatest vagabond-gossips, and Thag had found it to be almost universally true.

After leaving the others outside that coastal city, he had sprinted across the mountains and lands to the sea, then swam out to the islands Chalkos had found for him. It took hours to cross the miles of sea between the large peninsula the city was on and the first of the islands, so Thag arrived well after it was dark.

For the first few minutes after he swam ashore, some annoying dark creatures had attacked him. He assumed these things were some remnant of the gnome-wars, or maybe some twisted creation of the battle-mages. Either way, a few dozen of them had to be slain before the rest fled further inland and left him alone.

He wondered if those things were the reason there were no cities or villages of any sort on these islands. Chalkos had reported the islands strangely barren, and if these night-creatures were present all over them, that would certainly explain it.

Shortly after midnight, a wispy little wind spirit, barely a breeze, sped to Thag over the waves and sea and told him of the birth of his son. "The baby was born! The world thinks he's going to help it heal!" the spirit told him, and Thag pondered a while on what that could possibly mean. Though he tried, he couldn't get anything more coherent out of the spirit. As is common with air spirits, it promptly forgot its message to him the moment it had delivered it, and knew nothing of what it had said much less any clarifying details. Regardless, Thag interpreted the message as being a hopeful one.

Unlike his step-father, Thag had never been able to communicate well with other spirits than just the winds and storms of the world. With those, he was always on very good terms. But stone, water, fire, the living spirits of woods and animals and plants, and the clever spirits of cities and crafts and the machines of man, these had rarely appeared to him. Even Drew the dryad only spoke with him because she had once befriended his step-father.

A few hours before dawn, Thag swam into the sea and caught some fish for himself. He didn't have the appetite of a real troll, but he still liked to eat frequently, and the local waters swarmed with large tuna and a variety of their prey, which appealed to him far more than the twisted corpses of the night-creatures.

When he returned to shore a few minutes later, his stomach momentarily full, the night-creatures attacked him again. This second time, he only had to kill a few before the rest fled. Thag noted that they were learning, and decided they must be wizard-work, not mage-crafted. Crafting even rudimentary intelligence into their creations was far beyond the ability or desire of any of the battle-mages.

All the while, he pondered on the fact that he had a son. He'd never had a lover before Shina, and had never thought to have family. He knew Shina assumed he'd known what he was doing that first time, back in the sauna in Anytown, but he'd been as much a virgin as she had before that night.

A son! What a remarkable thing!

He knew Chalkos half thought of him as her father, and he more than half reciprocated the feeling, but a real son was something else indeed!

He wondered what he looked like, this son of his. "I hope he looks nothing like me, and can pass unnoticed amongst his mother's people!" he thought to himself. But he had little hope of that. Dragon-blood tends to carry its mark on the body it flows in, and Thag knew this better than most.

Of course, there was no telling what diluted troll-blood would look, or act like. So far as Thag knew, there had never been any half-blood trolls except himself and his long-dead siblings. What a quarter-blood troll would be, if anything, was a complete mystery. Trolls tended to kill and eat everything except other trolls, and only the powerful compulsions of the demoness Kamaia had kept his mother from trying to kill his father, as impossible as that would have been.

He knew it would be difficult to travel with a newborn. He hoped the trio would be able to travel soon, but he also counseled himself to patience. More important was for Shina and their son to be healthy, than for them to be fast. They only had a few years left if Sam was right about the plight of the world, but a few days or weeks to ensure better safety would be prudent even in that span.

A few hours after daybreak, Thag saw fishing boats leaving the docks from the city. He wondered what the city was called, and looked forward to Shina telling him about it. She wouldn't know much after a short stay, and probably wouldn't bother to read any of their books or listen to their stories, but she was highly intelligent and would learn somewhat of it before she left.

Koserana, eternally curious, clever and smart, would gather some stories. But they were likely to be gaudy things, like the time she once learned every bit of gossip, rumor and trade-craft she could gather from every whorehouse in a large city. She made the poor girls repeat their stories over and over till she had them memorized. He was sure there were people who would love to hear the detailed exploits of hundreds of sex-workers and exotic dancers, but to him they were boring. It had been decades since then, and she still sometimes quietly recited them to herself when she knew nobody could hear her except Thag. Those were the nights he wished he could sleep through it.

Brad, he knew, would probably spend the whole time drinking and wenching. He'd never understood his friend's single-minded focus on sex, but he accepted it without question, comment, or judgement. His idea of a good story involved at least two young women, a barroom brawl, and usually ended with him being chased out of town by an angry mob of young men, and an adoring mob of the young women who were the reason the men were angry.

He wished he dared cross the sea to the city itself, so he could be with Shina and their son. He wondered if she had named him after her grandfather, like she wanted, or if she had taken Thag's suggestion and named him Mornu. He had read that there was once a group of wizards who were dragon-friends, who had called themselves the Mor, and the singular of that in their old language was Mornu. He thought it would be a good name. But Shina was partial to Aramin, a name from the legends about the wizard Gem. He would be happy with either, or with anything else. He just wished he knew what it was to be.

The city, almost a hundred miles across the water, was interesting enough to watch through the morning. Thag knew most people couldn't see that far. Even those with excellent vision, like elves, were thwarted by the illusionary curve of the world. Only master-wizards and dragons could perceive the world's true flatness, and thus see the vast distances that were hidden from others.

From what Thag could see, at least half of the homes in the city were boats. Most simply anchored a little ways off from shore for the night. He assumed it was to avoid the night-creatures. He knew most people needed to sleep at night, and if the night creatures were as persistent on shore as they were out here on the island, they could prove annoying. At daybreak, many of the ships simply up-anchored and moved to docks, or out to sea. He enjoyed watching them for a while.

Shortly before noon, a much larger ship left the harbor and sailed out to sea. Thag saw that the boat seemed to be heading towards the waters off the island he was on. So he hid in the dunes and brush up from the shore. There was risk in letting any of those people see him. Though they were still miles from being able to even see the island, there was no reason to tempt fate by being out in the open.

After all, the city was human, and most humans would fear a monster like him. Given his ancestry and appearance, he couldn't even call it irrational. By any normal standard, they were right to be terrified by such as him.

When the ship was about twenty miles away, Thag recognized his friends on the deck. As soon as he made eye-contact with her, Koserana smiled and waved. Unsurprisingly, she had seen him even before he saw her. At twenty miles, Thag could just make out facial features clearly enough to identify people. Koserana could count nose-hairs at that distance. As keen as his half-draconic senses were, hers were made to see across worlds!

Koserana turned and spoke with someone, pointing Thag's location out to them. At the same moment, Thag caught sight of Shina and the tiny bundle held to her chest. Immediately, Thag dove into the water and began to swim rapidly towards the ship. Towards his son and wife!

His arms and hands extended straight ahead, he dolphin-kicked out into the waves. It took several minutes for him to close the distance, even with the ship coming towards him as he swam. The crew had a ladder ready for him when he pulled up along the bow of the ship.

A smaller boat would have tilted as he climbed aboard, but this large ship held itself steady, barely rocking in the gentle swells of the sheltered sea. When he got to the top of the ladder, a few brave sailors reached their hands to help him over the rail, but he knew all they'd get for their good manners was torn arms, so he merely took hold of the rail with one hand and vaulted over it.

Shina, waiting at the top of the ladder, presented tiny Mornu to his father as soon as Thag was aboard.

The baby had pale pink skin, with a wisp of barely-existent hair on his well-shaped head above a clearly human face. His eyes were closed, but he noticed the attention being paid to him and opened them in a moment. Thag stared into the pale blue eyes of his son, and his long life changed forever.

Shina knew her husband well, and addressed the thought in his swirling black eyes without Thag having to say a word. "You can touch him," she whispered gently.

Thag tentatively reached out a finger that was nearly as large as the tiny baby's whole arm, and gently ran it down the side of his son's face. The baby and the monster both broke into beaming smiles at the same moment.

"His name is Mornu," Shina told him.

Mornu quickly fell back asleep, sucking one of his oh-so-tiny fingers.

Shina quietly told Thag, "All he does is sleep and suckle."

Koserana, standing nearby, added, "He's a dragon, by his scent. Maybe somehow even more of one than you are, Thag. But he sleeps and drinks milk, so that makes him human. It's cute!"

Shina quietly told Thag, "All she does is talk about him and how cute he is."

For minutes, the crew stood around uselessly, trying to figure out why a sea-monster had been welcomed onto the deck, why it was making funny little noises at the passenger's baby, and why the baby's mother was letting her helpless child be exposed to a nightmare with giant fangs and claws and horns.

Finally, after thoroughly acquainting himself with his firstborn child, Thag looked around, a gigantic grin on his monstrous face. Some people mistook his toothy smile for a snarl and backed away apprehensively. Others just stared. Shina and Brad smiled at his gawking.

Brad gestured expansively. "So," he said, a laugh barely hidden in his voice. "You like my boat, I guess?"

Thag, scaly eyebrows raised in amusement, looked at Brad. "*Your* boat?" He paused for a moment. "Please tell me you didn't have this hidden in that bracelet."

Brad laughed. The crew seemed to take heart from this and some tentatively smiled. A few more, still staring at the giant monster on their deck, lost at least some of the fear in their postures and eyes.

"No," Brad replied. "No. I didn't have this with me. Gods but wouldn't that be incredible if this could hold that much!" He tapped the bracelet with his fingernail, which made the metal ring lightly.

He continued. "No. I didn't have this with me. I bought it this morning." He smiled and paused. It was obvious he wanted Thag to ask him about it.

Thag nodded knowingly, as if Brad buying a giant ship was an everyday thing. "You bought it. Of course you did," he muttered out loud. He peered around at the ship again, with a quick glance at Brad to let him know his bait had slipped the hook. Thag usually did get the better of clever conversations with anyone but Koserana, and even sometimes with her.

Shina rolled her eyes at the two men and their games. "Brad killed a nobleman in a fight that the nobleman started while he was being influenced by a demon. So Brad inherited a large house in town, a multitude of slaves, and a significant fortune in gold, art, and all the rest. They do that here — pass noble titles through nobles dueling each other. He used the money to buy the boat.

Shina quietly told Thag, "And all he does around Mornu is smile like his face is going to split in half and talk like his brain has gone to mush." She said it just loudly enough for Brad to hear.

Thag nodded and smiled. "Gone to mush?" He paused. "Of course, for him, mush is a move in the right direction. Do you think there's a chance that it will continue improving?"

Brad rolled his eyes, shrugged at the futility of it all, and walked off.

Koserana smiled indulgently at their decidedly amateur attempts at humor.

Shina and Thag went back to admiring Mornu and smiling at him.

Brad left them to it, and told the captain to get them underway as soon as possible.

The ship and her crew had made the long trip to the eastern continent a few times before. Trade with the elves on the coastal islands, and with the dwarves of the northern coasts, made the trip a prosperous one. Brad's was one of only a few ships that could do it safely. The captain assured the new owner that the trip would be as safe and fast as could be expected, and then quickly had them moving. They had spent all morning loading supplies and crew, and were fully ready for the long voyage.

The captain told Brad that it usually took about a month and a half to make the passage. Brad was able to drag Thag away from Mornu and Shina long enough to ask for help on that, but Thag told him the winds were already going that direction. Even if they would listen to him and push harder, all it would do is make for a rough storm, not a faster passage.

"Air and wind have certain rules, Brad. And they have to follow them," Thag explained. And then spent the next half hour going over those rules in great detail.

Brad both liked and respected Thag, and would follow him anywhere, but he did spend a large part of the lecture thinking that Thag having an affinity for moving air was not just about his talent for communing with wind and storm spirits.

Brad was comfortable with his role in Thag's crew. He was the best healer in the eastern lands, maybe in the world, and he'd proven his worth time and time again over the last year. He didn't know if his ability to almost guarantee healthy pregnancies and deliveries was something planned for, or just fortuitous, and he really didn't care.

He'd heard Shina's stories about what an awful person she'd been before meeting Thag, but Brad had only known her since, and he liked her immensely. It was obvious to him that she was struggling with her role and her responsibilities, but that was normal for someone finally becoming an adult, and it didn't worry him. She had Thag to keep her straight, and that meant she was in good hands. The power she was growing into was still immature, but it showed a promise of becoming something world-shaking if she had the time to develop it. She obviously didn't see it that way, but Brad knew she would accept it over time.

Koserana was something else. He'd never known a real dragon before. She was beautiful and amazing and fun and so sexy it hurt, but he had to agree with Thag that she was still immature. He would no more have taken her up on her offer of sex than he would take advantage of any other young girl with a crush on him. He'd known far too many of those, and he tried not to encourage them. Adult women, he couldn't resist. Sure, Koserana was physically mature, but she was still emotionally a long way from grown up.

Even so, given time, he knew it would be incredibly easy to fall in love with her.

He didn't often regret his heritage. He hated orcs, but he accepted he was half of one. He didn't know precisely who his father was. An orc raiding party had slaughtered everyone in his mother's village except a few young women. His mother had been only fourteen at the time. The orcs were busy gang-raping the girls when warriors from another human village showed up and killed every one of the orcs. So one of the dead orc raiders was his father, but nobody ever knew or cared which one.

When it came to Koserana, however, he did regret that he would never see her grown up. Half orcs like him are bigger and stronger and tougher than most human men, and smarter than most orcs, but they are also notoriously short-lived. Even those who didn't die in battle never lived past forty or so years.

And every time he healed a battlefield of people, he aged a bit. For him, old age would be thirty, and he knew it.

But he lived for the day in front of him. He truly believed that the amount of life that someone lived had very little to do with the quantity of days between birth and death.

So he enjoyed the voyage as much as he could. He watched pods of dolphins race the ship – sleek gray forms dancing in the waves as far as he could see in every direction! A huge group of leviathan whales crossed their path one moonlit night, and he stayed up all night in a state of awe. He spent whole days joking with Koserana, or chatting with Shina, or listening to Thag lecture about history and biology and cosmology and a dozen other subjects. Each day, the sun glinted off of endless waves. Each night, the sky was lit by countless constellations – though Shina, Thag, and even Koserana, all argued that he was "seeing things" and stars "don't really look like that at all".

The crew of the ship were amazed when he, the owner, wanted to know about ropes and knots and rigging and sails and navigation and currents and seasonal winds! He had never known that rope could be used for so many, many things, if you just knew how to tie it in a thousand different ways!

The crew were too terrified of Thag to include him in any of these lessons, but they were thrilled to teach Brad, and he passed along each lesson as he learned it. He was disappointed to learn that Thag already knew navigation better than the navigator and captain of the ship, since it meant he couldn't teach him anything about that. But Thag's deft fingers and quick mind absorbed braiding, knotting, splicing, and all the other things that could be done with the fine silk ropes of the ship, and Brad enjoyed passing those teachings to him.

Chapter 26: *A Short Story*

The weeks passed quickly, and the ship soon found the port it was looking for. It was a small fishing village with a single dock. The whole village was populated entirely by dwarves. From the deck of Brad's ship, the whole place looked like a physical manifestation of winter-depression built out of gray slate and badly weathered wooden planks. Shina thought the whole place looked like an old man dying of exposure to the salt water and cold weather. Visible mildew, mold, and salt-encrustations festooned every building like decorations dedicated to some abiding apathy.

There were brown and gray fishing nets strung up everywhere. Small, drab, utilitarian fishing boats covered the gray and black rocky beach. Even the seagulls added to the mood, floating around in the air and adding yet another touch of colorlessness. The people gathering on the shore and dock to watch the ship come in looked uniformly morose in their boring, gray-and-black clothing.

Hundreds of faces stared out at the ship from the shore and the dock. Every single one of them was covered with a heavy beard and thick mustache, and every head was as bald above as it was hairy below. There was no chatter, no excitement, none of the lively curiosity that a human crowd would have shown for the rare ship from over the wide ocean. Just a cold, dark mass-stare from all those dark eyes above black and gray beards. And every one of them built like a brick, with thick muscles covering wide, short bodies.

As they coasted to the dock, Thag briefed the other three. Neither Brad, Shina, nor Koserana had ever met dwarves before, and Thag felt that a few things would need to be explained.

"Don't mention gnomes or wizards. Dwarves were brought to our world as slaves of the gnomes, and they don't forget that. Talk of those things upsets them very badly. And don't buy anything from them – they are born for haggling, and you'll walk away impoverished, but think you're happy about it. We need some fresh supplies, but leave that to me.

"Brad, their women won't be interested in you. Koserana, their men won't find you attractive. Deal with that. Don't let it bother you. They're not human. Up till now, every intelligent race you've met, from elves to dragons, even the troll, were all descended from humans and altered by magic. Dwarves aren't like that. They look basically human, and they have some traits in common, but they think differently and they function differently. They come from a very different world, and they don't quite fit in here.

"They're honorable and trustworthy, except in bargaining. But they hold onto grudges like barnacles on rocks. Don't upset them. Got it?"

He looked Koserana directly in the eyes. "No tricks, no jokes, no teasing, okay?"

She pouted for a moment, then grudgingly gave in. "Okay. I promise I won't do anything fun."

Thag suddenly smiled. "Don't make that promise. I'm not sure you'll be able to keep it." But he wouldn't explain what he meant by that, he just kept a secretive grin on his face and pretended to be fascinated by the approaching shore.

As they came to the dock, Thag pointed out a few of the dwarves. "See that one, third to the left from that piling? And that one, just to the right of the one with the hat?" Shina nodded, the others just looked. "Take a closer look."

Shina stared for a moment. The ones he had pointed out were dwarves. Short. Stocky. Heavily bearded. Bald, or wearing a knit-woolen cap of a boring design. Nothing … then she saw it. Each of the ones he had pointed at had something in his arms. And one of the "somethings" was nursing at a small breast, the heavy beard pulled just enough to the sides to expose the nipple to the baby's mouth!

They were women! Women with beards, and bald heads! And just as stocky and muscular as the men standing around them!

Shina was still staring at the odd dwarf women when ropes were expertly thrown from the ship, and as-expertly caught on the dock. Dwarvish men with long pole-hooks worked with the ease of long-familiarity at bringing the large ship to a perfect docking. Still, the people on shore, even the ones on the dock doing the work, were eerily quiet. While the crew of the ship chattered and yelled commands at one another, the dwarves worked silently. But Shina noted they were the more efficient and more effective of the two teams.

When they finally went ashore, Shina had to be supported by Thag. The dock felt like it was swaying under her feet, and she had real trouble finding her balance, much less walking down the narrow gangplank. When they boarded the ship weeks ago, she had wondered why the plank had railings on it. Now she knew.

Shina was used to being the shortest adult she knew. She was only four feet and eleven inches tall, and had spent the last year surrounded by tall people. Even Koserana was slightly taller than most men, and Brad towered over her. Thag, of course, made everyone feel tiny. Suddenly Shina knew what they must feel like around her! The tallest man in the village barely came up past her lower ribs!

As Thag helped her ashore, first off of the ship, the dwarves on the dock all bowed till their heads were below their waists. One of them (Shina couldn't tell if it was a he or a she) came up from its deep genuflection and said, in a rumbling but pleasant voice, "My lord, Thag. It is good to see you again! The young'uns have sorely missed your stories, as much as we elders have missed your counsel."

Thag replied formally. "Councilman Elder Pott, it is my pleasure to visit you again. It has been too many decades since our last meeting." He nodded his head in the shallowest of acknowledgements of their deep obeisance, and all the dwarves stood up. Every single one of them was smiling and beaming like they'd just been granted titles of nobility.

An even tinier than normal dwarf ran up to the elder. Even this child had a beard, though it was only an inch or two of thin hair and not the wild bracken the older dwarves all sported. In a clear, high voice, the child asked, "Are we to celebrate, then? Shall there be revels for the noble visit?"

Thag scooped up the child in one giant hand and held it up in front of his monstrous face. "There shall be revels, young one. Yes!" He looked at the elder. "And council." Back to the child. "And stories!"

Every dwarf on the dock and shore cheered. Some began to dance. A few threw things into the air in wild excitement.

A dwarf that Shina thought might have some slight hint of breasts under all that beard spoke to her in a deep, gravelly voice. "Noble lady, you must be Thag's wife. The spirits of the earth have told us so much about you! Would you rest with your child, or would you prefer to join the revels? We have accommodations for you ready, if you like."

Shina gave a deep sigh of relief. "A hot bath? A real one, in a tub? Can you do that? We won't need anything special for accommodations, but a hot bath and fresh food would be wonderful."

The dwarf smiled. "A hot bath is definitely within our humble means, most noble. If you'll but come with me."

Shina smiled. Thag was standing a dozen feet away, surrounded by dwarf elders all talking to him at once, and covered with dwarf children who seemed to consider climbing onto his head some sort of game. He'd have heard every word that she and the dwarf had said, and would know where to find her.

She looked around, and saw Brad being led off by another dwarf, and Koserana following a pair. They were being separated, but she felt safe for the first time in months. Thag had said she could trust the dwarves, and she felt sure he was right.

Her dwarf was heading towards one of the drab, run-down, badly weathered buildings that fronted the bay. The back of the building was against a tall hill that led, she knew, to high mountains not far from the shore.

"I'm not really noble, you know. I'm just Shina. My name is Shina, and I would like it if you called me that," she told the dwarf she was with.

The dwarf smiled broadly. "Well, in that case, my name is John, and I'm to be your guest-host while you stay with us." He or she opened the door to the building, setting the hinges to creaking. Shina saw the wood of the door, salt-worn and wind-burned, actually bend as he pulled it open. As she stepped through, John continued. "Your husband won't need quarters, though he's welcome to them, of course. He'll stay up nights with the council, and spend all day with the children. He's like that, you know. But we considered his rank in assigning your rooms. They're humble compared to the luxury of the imperial courts, but we do the best we can."

The building was as ramshackle on the inside as it had looked from the outside. "Humble" wasn't the word Shina would have used. And definitely would never have compared the single room to any sort of court, much less the fabled imperial palaces. She started to thank John, while looking for anything resembling a bed or furnishings of any sort.

John brushed past her and went to a spot on the back wall. With a simple gesture, he opened a door so cunningly hidden she would never have suspected anything was there at all. Her mind balked a moment – the back of the building was straight up against a rocky hill, what could a door here possibly lead to?

The doorway thus opened revealed a passage into the rock itself. Easily tall and wide enough for Thag, it was spacious for Shina's small stature.

"To your real rooms, lady Shina. Back this way. The buildings up front are just there for pirates and the like. Fools them into never bothering to raid us. Even the elves mostly leave us alone these days!"

John led Shina deep into the hill. The tunnel was well-lit by strange glowing rocks – Shina couldn't see any magic in them, but they emanated a bright and steady light without fire. A hundred yards or more of rock, and a couple of bends in the tunnel, and then John gestured towards tall, wide double-doors made of polished oak with brass fittings.

"Your accommodations, Thag-wife," he said as he opened the doors for her.

Shina gasped!

The room beyond was furnished like nothing she had ever seen before! She'd been to the royal palace. Even to the king's own chambers, when her father had taken her with him a few times. Those paled by comparison! Imperial courts indeed!

Everywhere she looked, there was art, and gold and precious stones covered every available surface. The carpet was thick. The furnishings were covered in bright, colorful fabrics. Masterful paintings by the dozens covered whole swaths of the walls. The corners had statues of breathtaking beauty, and smaller statues and figurines covered every inch of massive shelves and a huge mantle over a giant fireplace.

It would have been shockingly easy to turn all that gold and all the fancy trappings into something gaudy and tasteless, but this room had been planned and decorated by master artisans and artists of the most refined taste and class. It didn't overwhelm, it welcomed with a rich warmth. It didn't overawe, it caressed the eyes with beauty.

"Will it suffice? I know humans generally like to have everything in separate rooms. Sleep in one room, eat in another, sit around bored in yet another. This is everything all in one room, but we hope it won't upset you or …"

Shina didn't give him time to finish. "It's wonderful! I love it!"

Before John could reply, she nodded towards one corner of the room, where a critical feature had caught her eye. "Is that a bath?" she asked, her voice full of hope.

"Um… yes… it is. Would you…?" he didn't need to finish his question, as Shina was already making a beeline towards it.

The bath was a raised, rectangular affair, lined with glazed tiles inlaid with gemstones. It could have easily fit a half-dozen people, more if they were intimate.

Shina didn't understand the solid gold fixtures at one end, nor the plated nozzles partway up the inner sides. She just recognized the basic shape and function.

She turned to John. "Please start some water heating. I'm sure this takes a while to fill, so I can't start right away, but I'd love to bathe as soon as it can be filled."

John gestured to the fixtures. "It doesn't take long to fill. Not if you … oh. You haven't used this type of bath before, have you?" He turned one of the knobs to full, and steaming hot water jetted out of dozens of nozzles along the sides of the bath. The thundering flow quickly filled the tub as Shina stared in awe.

John showed her how to control the flow and the temperature, and she quickly had it doing what she wanted.

She was used to tubs filled by slaves pouring buckets of water into them, but this was clearly vastly superior, and she knew before she even climbed in that she loved the whole thing.

Shina stripped naked, and quickly had Mornu out of his blanket. Then she soaked a luxurious towel in the hot water and wiped them both down with it. A bath will clean you, but she knew that the water would quickly become filthy without a little pre-cleaning.

She hadn't even considered John was a stranger before she undressed. She had been naked in her bath in front of servants and slaves her whole life. It was public nudity, or the helplessly naked feeling when she first met Thag, that bothered her. This was private, and in front of someone who was acting like a household servant.

What she didn't know is that John didn't care. Human nudity and sexuality were as alien to him as they would be to a lizard.

It took only a few minutes for the bath to fill, and then Shina settled into it and luxuriated in the hot water. She played with Mornu and set him to giggling and squirming in her lap. Barely more than a single month old, he was tiny and helpless, but he was amazingly aware for his age, and loved to smile at Shina and Thag.

She knew Koserana had arrived when she heard a gasp of unmitigated avarice coming from the general direction of the main doorway. Shina stayed in the bath, soaking in the heat and letting muscles relax and skin soothe.

Koserana took her time examining every precious item in the room. When Shina peeked an eye open the slightest crack, she saw that John was carefully watching Koserana – making sure every item went back where it had been picked up from.

Finally, Koserana came over to the bath and sat down on the edge of it. "Your room is even more glittery than mine!" she announced, still staring around.

She looked down at Shina. "Is the water nice and warm? You like that, right?"

Shina sighed and smiled indulgently. "It's beautiful! You should try it."

Koserana waved her fingers through the water. "It's wet. Too much to drink, and not big enough to swim in. I'll pass. But look at how shiny everything is!" A look that somehow combined pure joy and pure greed covered her beautiful face, lighting it from within.

Shina had only seen that kind of look of wonder on an adult one time before – when Drew first saw Brad. That had been pure love, or maybe just pure lust. This was clearly a close relative of those.

John, satisfied that Koserana's almost non-existent clothing couldn't be hiding stolen goods, finally spoke up. "Lady Koserana, we were led to understand your position is that of a noble freewoman. The room provided should live up to that standard, even in this provincial quarry. If you require more, or are unhappy with it, petition your lord, Imperatus Thag, and he'll let us know where you should be quartered. It's really quite simple."

Koserana looked him in the eyes. A predatory smile spread across her face. She was just about to say something wickedly sarcastic that would imply some horrible insult, but Shina touched her on the wrist and gave a quick shake of her head. Koserana settled for a grin that left the dwarf squirming in nervousness for reasons he couldn't quite fathom.

Koserana whispered to Shina, "I don't think they like me. I like their shinies too much, and they know it." She had such a wicked twinkle in her eyes that Shina couldn't help giggling. Then Mornu reached up and poked her in the nostril with his finger, completely changing the rest of the conversation.

For the next hour, the two women relaxed for the first time in ages. Koserana helped Shina finish bathing, then they ate a strange but filling dinner – it had some unfamiliar yellow plant in it that resembled the rice they were both used to, but much larger and softer. Finally, Thag sent a young dwarf (his or her beard was only a few inches long) to fetch the two women to a conference.

John stayed behind to clean up, and the young dwarf, who hadn't been introduced by name, led them through about a hundred yards of tunnel, mostly going downwards, to a large meeting hall.

Unlike the guest chambers, this wasn't completely ostentatious with gold and precious stones. It was, nonetheless, much more lavishly decorated than anything they'd ever seen before in the western continent.

The hall was about twenty yards on a side, had a raised lectern at the far end, and many benches and stools that held dozens of dwarves. In a human hall, the benches would all have lined up and faced the same direction. In here, they were all over the place – different sizes, pointing different directions, aligned to nothing. The only thing all the benches and seats had in common is they were all obviously made for people with very, very short legs.

Every spot big enough to hold one had a dwarf in it. Thag, even sitting, towered over them. In the dwarvish glitter and gleam, his gray skin and dull black scales looked even more drab than usual – suffering in comparison to even the boring garb of the dwarves.

Koserana's tattoos looked like liquid gold flowing over shimmering gems. As she strutted through the crowd to Thag, she stood out like a beacon. The dwarves ignored her, much to her chagrin.

Shina watched from the side for a minute, then quietly walked to Thag. As always, she had Mornu in a wrap on her chest, and the magical book-gems in a purse on her shoulder. Nothing to attract attention. She needn't have bothered to be polite and unassuming – all attention in the room was on Thag.

Nobody even noticed when Brad came in by a side door. He stood silently and just watched. He had bathed ("Western kingdom baths just don't clean the pores like a real sauna," he had told his companion-dwarf, who had simply replied that, "If you want to bake, we have a lava lake a few miles from here.") and dressed in simple but presentable clothing. He carried no visible weapons, just those in his bracelet, but he looked like a warrior – ready but relaxed.

Thag finally broke the silence. He spoke in the informal imperial language, the old language of the battle-mages, that the dwarves were most comfortable with. Shina could follow it, just barely. Like most nobles, she had been taught it as a child, and also like most nobles, she had forgotten it just as fast. Brad couldn't speak it, so he listened only for the tones and watched the body language in the room. Koserana, dragon-fluent in every language of every world, merely stood and smiled. Shina didn't cast her usual translation spells, since Thag had asked that she avoid wizardry around the dwarves.

"Elders, we need your help. We'd like passage through your domain to the east side of the Redstone Mountains. You do not owe us this, we ask it – I ask it – as a favor."

One of the dwarves, with a beard that had dust on it from dragging on the floor when he walked, replied. "You could buy passage, my lord. It is a long walk, and not without hazard, even for us. We would need to send bearers for food and supplies, guides, guards, and the people to support those. That would mean many strong backs and skilled hands away from our village, not doing our work, for some months."

Thag nodded, but replied, "We haven't much money, Eldest. I have helped your people in the past, and if we succeed will do so again. Will that promise pay our passage and a guide? We have supplies of our own."

"Why not pay with one of the precious stones I sense in her bag?" the Eldest asked, pointing at Shina's purse.

Thag muttered under his breath for a syllable or three. "Eldest, those are not ours to pay with. We but guard and carry them. They belong to another."

The dwarves muttered amongst themselves for a minute. A couple of elders whispered to the Eldest. Shina saw Thag's posture change and braced to defend herself and Mornu if she needed to.

Brad, outside the crowd, suddenly and silently had a pair of long, thin swords in his hands. He stood still, poised for action, but awaiting Thag's signal or some more measurable threat than dwarvish whispers that Thag had heard but Brad had not.

Koserana sneered at the dwarves. She'd heard their whispers just as easily as Thag, and understood even their secret speech amongst themselves. "Why should we pay? We've walked half across the world, and can walk across the rest if we have to! We don't need your guides and porters and impedimenta!"

If Thag's eyes could have rolled, he would have rolled them. Shina and Brad could, and did.

"You will pay! And you will walk!" shouted the Eldest, and dozens of dwarves stood to their full miniscule heights. Anyone with sense would have been intimidated by the looks on their faces and their sheer numbers, despite their diminutive sizes. So Koserana was unimpressed.

With a snarl, she blurred, and Lord Chalkos stood in her place, rearing her neck and head like an angry serpent, flapping her wings, and hissing through razor-edged teeth. Needle-claws scarred the stone floor where she pawed at it.

Dwarves shrieked. Yells of "A dragon! A dragon!" echoed through the halls as they stampeded out of the room. The Eldest fell to the floor and lay there shaking while pandemonium erupted all around him.

In moments, he was the only dwarf left in the room.

Thag paused.

Brad stared wildly around, wondering what the hell he should do.

Shina stared at her friend and wondered what had gotten into her. Turning into her dragon-form in front of people was normally the last resort of desperation, not something she did in a fit of peevish temper.

A moment later, Thag looked around with alarm and confusion on his face. Just as he began to announce, "They're coming back", the first dwarves charged into the room.

Brad leapt to defend Shina, his swords ready to fend off as many as he could. His skin took on the rigid sheen of stone-armor, and his muscles corded with the power of his battle-spirit.

Chalkos inhaled and readied to loose fiery Armageddon on the charging mass of dwarves.

Then the dwarves started dropping armloads of gold, gems, pearls, silver, platinum, and everything else they could grab and haul in their racing haste.

Dwarvish eyes were wide with excitement as they raced in and out of the room. Whispers and shouts of "A dragon!" came from every set of dwarvish lips.

Some paused for a moment and stared wide-eyed at Lord Chalkos. Some merely glanced and then ran back out of the room, to get another armload of treasure. All had the look of excited, bearded children.

Chalkos looked confused. Then she began to stare in awe as the pile of treasure piled higher and higher and higher. She started rocking back and forth and side to side. Her tail swirled back and forth on the floor in excitement. She craned her long neck around, delighting in every aspect of the incalculable wealth being heaped in front of her.

Finally, Shina gained enough composure to ask, "Thag, what is going on here?" She couldn't take her eyes off of the haphazard heap forming all around them.

Thag shrugged, his eyes wide. After a few minutes, as the piles grew together into a solid ring, taller than the dwarves themselves, all around them, he picked up the Eldest and spoke to him. Shina couldn't hear what he said over the clatter of armloads of metal being thrown around.

The Eldest replied and Thag nodded, then spoke again. The conversation continued while the clanking cacophony carried on.

The pile was almost up to Shina's neck when Thag suddenly bellowed something so loud Shina couldn't hear it, but it overcame the shattering clamor around them. When her ears stopped ringing, the room was silent.

Dwarves climbed and slipped over the piled abundance.

Chalkos muttered something in her deep voice. Shina wasn't entirely sure, but it sounded kind of like, "But they could bring more".

"Elders and Eldest, miners and smelters and simple-folk," Thag orated. "Lord Chalkos gladly welcomes the gifts you have saved for her. The work of thousands of years, carefully kept and hoarded, just for her – counted carefully and systematically, just as she likes it – is appreciated more than she can express in simple words.

"However, she needs passage with us at this time. Will some of you guide and protect her on her journey, that we accompany her on?"

Excited discussions took hours. Apparently, every dwarf house wanted every one of its adults to go on the expedition to get Chalkos to Sam's lands. Thag pointed out, repeatedly, that this wasn't practical. They didn't care. Everyone had to go, or whoever was left behind would be dishonored forever.

While Chalkos wallowed in gold and diamonds and other "ooohh shiny" things, Thag argued back and forth.

Shina finally pointed out, "How will you keep gathering treasure for her if you all go?" Then the arguments started in earnest. Which was the greater honor? Who deserved which?

Chalkos tried to suggest something to them, but the dwarves shushed her and went and got some new treasures for her to play with. Apparently they wanted her rich and quiet – and when Shina thought about that, it made a lot of sense. If gathering treasure for dragons kept the dragons from fighting and eating them, then it was very sensible for dwarves to gather treasure.

During a lull in the verbal storm, Shina asked Thag about that. He agreed, and then lectured a bit about dwarvish history and their relationship with dragons. He had apparently learned it all from the Eldest just that day, and was excited about the whole thing – so he segued off a lot on theories about details the dwarves hadn't supplied.

In sum, dwarves were natural miners and smiths, and they focused on practical things at first in their far distant history, but then learned that they could gain a guardian dragon for their mines if they made things of gold and other rare metals for them. After that, they split their efforts on what they themselves needed, and gathering hoards that would gain them a … pet.

Shina was very careful to only think that, and not say or even mutter it, since Chalkos would easily hear even a mutter from a cave away, and she knew her friend and lover well enough to know exactly how poorly that thought would go over.

It took a week for the dwarves to organize their expedition. Apparently, mapping out tunnels that Thag would fit through was one of the biggest challenges. They needed to accommodate his size, and Shina's "fragile, human body" was a common phrase when mapping around things like underground seas of lava or pockets of toxic gas. Finding a path that did both was cause for a lot of heated discussions and a lot of digging through archives for rare and unusual maps.

Shina asked about the fragility thing. She thought maybe they were over-worrying about her because of her recent pregnancy. It turned out that, so long as they're underground, dwarves can swim in lava and survive poison gas. Unlike a dragon, they can't do that except when they're surrounded by natural bedrock, but so long as they stayed in tunnels, they were immune to the natural hazards of underground living. Even to the point that, under normal circumstances and above-ground, they needed to breathe, just like Shina did, but in a cave-in a dwarf can survive just about indefinitely without fresh air. So they needed caves and tunnels that would support human life and not require lava-immunity and similar traits. That severely limited their choices of paths.

They explained to her that the titan that originally made them, on a different world-shard, made a world of caves and rocks, without any useful surface anywhere on it. She (the titan was a "she" to the dwarves) made dwarves to populate that world, just as Shina's home-world had humans on it, made by the world-titan of this shard.

The conversation about world-shards excited the dwarves when they concentrated on how dragons could travel between shards, and survive on any world. But they quickly grew surly and reticent if the subject of wizards or gnomes came up – those could travel between shards, but they weren't "suitable subjects for a nice girl like you to talk about".

While they waited for the dwarves to plan and prepare the trek, Shina and Thag spent most of their time playing with Mornu. Chalkos spent most of her time playing with stacks of "pretty, pretty, shiny, glittery". Brad, stifled by the tunnels of the dwarf town, went hunting in the hills and woods nearby – the dwarves appreciated the fresh food and meat he brought in every day, and he quickly became popular for it.

One day, while visiting Chalkos in her gold-filled meeting room, Shina noticed something odd.

Later, with Thag and Mornu, she asked her husband, "Thag, is

Chalkos growing? She seems bigger than when I first saw her."

Thag replied, "Growing? Yes. And you've probably noticed her more aggressive moods, too. Right?"

Shina definitely had and nodded in agreement.

"You can't tell from her scent, of course," said Thag. "But it's normal for her age. I went through a lot of the same thing when I was that old. It was different for me, of course. Because of my mother, you understand." He looked at Shina like he expected that statement to make sense.

Shina just looked puzzled. "Um. Do you mean dragons get moody and kind of aggressive and such when they grow?"

Thag chuckled. "No. People, including dragons, get moody and such when they hit puberty. It's normal."

Shina's jaw dropped. She tried to speak a couple of times, but stopped before any words came out. She finally managed, "Puberty? But …"

Thag nodded sagely. "Yes. The next half-century is going to be very interesting for all of us. No way around that."

Shina remembered the awkwardness of her own body during her own maturing. The unexpected cramps and bleeding, her single-parent-father's complete incompetence in shepherding a young woman through changing moods and desires – all those complex aspects and changes had been overwhelming for a couple of years.

"Fifty years?" she asked Thag.

He nodded. "More or less. Took me about that long. She might take longer, or less. It's going to be a bit different for her, because of my mixed ancestry and because of our gender difference." He shrugged like this was no big deal. "Could be longer. There aren't any reliable records available."

He chuckled again. "My poor step-father. He had no idea what was going on for the first decade or two. Can you imagine what I was like during my 'rebellious phase'?"

Shina had an incongruous mental image of a scholarly, overlearned, surly "teenage" Thag, suddenly growing from merely big to truly gigantic, and rebelliously lecturing his step-father in erudite, grammatically perfect teen-sarcasm. "I bet," was all she could say without giggling.

Then she sobered. "Fifty years, you say. So I probably won't live to see the end of it," she said.

Thag comforted her, "Little One, don't worry about that. We're almost to Sam. This world can still be saved. We'll all live to see Chalkos all grown up and amazing."

"That's not what I meant," Shina answered. When Thag just looked at her, she continued, "I'm human, Thag." Tears she hadn't expected tried to form in her eyes and she swallowed around a lump in her throat. "I'll be lucky to live another thirty years. Maybe fifty if I live as long as my father has."

Thag folded her into his arms and held her head to his chest. She felt the warmth and comfort of him, but this time it didn't ease her distress. She knew she'd lose those things one day. He would live on, immortal dragon and immortal troll blood never fading in age. She would live a mortal's few decades and then fade and die.

Thag looked down at her. "Little One, what do you mean?"

She realized he really didn't know what she was talking about. "I'm human, Thag. We only live a little while. You know that."

Thag smirked. Shina knew he was hiding laughter, and a tide of temper began to rise inside her.

Thag spoke before anger could break through. "My dear, you're a wizard. What does that mean to you?"

The tangent and the question broke the emotional tide before it could crash to shore. She thought for a moment as tears dried and anger faltered. "A wizard? It means I can use magic. I can channel power left over from the creation of the universe and the world-shards, and use it to make things or twist the laws of the world. What does that have to do with…?"

Thag nodded. "Gem's books don't mention what effects that has on you?"

Shina shook her head. Then a look came over her face. "What effects?"

Thag nodded briefly. "Ah. I thought you already knew. This explains a few things." He looked at her and suddenly looked like he was about to tease her. "But maybe I should leave it to Sam to explain all this. After all, she knows wizards better than I do…"

Shina punched him in the arm. "What effects?" she demanded.

Thag pretended pain from the light punch. "Well, since you're torturing it out of me, I guess I have to have to answer….

"Little One, you're a wizard. Wizards are one of the two full-users of real magic.

"Elves, sorcerers, battle-mages, and others, use tiny bits of limited magic. And they all end up essentially immortal. Magic is the force that creates the worlds themselves – and is itself eternity incarnate. Using it, even limited use, stretches life such that no one yet has ever measured the full years of an elf or a battle-mage. Your own father is much, much older than you think. He has advised and manipulated the military leaders of Berdonia since before it was a kingdom.

"But the real users of magic, the ones that can do more than a few mind-tricks or shape their own bodies a little bit, are dragons and wizards. Dragons turn magic inside themselves and become what they are – powerful and beautiful and fire-breathing, able to survive any world, immune to the elements, and possessed of far more mental power than any sorcerer.

"Your father is as powerful a sorcerer as has ever lived. Chalkos was born mentally stronger than he – as much more powerful than he as an orc warrior is stronger than a newborn kitten – and she's growing stronger yet as she matures.

"Elves make themselves 'perfect' and beautiful and graceful and strong and tough. But you've seen how they envy Koserana. They're not even candles compared to her noontime sun.

"The battle-mages were like that with wizard-magic. As strong in their own way as your father. They could shape purpose into weapons and armor so that they transcended their physical structure. Their other abilities were comparable. But, like wizards, their magic went outwards not inwards. They didn't shape themselves the way elves and dragons and sorcerers do, they shaped the things around them.

"Wizards, like you, are to battle-mages what dragons are to elves or sorcerers. You barely qualify as an apprentice, but you ripped battle-mage magic out of Antain's weapon almost by accident. Like stepping on an ant and accidentally killing it – the difference in strength and power is that extreme.

"No matter what channel, no matter if a trickle or a flood, magic flows through all of these. And it leaves behind life.

"You aren't truly mortal, my tiny love. You never have been. From the moment you were born a wizard, you've been a conduit for the force behind the forces of nature.

"Learning the techniques of the wizards of old will save you from having to re-invent those techniques. The 'spells' you'll learn are the tools of your trade. But magic itself is not your craft, it's what you are. Techniques will help you use magic effectively. The very first wizards had to figure everything out on their own. You won't have to do that. That's all. You are a wizard no matter what you learn or don't learn."

Shina just stared at him in shock.

"I'm sorry, Little One. I would have told you, but I thought Gem's books already had, and better than I can hope to. I thought you already knew."

Shina did the only thing she could. She threw a temper tantrum.

"I was worried forever that I was going to die and lose you! I hate you! Never don't tell me something again! I need you!"

She pounded her fists against him futilely. She cried tears of frustration, grief, and rage.

Thag silently held her close.

She hiccupped and cursed and cried.

Thag patted her hair back from over her face.

She breathed deeply and clung to him.

He stroked the back of her head and neck with his hand.

She reached up and kissed him. "I need you, Thag. I was so worried. Promise me you'll tell me things from now on. Even things you think I already know."

Thag nodded.

After a time, Shina reached between them and put her hand down inside the front of his pants. "Good. Then that's all settled, but you still owe me for it. You owe me a big … debt." She smiled up at him as her hand found what she wanted.

"You owe me big-time, and it's going to be very hard to pay off…"

Chapter 27: *Am I Bugging You?*

After months of crawling around in cold, dark caves, Shina and Brad were not in the mood to wait before finally going outside, but Thag insisted that Chalkos needed to scout the area nearby before they left the safety of the dwarf-paths.

The cave they were in was just big enough for the three of them. The opening was barely big enough for Thag. A long, dark, cold, boring tunnel went from the back of the cave deep into the mountains that loomed over the western horizon of the part of the world just outside their subterranean hideout.

As soon as the dwarves left, Shina conjured up a ball of pure wizard-light, and then put it on a small finger of rock that looked like it was dripping down the wall of the cave. It shed no warmth, but the steady white light was comforting to the two non-dragons.

Mornu had watched with knowing eyes while Shina conjured the light. Once it was steady, he went back to playing a game of "grab Mommy's hair and pull it" that he had momentarily been distracted from. Shina indulged him and boosted him up higher in his bundle on her chest.

In the spirit of "tell me things", Thag explained the plan while they waited.

"There's a large plain out there. It's more temperate than the part of the Eastlands we went through, but it's comparable in size. We have about five hundred miles to cross, no cover anywhere in sight, and it's not friendly territory.

"There's another old wizard-weapon out there. It's big, fast, and very, very dangerous. I can't outrun it, but Chalkos can outfly it, so we need her to scout first. If it's anywhere nearby, we won't go out till it's gone. It wanders a lot, so we shouldn't have to wait too long for that, if she even finds it nearby."

Shina interrupted. "What if one of us sees it? How will we know?"

"It's about thirty feet tall, and looks kind of like a centipede with stinger-tentacles coming out of its face. Don't worry about recognizing it — you'd run even if you'd never heard of it.

"

"It can outrun us, and outfight us. It's immune to things like dragon-fire, gnomish energy cannons, and most wizardry. The only thing it's afraid of is Sam, so we need to get to her territory as fast as we possibly can."

Brad stopped him. "You keep talking about Sam as our destination. She sounds dangerous, if something like that is afraid of her. What is she?"

Thag paused a moment, looked at Shina knowingly, and finally said, "I really can't answer that. You'll have to see for yourself and draw your own conclusions. But I can tell you, if you see red wasps or golden ants, then we've arrived in her territory and should be safe so long as we don't anger her."

Brad replied, "So … don't swat at the red wasps or step on the golden ants? Is that about it?"

Thag nodded. "Definitely don't swat them. They're important to her, and she's important to us."

Brad and Shina nodded.

"Sam's territory is pretty much east of here. If you go east, and maybe a tiny bit north, you'll find her. I don't expect to get separated, but you need to know just in case.

"I don't know what we'll do once we get to Sam. I know she has a plan of some sort. It involves both of you, but I don't know what it is. I trust her, because Llwddann trusted her. But I don't know her very well – we've only met once and that was a long time ago.

"I do know she's been around almost since the titan made the world. The gnomes couldn't kill her, and the battle-mages were afraid of her. She likes wizards and druids and some dragons, and she's given her word that the four of us will be under her protection once we get to her."

"So, we wait for Chalkos to scout. And when we go, we go fast and we don't stop for anything." Everyone nodded understanding and agreement.

Chalkos only took a few minutes to fly around for a good look at things. The land was so flat, between the high mountains to the west and some lower mountains far to the east, that she could see every detail for hundreds of miles in all directions.

When she was satisfied there really was nothing to see, and the scary, big creature was hundreds hundreds of miles to the north, she returned to the cave and told everyone it was safe to come out.

Shina, carrying tiny Mornu, followed Thag out of the cave. She stood quietly in the sunlight, enjoying the warm radiance and the light breeze that caressed her skin.

Brad scrambled out right behind her, and stood full up and stretched intensely. Eyes closed, he raised his face to the sun and soaked it in. His arms stretched above his head and he filled his lungs deeply with fresh air.

After a minute, Shina opened her eyes and looked around. It was beautiful, and the sky looked huge, but it was also monotonous like no land she had ever seen before. Far to the west, she could make out the shapes of distant mountains. Far, far to the east, she could barely make out the hazy outlines of some irregularity that might be the eastern mountains Thag had spoken of. Above, the glorious sun was surrounded by the world-shards that others called "stars". She was comforted to see that, even this far from home, those were the old familiar ones she had seen all her life.

But there was something here she had never sensed before… something that touched on senses that had only awakened when she began to actually practice magic. A thrumming pulse, slow and regular like a resting heartbeat, that seemed to come from all around, but mostly from just a little north of east.

"Thag," she said, and pointed towards the source of the sensation. "Is that where we're going?"

Thag looked up at the "stars", quickly orienting himself, and then nodded. "Yes. Exactly. How could you tell?"

She shook her head a tiny bit. "I'm not sure. I just can sort of feel that there's something that way that … calls to me. A beacon, maybe. Like I'm supposed to go there."

Thag nodded. "We should get moving. Yes, that's the right direction. It's good to know you can feel the way. If we run into Colossus – the big bug – I'll try to distract him and lead him off. You and Brad need to stick together and get to Sam's tower."

Shina and Brad were soon moving at the quick trot they had adopted over thousands of miles of trekking. With Brad's magic, they could keep up that pace all day, and miles would melt under their feet. Chalkos, flying above, swooped and looped and paced ahead and behind and all around. Thag kept pace with them, occasionally racing one way or another to scout the ground.

As flat and easy as the terrain was, with no hills and few rivers, Brad calculated that he and Shina could cross the plains in about a week, given the distances Thag had described. By himself, Thag could cross them in half a day, and Chalkos in less than an hour, but the pace was set by the slowest – which was still Shina, even when Thag carried Mornu for her.

They didn't want to draw attention across these vast distances by using mage-light, so Shina and Brad had to stop when the sun was down and the land was too dark to safely run across, and wait for the sun to rise enough in the morning before starting each day. They ate on the run, small handfuls of nuts and grains, and stopped at streams to drink hasty mouthfuls of the silty water that predominated in this land.

Unlike the Eastlands, there were no large animals living on these plains. The grass was waist- or even shoulder-high, and looked like it could have supported vast herds, but Thag said the Colossus kept large things from living there. The battle-mage empire had never settled this land.

In some places, the grass was eaten down, and they had to avoid those places because some small animals had filled them with mile after mile of holes and burrows that could sprain ankles or even break legs.

It was a strange land, wide and flat and full of marvelous grasses and flowers and bushes, with occasional patches of trees and bogs full of reeds and herbs. Not a hill in sight. Huge flocks of birds, some so vast they darkened the noontime sky, were almost the only animals they saw.

Insects, on the other hand, abounded. Bees and grasshoppers and a million other creepers and swarmers filled the land and the air. None, yet, of the golden ants or red wasps they'd been told to watch for, but every other type in uncountable throngs.

They had to cross one huge river, like nothing Shina or Brad had ever seen before. Wide and slow and muddy, it was full of strange fish and small creatures. Chalkos flew Mornu across while Brad, Thag, and Shina swam.

One day, Thag pointed out a huge storm tearing through the land south of them. At the core was a funnel of furious wind, howling and smashing everything in its path. While Brand and Shina stared in awe, Thag asked the local winds to keep the storm away from them, and the spirits agreed after he told them Sam was expecting them. Chalkos flew into the storm and flitted around in the roaring tornado. Nobody was surprised when she came back and told them it was fun.

Finally, after weeks of flat horizons, Shina saw they were coming to hilly areas covered in forest. That night, they camped on the plains for the last time and prepared to enter rougher lands, where they wouldn't be able to travel anywhere near as many miles per day.

"We're getting close to Sam's territory," Thag told them that night. "We might arrive tomorrow. I'm not sure exactly where her borders are in this area. The one time I came here, I arrived via dryad trees with my step-father. The wind spirits here are familiar, though, so we're definitely getting close. I've met some of these spirits before, and they know me."

Brad asked why there were no dryads in the west. Or were there and he just didn't know it?

Thag explained that the only dryads left were in the elf-lands and Sam's lands. The ones in the west had all been killed by the invading gnomes millennia ago, while most of the ones in this eastern continent had been destroyed by the Empire. The battle-mages had been careful to avoid antagonizing the elves and so a few remained in their lands. And the gnomes and the battle-mages had both been kept out by Sam, so there were numerous spirits in her lands that no other land had seen since the invasion.

In the middle of the night, Chalkos suddenly bellowed out an alarm and took flight in a rush. Thag jumped to his feet and, without the slightest hesitation, grabbed up Shina and Brad. Shina held Mornu in her arms while Thag held her across his chest. Brad clung to Thag's neck and shoulders, carried piggyback. In seconds, Thag was running and leaping across terrain he could see as clearly as day.

Nobody had to ask what Chalkos had seen. There was only one thing in this land that warranted alarm!

Mornu began to cry at the rushing jostle. Shina tried to comfort him, but there was little she could do but try to protect him from the worst bumps. She was getting bruised and strained by the mad pace, but she did her heroic best to shield the tiny infant, paying no heed to her own needs.

Chalkos, airborne, could see the creature gaining on Thag's fleeing form. It was still miles behind, but gaining with every minute. If Thag hadn't forbidden it, she would have tried to distract the monstrous thing herself, but he said it was too dangerous and she was too important.

If Thag could find a suitable hiding place for Shina, Mornu, and Brad, he would drop them off and try to distract the creature himself. But he couldn't just leave them where it might find them — they could not count on luck when so much was at stake!

His massive legs pumped tirelessly, blazing through mile after mile through the dark! Every stride took them closer to Sam, closer to safety.

At first, he heard nothing but his own pounding footsteps.

Then he heard it behind him. Miles away, but gaining fast!

More miles sped beneath his steps, and then he could feel the shake of the ground at the creature's thunderous onrush!

It was getting too close!

Thag leapt a twenty-foot river and landed smoothly on the other side. Maybe the mass of the water would slow the thing a tiny bit.

But finally he knew it was going to be upon them. There was no avoiding it. No place to hide. He could hear it crashing through trees without pausing or slowing. He could feel the shake of the land beneath him.

No storm he could summon would slow it.

No fight would protect them.

It was done.

But still he ran. There was one hope. Faint, but hope would last as long as breath did.

Then, as the predawn light spread over them, the creature less than a mile behind, Shina suddenly screamed in his arms.

Still running, Thag glanced down at her. She was staring in horror at something on Mornu!

Thag stopped and set Shina down. Brad jumped off of his back and set himself for battle with the creature moments behind them.

Thag stood relaxed.

A nasty looking wasp, as long as a grown man's thumb, colored with bands of blood-red and metallic gold, was crawling over Mornu's tiny face. Its feelers patted at his skin.

Shina looked in horror at the creature crawling on her son. Its stinger poised threateningly near his eye, its jaws twitching near his tender skin. Instinctively, her hand moved, almost on its own, poised to violently swat the thing away from him, but Thag's fingers closed on her wrist and held her immobile.

The Colossus crashed through the last trees between it and its intended prey just as a black cloud rushed out of the sky between it and Thag's tiny group.

Rising sunlight flashed on millions of buzzing wings and glinting bodies, and all hearing was drowned in the whirring roar of the cloud.

The creature crashed to a quivering halt, roaring in frustration and rage.

Part of the immense cloud of wasps thickened, became opaque, and settled to the ground.

Shina, Koserana, and Brad watched in a mix of amazement and horror as that congealing cloud took on the shape of a girl. A girl made of millions of insects crawling over each other.

Then the multitude of wasps began to melt into each other. It looked like blood-red candle-wax melted into a nightmare shape of almost-humanness.

And then she stood there in the appearance of a perfectly formed ten-year-old girl with gold-red hair, pale blue eyes, and lightly tanned skin. She wore no clothing, but stood with a dignity and poise that completely precluded any need for covering or modesty.

She looked at the raging Colossus and spoke to it quietly, calmly, with assurance. "Approach, and I will consume you. Flee and you may yet serve your creator's purpose one day."

The thirty-foot-tall, hundred-foot-long monstrosity turned and fled. Its passage shook the ground, but soon faded to silence as it withdrew from the most dangerous predator in the world.

The little girl turned to Thag and his companions. She smiled sweetly and her eyes twinkled in joy. "Thag! You brought them!"

Thag bowed. "My lady, may I present to you Lord Chalkos, the last dragon in our world, Life-Husband Angbarad, the first Great Healer in over a thousand years, and Empress Shina, the only living wizard in all of our shard. She has been to Xalax, where the school accepted her and lent her Gem's learning-stones.

"Shina, Brad, Chalkos, this is Sam."

Chapter 28: *Towering*

When Sam first showed them to the island of her tower, Shina was a little confused. There was no tower, but Sam and Thag kept referring to the whole place as Tower Island.

The "Island" part of the name was clear. About thirteen miles north-south, and a little over two miles wide, with rivers on three sides and a bay facing onto the Western Ocean on the south, it was, without a doubt, an island.

But there was no tower anywhere to be seen when they first arrived.

Sam explained that her tower travelled between worlds. It would only be there during the bright phases of the moon, and only fully there during the full moon. During the dark of the moon, it was in another world-shard. In between, while the moon waxed and waned, it was travelling.

Naturally, Shina asked, "What other world? What's it like?"

Sam replied, "I've heard that it's a gigantic forest, centered around two titanic trees. Each of the two is the size of a mountain. One is in perpetual darkness, and the other is in sunlight. And the residents of the trees are caught in eternal war with each other. A few elves have gone there, taken by the tower, and live in the forest. It's supposed to be terribly dangerous and hauntingly beautiful. But I can't go there. This world is the only one I can live in."

Thag didn't know much more than that, but added that only wizards could enter the tower, unless they took others as guests. Much like the school at Xalax, but even more so, since dragons couldn't enter here and could there.

*****

Shina sat on the grass near the foot of the tower.

Mornu played nearby, running and leaping and mocking fights with shadows crafted by Sam's wasp-clouds. He and Koserana frequently took the roles of Gem and Ariel in battles against swarm-crafted gnomes.

Thag sat, leaning against a large rock, relaxed and comfortable.

Brad was off "exploring" – which was the word he used when he was meeting with the myriad of female elemental spirits that found his company as fascinating as Drew had. Naiads from the local streams, sylphs, even storm-maidens, always accompanied him when he went "exploring". Shina knew he wouldn't be back for a couple of days.

Sam, or maybe an avatar of her, sat with Shina while Shina practiced the lessons from Gem's books. In the five years Shina had known Sam, she had never yet been able to discern whether Sam was really a girl who turned into an insect-hive, or was just a projection of the hive and had no reality beyond that. She wasn't even sure Sam had to be in one place at a time – whether her ability to know every going-on in her territory was because of insect eyes and antennae reporting to her, or whether those very eyes and antennae were truly part of her. Sam willingly tried to answer questions about herself, but generally left both Shina and Thag more confused rather than less.

"I think I understand this lesson, Sam," said Shina. "I will channel power to Brad's spirit-wife, and she'll channel power to him, and we'll heal the titan that way. Right?"

Sam nodded agreement. That part of the plan had been gone over many times over the years.

"But, per this, I need to also channel living power into Brad directly, so the other power won't kill him. But I also need to drain any excess power out of Brad, so he won't overload. I'll need to have three streams going at once, but I must not cross the streams – that will tear the whole thing apart and might kill the world with the sudden shock."

Sam nodded. "That sounds correct. I can only help you find the way, I can't guide you along it. Only another wizard could do that. Is there a way to practice these streams, to learn to keep them uncrossed and flowing, without danger? Most practices involve the same skills but lower levels of raw power. Can you do that?"

Shina nodded. "I think so. Should I try?"

Sam and Shina looked to Thag, who, of course, had heard every word despite distance and the appearance of sleep. He nodded.

Koserana stopped her play with Mornu and walked over. "Are you going to do something exciting? Will it be less boring than watching Thag nap all day and listening to Brad's never-ending sex at the other end of the island?"

Shina didn't bother pointing out that Thag didn't actually nap. "You can watch. It might be exciting, or it might kill us all and doom the world completely. Hard to say."

Koserana rolled her eyes. "Better than being bored."

There were times when Shina felt like she had more than one child. And the five-year-old seemed more mature than the one that was over a century old.

The level of concentration the spell required was far beyond anything she'd ever tried. Her father had taught her how to focus, but his old exercises were more of a distraction than a help in this. Sam had been teaching her new methods, ones that worked better for wizardry, but she was mastering them slowly.

Sweat broke out on her forehead as the tiny threads of controlled power formed. They danced and wove like ribbons in a breeze. Keeping them close enough together to work, but far enough apart to avoid crossing, was impossible!

In seconds, she gave up and let the whole construct fade. Sparks of power shot off of her like the hot metal grains from a grinding wheel as the spell faded.

Sam, patient as eternity, looked her in the eyes, and said, "Excellent. Do it again."

***

Shina watched intently as Brad reached out to his totem, his spirit-wife, and drew healing power from her. She could see the cord of energy as clearly now as she could see Brad himself. The power was both like and unlike what had been woven into Antain's weapon all those years ago. She couldn't express it in words, but she could see how both came from the same source, but also how they were as unlike as milk and sweat though both came from the same body.

She reached out to reinforce the connection Brad had formed. Then she spun a second tiny thread parallel to it that connected to the source of Brad's power. Two opposite flows, one of raw magical power, one of spirit-magic that contained and became the essence of healing and living. It was hard, impossible even, but somehow she managed to hold them steady.

As power trickled into Brad, he took on a glow that only Shina and the dragons could see. If it got too strong, it would overwhelm him. She had to put a third thread of power onto him, to drain off any excess that he wasn't using.

For a moment, it was too much. Pain exploded in Shina's skull, and she doubled over in agony! But then she took the excess pure-healing that she was pulling into that third thread and put it into her own body. She was looking down on her own physical vessel, the body she had known since birth, and healing it with Brad's magic powered by her own magic.

The pain disappeared. She found herself once again seeing from her own eyes. The threads of power were steady. She barely managed to extinguish them before she fainted from the strain of the whole thing.

***

The tower stood behind her, like so many times over the years. It was over 1,000 feet tall, with 102 floors and a strange metal spire on top of its pointed roof. The construction was unlike anything else in the world – beautiful and majestic despite the oddly square outline. Shina was used to round towers, better able to deflect the stones from catapults and trebuchets. It was also covered in thousands of windows sealed by the most perfectly formed glass Shina had ever seen. It had obviously been designed for wizardly work, not for warfare, and it suited its true purpose very well.

Sam spoke. "The tower is here. If we fail, at least some of you may escape in it. The death of this world will not touch the tower, for it is of the void and not tied to the life of the worlds made by titans. It is time."

Shina was not ready. She knew she wasn't.

She also knew that the world had only months left. No amount of practice would ever prepare her for this. Every delay made the final healing more difficult.

Brad had told her he could sense the wound in the world. "It was worse when we stood in the wastelands around Xalax, but I can feel it from here. It's growing, and it's already infinitely larger than any power I can imagine."

Thag had tried to comfort her.

Mornu held her and told her, "It'll be okay, Mommy. You'll make it right." She put him in the tower, along with Koserana. If everything went wrong, at least those two would survive.

Thag refused to hide in the tower with them. He gave reasons for it – if they needed to escape quickly, he could carry Brad and Shina faster than they could run – but Shina knew that really he was there to support her, and she knew she needed him there.

It was time to begin.

***

Duke Antain looked over the battlefield from atop his warhorse,

Sachem. The horse hadn't been born for this, but Antain knew the changes that had been wrought by his Empress-Wizard on her favorite mount, and knew he was better served by that magic than by any mortal steed.

The battle was desperate for both sides. King Yonind's forces had more battle-mage armor, but Antain's had more spirit-warriors and even had a few elves in it.

Though Antain had kept to his promise not to lead an army into Kingdom-lands, Yonind had not ignored the growing threat on his doorstep and had brought his own army to Antain's growing city/encampment.

Yonind made his intentions more than clear by sacking and burning Antain's home-city of Herztad on the way. Refugees had been murdered wherever Yonind's ruthless soldiers had found them, no prisoners or slaves taken, no survivors left behind. It was an atrocity, but not an unprecedented one – the battle-mages had fought that way for millennia. It was one of the things Antain hoped to change.

Suddenly the ground shook under him!

Storm-wind from nowhere ripped through the sky and over the battlefield, smashing men to their knees!

The mountains across the northern horizon spouted flame and blasts of black smoke into the tortured sky!

The ground pitched like a ship on storm-waves and Sachem staggered.

All around, less sure-footed mounts fell and crushed the men on and around them.

Wyverns and griffons were torn from the air and scattered like leaves or smashed to pulp against the ground.

Antain knew Thag's predictions that the world would die. He had assumed it would be quietly – he realized he didn't know why he'd thought that, but he realized he had. "She failed," he thought, and mourned. "I should have been there with her."

He knew it was the terrible day.

***

Lisa the werewolf leapt out the window the moment her cottage started shaking, her children seconds behind her.

It was mid-day, but the sky was black!

The trees and hills and the ground itself were moaning and shaking in terror, and it was all Lisa could do to keep her family from panicking and fleeing into woods that offered false-refuge.

Momentarily, as she danced for balance, her thoughts turned to Thag and the strange young human girl he had travelled with all those years ago. She didn't know why she thought of them, but wolf-instinct didn't require rationality.

***

In Anytown, flame erupted from gigantic holes in the ground and air was filled with ash and poison gas. Thousands died in the first seconds. Thousands more fled in terror.

***

On an island in a distant sound, the elves paused their fights and parties and lovemaking and watched in terror as the sea around them rose into a wall hundreds of feet tall, and crashed towards them.

***

In the ruined lands around Xalax, where no living thing could grow or dwell, an errant gust of wind dropped a grass-seed on the moist verge of a stream so dead neither fish nor plant had lived in it for thousands of years. The seed, sensing the moisture around it, split and sent a tiny thread of root into the soil. The first living thing to grow in the devastation since the ancient war, took root and survived.

***

Dwarves caught in countless cave-ins and eruptions, even ones crushed under collapsed rocks and tunnels, stirred and began to patiently dig themselves out.

***

The land settled and stopped shaking, and Sachem no longer had to dance to stay upright.

Far across the field, Antain saw Yonind himself trying to get to his feet, his heavy armor weighing him down almost as much as his age and obesity.

Without hesitation, the duke put Sachem to an all-out charge. The battle, interrupted, could be won by a single, bold stroke, if Antain could make it before the king's bodyguards could recover.

329

He knew it was a glorious day!

***

The mountains stopped shaking, and Lisa and her pups and her mate watched as the sky faded to the pale blue of the extreme north. They didn't know what had happened, but they sensed it was over.

***

Power raged through Shina!

Her own body was torn apart into raw light and then rebuilt, thousands of times every second!

Swollen rivers of awesome power raged, barely under her tenuous control, their borders never quite touching but only the slightest lapse of attention away from catastrophic short-circuit!

Brad reached his healing into the world itself, and felt his life fading from him even as unimaginable force overfilled him and amplified him beyond mortality.

Thag and Sam were forced away from Shina and Brad by the overspill, pushed by strength that made even Thag feel weak and helpless against it.

***

Deep in the southern continent's endless jungles, a ten-foot-tall, ton-and-a-half monster paused in its gorge on the herd of buffalo it had killed, and looked around itself in confusion. The pain, the hunger, the endless and mindless corruption, faded. It couldn't remember what it was doing and why it was surrounded by dead and maimed creatures, nor why its stomach was so full that it hurt, but slow intelligence came back to it and it realized it needed to find out.

Eating could wait.

***

Deep in a hidden wizard-school, a spirit hovered over a dead, dried out body, and let wonder come over itself. The pain, the insanity, the horror it had suffered since the gnomes used their weapons on it, faded like mist before the hot sun, and the spirit known as Kamaia stopped her raging and settled to wait and see what would come next.

She knew the place she was in. Knew she could not leave without the help of a wizard. She had the patience to wait for one, and was sure someone would be by sooner or later to help her out. Especially if she asked nicely. After all, most wizards were good, just like most people.

***

Shina could feel that Brad was dying. She longed to stop the spell, but knew that would be impossible until it was complete.

Then, suddenly, something changed. Something outside of her took hold of her primary stream, the one feeding power to Brad's spirit-wife, and effortlessly, irresistibly, took the power from it into itself.

The power faded instantly from the flow into and out of Brad. Not the slightest trickle remained.

But the primary stream grew in strength beyond anything Shina had any slightest hope of controlling!

She looked at it, terrified of what it would do now that it was out of her control.

The stream was perfect!

It was steady, smooth, purest white and flowing with a strength and certainty beyond imagining.

Then the stream was gone.

No! It just wasn't flowing through her any more. It was there, but it was straight from the Void to the world. Not a stream, not a river, instead it became a perfect flow of life and creation to a spirit that was the master of both.

The titan was awake.

It was healing itself.

Brad was nearly dead and fading fast.

Before Shina could move to him, before she could react at all, an intention flooded into her mind from outside. It wasn't words. It was more than that. But it contained a word. One word too big for a mind, even a wizard's mind, to grasp.

Brad stood up. His eyes were pure silver pools of swirling liquid steel, and there was a beauty to him, a perfection, that Shina wept to see.

Appendix

People	Notes
Thag	Monstrous male humanoid. 8'6" tall (2.6 meters). Horns, claws, gray skin with some dull black scales. Part-dragon. Over 500 years old.
Shina	Human female. 4'11" tall (1.5 meters). Redhead, blue eyes, tan complexion. 18 years old. The world's only living wizard.
Koserana	Appears to be a human female. 5'10" tall (1.8m). Blonde hair in a long mohawk style. Animated tattoos across shoulders, arms and thighs. Appears mid-20s age.
(Lord) Chalkos	Dragon female. Copper/gold scales. 135 years old. About the size of a small pony or very large dog.
Brad/Angbarad	Half-human, half-orc humanoid male. 6'4" tall (1.9m). Brown skin. Straight, black hair. Very handsome. Large tattoo of a rose and vines on chest. Can heal people and control plants through spirit magic.
Duke Antain	Human male. Medium-height, athletic build. Dark-complexion Caucasian. Warlord and rival to King Yonind.
Emstone	Human male. Middle-aged. A powerful sorcerer in the employ of King Yonind.
King Yonind	Human male. A tyrannical despot and military conqueror. Rules through force, fear, and military magic.
Kamaia	Demoness. No body of her own, possesses young women and shows as glowing green inside their eyes. Driven insane in the wizard-war against ancient gnomish invaders from another world. Wants the world to die to end her pain.
"Brad's wife"/ "Brad's totem"	Powerful healing and plant spirit. Sister of Kamaia. Not named in this book. Patroness of Brad and source of his magic.

Gem	Ancient archmage. Infamous as the creator of the undead. Famous as a leader of the army that drove the gnomes out of this world.
Ariel	Ancient dragon. Famous as a leader of the army that drove the gnomes out of this world. ("Second Story" has more about her and Gem.)
Sam	Hive-mind insectiform polymorph. Not a wizard, but spent enough time around them that she can help teach apprentices. Appears in "Story", "Second Story", and "Third Story".

Places

Anytown	Large city in the plains. Where Thag and Shina meet Brad.
Berdonia	Kingdom Shina was born in. Yonind is king.
Klosia	Duchy within Berdonia. Antain is duke.
Xalax	Ancient city ruined by gnome wars. Site of a defunct wizard-school founded by Gem. Central to "Second Story".

Terms

Battle-Mage	Human warriors granted extraordinary power by the wizards of Xalax at the end of the gnome wars. They can imbue martial power and utility into anything, including even living organisms. Absolute masters of combat, including tactics and strategy. Hyper-aggressive and competitive, they conquered an empire over the world and ruled it ruthlessly and despotically. Their legacy is constant warfare and corruption. The most powerful of them were the Imperial Battle-Mages. Even the least of them could turn the tide of almost any battle. Thag killed the last of them and they are extinct at the time of "Story". More about them will appear in "Third Story".

Dragon	A race of humans who used immensely powerful magic, with the help of world-titans, to transform themselves into semi-reptilian demigods that can survive on any world and can travel the void between worlds. Most can assume a human form that corresponds to who they would be without magic. Some can take multiple humanoid forms. All are immensely powerful, effectively immortal, and very dangerous.
Dwarf	A race of humanoids from another shard-world with different rules. They mostly live underground and are very good at mining and smithing.
Elf	A race of humans who use internally directed magic to "perfect" themselves and achieve a form of limited immortality.
Orc	Human warriors enhanced and modified by the war-magic of the battle mages.
Troll	Human warriors transformed by the wizards of Xalax into war-machines. Average 10' tall (3m), with claws, fangs, armored skin, and the ability to recover from wounds almost instantly. Effectively immortal unless killed by magic, or burned to ash. Driven insane in the gnome wars. Incredibly dangerous and ravenously hungry no matter how much they eat.
Void	The space between worlds. Perceived by humans as the space between worlds and stars. Perceived by wizards as a chaos of power and creative potential. Perceived by dragons as a vortex of energy that can be flown through by adult dragons. Deadly to anyone exposed to it in its raw form.

Wizard

Any living creature that can use the creative power of the void between worlds to corrupt, override, or manipulate the rules of the world-shards. Most start out human. There are no elf-wizards or dragon-wizards (one exception). Much more about them in "Second Story".

World-Shard

A partially or fully formed world placed in the void by the gods during the creation of all reality. Look like planets or stars to humans. Look like "islands in the sky" to wizards and dragons. They have different elements and different rules, but humans can only experience the rules of their own birth-world, so perceive them as variations from their own world. Only wizards and dragons can see worlds as they truly exist in the Void.

World-Titan

Worlds are made of spirits. Wind, Earth, Fire, Water, Life, and sub-forms (examples: Fox spirits, Storm spirits, Wave spirits). The most powerful of these spirits are the world-titans, who are the incarnations of the power that makes whole worlds. These spirits have the potential to become totems for people, usually human, who then gain some degree of the essence and power of the spirit.

Notes on Shina's journey:

The geography is "based on a real world" in the Hollywood sense of "it's mostly made up, but there are semblances to something you might recognize".

Assume the base-geography is Earth in the physical spaces and arrangements. There is a peninsula where Scandinavia is on Earth, of roughly analogous shape, terrain and climate. There's a large continent that corresponds physically to Eurasia, and another for Africa, and again for the Americas. The details are frequently different, but the overall shape and terrain would be familiar.

Given that, and with the understanding that these places don't match in culture, history, or any other particulars:

- Shina was born and raised in a city that would be on the Med coast of southern France or northern Spain in our world. That city is the capital of Berdonia and is ruled by King Yonind.
- Antain took her to a castle in what would be Scandinavia in our world. Somewhere on the south-west coast.
- The werewolf village is inland on that peninsula.
- Anytown would be in the plains of western Russia in our world. Around the location of Moscow or one of its suburbs.
- Bart Pass would correspond to a pass over the Urals.
- Brad comes from mountains similar in location and geography to Afghanistan or Nepal.
- Chalkos was born in what would be Turkey on a map of modern Earth.
- Thag is from what would be South America in our world.
- Xalax is roughly in the Tibet/Siberia area. To get there, they fly across their analog to southern Siberia. (Despite popular conceptions, Siberia isn't all snow all year. That area is beautiful in the summer.)
- The dwarvish village would be on the coast of British Columbia or southern Alaska in our world.
- They cross most of their world's version of North America in dwarf-tunnels and come out on the east side of the Rocky Mountains.
- Sam's tower is an obvious rip-off of the Empire State Building and corresponds to it in most particulars.
- The rest can be extrapolated by looking at a globe and tracking between these points.